DARK WATERS

A MACY ADAMS MYSTERY

DARK WATERS

SIBYLLE BARRASSO

FIVE STAR
A part of Gale, Cengage Learning

GALE
CENGAGE Learning

Detroit • New York • San Francisco • New Haven, Conn • Waterville, Maine • London

GALE
CENGAGE Learning·

Set in 11 pt. Plantin.
Printed on permanent paper.

LIBRARY OF CONGRESS CATALOGING-IN-PUBLICATION DATA

Barrasso, Sibylle.
    Dark waters : a Macy Adams mystery / Sibylle Barrasso. — 1st ed.
        p. cm.
        ISBN-13: 978-1-59414-639-8 (alk. paper)
        ISBN-10: 1-59414-639-X (alk. paper)
        1. Women private investigators—Massachusetts—Boston—Fiction. 2. Boston (Mass.)—Fiction. I. Title.
PS3602.A77746D37 2008
813'.6—dc22   2008016366

First Edition. First Printing: August 2008.
Published in 2008 in conjunction with Tekno Books and Ed Gorman.

Printed in the United States of America
1 2 3 4 5 6 7 12 11 10 09 08

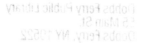

To my Mother and Father,
their lives' work
the printed word

ACKNOWLEDGMENTS

The author wishes to acknowledge the following people:

First and foremost, my husband David, my own personal rock of Gibraltar whose support I count on daily, and Lane, who lights up my life and sparks my creativity.

This manuscript went through many drafts. I am deeply indebted to my two writers' groups and their countless suggestions to improve this novel. In Cambridge: Jeremiah Healy, James Barretto, and Gary Chafetz. In Natick: Judy Copek, Jane Freeman, Sheryl King, Joan Scott, Barbara Glynn, and Julie Hennrikus. I also owe thanks to Hank Phillippi Ryan for her insightful suggestions. For help with earlier drafts or portions of the text, I thank Stacy DeBroff, Valerie von Rosenvinge, Katherine Prins, Margo Lemieux, Alice Calderon, Michael St. Clair, the late Al Blanchard, and Marisa D'Vari.

At the Santa Barbara Writers Conference, I'm indebted to Robert M. Morris, S. L. Stebel, and Leonard Tourney for giving me a crash course in writing fiction, as well as Joyce Spizer, a real life private eye, Kay Mouradian, and W. Hansford Watford Jr.

Thanks to John Helfers and all the people at Tekno Books, and especially to Denise Dietz, my wonderful editor, and Gretchen Gordon, my eagle-eyed copy editor. Thanks to the people at Five Star Publishing, who besides producing beautiful books make authors' dreams come true.

For technical information, I am deeply indebted to Joseph

Varlaro of the Boston Police Crime Laboratory Unit. Also Charles J. Walsh, Special Agent, FBI; Terrence M. Cunningham, Chief of Police, Wellesley; Paul C. McLaughlin of the Boston Police Homicide Unit; Tim Roberts, Detective Homicide of the City of Santa Barbara; and Stanton Kessler, Office of the Chief Medical Examiner.

I'm grateful to Kate Mattes, who first introduced me to the world of mysteries, and to the first authors I read in the mystery genre: Sue Grafton, Robert B. Parker, Jeremiah Healy, Kate Flora, and Thomas H. Cook, among countless others. I thank Bill Eidson, from whom I learned about editing, and Otto Penzler, for explaining the business side of publishing to me. I'm grateful to Charles Raisch, for giving me a start at *New Mystery Magazine,* and Steve Glassman, editor of *Bad Boys and Bad Girls in the Badlands.*

On a more personal note, I'm grateful to Catherine Lucchini Gerson, for being a great friend, and to my two tennis partners, Sue Iodice and Cynie Simon, for putting up with my many unforced errors. I'm indebted to Miriam Dougherty, M.D., and Bradford Shingleton, M.D., for restoring my failing eyesight, and to Erica Johnson, M.D., for keeping my body and soul together.

Hildegard and Achilles, I am blessed with your ever constant guidance, support, and love.

Last but not least, I wish to thank Michael A. Black, an immensely talented writer, for helping me in so many ways. Thank you, Michael, not just for so much good advice, but for being a very special and wonderful human being.

ONE

Ten days ago Mitchell Browne's body washed up on the marshy riverbanks of the Charles, just a short distance from where I was standing. It was late afternoon. A gusty, dank breeze was blowing in my direction. Directly across the river I could see the Citgo sign, just six blocks from where the Red Sox played. Behind me the Hyatt Hotel rose up like a modern version of the Mayan pyramids.

Steadying the Nikon in my hand, I took several snapshots of the scene. Next to me a Hyatt Hotel security guard, an attractive dark-haired man in his thirties, was taking a deep drag from a cigarette. Like an addict getting a fix, the coiled tension left his body.

"What's your interest in this thing? Are you a reporter?"

His Boston accent was pronounced. Park the car would have rolled off his tongue as *pahk the cah.*

"Private investigator," I said. "I'm Macy Adams."

I walked to the edge of the water, trying to remember the exact details of the newspaper accounts I'd reviewed that morning. The *Boston Globe*'s front page headline read "Nation's Foremost AIDS Expert Drowns in Charles." Two days later, "Drowning Ruled as Homicide." A week later, the arrest of Evelyn Browne created a media frenzy. "Widow of Wadsworth Professor Arrested for Husband's Murder."

Evelyn Browne had retained David Silverman, one of Boston's most prominent defense attorneys. I had done investigative work for David before on a number of lesser cases. Still, I was surprised when he called the previous evening. Even more surprised when he asked me to join his team as an investigator. The Mitchell Browne murder case was bound to be the most prominent of Silverman's career thus far.

The security guard looked skeptical as he inhaled another dose of nicotine. "A private eye, huh?"

It was obvious the man didn't know what to make of me. The ultra-short, white tennis getup I was wearing didn't help. I'd dropped by the Hyatt on impulse, on my way home from a tennis match. Before David's call, I'd been essentially unemployed, meaning I could pick up a game of tennis anytime I felt like it.

Wearing something skimpy to a crime scene was unprofessional. I vowed to myself that from here on out I'd conduct myself in a more fitting manner.

I reached into my handbag and pulled out my P.I. license.

He scrutinized it. "Macy," he finally said, "that Irish or what?"

"On my mother's side."

"Charlie O'Toole. I'm head of security." He stretched out his hand and we shook. "What outfit are you with?"

"Investigative Enterprises."

The firm's name stuck in my throat. It was a lie. Why was it so hard for me to admit even to a complete stranger that I was no longer gainfully employed by IE? The plain truth was they'd fired my ass six weeks ago. At the moment I was freelancing, trying to figure out what to do with the rest of my life.

Charlie brightened. "Hey, you must know Harry Luger."

"Sure, he is—was—my boss."

"Was?"

"Harry retired a couple of months ago."

"He's not old enough to retire." The skeptical look returned.

"We had some management changes at IE, and Harry wasn't pleased with what was happening. He decided to take early retirement. You know Harry, he doesn't suffer fools gladly."

I smiled, flashing back on Harry muttering under his breath as he left the building, a file box tucked beneath one arm. *"Damn wet-behind-the-ears computer nerds trying to tell me how to run an investigation, when they can't find their way to the John without a GPS."*

I felt a stab of regret. I missed Harry, and his wacky sense of humor and fatherly attentiveness.

Charlie caught my expression. "Yeah, he's a regular guy, that Harry. Calls a spade a spade. No bullshit. Real smart, too." He gazed out at the river. "Give him my best if you see him."

I wanted to get Charlie O'Toole off IE and back onto my case. "Could you show me where the body was found?"

"Sure, just downriver a bit." We started walking east along the bank. "A rower found the body. Once he figured out what it was, he rowed back to the B.U. boathouse and called 9-1-1. The state police arrived soon after. And then it was divers, the M.E. and his staff, press and TV people camped out here for the rest of the afternoon. Even a freaking helicopter kept circling, whipping up the water like a blender. Not exactly great publicity for the hotel, if you catch my drift." He took one final drag before crushing the cigarette butt into the ground.

"I thought there was no such thing as bad publicity." I grinned at him, and then aimed my camera at the area between the riverbank and the hotel.

Out of the corner of my eye, I saw O'Toole checking out my legs. My own fault for wearing the skimpy tennis skirt. Not that I cared much. Boys will be boys. I have runner's legs, bony in the knees and more muscular than the Barbie dolls featured on the pages of *Cosmopolitan* and *Glamour*. But I could beat any of those *Glamour* girls in the hundred-yard dash—not to mention longer distances. Charlie's eyes paused briefly on my chest, nothing spectacular there, before returning to my bare legs. I re-aimed my camera and took a picture of O'Toole. *Caught you in the act.*

He colored and gave me a sheepish smile. Maybe wearing the skimpy outfit hadn't been such a bad idea after all. Perhaps from now on I'd conduct all my interviews with male witnesses in skimpwear.

"What do you use the pictures for?"

I was tempted to reply "blackmail." Instead I said, "To help me visualize the scene, refresh my memory."

He pointed to a boulder twenty yards in front of us. "They pulled the body out of the water right there."

I aimed and clicked the shutter, then walked to the spot he'd indicated, perusing the ground. Lots of footprints, but nothing else of interest. The Charles curved and widened considerably where we were standing, allowing the river's current to slow, undoubtedly accounting for the fact that the corpse had wound up here. Footpaths rimmed the river on both sides. Joggers and bicyclists were utilizing them with faint hope of pushing back time and gravity. Thirty yards away a flock of white geese pecked the ground where a passerby had spilled a bag of popcorn. The tableau looked peaceful, even idyllic.

"Did you get a look at the body?"

"Nuh-uh, the staties kept everybody away. By the time the divers brought him up the slope, they'd already bagged him."

"What about the officers? Recognize anyone?"

"There was that Pascucci guy from the Underwater Rescue Unit. I didn't recognize the homicide guys, but they were from the MDC." He paused. "Oh, yeah, and a couple of Fibbies showed up."

I raised an eyebrow. "The FBI? Why would they get involved?"

He shrugged. "Beats me."

The feds, on what had initially looked like an accidental drowning. That was odd.

"Anything else you want to know?" He jingled some coins in his pocket. I could sense his restlessness.

I took one final picture of the terrain between the river and the road. "No, that's all. Thank you for taking the time."

O'Toole pulled a business card from his wallet. "Call me if you think of anything else. And if you're in the neighborhood, stop by for lunch, on the house."

"Thanks, Charlie," I said, doubting I'd take him up on his offer.

We walked up to Memorial Drive. I found my car in the garage and headed west toward Wadsworth Square. A mile and a half upstream were the staid brick and ivy walls of Wadsworth University, considered by many to be the most prestigious institution of higher learning in the world. Dr. Mitchell Browne had been an esteemed expert in the field of molecular biology, on the faculty of Wadsworth for the past nineteen years, and the author of a best-selling book on HIV. He had also served on the board of directors of two Boston-based biotech companies. It seemed incongruous that a man who traveled in such lofty circles should be found floating face down in the cold, murky waters of the Charles.

Nearing Wadsworth Square, I took a right onto Elmwood and a left onto Brattle for several blocks to my new home, a former mews stable in back of a mansion. I'd gotten the place for a song through my cousin Deborah, a realtor.

I showered and dressed in a conservative, dark-blue dress, adding a gold necklace and Monet earrings. The finishing touch was rolling my ash-blond hair into a French twist. A glance in the mirror told me that I looked just right for a meeting with a prominent attorney at the Ritz-Carlton.

By five-thirty I was behind the wheel of my blue Jetta, heading east on Storrow Drive.

Two

Boston's Ritz-Carlton exudes the charm and elegance of a bygone era. Marble floors, oak-paneled walls, a cozy fireplace in the bar. Paintings scattered throughout showcased nineteenth-century gentlemen, surrounded by stately horses and noble canines, in pursuit of manly pleasures: riding, foxhunting, shooting. A decor designed to put Anglophiles and masters of industry at ease—also lawyers.

David Silverman was sitting next to a huge window overlooking the Public Gardens, immersed in the *Globe*, a look of intense concentration on his face. The martini glass in front of him was half-empty. He glanced up as I approached, and stood, towering above me in his six-four frame.

"Macy, so good to see you. I always knew you'd hang out your own shingle. How's it going?"

"Fabulous," I lied.

I wasn't about to tell him he was only my second client in six weeks since I'd left Investigative Enterprises. At this rate I'd end up knowing more about bankruptcy than entrepreneurship.

"The *Globe* is crucifying Evelyn Browne."

"What are they saying now?"

"Something about rumored infidelities, the couple allegedly sleeping in separate bedrooms. It's mostly innuendo. I don't understand why this is turning into such a big story."

Slipping into the seat opposite him, I ordered a glass of Chardonnay from the elderly waiter whose pinched expression

14

mimicked that of the dogs in the paintings. Maybe he'd been looking at the paintings too long. Or maybe he was constipated.

Silverman said, "I met with IE's new head honcho yesterday. And I must say, I was not impressed."

I smiled, delighted to hear someone whose judgment I respected share my own low opinion of Dan Colburn, IE's new chief operating officer, the man who'd caused Harry to retire prematurely. The COO slot should rightly have gone to Harry.

"Colburn struck me as an unsophisticated computer geek," David continued. "I don't see him possessing the brains or refinement to conduct a high-level investigation at Wadsworth."

I sensed irony here. When I'd first met David Silverman, I'd thought of *him* as a little rough around the edges. He'd been twenty-seven then, a newly minted Wadsworth Law grad, top of his class. For our first meeting, David had worn white socks, thick black-rimmed glasses, and an ill-fitting polyester suit. His hairstyle resembled the cartoon character's who'd accidentally stuck a finger into a light socket, reproducing that Albert Einstein Academy of Hairstyling effect.

In short, the man was brilliant but lacked polish.

Since then David had undergone a transformation. He'd graduated from discount off-the-rack Sears to custom-made suits from LouisBoston. Gone were the bright power ties. His hair had been sent to obedience school, each strand perfectly in place, forming a nice reddish-blond frame around his face.

Professionally, David's rise had been meteoric. He was one of the most sought-after litigators in Boston, the youngest partner in his law firm. David possessed an uncommon flair for courtroom dramatics. If he had gone to Hollywood instead of law school, he could have been an Oscar contender.

"The police are real slow about sharing their files." David signaled to the waiter, pointing to the bowl of nuts on the table. "Things aren't going well, Macy. The case against Evelyn is stronger than I initially thought. I wish I'd known more before signing her on as a client." His demeanor was serious. "To top it all off, I find Evelyn difficult to deal with."

"How so?"

"We'll get to that later." David leaned closer and looked around to make sure we weren't being overheard. "Let me lay out some of the police findings first. Evelyn and her husband had dinner at the Hyatt the night he was killed. The maitre d' remembers them leaving around nine-thirty. That makes Evelyn the last person on record to see Browne while he was alive."

"What happened after dinner?" I asked.

"According to Evelyn, they drove home together, and she went straight to sleep."

"But the police don't believe her? Why?"

"Easy. Evelyn returns to her house, as does Browne's Jaguar. So how does Browne's corpse end up in the water back at the Hyatt?"

I nodded. If Evelyn was telling the truth, it meant that Browne must have backtracked to the hotel. But how, since he obviously hadn't driven his own car? And why?

Or had Evelyn overpowered her husband after dinner and dumped his corpse into the river, then driven home? Was she lying?

The waiter brought my Chardonnay and a fresh bowl of nuts. I sipped my wine while David sorted through the nuts, foraging for cashews.

"David, have you walked that stretch in front of the Hyatt?"

"No. Why?" He fished the olive from his martini glass and popped it in his mouth.

I placed the photos I'd taken earlier that afternoon in front of him. They showed a thirty-foot-wide strip of mowed weeds leading to the water.

"Does this strike you as the kind of place you'd take a late-night stroll?"

David scrutinized the photos, chewing, and shook his head. "No."

"I can't see Browne doing it, either," I said.

"Good point. Clever of you to take these photos. They help. It's something you will need to discuss with Evelyn." He rummaged for more cashews. "It gets worse, Macy. This next bit is something I just heard from my contact at the M.E.'s office. Browne ingested a substantial quantity of Valium that night. Enough to knock him out cold."

"That could suggest suicide," I said hopefully.

"My thoughts exactly. Which is why I called Browne's physician. And I got an earful. Listen to this. Two years ago, Evelyn suspected her husband of having an affair. So she arranged for Browne to be too sleepy after dinner to engage in any extracurricular activities. Eventually, Browne goes to his doctor. They put him through a series of tests, all negative. Finally they run a toxicology battery, and bingo. Browne had been overdosing on tranquilizers. Valium. Except Browne claimed he wasn't taking any."

I stared at David wide-eyed. "Evelyn slipped him the Valium?"

"That's what Browne claimed. He suspected Evelyn of mixing the stuff in with his food. I don't have to tell you how damaging this will be."

As schemes went, I had to admire Evelyn's creativity in dealing with marital infidelity. But it would wreak havoc with our defense case.

David toyed with the martini glass. His gold cufflinks caught my eye, engraved with a square-lettered DJS monogram. Fancy stuff.

"What does Evelyn say for herself?"

"That's just the problem. She refuses to talk about it. Or at least, she refuses to discuss it with me."

"Doesn't she realize you're on her side? Did you explain to her that everything she tells you is confidential?"

"Of course I did. But she won't talk. Claims it's all too personal. But something she said yesterday led me to believe that she might open up to a woman." Silverman looked at me. "My hope is that she'll talk to you."

Professionally, being female often worked against me, as it did most recently when Colburn took over as managing partner of IE. Wouldn't it be nice if, for once, being a woman would give me an edge? My former boss, Harry, claimed that women made better P.I.s than men because they could lie through their teeth without batting an eye. True enough, but I'd also seen plenty of men mangle the truth while maintaining choirboy expressions. Lying was an equal-opportunity activity.

I sipped my Chardonnay, letting the liquid roll around on my supposed forked tongue. "I'm surprised Browne didn't divorce Evelyn right there and then," I said. "Would you share a house with someone you suspected of slipping you drugs?"

Silverman shook his head. "They did separate. For three months. But there was a child involved, and then Evelyn tried to commit suicide, so Browne moved back in. But he was planning to divorce his wife. He'd hired Samuel Kane, a real hotshot divorce attorney, to handle his divorce, all the while leaving Evelyn under the impression that they were getting along splendidly. Or so Evelyn claims. I had a long talk with Kane yesterday. Between the tranquilizer incident and her alleged suicide attempt, they were going to make Evelyn look like a mental case. Plus on Kane's advice, Browne had begun spending more time with his son. He was going for sole custody."

Not having children myself, I could nonetheless imagine a mother turning nasty, if not downright homicidal, when faced with the threat of having her offspring taken away—an argument that wouldn't be lost on the D.A.

"Any idea when he was planning to file for divorce?"

"According to his lawyer, it was imminent."

"This is not good," I said quietly.

"No. Not at all."

Silverman removed his horn-rimmed glasses and rubbed his eyes. He looked more tired without his specs.

"Okay, so Browne was planning to divorce his wife," I said. "Things between them had to be bad. If he also believed her to be mentally unstable, would he agree to go for a late-night stroll with her along a deserted stretch of the Charles? It doesn't make sense."

"No, it doesn't."

"And if they didn't go for a walk, then how *did* Mitchell's body end up in the river? With Mitchell zonked out on tranquilizers, his wife couldn't possibly have managed to drag him across Memorial Drive, not to mention across a thirty-foot embankment. She must have had an accomplice. Unless she's one hell of a strong woman."

"She isn't. In fact, Evelyn's tiny. She wouldn't have been able to drag him alone."

"You think someone else is in the picture?"

David thought for a moment while we sipped our drinks. "Honestly, I don't see it," he finally said. "But I guess anything is possible. Wait until you see her."

I looked at him quizzically. "Why?"

"I'd appreciate your assessment of Evelyn." He smiled. "In fact, I can't wait for you to meet her, Macy."

"The suspense is killing me. What are you thinking?"

Plenty of press photos of Evelyn had been taken the day she was arraigned, but she'd managed to shield her face for every single one of them. I had no clear visual image of my client.

"Well, let's just say she isn't what you'd expect for the wife of an eminent Wadsworth professor."

My mind started spinning images of Evelyn, from total mouse to absolute sex kitten. "How about a hint?"

"You'll see for yourself. I don't want to bias you. Then we'll talk." He pushed a legal file across the table. "You'll find her at her Cambridge address."

"She's not in custody?"

David shook his head. I'd expected Evelyn to be holed up in a correctional facility. It was inconceivable that she should have been granted bail on a capital charge.

"How the hell did you manage that?"

"Oh, we lawyers have our ways."

"I'm impressed. I'll talk with her tomorrow."

The waiter approached and asked if we wanted another round. David shook his head. "Just the check."

"So what do you think?" I asked.

"About . . . ?"

"About what happened. Did she do it?"

He paused, ostensibly giving the question consideration. "To be perfectly honest, I'm not sure." He steepled his fingers. "But it doesn't matter whether she did it or not. Evelyn hired me to defend her, and that's what I'll do. The same goes for you, Macy. The police are doing a bang-up job discrediting her as it is. I get the impression that they really want to nail her ass."

"Even if she's innocent?"

"It's an election year. The D.A. failed to get convictions on several high-profile cases last year. He desperately needs a win on this one."

Nothing like politics to mess up a case.

"There are a number of leads you can pursue," he continued. "Mitchell was on the board of two biotech companies: BioCorp and Genetechnology. Big bucks. There may be a motive for murder there."

Silverman drained the last of his martini. "Obviously, I'd like to see this whole damn thing dismissed before it gets to the grand jury, never mind a trial. You know the drill. If we don't come up with enough for a dismissal, we'll have to work the reasonable doubt angle. I want you to talk to everyone: Mitchell's colleagues at Wadsworth, friends, family, the people at Bio-Corp and Genetechnology, neighbors, you name it. Find me another suspect, anybody. Are you with me?"

"Does that mean you're ruling out suicide?"

"No, no. Find me a credible reason why the good professor might have been suicidal, if you can. Maybe we get lucky and find out Mitchell had an inoperable brain tumor."

The waiter returned with the check. Silverman handed him a credit card without glancing at the bill.

"My forensic accountant is digging into Mitchell's financials as we speak. We're scheduled to meet on Monday. Can you join us? Ten o'clock?"

"Sure."

"How much of a retainer do you need?"

"Five thousand."

David didn't even blink. Probably considered it a bargain. His retainer for this case was undoubtedly well over a hundred thousand. He made out a check to me with his fancy Montblanc fountain pen. I slid a copy of my contract across the table for him to sign. Under Massachusetts law, I couldn't work a homicide investigation unless I was in the employ of a lawyer. I liked having my paperwork in order.

The waiter returned with Silverman's credit card and receipt. David stowed both in his Cordovan wallet. I noticed the "DJS" on the leather, the same design as on his cufflinks and briefcase. Silverman was keeping an army of engravers and imprinters in business. I bet his shirts were monogrammed, too.

"We'd love to have you to the house for dinner." David smiled broadly. "Did I mention I'm a brand new daddy?"

"No, you didn't. Congratulations."

"Rachel's four weeks old—and she's gorgeous. Looks just like her mother, thank God."

I'd barely had time to get used to Silverman being married. The news of a kid was a shocker. Only three years separated us, but in some ways we were a generation apart, with his being married, living in a mansion in Weston, and now being a parent to boot. An unpleasant reminder that my own biological clock was ticking. I pushed the thought aside.

"Are you getting any sleep?" I asked.

"My wife's doing all the middle-of-the-night feedings."

"Lucky you."

"Don't I know it."

David looked terribly pleased with himself.

"What about Mitchell Browne's will? Who inherits?"

"With the divorce proceedings imminent, Browne had asked his lawyer to draw up a new will. But as of now his new will isn't legal, because Browne's lawyer can't seem to find a signed copy of it. But here's the clincher. Browne had a two-million-dollar life insurance policy. Payable to Evelyn."

I let out a soft whistle. "No wonder the D.A. smells blood. With Mitchell planning his divorce so meticulously, it's surprising the life insurance policy should have slipped his mind."

David tapped me on the arm. "Guess who signed the monthly checks?"

"Evelyn?"

He nodded meaningfully. "The insurance company is doing its own investigation. Apparently there's some question about the signature on the policy. But since they've been cashing the monthly checks all along, they don't have any choice but to pay up—unless Evelyn is found guilty, of course."

I did not like what I was hearing. Everything David was telling me pointed to Evelyn as the most likely suspect.

He leaned forward, his eyes boring into mine.

"Macy, I haven't lost a case in three years, and I don't wish to taint that record. I hired you because I need a woman investigator, and I happen to think you're the best female private eye in Boston. Get me stuff that'll clear our client. Or at least enough to muddy the waters. However," he raised one finger, "if for any reason you don't feel up to the task, now is the time to tell me."

I tried not to swallow.

"I'm up to it."

I'd said it with more conviction than I felt.

We stood, with him towering above me. With his height and that look of perpetual amusement on his face, David Silverman somehow gave the impression that he was privy to inside information. He was aware of his own power.

We retrieved our almost-matching Burberry raincoats and exited through the hotel lobby.

A valet opened the glass doors to Arlington Street. Outside the Ritz, Silverman shadowboxed me on the shoulder and wished me a nice weekend.

I watched his tall figure recede from view on Newbury Street, before walking myself in the opposite direction, toward Beacon Hill.

I mouthed a silent prayer. Prayer wasn't part of my regular investigative routine, but it couldn't hurt. Things were looking bad for Evelyn. I'd need all the help—spiritual or otherwise— that I could get.

THREE

My Aunt Esme had invited me to one of her fancy dinner parties. I'd be fashionably late for the six-thirty cocktails. Beacon Street was a short walk from the Ritz. I crossed Arlington to the Public Gardens, admiring the sea of tulips with their bursts of red or yellow blossoms. The enormous weeping willows skirting the water of the swan pond were covered in yellowish-green fuzz. As I walked across the footbridge that spans the pond at its hourglass center, I wondered who else might show up at Aunt Esme's party.

I was hoping to run into my cousin Deborah. As the real estate agent equivalent of the Energizer bunny, Deborah was on a first-name basis with most movers and shakers in town. She was bound to know people who worked for BioCorp or Genetechnology, the two companies that had invited Mitchell Browne to serve as a board member.

Minutes later I reached my aunt's town house, a stately five-story brownstone on Beacon Street that had been in her branch of the family for five generations. Esme was holding court in the parlor. When she saw me, she stretched out her arms and hugged me, enveloping me in an almost overpowering cloud of Guerlain.

"Macy, my darling, darling child. It's been ages. You really shouldn't disappear for months at a time."

I kissed her on both cheeks. "It hasn't been that long," I protested.

"Has too, darling. Christmas, at the Winthrops. That's all right. You're here now and I forgive you."

Tonight Esme looked like the Queen of Sheba, dressed in a floor-length purple caftan with gold trim, rings on all ten fingers.

"How is your father?" she asked.

"Daddy's fine," I said. I hadn't seen my father in a month, but we talked on the phone. People always asked me about him—never about my mother, though I'm sure she's a big source of gossip behind my back. My parents divorced when I was ten. My mother currently lives in California with husband number four. Raised as a devout Catholic, hers was a total rebellion against her upbringing, for which the WASP side of my family has never forgiven her.

Esme's assembled guests included the usual crowd of assorted upper-crust Bostonians, some of them distant relatives of mine. The Adams surname descended from one of the four siblings of the fifth American president. My brother was big into the pedigree and ancestor worship and its accompanying snob appeal. As far as I was concerned, the only things I got out of being related to some rather illustrious townies were relentless requests for contributions to countless charities—with an occasional dinner party invitation thrown in for good measure.

I was about to pick up a lobster ravioli from a passing server, when I spotted someone I had not expected to see tonight. Prentice Porter, the person responsible for my dismissal from Investigative Enterprises.

Prentice spotted me a split second later, and his double take was almost comical. He was trim and aristocratic-looking, black hair slicked back. The direct gaze of his blue eyes gave him an air of studied sincerity. I watched as he disentangled himself skillfully from the crowd surrounding him and ambled over to greet me.

"Macy, what a pleasant surprise."

He gave my arm a slight squeeze.

Prentice Porter had recently announced his bid for the Bay State's gubernatorial seat. A Democratic opponent had hired IE to do a background check on Prentice. Since Prentice's image was squeaky-clean, the Democrats were desperate for any kind of innuendo or rumor that could be used in a down-and-dirty smear campaign.

That Prentice Porter had been a longtime acquaintance of mine was common knowledge around IE. Therefore, I wasn't surprised when the new head honcho, Colburn, waltzed into my office to inquire about him. But it never occurred to me that refusing to work on Porter's investigation would result in ending my career with IE. Harry had never operated that way. But then, Harry was a class act, while Colburn was a world-class jerk. As it happened, I *did* know something about Porter's past that had the potential of stopping his political aspiration dead in its tracks. But Prentice was a close friend of my brother's. Divulging Porter's secret could damage my brother's reputation equally as badly as Porter's.

"IE's doing a bang-up job," Prentice said. "I feel like my past is being put under a microscope."

"Welcome to politics. Have they found any skeletons?"

"Nothing yet, as far as I can tell. What do *you* hear?"

I shrugged. Prentice guided me to a quiet corner of the room.

"I'm out of the loop, Prentice. Honest."

"No old buddies you still stay in touch with?"

I looked at him surprised, if not dismayed. Did everyone in Boston know that I no longer worked at IE? "Who told you I left the firm?"

"Word gets around."

Great. "Well, to answer your question, no, I have no old buddies left over there. Colburn runs the place with a tight fist. You'd have an easier time getting information out of the CIA."

"That's not saying much." Porter shifted his weight uncomfortably. "By any chance, did Colburn ask you to work on, um . . . my investigation?"

"I was top on the list."

"I thought so. Did you refuse?"

"Of course."

He was trying to be subtle about it, but I could tell by the minimal relaxation in Porter's stance that he breathed a sigh of relief. "Is that why you left the firm?"

"Among other reasons."

"I owe you, Macy." He placed his hands over mine. "And I'm a man who never forgets a debt."

I was contemplating ways to collect, when I heard a husky voice behind me.

"So when do we start calling you Governor Porter?" Deborah "Dubs" Smythe, real estate agent extraordinaire. My cousin.

Porter beamed. "Hopefully soon. Come January. Hello, Dubs."

My cousin kissed Porter lightly on the lips, gave my cheek a peck, and started chatting up a storm, oozing poise and charm. Her auburn hair cascaded loosely in soft waves over her shoulders. Five-eleven in stocking feet, Dubs dwarfed most women. She was so painfully thin, there wasn't a stitch of clothing that didn't look sensational on her. If it weren't for her deep-set, slightly hooded eyes, she might have been a raving beauty. But those vigilant eyes gave her face the air of a watchful hawk.

I'll be the first to admit that I've always been more than a little envious of my cousin. It started in the sandbox, where Dubs always managed to build the biggest, most creative, and elaborate of sand castles—no doubt early training for her future real estate career. My green monster grew as we got older, as

Dubs's sparkling personality and riotous sense of humor blossomed and made her the instant belle of any ball—with me invariably playing second fiddle. To top it off, nowadays Dubs was making serious money—while I was trying to figure out what to do with the rest of my life.

So why did my cousin, a woman who ostensibly had everything going for her, experience perpetual man-trouble?

Porter soon extricated himself, and Dubs linked her arm through mine and pulled me in the direction of a waiter who was dispensing shrimp.

"So how are your new digs?" she said. "You like?"

"I *love*."

Dubs picked up a shrimp and dunked it in cocktail sauce. I followed suit, almost swooning from the delicious taste. I let out a groan of delight.

Dubs gave me an accusing glance. "God, why don't you try sex every once in a while?"

"Look who's talking."

"Hey, I get plenty," she protested.

She probably did. Quantity wasn't her problem, quality was.

"And how's Jack?"

"Jack?" I scooped up a second shrimp.

"Jack Hamilton. Your landlord?"

"He hasn't been around."

In the six weeks since I'd been at my new address, I had yet to catch a glimpse of the man. I'd begun to wonder whether Jack Hamilton actually existed.

"What?" Dubs said, astonished. "You haven't met Jack yet?"

I shook my head. "Nope."

"Oh Honey. That's so odd. You've been there what? Two months?"

"Six weeks."

"That's so strange. I should call his office and find out what the deal is."

Dubs was a personal friend of my landlord's. She'd called me the instant he decided to put the carriage house up for rent. The listing never even made it into the MLS computer.

I changed tack and made my plea for introductions at Bio-Corp or Genetechnology.

"Sorry. I don't know a soul at either one of those firms." Dubs grabbed another shrimp. "Well, actually . . . I take that back. I dated a guy. A postdoc. He does research at BioCorp."

"Excellent. I knew you'd come through."

"BioCorp was going public when I dated him. Months of overtime for everyone, and then, poof, the deal fell apart."

"Why? What happened?"

"It was all very hush-hush. But according to the rumor mill, it involved some fraudulent experiments."

I couldn't wait to pick the brains of Dubs's former lover.

"I'd love to meet him."

"No you don't, Macy. The guy harbors a death wish for me."

"Okay, just give me his name then. I won't mention you."

"He's a creep, Macy."

"I don't plan to marry the guy. All I want from him is some information."

Dubs's hawk eyes were suddenly hard and stubborn. "Macy, no. I meant it when I called him a creep. He's crazy. A sicko. You won't be safe if I tell you his name. The man handles deadly viruses. Not someone you want to know."

FOUR

The Browne residence was a white Victorian in an upscale section of Cambridge. A wooden porch skirted the front of the house. While lovely, Victorians always struck me as twisted somehow, a setting begging for an Agatha Christie mystery. All those circular staircases and secret hideaways to stow away corpses. All that repressed sexuality.

I should talk—if my cousin was to be believed.

A light rain was falling. Baskets of pansies hung from the porch beams, soaking in the raindrops. If flowers had thoughts, they'd consider themselves off to a great start for the weekend.

The repeated clicking of a camera shutter interrupted my thoughts.

I put up a hand to shield my face, but I was too late. The photographer—who'd come out of nowhere—already had several pictures of me. She looked overweight despite her black jeans and turtleneck. Her pug nose and jowly face reminded me of a bulldog. An ill-tempered bulldog. Her blunt-cut, blond hair hung artlessly around her face. No makeup. Meet the press.

"What's your name? Are you a friend of the family? Do you think Evelyn is guilty?" Her questions came like rapid machine gun fire.

I didn't reply, did not even break stride. The woman followed closely as I approached the house, camera at the ready.

Before ringing Evelyn's doorbell, I turned and addressed the photographer, "Would you please step back. You're on private property."

"I'm with the *Globe.*"

A non sequitur if ever I heard one. "I don't care who you're with. Show some respect for people's privacy. The woman in this house just lost her husband."

She didn't move. I took a couple of steps toward her, feeling my fists clench.

Okay, I had tried to be nice.

"I'm warning you. If you don't step back to the sidewalk you're going to need a new camera."

We glared at each other, and I felt a rush of adrenalin. The woman retreated. I took a deep breath and rang the bell.

A muffled voice came from the other side of the door, "Who is it?"

Since the reporter was still within earshot, I did not say my name. Instead, I fished a business card from my pocket and dropped it through the mail slot.

Seconds later the front door opened a crack. I slipped inside, entering a large, oak-paneled front hall. I was about to ask the child who'd opened the door if I could talk to her mother. Belatedly, I realized that the toy-sized person in front of me was Evelyn Browne.

She was a far cry from the sex kitten I'd conjured up in my mind. But David had been right. She did not fit the image of the wife of a high-profile Wadsworth professor. She seemed altogether too childlike and inconsequential.

"Hi. Mrs. Adams?" Even her voice sounded young, almost like a child's.

"It's 'Miss.' But I prefer Macy."

"Mr. Silverman said you'd come by this morning."

Evelyn wasn't even five feet tall. She was tiny and slim, but beneath her khakis her body lacked muscle tone. She had the build of someone who watched calories but avoided exercise.

I followed her into the living room, where she went to the window and peeked through a crack in the curtains.

"Damn vulture. How much longer is she going to stay out there?"

Again I was taken aback by her voice, so tiny and bell-like.

"She'll give it up in a day or two."

Evelyn pointed at a pair of love seats in front of the fireplace. She sank into the nearest, all but disappearing in the huge beige cushions, her feet failing to reach the floor, making me think of the Lilliputians on Gulliver's island.

"Nice house," I said, taking in the cream-colored walls, skirted tables, fringed lampshades, and potted areca palms.

She smiled and played with her mop of brown hair, which dwarfed her face. I had an urge to push the thick bangs away from her forehead to get a better look at her. Pale skin with a multitude of freckles, large hazel eyes.

"We have a lot of things to talk about," I began, hoping to put her at ease. But I was interrupted by a tall teenage boy who appeared in the hallway, backpack slung over a shoulder, baseball hat with the Red Sox emblem pulled low over his face.

Evelyn shot up as if stung by a bee.

"Tommy. You can't go out. The reporter's still there."

"I have to, Mom."

"Tommy, we don't want your picture in the paper."

The boy pulled the baseball cap even further over his face. He shrugged. "I can't afford to miss any more practices. I've got an important meet coming up, Mom."

"Just one more day," Evelyn pleaded.

"What if that damn reporter is still out there tomorrow? You can't expect me to stay cooped up in my room for the rest of my life!"

"I'm sure she's getting tired of camping out on our front

lawn, Tommy."

"That's what you said yesterday. It's going to be a close meet. We could lose if I don't swim well."

"We're only talking a couple more days, Tommy."

"See. You're lying. A minute ago you said just *one* more day." He turned. "I'm leaving."

"Tommy. No. Please. Don't."

"See you, Mom."

He hesitated for a split second, and I sensed that if Evelyn had put her foot down, her son would have caved in. But she didn't, and the moment passed. Browne Junior crossed the front hall and lowered his head as if to brave an oncoming gale. He slammed the door hard on his way out, causing the hall windows to rattle.

Evelyn rushed to her observation point to spy through the crack in the curtains. She looked exhausted when she sat back down.

"Rough day?" I asked.

"It's been a nightmare." She let out a deep sigh. "I don't think she got a decent picture of Tommy. He was too fast for her." She looked up. "I'm so sorry we argued in front of you. We don't usually fight."

"It wasn't much of an argument. Besides, I rarely see people at their best. People hire private investigators when they've reached a low point and need help."

"I only wish I could protect Tommy from all this."

She'd started twisting her wedding band around her finger. At this moment Evelyn Browne looked frail and defeated. She smoothed her mop of hair with both hands.

"The last few days have been hell. Mitchell's death, the photographers on the lawn, my arrest. Tommy's a great kid, but it's too much even for him. He got into a fight yesterday with another kid at school. The kid made fun of me, and Tommy thought he had to defend me. He should have let it go. Stupid."

I nodded. I knew about as much about raising kids as I did about skydiving. And her son wasn't a kid. He was a teenager, meaning—in my experience—that he would exhibit sporadic tendencies of acting like a visitor from another planet.

Evelyn's eyes filled with tears. She pulled a tissue from a box, dried her eyes, and blew her nose hard.

"Your son mentioned a meet?"

"Swim meet." She attempted a weak smile. "He's one of the top swimmers in Massachusetts." Pride was audible in her voice. As if taking strength from her remark, she sat up straighter. "How do we do this?"

"I know this can't be easy for you, but it would help if you told me what happened on the night your husband died."

She shrugged. "Mitchell and I had dinner at the Hyatt. God, it was such an ordinary evening. The food was great, and we had a nice conversation over dinner . . ."

"What happened after you left the restaurant?"

"We came straight home. Mitchell had an early flight the next morning. I felt tired—too much wine I guess—and went straight to bed . . . and . . . and . . ." She stopped, reaching for another tissue. She dabbed her eyes and blew her nose before continuing. "That was the last time I saw him. Three days later the police knocked on my door and told me he was dead. Then they asked me all these questions. I told them everything I knew—I mean, I had nothing to hide. It never occurred to me that they would suspect *me* of killing Mitchell. I couldn't believe it when they arrested me."

I wondered whether she realized just how lucky she was to be back in her own home. David Silverman must have moved heaven and earth to swing bail on a murder charge.

"Why didn't you report your husband missing?"

She seemed puzzled. "I just assumed that he'd left on his

trip. I hadn't expected to see him the next day."

"But wasn't it unusual for him not to call for three whole days."

Evelyn looked confused. "No. Not really."

Sounded like the bloom was off their marriage. Evelyn smoothed her hair again, something she apparently did as a nervous habit.

"Evelyn, were you and you husband happily married?"

She looked down. "Oh . . . this is so hard."

"It's okay. Take your time."

Evelyn was silent for what seemed an eternity. Sighing deeply, she said, "I think Mitchell had a string of affairs. With his graduate students. I know he was involved with one of his doctoral students just before he died."

"Do you know her name?"

"Dawn Halebrook. Mitchell was her advisor. God, the nerve of that woman. I invited her to our Christmas party. So here she is, in my living room, sipping eggnog, and all the while she's screwing my husband."

"Did you confront Mitchell about it?"

"What would be the point? He wasn't going to stop having the affair just because I found out. It never stopped him before."

She studied the pattern of her Aubusson carpet.

"Evelyn, there is one other thing we need to talk about."

"What?"

"The Valium."

Her face colored. "That was two years ago. You probably think it was an incredibly stupid thing to do."

Actually, as a means of dealing with an unfaithful husband, her idea had been pretty ingenious. But I kept that thought to myself.

"Well," she said, "given how Mitchell died, it really was stupid. But I was desperate. The assistant to the dean of the biology department, she's a friend. Well, maybe not a friend exactly, but Jocelyn bought a puppy from me a few years back, and I helped her get it housebroken. One afternoon she calls and asks if she can come over, that there's something we need to discuss. I say okay, and she tells me there's a rumor circulating that Mitchell is having an affair with a student. It had come to the dean's attention. It had to stop, or Mitchell would be reprimanded. Wadsworth has a strict code about sex between students and professors. Mitchell could have been suspended. Even fired."

Evelyn started fiddling with her hair again. "Jocelyn suggested I talk to Mitchell. He and I discussed it. Little good that did. I'm sure they kept seeing each other. They were just more careful, about meeting in public. But *I* knew. Mitchell was away a lot at night, and when I called the lab, he wasn't there. He gave me lame excuses about doing research in the library. God, how dumb did he think I was? Then one evening I followed him. Right to *her* house. I kept driving around the block until he finally came sneaking out at midnight."

Ouch. "Did you confront him?"

"Well, not exactly. I didn't know what to say. I asked him the next morning where he'd been? That I'd tried to reach him. He said he was in the lab. The liar. I let it go. What could I say? I followed you last night?" She grimaced. "What would *you* have done?"

I would have documented his nocturnal escapades with my digital camera and changed the locks to our house. But I kept my mouth shut. Her question had been rhetorical.

"I didn't know what to do," she continued. "I mean, he was risking everything—his career, his reputation. All because of this . . . girl. Meanwhile I was a nervous wreck. My doctor gave me some Valium, and that's how I got the idea of slipping him some. I mean, *he* was the one with the overactive sex life. I fixed it so he wouldn't have the energy to go catting around at night."

I suppressed a smile. "And just how did you manage to slip him tranquilizers without him noticing?"

"Oh, that was easy," she said lightly. "I ground the tablets into a powder and stirred them into his spaghetti sauce. Or mixed them in the butternut squash. He always ate dinner at home, even when he planned to go out later."

What a prince Mitchell Browne had been.

I also changed my original assessment of Evelyn. She wasn't small or frail or helpless. She had spunk. I just hoped she wasn't a murderess.

"Weren't you afraid he'd eventually catch on?"

"I wasn't thinking that far ahead. You have to understand. I was at the end of my rope. I just wanted him to stop."

"But eventually he did find out?"

"Oh yes. Ohmigod. He was so pissed." She slumped back in her seat, creating once more the impression of disappearing into the oversized cushions. "He locked me out of the house. Can you believe it? He's the one screwing around, and I get the boot. He packed my things and put them out on the street."

Evelyn moistened her lips. "Eventually, a judge allowed me back in my home, and told Mitchell to move out. Mitchell traveled abroad, often for weeks at a time, leaving Tommy with a nanny. The judge decided that a child's place was with his mother."

"Why didn't you divorce him?"

"Because Mitchell wouldn't give me custody. At best we'd have joint custody—if I was lucky. Mitchell would have hired the best lawyer in town. The thought of my being only a part-time mother to my son was more than I could bear."

"You could have hired a first-rate lawyer yourself. Most judges would think it preferable for a child to grow up with a full-time mother than with a nanny and absentee father."

Evelyn shook her head. "Mitchell owned this house when we got married. He made me sign a prenuptial. I had no cash, no marketable skills, not even a college degree. I had no money to hire some fancy lawyer. And besides, courts don't automatically give custody to mothers anymore. I could have ended up with no custody, just visitation. I wasn't taking that chance."

"Who all knew that you had slipped Valium in your husband's food?"

"I don't know."

"You mentioned that Mitchell's doctor knew. Who else might Mitchell have told?"

She shrugged elaborately.

"Come on, Evelyn. This is important. I need a list of people who knew. Your husband's murderer used that precious piece of information to make it look like *you* killed him."

I could see from her suddenly alert expression that she was finally getting the point. "Mitchell wouldn't have told anyone. Certainly not at Wadsworth," she said thoughtfully. "He did have a reputation to maintain. Mitchell's brother knew. He stopped seeing us. Mitchell told me Phillip couldn't trust me, especially around his kids. That I was a danger to his family and I might poison them all."

"Mitchell's brother doesn't sound very nice."

"Oh, I don't mean that . . . Phillip is a great person. Not like Mitchell at all."

I felt suddenly sorry for Evelyn. A loveless marriage. And now she was in a lot of trouble.

As if realizing what she'd said, Evelyn colored. "Hard to believe Mitchell and Phillip came from the same family. I mean, Phillip works construction . . ."

That last sentence surprised me. Working construction wasn't exactly the intellectual fast track. I would have expected Mitchell's brother to have a desk job, doing something cerebral. I made a note to talk to Phillip Browne.

"How did you find out about your husband's latest affair?"

She shifted in her seat, her expression as guilty as a puppy's that had just peed on the carpet.

"Oh, you know . . . you pick up clues."

"What kind of clues?"

Evelyn seemed to be struggling with the response. I could practically see her mental wheels grinding for an answer that wasn't coming. If she thought much longer, I might see smoke rise from her ears.

To spare her further agony, I jumped in, "I take it we're talking more than intuition here, Evelyn. What happened? Did someone tell you about them? Did you see them together?"

Evelyn shook her head. "Promise you won't tell?"

"I promise."

"Okay. I was taping Mitchell's telephone conversations. You know, with one of those little voice-activated tape recorders? I hooked it up in the guest bedroom."

"Do you still have the tapes?"

"Just a few of them. Mostly, I'd tape over a cassette once I'd listened to it."

"I'll need to hear them. I'll take whatever you have."

Evelyn looked distressed, the room suddenly very still.

"Could I go to jail for this? I mean, isn't it illegal to tape someone else's phone conversation?"

I felt my eyes cross. "Evelyn," I said. "You don't seem to be getting the big picture here. Right now you're going to jail for *murder*. Electronic eavesdropping is peanuts in comparison. We have to figure out who wanted your husband dead. Those tapes could help."

"Okay, okay. I'll get them." She stood and disappeared into the hallway, her footsteps echoing as she climbed the stairs.

She returned a minute later and placed three cassette cases

on the table—Bonnie Raitt, Britney Spears, and Anita Baker. Again, I had to admire her slyness, the clever camouflage she'd used to hide her loot.

Her expression remained troubled. "You won't tell anyone about the tapes?"

I crossed my heart. "Your secret's safe with me."

She gave me a tiny smile.

"Tell me what you know about your husband's mistress," I said.

She shrugged. "It's all on the tapes. Her name's Dawn Halebrook. Did I already mention that? She used to call here all the time. Can you believe it? It wasn't until I started listening in on their conversations that I realized there was something going on between them. What kind of woman calls the man she's having an affair with at home?"

I had never given any consideration as to what constituted proper etiquette for mistresses, though I assumed it was bound to be pretty much a free-for-all.

Evelyn began working a cuticle. "Hell. It's no big mystery why Mitchell was attracted to her. She's smart and young and talented. She was on some gymnastics team. Not the Olympics, but she placed nationally." Evelyn sighed deeply. "What I can't understand is why a girl like that would waste her time with a married guy who's old enough to be her father."

"I'm sure she got something out of the deal. Brilliant advice on her research project, perhaps? Help with her dissertation?"

"But Mitchell said she *was* real smart. Why did she have to sleep with him?"

It was obviously a question that had been bothering Evelyn for a long time.

"Where does Dawn live?"

"In that high-rise across the river from the B-school."

I knew the building she was talking about.

"Evelyn, can you think of anyone else who might have wanted your husband dead?"

She gave me a sardonic look. "You mean, besides myself?"

"No." I grinned at her. "Besides Dawn."

For the first time since we started talking, Evelyn cracked a genuine smile, lighting up her little face. Her teeth were tiny, again creating that childlike illusion.

Immediately, her expression turned serious again. "You live with a man for seventeen years. You cook for him. You raise a child with him. You'd think you'd know him. But you don't. Or at least, I didn't." She looked defeated. "To answer your question, no, I can't imagine who would have wanted to kill my husband."

"I'll need to talk to your son as well."

She bristled. "Why? Tommy doesn't know anything."

"We can't be sure of that until I talk with him."

"I don't want him involved in this."

"Evelyn. He already *is* involved. His father is dead and his mother has been accused of murder. Tommy may know something that could clear you."

She sighed. "All right. Drop by later. Say after six?"

I had better agree before she changed her mind. So what if it was Saturday night? It's not like I had Mel Gibson on hold for the evening.

"And Evelyn, I need to go through your husband's personal belongings. Did he have a home office?"

She nodded. "Do you need me to help?"

"No. Just show me where his study is. I'll call you if I have any questions."

A sigh of relief escaped her tiny mouth.

"Thank you," she whispered. "I don't think I could stand looking through Mitchell's. . . . through his things."

FIVE

On the way to her deceased husband's study we passed through the front hall, with the dining room on our left. To the right I caught a quick glimpse of the kitchen. Oak cabinets, brass pots and plants hanging overhead, white and black tile floor; a setup straight out of *Architectural Digest*. Beyond the kitchen were two closed doors—a bathroom and a closet, I guessed. The next door on the left was Mitchell's home office.

The study was spacious. Two big windows faced the backyard. Through the painted shutters I could make out a pretty view of flowering azaleas. A dark-green wallpaper with a subtle plaid pattern covered the walls. Two framed hunting scenes hung on the wall over a leather couch to my left. An enormous, eye-catching antique desk dominated the center of the room. A genuine period piece. Even my untrained eye saw that this wasn't a reproduction. The desk was intricately crafted, the luxurious wood luminous.

"Holler if you need help," Evelyn said. She left, shutting the door softly behind her.

Alone at last. I always feel a little strange snooping through other people's belongings, but it's part of my job.

A number of photographs were strategically scattered around the room. I recognized Mitchell Browne immediately from the newspaper clippings. He looked like a little geek. He had wavy, light-brown hair, thick glasses, a square face with a high forehead. His smile for the camera was innocuous, almost shy.

In most of the pictures he held his arms in front of his body, as if protecting himself. I judged him to be fairly short, five-eight at most, with a portly build and a small potbelly. Definitely no sex symbol. His young, nubile grad students had obviously been attracted by his brilliant intellect or his scintillating personality rather than his physique.

In most of the displayed photographs Browne was posing with some famous personality. Governor Weld, Governor Romney shaking Browne's hand, and a younger-looking version of Mitchell Browne with George W. Bush, also shaking his hand. Another photo was of Browne with a distinguished-looking gentleman holding a pipe, no handshake. Not a single picture of his wife or son. Browne's priorities were clear. Already I didn't like the man.

I started going through the desk drawers. Envelopes, pen and pencils, a dictionary, Scotch tape, stamps, some files that looked like biological research. So far I'd found nothing you wouldn't expect to find in an office. I put his address book and telephone bills aside, the only items of interest so far. His long-distance calls were mainly to California, to the 650, 415, and 408 area codes.

At the bottom of the drawer was an envelope containing several faded photos, school portraits of a girl in her early teens. They were like time-lapse photography, showing the subject grow older and more sophisticated with each successive shot. She was ordinary-looking, neither pretty nor homely. Her hair the color of honey, crinkly, and teased into a beehive hairdo reminiscent of the early sixties. I wondered what she'd meant to Browne. An old flame? I put the photos with the address book.

The top drawer was locked. I looked for a key. No luck. It was so shallow—a mere two inches—that I wondered whether the drawer opened at all. Maybe it served as a fake front. I scooted under the desk. Smooth polished wood without a hint of a drawer mechanism.

I rummaged through the folders in the file cabinets behind the desk. There was a slew of articles on HIV, some authored by Browne. The remaining files were about recombinant viruses. As I skimmed through the papers I got the gist of it: attaching virus particles from one species to those of another. The mere thought of some deranged scientist attaching parts of an AIDS virus to a different, innocent, and more prolific virus wasn't comforting. There were entire folders filled with DNA X-ray strips, autoradiographs, and images of EcoRI fragments.

Another folder held replications with seemingly endless strings of capital letters. They looked like the output from a computer with a personality disorder. Cleavage sites, on the other hand, sounded sexy, kind of like bacteria with boobs. Next I found charts of circular vector plots, with labels like "pJE 253 plasmids" attached, with explanations of restrictive enzymes and restriction sites. Straitjackets for viruses to me. *Make my day. Send those suckers to jail.*

I was getting punchy. I had no idea what I was looking at, but rocket science had to be simple compared to this stuff. How smart did these biotech people have to be to come up with all these graphs and charts? Not to mention the genome project?

I turned on Browne's computer, scanned the directory, and opened documents at random. The documents looked like electronic versions of the hard copy files I'd already gone through, except that virtually all of Mitchell's computer files were about HIV.

Rummaging through Brown's office took about an hour. I found no death threats, love letters, extortion demands, or suicide notes. Really, the only intriguing item had been the school portraits of the girl. She had obviously been important to Browne at some point in his life. Moreover, how odd that he'd kept the multiple pictures of this girl, when there wasn't one photo of his wife or son in his office.

Probably just idle curiosity on my part. I had no reason to believe that the mystery girl would tie in with Browne's death in any way. But I stowed her photos in my briefcase nonetheless.

Six

I found Evelyn in the kitchen. She was Scotch-taping newspaper clippings into a scrapbook. A small, buff-colored dog with large soulful eyes and big ears gave a bark.

"It's okay, girl." Evelyn got up and the dog, tail wagging, stayed close on Evelyn's heel, eyeing me with distrust.

"We're going to have puppies."

"Cute pooch. What breed is it?"

"Cocker spaniel. Come on, girl. I'll get you some fresh water."

While she poured Poland Springs into a stainless steel bowl, I noticed newspaper clippings on the table.

"May I?" I asked.

"Be my guest."

The articles were about her son's swim meets and academic accomplishments. Most came from the BB&N school newsletter. By all accounts, Tommy was an honor student who was also active on the basketball and swim teams. There was a photo of him playing the saxophone, with an accompanying article about an upcoming concert of the school's jazz band. Two of the articles had come from a local newspaper. The previous winter, Tommy had risked his life to save a classmate after she'd fallen through the ice on Spy Pond.

Interestingly, there were no clippings about Mitchell's murder, though the papers had been full of them all last week.

"I'm impressed," I said, scanning the articles and returning them to the pile. "You must be very proud of your son."

"I am." Evelyn flashed a smile. "You took a long time. Did you find anything?"

"Not really." I showed her the school portraits. "Do you know who this is?"

She examined the photos and shook her head.

"I've never seen this girl before. Where did you find these?"

"In Mitchell's desk. Oh, and I think the top drawer is locked. Do you have the key?"

She hesitated.

"What is it, Evelyn?"

"The police asked me the same thing. I told them there is no drawer. It's just wood."

My bullshit meter went on the alert. Was she lying?

"Well, I'm not the police. And I'm not stupid, either. There is a drawer, isn't there?"

"Yeah. Mitchell kept the key on his key ring."

"And you don't have a duplicate?" I asked.

I was already making for Browne's study, with Evelyn close on my heels.

"Mitchell didn't like me coming in here. He'd have killed me if I tried to get into his desk."

She shrank away, staying by the door. I got the impression she feared lightning would strike if she entered Browne's inner sanctum. Or that his ghost would return to haunt her.

"His keys are gone," she said. "They weren't in his pants pockets when they pulled him out of the river. And they're not in the house." She was quiet for a moment. "I guess I'll have to call a locksmith. The desk is a rosewood antique. I don't want some incompetent to ruin it."

Frankly, I thought the woodwork was the least of Evelyn's worries.

Browne's murderer might still have the keys to the house.

"Change all your locks. Today. Now."

"Why?" she asked innocently. Then her eyes widened. "God. I hadn't thought of that."

She raced to the family room and started flipping through the yellow pages.

"Where else in the house did your husband keep his belongings?"

"It's all in the study. He didn't have much. And in the bedroom. But just his clothes. And he kept some old boxes in the attic."

Going up to the attic or sorting through Browne's clothes wasn't an enticing prospect. Besides, I'd had my fill of rummaging through other people's stuff for one day.

"One more thing, Evelyn. Do you know anything about Mitchell's updated will?"

She was copying a number from the phone book, writing slowly and pressing down hard. She looked up. "No. Is that why the police think I killed him? Because of the money?"

I didn't answer.

"It's the life insurance, isn't it? And if they convict me, I won't get to collect any of it. Why couldn't Mitchell have died in an accident, or of a heart attack? Why did he have to get himself murdered?" She looked straight at me. There was no guilt on her face, just indignation.

"So who killed him?" I asked.

"I don't know. I wish I did."

"Evelyn, one last thing. Your husband's attorney says you tried to commit suicide two years ago."

She looked at me like I wasn't playing with a full deck of cards. "Where on earth did he get that idea?"

"From Mitchell."

"But that's ludicrous. I wouldn't commit suicide. Not after everything I've been through. I'm lucky to be alive. I was a sick child. I barely made it. I wouldn't throw away my life now. And who'd raise Tommy? I can't imagine Mitchell saying such nonsense. His lawyer must have heard wrong."

I understood only too well why Mitchell Browne had said it. Selfish and calculating, this was how he dealt with his wife. If this was how he'd treated members of his family, there had to be plenty of other people who hated his guts.

"Macy, don't let them put me in prison for a crime I didn't commit. Because the thought of some stranger raising my son makes me ill. You have to find out who killed Mitchell."

"I'll do my best, Evelyn."

As I left the house, Evelyn was telephoning the locksmith. It was a little before noon. I pushed past the reporter outside, hand raised to shield my face.

While I drove home, thoughts of Mitchell Browne's missing keys kept buzzing around my brain like a pesky fly. Most likely they lay buried in the primordial muck at the bottom of the Charles. Or maybe Browne's killer had them.

I couldn't figure out the point of taking the keys? If the murderer wanted to break into the house, he would surely have done so by now.

It probably meant nothing, but I hated loose ends.

Once I got home, I found Phillip Browne's phone number via directory assistance, master sleuth that I am. A woman picked up on the third ring. She had a friendly voice. I stated my business and she said her husband would be home after four. I was welcome to drop by and speak with him then. The directions to their house in Concord were simple enough.

I changed into my running shorts and went for a jog. I ran slowly at first, picking up the pace when I reached the Charles. The ground beneath me was still damp from the rain, and a white mist rose from the footpaths. The sun had come out and was making a brilliant display on the surface of the water. I thought of Mitchell Browne's corpse floating in the river for days.

My legs protested for the first half-mile, until the endorphins kicked in and I felt like a racehorse that had been stabled too long. I headed all the way to MIT, crossed at the Mass. Ave. Bridge and backtracked on the opposite side, delighted by the mild weather and budding trees.

By the time I got home from the run I felt as relaxed as Seabiscuit in the home stretch. And I had an idea.

SEVEN

Concord is about twenty miles northwest of Boston. It's a pretty town with lush green fields, fieldstone walls, lots of antique houses on big plots of land—even an occasional farm. Home of Thoreau, Walden Pond, Minuteman National Park, and the Old North Bridge, Concord is steeped in history, proud of its role as the Yankee cradle of the American Revolution.

Phillip Browne lived southeast of the town center, in a heavily wooded section. A narrow driveway, flanked by rough stones on both sides, led up to the house, a stately light-gray colonial with blue shutters and trim. A series of brick steps snaked from the driveway up to the front door. The overall effect was charming. The size of the house and the generous proportions of the property struck me as too grandiose for someone working construction. I wondered how Phillip Browne managed to pay for it all.

I stepped out of my car. To my right, through a large bay window, I could see two youngsters sitting across from each other, engrossed in some sort of game.

I followed the sound of voices to the backyard, where two women were discussing the fate of two flats of budding annuals. The younger of the two was in her thirties, and pretty, even if somewhat on the heavy side. The other woman had to be in her sixties. She was very tall and big-boned. A bandana covered her hair. Their conversation stopped when they saw me.

"Hello, I'm Macy Adams. I called earlier."

The younger woman smiled. "I'm Amanda, Phillip's wife." I recognized her pleasant voice from our phone conversation. "This is Claire Browne, my mother-in-law."

It took a split second to sink in. The older woman was Mitchell Browne's mother.

"My condolences," I murmured, extending my hand.

Claire Browne took my hand, her grip firm. Her skin felt dry and calloused.

"Amanda mentioned that you're looking into my son's death."

The statement was delivered in the flat tone commonly used to discuss the weather. I had expected Mitchell's mother to get tearful at the mention of her son, but her face remained impassive. Whatever grieving she was doing, she seemed to be doing it in private. I wondered if she planned to stick around for the meeting.

As if reading my mind, she said, "Well, I had better run along." Her pale eyes shifted to me. "I assume you won't require my presence." She was already stepping back.

"Actually, I would like to talk with you at some point, if today isn't convenient."

"I don't think there's anything useful I could add to your investigation. Besides, it's my understanding that the police already found and arrested my son's murderer."

That last statement was delivered with an edge. Her eyes were hard and dry. She shifted her gaze. "Amanda, remember to move the plants into the garage if the forecast calls for frost."

The older woman gave a small wave. I watched her print skirt billow behind her in the breeze as she walked away, troubled by what she said. Accusing someone of murder was serious, going beyond mere mother/daughter-in-law animosity.

"Come on in," Amanda said.

She led me through the back door into her lovely kitchen. "I guess Phillip's running a little late. Can I get you something to drink? A soda, some juice?"

"No thanks, I'm fine."

She pointed to a bar stool at the kitchen counter, turned on the stovetop, and reached for a pot on a shelf. Her hair was bleached blond with some dark roots showing, her complexion rosy, her cheeks flushed. She had a pug nose and laugh lines around her mouth. Her facial expression was happy as she filled the pot with water, added salt, and placed it on the stove. She would have looked great in one of those Crisco ads in women's magazines.

She caught me watching and smiled. "Sorry, this'll only take a minute. Phillip gets up at the crack of dawn, so we tend to eat dinner early. I hadn't expected Claire to drop by this afternoon."

She removed the wrapping from a tray of chicken fingers, sprinkled them with salt, and popped them into the oven. Next she emptied a package of rice into a simmering pot of water on the stovetop. She opened the refrigerator and took out a tray of butternut squash, transferred it to a Pyrex dish, put it in the microwave, and set the timer. Her movements were swift and exact. I was astonished. Thus far her dinner preparations were under two minutes.

So what if it wasn't gourmet? Who was I to criticize? My meals consisted of turkey sandwiches and Chinese takeout.

"I take it you and your mother-in-law are close?"

"You could say that. And Claire's terrific with the kids. They love her."

Amanda attacked a head of romaine lettuce, chopping it with military precision.

"That's nice. You hear so many horror stories about mother-in-laws."

She laughed, "Don't you, though? Phillip's always been her favorite. I'm sure that helps."

Our exchange sounded stilted. I felt like we were stuck in a holding pattern, waiting for her husband to arrive. I shifted my weight on the bar stool and crossed my legs.

"From what she said, it doesn't sound like she's crazy about Evelyn."

Amanda gave a nervous laugh. "No, I shouldn't think so."

"Why is that?"

She shrugged. "Oh, I don't know. I guess their personalities clash." She gave me another smile. Miss Congeniality. But her smile seemed forced. She was clearly uneasy.

"I get the impression that she thinks Evelyn killed Mitchell."

Amanda said nothing, her face set in an expression of displeasure. While she grated carrots, the silence stretched on, thick and uncomfortable.

"Nice house," I finally interjected, a clumsy attempt to break the conversational ice drifts forming between us. I glanced around the kitchen, taking in the granite counters, cherry cabinets, Viking stove, twin dishwashers, and Sub-Zero refrigerators. The windows had half-moon arches and the polished flooring was golden oak. Again, I wondered how Phillip could afford all this.

"Thank you. My husband did most of the work himself."

Still, the kitchen appliances and cabinets alone had to price out at over a hundred thousand. "Your husband works construction?"

"Actually, he runs his own company. He has a crew of eight working for him. They're doing a development in Carlisle. It'll keep him busy until the end of the season."

Her eyes lit up and there was pride in her voice when she talked about her husband. She tossed the salad fixings into a bowl, which she transferred to the refrigerator. With quick, efficient movements she picked up a sponge and wiped the counters.

"Were your husband and his brother close?"

"God no. Mitchell was positively antisocial."

"Sounds like you didn't care much for your brother-in-law."

She shrugged. "I didn't. We hadn't seen Mitchell in years."

Her statement confirmed what Evelyn had told me.

"Not even for holidays?"

She shook her head.

"How come?"

We both looked up. A car was pulling up outside.

"That's Phillip," Amanda said, sounding relieved. She dried her hands and rushed to the back door.

"Honey, the private investigator is here," she called out. To me she said, "I had better put the plants in the garage before I forget."

I slid off the bar stool and spotted Phillip at the back door. He was bent over, slipping off his shoes, which were caked in mud. When he stood, I was stunned by how good-looking he was. Being Mitchell's brother, I had assumed that both men would share Mitchell's geeky looks. This guy was a hunk: well over six feet tall, tanned, with broad shoulders and slim hips. Even with his shirt on, I could make out the bulky muscle tone of his arms and chest. Sexy.

A crooked grin formed on his face. "So you're the private eye? This should be interesting. I've never met a woman P.I. before."

"There are a few of us around."

Handsome men occasionally have a negative effect on my I.Q. I was trying not to let that happen here.

As Phillip stepped into the light, I could see him more clearly. His hair was dark brown and thick, his eyebrows nearly straight. His eyes were hazel, set far apart, and he looked at me with an amused gaze. He did not look like a suspect.

"Hey, I think it's great, you being a detective, I mean." His smile came easy. He opened the refrigerator and scanned the interior.

"How about a beer?" he said.

"I'll pass, thank you."

He frowned. "What's the matter? Big bad P.I. like you, you don't drink?" He took out two cans of Michelob and, with a flick of his wrist, tossed one toward me. I was so surprised by his sudden move that I almost let the can drop on his glossy oak floor.

"Nice catch," he remarked.

I placed the can on the kitchen counter. He surveyed me with a long, lazy look while he flipped open his own can. Was he flirting with me? It didn't make any sense with his wife just outside the door.

Phillip led the way to the family room. I followed warily, aware of the awkwardness of being alone with him, and felt relief when I saw the kids were still playing Monopoly.

Phillip kissed his daughter on the top of her head. "Who's winning?"

"I am." She gave him a triumphant smile. His daughter had her mother's blond hair and her father's stop-traffic bone structure and serious eyes. She looked about twelve. Another year or two, and she'd be giving her parents serious headaches.

The boy seated opposite her looked a couple of years older than his sister and was going through that awkward stage of puberty of arms and legs growing too long and fuzz sprouting everywhere. Compared to his gorgeous sister, he was an average-looking kid.

Phillip nodded and motioned to the conversational grouping at the other end of the room. We sat down.

"Getting hot out there," he said, taking a swill of Michelob. He gave my Brooks Brothers shirt a once over.

I didn't respond.

"Evelyn hired you?"

"Evelyn's lawyer."

"What a mess," he said. "I can't believe they're accusing Evelyn of murder."

Amanda had reappeared and took a seat next to Phillip, her big brown eyes bright.

"Did I miss anything?" she said.

"Not at all," I said. "We were just getting started. Tell me about your brother, Phillip?"

"My brother, the genius? This may sound strange, but I always thought that if someone in the family died a premature death, it'd be me. I was the one always getting hurt—doing sports, or on the construction site."

He shifted his weight forward and put his beer can on the table. "Okay. Mitchell and me. Clearly, my brother ended up with the brains in the family. Big bro' and me were never on the same wavelength, even when we were young. He'd spend entire days off by himself, usually in the library, while I was playing ball with some team. My brother was a loner. He kept to himself, his nose buried in a book." Phillip looked at his wife and winked. "I guess I'm more of a hands-on type of guy."

With his last comment, he tickled her stomach. She let out a tiny shriek and gave him a goofy smile. *Weren't they cute?*

"When was the last time you saw your brother?" I said.

Phillip glanced at his wife, as if looking for instruction. "When was that, Amanda? Maybe two, two and a half years ago?"

She nodded. "That sounds about right."

I found it peculiar, especially since Mitchell was Phillip's only sibling. On top of that, they'd lived only ten miles apart.

"What happened?" I asked. "Did the two of you have a falling out or something?"

"Not at all." Phillip shrugged. "Mitchell's career was keeping him pretty busy, and I had my own business to get off the ground. Plus we were building the house . . ."

"What about Thanksgiving, or Christmas?" I said.

"We go skiing over Christmas break, in Vermont. My brother didn't ski. His thing was to attend some conference, at some fancy resort in the Caribbean, where rooms go for five hundred dollars a night. Too pricy for our tastes. Besides which, to be perfectly honest, Mitchell wasn't my first choice of someone to pal around with. He could be a royal pain in the butt, if you pardon my French."

He fixed his eyes on me again, another lazy look. He had bedroom eyes with incredibly long eyelashes. I shouldn't be staring at Phillip, not with Amanda sitting right here in the same room. But he was a visual magnet. I had trouble tearing my gaze from those terrific cheekbones.

How had an average-looking, slightly overweight female like Amanda managed to snag an absolute hunk of a man like Phillip? She had to be really good at something—and the kitchen was obviously not the place. Good in bed perhaps? Or maybe Phillip wasn't such a prize? Maybe he was all packaging and no substance.

"You said your brother was a pain in the butt? How so?"

"Let's just say that Mitchell didn't cope well when things weren't going his way."

Phillip finished his beer. Amanda took the empty can from his hand. Noticing my untouched can of Michelob, she said, "I'm getting a glass of white wine for myself. Would you like one as well, Macy?"

"Sure. Wine would be great. Thank you."

Phillip shook his head and leaned back, stretching his arms along the back of the couch.

"Can you explain something to me? And this is something that has bugged me for years." He waited a couple of seconds, as if to make sure he had everyone's undivided attention. "Why is it that women drink wine when beer tastes so much better and is so much more refreshing?"

I had expected some important question relating to his brother's death, not trivia.

Amanda laughed, breaking the tension. "Maybe it's because women don't enjoy burping as much as men do."

"Maybe it's because beer smells bad and tastes like throw-up," Phillip's daughter chimed in from across the room.

"Who asked you?" Phillip called to her. Then to me, "That's what you get. You feed them, pay for their clothes and schooling, and room and board, and then you get a lot of lip." He winked.

"Your daughter is beautiful."

"Too beautiful for her own good. She thinks she owns me." But he said it good-naturedly.

"*Mom* owns you," his daughter shot back from across the room.

Amanda returned with a tray bearing two glasses of wine and a can of Michelob.

"Well, I can't speak for Macy, but I do prefer wine."

I took the glass from her hand. "So do I." I sipped the wine, which had a slightly fruity bouquet.

"Evelyn thinks she was responsible for a rift between you and Mitchell," I said, getting back to the topic of his brother's murder.

"Where on earth did she get that idea?" Phillip sounded genuinely surprised.

"It's not true then?"

"God, no." He shook his head. "Given a choice between spending time with my brother or Evelyn, she wins hands down. Besides, she's a terrific cook. The thing I miss from our get-togethers are Evelyn's dinners."

I was confused. Mitchell had told Evelyn they stopped socializing with his brother's family because Phillip deemed her to be a potentially dangerous cohort, especially around the kitchen. Had he lied?

"You knew about the tranquilizers?" I probed.

Amanda and Phillip looked at each other. Amanda finally broke the silence.

"You mean two years ago? Yes, we knew. When you see Evelyn, please tell her that we're really sorry. But we had to tell the police about the Valium. The detective brought it up. He already knew. We don't want Evelyn to think that we're responsible for her getting arrested."

Amanda's regret seemed sincere.

"Did the detective mention who first told him about the Valium?"

"No, and we didn't ask," Phillip said. "But he knew. Could you tell Evelyn that we had no choice but to confirm it? We do feel bad about that. She's family, after all."

I was getting strange vibes here. They were making too much of it. And both of them looked ill at ease. Amanda especially had been on pins and needles from the second she saw me.

"When did Mitchell tell you about the Valium?"

"Actually, Mitchell didn't tell us," Phillip answered.

"Who then?"

"Tommy brought it up. He asked me what Valium was. After I explained, he said that was the medicine his mother had accidentally given to his father, and that his dad was real mad about it."

"And what was Mitchell's version of the story?"

"As I said, we never discussed it."

Not according to what Mitchell had told Evelyn. Somebody was lying.

"Did *you* tell anyone else? About the Valium, I mean."

"Not a soul." He shrugged. "Why would we?"

Amanda spoke up, her voice suddenly intense. "Why does it have to be anybody's fault that he's dead? Hasn't it occurred to the police that Mitchell might have committed suicide?"

"Do you know of any reason why your brother-in-law might have wanted to take his own life?"

"Well no. But Mitchell had always been such a secretive person, who knew what was going on in his mind? I just can't believe Evelyn could kill anyone. It's ludicrous. Crazy."

Amanda was getting herself all worked up. Phillip put an arm around her shoulder.

"It doesn't make any sense to me either," he said quietly. "I even told the police so."

"Well, if it wasn't Evelyn, then who?"

Neither of them answered. Phillip just sat there, while Amanda sipped her wine.

"I'm almost ashamed to admit it." Phillip's voice was soft. "But when you get right down to it, I really didn't know my brother all that well." He leaned forward. "But with the millions involved in his research, wouldn't you think that his death had to be linked to his work?"

"Like how?" I asked.

"Maybe someone was trying to steal his research. Or maybe someone tampered with his medical trials and he found out. But Evelyn? She wouldn't hurt a fly."

Phillip looked at his wife, and she nodded thoughtfully. "Phillip's right. Evelyn is like Mary Poppins, always rescuing things. She'll find a bird that fell from its nest and nurse it back to health. She's forever taking in stray dogs and cats and finding homes for them. That's just the kind of person she is. She's no murderess. We went fishing three, four years ago. She wouldn't even let us kill the damn fish. She insisted that we toss them back in the water."

I could easily picture that side of Evelyn, thinking back on the affection she'd lavished on her dog.

But plenty of people who were squeamish about hurting small animals didn't think twice about doing their fellow human beings in. Animal activists had killed people for the sake of saving laboratory rats.

I left shortly thereafter. The main thing I took away from our meeting was how truly sorry Amanda and Phillip felt about ratting on Evelyn. But I couldn't discern their motive. Was it because they believed her to be fundamentally incapable of murder—or because they themselves were hiding something?

EIGHT

The drive back from Concord was scenic, the sun a bright red ball in my rearview mirror. I stopped by my office to pick up the mail and messages, and most importantly, the 9 mm Glock pistol I kept in a safe. I had to renew my firearms license, a royal pain. In five years of being a private investigator, I'd never once discharged a firearm in the line of duty. But I'll admit that the mere knowledge of possessing the handy, lightweight gun made me feel more secure. In order to keep my Massachusetts firearms license current, the law required a shooting test every five years. I needed to spend a couple of hours at the practice range to avoid acute embarrassment before the examiners. Since I didn't want to walk around with a loaded weapon, I removed the magazine, stuck it in my briefcase, and dropped the 9 mm cavalierly into my handbag, right next to the emergency supply of Tampax.

From the office it was a short distance to Evelyn's house. The *Globe* reporter was nowhere in sight. Even the press had more sense than to work on a Saturday night. I rang the bell.

Evelyn opened the door, dressed for a night out. It was the first time I'd seen her made up, and the effect wasn't flattering. Instead of rendering her more attractive, the paint job she'd done on her face made her look older and harsher. The boxy cut of her mid-calf black dress didn't help, as it seemed to shrink her further. She looked like a kid who played dress up in her mother's clothes. The fire-engine-red lipstick clashed with her delicate coloring, and her hair was teased way too big. In short, she looked like the before version of a makeover candidate.

Evelyn steered me toward the living room. Tommy sat on the love seat, his back stiff and ramrod straight. He stood as I entered. On his feet, he positively dwarfed his tiny mother. He wore chinos and a white dress shirt. His slender, streamlined swimmer's physique swimmer lent his clothes an air of casual elegance. Hazel-eyed and handsome, he more closely resembled an offspring Phillip might have fathered instead of Mitchell. Somewhere among Mitchell Browne's ancestors lurked an individual who'd passed down the good-looks genes.

"Tommy, this is Miss Adams," Evelyn said formally.

"Just call me Macy," I said.

Evelyn and Tommy sat down, looking at me expectantly. It was all so polite. Too polite.

I stayed on my feet. "Could I talk with Tommy alone?"

Tommy's eyes brightened, while Evelyn's face tensed.

"Is that really necessary? Tommy doesn't have any secrets from me."

"It's okay, Mom," Tommy piped up eagerly.

"Tommy and I could go down to the Square and grab a quick dinner?"

The boy bounded to his feet. "I'll grab my jacket."

Evelyn looked upset and lost. The evening wasn't proceeding according to her plans. But what was the big deal?

"I don't know . . ." she said. "I was going to the symphony. Mozart. My favorite. I bought the ticket last month."

"Perfect. Go," I said encouragingly. "Tommy won't be alone. He'll be with me."

"Maybe I should just stay home."

"Go out, Evelyn. It'll help you get your mind off things. I'll keep an eye on Tommy and make sure he gets home safely."

The kid was already standing by the door, a coil of tightly wound nervous energy.

Evelyn sighed. "Be sure to set the alarm when you get home. I'll call during intermission."

Tommy rolled his eyes. Evelyn kissed his cheek, as he stood stiff as a board, visibly embarrassed by all the fuss.

As soon as we were out the door, he said, "Can we go to Fire and Ice?"

"Sure."

I told him that we would walk the short distance to Wadsworth Square.

I said, "Where do you go to school?"

"BB and N."

Buckingham, Browne, and Nichols, a prep school located in Cambridge that was very popular with the Wadsworth professorial set.

"How do you like it?"

"My father liked it."

The caustic undertone in the word "father" was unmistakable.

"What's your favorite subject?"

"Math, or science . . . I hate English. All those essays . . . I never know what to write. I'm doing this totally awesome project for science fair." He started telling me about his project, losing me after two sentences. But what came across was his complete enthusiasm. His demeanor changed, as he became more self-assured. Tommy must have inherited his father's brains for research.

We arrived at Fire and Ice. I liked the place, with its colorful interior and all-you-can-eat buffet. I packed my bowl with chicken and Chinese vegetables, and presented it to the cook for stir-frying. Besides his bowl of stir-fry, Tommy also asked for a hamburger. I remembered from having an older brother that adolescent boys manage to pack away mind-boggling quantities of food.

While we waited for our food to cook, we sipped our drinks and talked.

"This thing with my mother," Tommy said. "Will they put her on trial?"

"I hope not."

Tommy swirled the ice cubes in the drink around in circles. "I think I screwed up."

His casual demeanor had evaporated, replaced by a bereft look.

"How so?"

"The night Dad died . . . the police asked me a bunch of questions. And I lied to them."

"About what?"

"I didn't want to get my friend Kevin in trouble. How could I know that I was screwing things up for Mom?"

"You told a lie?"

He swallowed hard. "Yeah. I told the cops I was at Kevin's all night, 'cause that's what I'd told Mom. Except, what we really did was go to this party . . ."

He smoothed his hair back, a mannerism he must have picked up from his mother. "Okay, things got a little wild at the party, and the neighbors must have called the police. When we saw them pull up, Kevin and I slipped out the back and took off. When we got to Kevin's car, it was gone. It was his dad's car— his dad's new Beemer—and Kevin wasn't supposed to drive it. We thought it had been stolen. Turns out it had been towed. And we did not have the hundred bucks to get it back from the tow lot. Kevin was in big trouble.

"I can imagine. But what does this have to do with your mother?"

"I'm getting to that. I ran home to get some money. From

Mom. Except she was already asleep. I didn't want to wake her, so I took a hundred bucks from her handbag."

"She allows you to just take money from her wallet?"

"It was just a loan."

What's a little petty larceny among family members?

"I still don't get what this has to do with your mother."

"Don't you see? I could have been her alibi. If she was home asleep, she couldn't have killed my dad, right? If I had told the truth, she wouldn't have been arrested."

"What time did you get home?"

"A little before ten."

I thought back. Mitchell and Evelyn had left the restaurant at the Hyatt around nine-thirty. Awfully quick work to drown the husband, drag him down to the river, drive home—a ride that took a good fifteen minutes—and be undressed and in bed by ten.

I didn't think it could have been done in less than thirty minutes. If Tommy was telling the truth, he could provide an alibi of sorts to his mother. Not airtight. But sufficient to raise doubt.

Pity he hadn't spoken up before.

"How sure are you of the time frame?"

"I checked my watch when I got home."

I hoped Tommy was telling me the truth, and not merely lying to protect his mother.

"What about your dad? Did you see him? Was he home?"

"No. And his car wasn't in the driveway."

Tommy's last comment peaked my attention. So Mitchell had driven his wife home, and then left again. To go where?

"Too bad you didn't tell this to the police when they first questioned you."

"Kevin made me promise not to tell. He was in a shitload of trouble if his dad ever found out that the Beemer got towed.

And how could I know that it would turn out to be important?"

"Was there drinking at the party?"

Tommy hesitated.

"Come on, Tommy. If there was booze at the party, the cops will have a record of it."

"I only had one beer. Honest."

I sighed. Unfortunately, the availability of alcohol at the party weakened Tommy's credibility. Should Evelyn's murder case ever get to trial, any prosecutor worth his salt would argue that Tommy had been too intoxicated to remember the details of the evening accurately. On top of that, stealing money from his mother's wallet didn't exactly showcase a stellar character.

"Do you think this will help Mom?" Tommy's tone was hopeful.

"Yes, it will."

"Will I have to tell the police about the party and the Beemer getting towed?"

"You'll have to tell them everything. It's what makes your story plausible."

"God, Kevin's gonna be so pissed."

Obviously, the gravity of his mother's situation hadn't sunk in yet.

"Frankly," I said, "your main concern shouldn't be that you might make a friend angry. Your concern has to be for your mother—and to make the police believe you."

"Why wouldn't they?"

"Because you could be lying to protect her."

"But I'm telling the truth. I'd be willing to take a lie detector test. Or they could give me truth serum."

Truth serum? Oh my. I suppressed a smile.

"By the way, do you make a habit of using your mom's wallet as an ATM?"

"If I take money, I always give it back. I do earn my own

way, you know. I coach swimming at the Y and I tutor seventh grade math."

My estimation of Tommy went up a notch. He wasn't just another spoiled rich kid.

Our food arrived. I ate with gusto and marveled at the quantity—and the speed—with which Tommy demolished his two plates. More astonishing still in view of his being rail thin.

I said, "How did you and your father get along?"

"He was a jerk."

"How so?"

"I swim with a U.S. swim team, at Wadsworth. I'm one of the fastest swimmers on my team. But would Mr. High and Mighty ever say 'well done'? No. 'You're not rolling your hips. Your kick's too slow. You need to get off the blocks faster.' " Tommy's voice had dropped in an older man's imitation, and his jaw was clenched. "I wanted to scream at him, 'Why don't you get in the pool, Dad? Want to have a little race, Dad?' Not that he could have kept up with me for even half a lap. My father was a couch potato. It pissed me off that even when I placed well, he still made me feel like I could have done better."

"He doesn't sound like a nice man," I said sympathetically.

"And he was always hassling me about my grades. He said he'd only pay my college tuition if I got into Wadsworth. But back in the dark ages when Dad went to Wadsworth, if your parents had the bucks and knew the right people, you were in. It's different now. You have to have straight As, SATs in the high fifteen hundreds, *and* be a superstar in something. Unless you're a minority. It just isn't fair." Tommy was really working himself up, with a lot of anger spilling out. "You know what? I don't give a shit. Wadsworth is overrated, you ask me."

I nodded, sensing the pressure he'd been under, and feeling sad for the picture he painted of his relationship with his father. Having one's ego assaulted by a parental figure was too heavy a burden for a child to bear.

"How did your mom and dad get along with each other?"

"Dad treated Mom like shit. He always acted so superior, like she was stupid or something. I don't know why she put up with him. I'd have told him to take a hike."

Me too, I thought. Probably the reason I was still single. This need for independence seemed to run in our family. My mother didn't put up with any crap either—which may explain why she's with husband number four.

"Mom's great." Tommy smiled. "Most of the time, anyway. And she isn't stupid. Did she tell you she wrote a book?"

"No." Somehow I wouldn't picture Evelyn as the literary type.

"It's about raising puppies. She got it published and everything. The publisher even put her on a book tour. When Dad found out about the tour, he cancelled all her credit cards. She got stuck in Springfield without gas for the trip home."

I winced. "That's way cold. Why would he do something like that?"

"He said her job was to take care of me. Not to go gallivanting all over the place, promoting some stupid book."

Tommy was painting a sorry picture of the state of Evelyn's marriage.

"See," he said. "I told you he was a jerk. You get it now? And that's not half of it."

NINE

Tommy had started circling the ice cubes in the glass again. The rattling sound they produced was driving me crazy. I was tempted to grab his damn Coke.

"Come on, Tommy. I can see that you want to tell me something."

I could barely hear the next sentence, his voice was so low. "He was screwing around."

"You mean sexually? How do you know?"

"I went to his office. This was last fall. It's closer to school than our house. I was feeling sick to my stomach, and I wanted him to drive me home. He was still in class, so I lay down in his office, on the floor behind his desk. I guess I fell asleep. Next thing I knew, there was Dad and this girl, groping each other on the love seat. I mean, she wasn't much older than me. Talk about gross. It was, like, totally embarrassing. I didn't know what to do, so I hid under his desk while they went on and on." Tommy's face reddened with embarrassment. I wondered how much he had seen.

"Could you describe the girl?"

"All I saw of her was from the waist down. She was short and skinny . . . and she had on panties with yellow smiley faces."

It was an awkward moment for the waitress to arrive. She asked whether we wanted anything else. I looked at Tommy. He shook his head.

"Just the check," I said. The waitress gave Tommy a big smile and left.

"I'm sorry you had to see your father do that, Tommy. Did you tell your mom?"

"Hell, no. It'd have killed her. Plus I was afraid she'd divorce Dad if she ever found out, and I didn't want that either."

"Why not, if you couldn't stand your father?"

He shrugged and started playing with the ice cubes again, jabbing the straw angrily into the glass.

The waitress returned with the check. I pulled some bills from my wallet and paid.

The tip I'd left was too big, but I didn't want to wait for the change.

Tommy and I headed toward my office building, where I'd left my car. Sometimes we got separated by the multitude of people milling about in Wadsworth Square. Gradually, the boy regained his composure.

"You're not married, are you?" he asked.

"No."

"I thought so. No ring. I bet you don't even have a steady boyfriend."

"What makes you think that?"

He shrugged. "I don't know. It's Saturday night. The way I figure, you wouldn't have agreed to have dinner with me tonight if you were seeing someone."

"You think so, Sherlock?" I was amused. Was his assumption correct? Would a hot date have taken precedence over the case? I honestly couldn't say.

"I'm right, I knew it." There was a note of triumph in Tommy's voice. He cocked his head to one side and narrowed his eyes in an appraising, almost flirty, way. *Precocious little bugger. Also very cute.* Too bad he was too young for me.

"Why aren't you married? You're okay-looking." He reddened. "I mean, you're better than okay-looking."

"Well thank you. I think."

"So why aren't you married? Are you gay?"

I laughed out loud. "God, you sure don't pull any punches. No, I don't happen to lean that way. Not that it's any of your business."

"I bet you get asked out a lot."

"Relationships are complicated, Tommy. The way someone looks is only part of it. A small part, as you'll find out when you grow older."

"Has anyone ever asked you to marry them?"

"Yes."

"And why didn't you?"

I shrugged. "It just didn't work out."

We walked in silence, dodging the other pedestrians.

He exhaled. "Might have been better if Mom and Dad hadn't gotten married."

"But then you wouldn't be here, now would you?"

"I guess not." He cleared his throat. "Have you seen my Uncle Phillip yet?"

"Earlier today, in fact."

"Are you gonna see him again?"

"Probably not. He wasn't much help."

"What did you think of him?"

"He seemed like an okay guy."

"He is. They have a really cool marriage. Aunt Amanda isn't like a total knockout or anything, but she's so nice. They always made me feel good when I went to their house. They joked a lot. And you didn't get your head bitten off when you made a mistake."

He made them sound like the Waltons.

"How's Chrissy?" he asked.

"Chrissy?"

"Their daughter. Was she there?"

"Is she that absolutely gorgeous girl?"

"I guess she's okay-looking." Tommy blushed. "Could I ask you a favor? If you go out there again, could you take me with you?"

"I doubt I'll see them again, but sure. Yes." I'd have to ask Evelyn first, but I couldn't see that as an obstacle. Was the dazzling Chrissy Tommy's motivation for wanting to visit?

"I'm curious, Tommy. Why this sudden urge to reconnect with your uncle?"

He hesitated for a few beats. "I was thinking. If Mom gets convicted, well . . . it is possible, isn't it? I thought . . . maybe I could live with Uncle Phillip?"

I slowed my pace. I'd spent a lot of time thinking about Evelyn's predicament, but in all honesty, I hadn't given a single thought about the impact on Tommy. *Poor kid.*

"Have you and your mother discussed this?"

"No. She's got enough to worry about. So will you take me?"

"Let's not get ahead of ourselves. Our goal is to clear your mom. If we succeed, you won't have to live with your uncle. And what you told me tonight could help. But yes, if I go to see your uncle again, I can take you."

"Great. Thanks." He cracked his knuckles. "You know, we used to rent a house on the Cape with them every August. Dad and Uncle Phillip would come down for weekends, and Aunt Amanda, Chrissy, Jake, Mom, and me would be there all week long. It was such fun, like having a real brother and sister. We'd hang out on the beach all day . . . I really miss them."

I gave him a surprised look. From what he was telling me, the relationship between the two brothers had been a lot closer than either Evelyn or Phillip had intimated. Why had *both* of them been downplaying it?

"You used to be close. Why did your family stop seeing them?"

"You got me. The last time we were all together was at my grandfather's funeral. I asked Dad a bunch of times why we didn't get to see them anymore, but he just said we were too busy. Which was bullshit. He tried to be calm about it, but I could tell he was pissed at me for asking."

"How could you tell?"

"When Dad got mad he'd get this look around his eyes."

Tommy scowled, in imitation of his father. The boy was a keen observer.

We reached the Jetta and I drove Tommy back home.

I pulled into Evelyn's driveway, but Tommy just sat there, not making any moves to get out of the car.

"Listen Tommy," I said softly, "for now please don't jump to any conclusion as to what might happen with your mother. She's innocent until proven guilty. Should that change, we'll cross that bridge when we come to it."

He didn't look convinced.

"No plans for tonight?" I asked.

"Nah. Everything's just too weird right now."

"This whole thing is really hard on you, isn't it?"

"I feel like we've been prisoners in our own house. And school's been bizarre too—lots of whispering behind my back. I'm always wondering what they're saying. It's like we're celebrities. It's sick."

Tough enough being a fourteen-year-old coming of age these days even without having a murder charge hang over your mother's head. Things had to be damn uncomfortable for Tommy at BB&N, a tight-knit school community where appearances and propriety counted for much.

"Have you thought about transferring to another school?"

"Like to Concord?" he asked. He sat perfectly still for a moment, staring straight ahead. "I've thought about it. A lot, actually. It would be nice to be somewhere else—for a while at least.

Or even to drop out for a semester. But no matter where I go, someone would make the connection. I can't run away from this. Besides, Mom needs me. What kind of a son would I be if I left her now? And wouldn't that make her look guilty?"

I touched his arm and smiled at him.

"You know, Tommy, I think Evelyn is pretty lucky to have you for a son."

We said good night and he made his way up the steps to the house, a lone figure in the dark. I waited until the front door closed before driving off.

TEN

It was just after eight, and I was keyed up. Tommy had been perceptive: there was no significant other in my life. But would I be any happier if I had a steady date on Saturday nights?

As it was, I wasn't feeling all that peppy tonight. Tommy had reminded me that everyone seemed to be out, having a grand ole time, while my evening consisted of dinner with a fourteen-year-old who happened to be the son of a murder suspect. Tommy had to be feeling lonely as well, cooped up by himself at home when all his friends were out partying.

My heart really went out to the boy. He seemed like a decent kid, well mannered and smart. Evelyn had done a fine job raising him.

Being with Tommy brought back memories of my own youth. When I was his age, my parents' divorce decree had just been finalized—although my mother had walked out on us three years earlier. With Mommy gone, my brother and I had been shipped off to boarding school. I felt like I'd been orphaned. No mother. No father. Even my brother had been sent to a different school. I remember those years as being the most painful of my life.

Maybe that's why the thought of Tommy's mother going to jail churned my insides. As bad as things had been for my brother and me, they had to be worse for Tommy. And if Evelyn were to get convicted—

My ruminations about Tommy got interrupted when I pulled

into the graveled driveway of the carriage house. I was startled to see a stranger caught in the beam of my headlights. He stood in the entry of the main house, apparently trying to jimmy my landlord's lock.

The guy looked like a derelict. I'd been afraid someone might try to break into the house. The place had an abandoned air about it, especially at night. Two lamps in the living room, set on automatic timers, gave scant illumination, an open invitation to a burglar.

My heart skipped a beat, then started pounding insanely. I took the gun out of my purse. Then I remembered that it wasn't loaded. The magazine was in my briefcase in the trunk. *Great.*

I hoped the mere show of a 9 mm would be sufficient to scare the creep off.

Just then, the man turned and approached, his hand raised to shield his eyes from the bright headlights. His hair was unkempt, in need of a cut, his beard scraggly. He wore a wrinkled shirt and Bermuda shorts.

I reluctantly cracked the car window an inch to hear what he was saying.

"You must be Macy Adams."

"And who are you?"

"I'm Jack Hamilton, your landlord."

He took one giant step back when he saw the gun in my hand. "Do I look that bad?"

"You're not exactly leaping off the pages of *GQ*, buddy. You gave me a scare."

"I gave *you* a scare? Is that thing loaded?"

"Well, of course it is," I lied. "What good is a gun without bullets?" I still wasn't entirely convinced the guy standing in front of me was really Jack Hamilton. This man looked one step up from the Pine Street Inn. Certainly not like the owner of a small mansion in Cambridge.

"Would you mind not pointing that thing at me?" The nervous tension in his voice made me feel good somehow. But I lowered the barrel of the gun.

"Well, well. Dubs mentioned that my new tenant was a private eye. I guess the gun proves it. Have gun, will investigate?" His laugh was inappropriate.

But the mention of Dubs's name took the edge off my own anxiety. I put the gun on the passenger seat. The expression on Jack's face changed, taking on an amused look. People sometimes react that way when I introduce myself. Like private investigators exists only in TV-land.

"Listen, if it isn't too much trouble, I'd like to pick up my mail. Could I stop by in a few minutes?"

"Be my guest. I'll be only too happy to be rid of it." Jack Hamilton's correspondence filled three grocery bags, taking up precious space in the closet.

"I hope you threw out all the junk mail."

Now he tells me.

While he ambled toward the main house, I jumped out of the car and *ran* to the carriage house, stopping short only when I heard the piercing shriek of the house alarm. I watched Jack fiddle in the entryway, curious what would happen next, feeling my tension mount for an instant until the alarm ceased.

My own place was a mess, totally unfit for the critical eyes of a visiting landlord. I swept through the room like a whirlwind, picking up stray socks and underwear and dumping them into the clothes hamper, straightening the bedspread, rounding up dust balls with a used tissue. Dirty dishes went into a pail under the kitchen sink, while stray newspapers, mail, and magazines went under the bed. I straightened and fluffed pillows. Five minutes of frantic activity, and I was satisfied. One benefit of living in a small space is that there isn't much to clean.

I liberated the three grocery bags with Jack's mail from the closet.

A quarter hour later, I heard a knock on my door. In the bright light of the room my landlord looked like an updated, light-haired version of Captain Hook. The deep tan caused his blue-green eyes to jump out of his face. His hair looked unwashed and his beard straggly and neglected. I've never been a big fan of men's facial hair. It's a trap for stray food crumbs.

Jack sat down and started flipping through the mail.

I was taken aback that he made himself all comfy in *my* living room, like he owned the place—which he did, but I was the one paying the rent. A letter caught his eye. He opened it, scanned it, and tucked it into his shirt pocket.

He looked up with interest. "Everything all right with the place?"

"Fine."

"Plumbing, appliances, all in working order?"

"So far."

"Good. Any problems, you know where to find me . . ."

"You're not planning another extended trip, then?"

He chuckled and shook his head, as if what I'd said was funny. "No, I don't think so."

"If you don't mind my asking, where have you been all this time?"

"Oh, here and there," he said vaguely.

"Actually, since I've got you here," I said, "there *is* one thing. I'd like to paint the walls."

He looked around the room.

"Yourself?"

"Sure."

"Have you ever done any painting before?"

"Lots of times," I lied.

"Well, I guess if the licensing board trusts you with a firearm,

I can trust you with a paint brush. Okay by me, just as long as you don't paint the place pink." He winked.

Pink walls. Now there was a thought. All along I'd waited for my landlord to show up, and now that he'd finally materialized, I had to wonder what hole he'd crawled out of.

"Pink would be a big improvement over *this* yucky pea-soup green."

"Hey, what's wrong with Tequila Lime green? That's Benjamin Moore paint."

"It makes everyone in the room look seasick."

"Careful, or you'll hurt someone's feelings. This particular color was personally selected by yours truly."

Was he serious? Were we having an argument over wall paint?

Jack laughed out loud. "Where's your sense of humor? Save the receipts. I'll reimburse you for the paint supplies."

I held the door open for him, not out of courtesy, but because I wanted him gone. I suppose pulling a gun on someone the first time you meet is bound to start things off on the wrong foot. Still . . .

Jack trudged out the door, the third heavy bag of mail awkward under his arm. I did not offer him a hand. After he left, I wondered why he was so mysterious about his whereabouts during the past two months—especially as he'd come back looking like a refugee from an archaeological dig.

Strange man.

ELEVEN

Sunday started as a perfect day. Bright sunshine with a scatter of cumulus clouds. The air was dry, and there was even a slight breeze.

Decked out in my tennis whites, I headed to The Country Club in Brookline for a game of doubles. With Dubs as my partner, we won easily in straight sets—6-4, 6-2.

Afterwards we feasted on mimosas, fruit salad, coffee, eggs Benedict, and those tiny Danish pastries I adore. Unfortunately, so do my thighs.

By the time I got home it was after eleven. I opened the *Globe* and gaped at the headline, "Widow Hires Private Eye." The article not only mentioned my name, which was bad enough, but went on to insinuate that my leaving Investigative Enterprises hadn't been entirely voluntary on my part.

I cursed, recalling the unattractive reporter who had been camped out in front of Evelyn's house that first day. How had she found out who I was? Doubtless the same way I would have done it: by running my license plate. Nice payback for my threatening to break her camera.

At 11:44 the phone rang, interrupting my perusal of the paper. David Silverman was thrilled when I told him about my conversation with young Tommy.

"I'll schedule a deposition with him," he said. "Also with that friend of his, Kevin."

We chatted for a bit longer. My plans were to spend the

afternoon at home, listening to the cassettes Evelyn had made of her late husband's conversations, courtesy of an illegal wire-tap.

I was tossing the *Globe* into the trash when I heard an engine spring to life outside. Through the window, I saw my landlord's Jeep pull out of the garage. Instantly, I remembered our discussion of the previous evening. I stared at the walls, that shade of green favored by asylums and prisons—a color so offensive it constituted cruel and unusual punishment. Jack Hamilton had to be color-blind.

I might just as well get a move on the paint job before my landlord reconsidered and subjected me to yet another one of *his* color schemes. I picked up my handbag.

On the way to the hardware store I wondered why the walls were irritating me so much all of a sudden, when they had never bothered me before?

Half an hour later I was back, toting two large cans of Peach Parfait. Not pink, but close enough. The clerk in the paint store had recommended I wash the walls thoroughly with TSP before painting them.

I retrieved the three audiotapes Evelyn Browne had given me. They weren't labeled. On a whim I inserted the one in the Bonnie Raitt jacket. A few seconds of white noise, then a man's booming voice. *"Did you get my note, Dawn?"*

I felt a slight shiver, aware that I was listening to a dead man.

"Yes. Tomorrow afternoon works for me." A young, breathy voice.

I pulled on plastic gloves, dipped a sponge in the mixture of TSP and warm water, squeezed out the excess, and started washing the walls.

"Good. Excellent. How did your latest trial go?"

"It didn't. I'm going back to E. coli."

The sound quality was excellent. I sure do odd things for a living, like listening to a deceased man's telephone conversations with his alleged mistress while painting walls.

Browne's voice was low and gravelly and he spoke with the authority of someone used to addressing large groups. Most of what he said was too technical for me. His conversation with this woman, whom I assumed to be his mistress, was hardly pillow talk. He'd spend ten minutes at a stretch discussing crystal structures of DNA binding, cytokines, isoforms, and receptor proteins. Only occasionally would they slip into a more personal vein.

Once he called her "darling," right before he worked himself up to a fever pitch of whispering, *I can't wait to see you.* That last constituted steamy stuff for him.

I stepped on a chair to reach the top third of the wall. As I worked my way around the perimeter of the room, the water in the pail gradually turned dark.

Dawn's snippets of conversations were equally matter-of-factish. Romeo and Juliet these two were not, at least not when giving phone. I couldn't help but wonder what they'd talked about in bed. *E. coli?* Uggh.

The tape ran forty-five minutes each side. I'd finished my scrub job when the tape stopped, and so I ate lunch—a turkey sandwich—while the walls dried. Then I started applying the peach-tinted primer. I spread it over half a wall and stepped back. Not bad.

I inserted the next cassette, the one in the Whitney Houston jacket, and listened to Browne and Dawn continue their shoptalk. The subtext of the conversations was interesting. Browne was in heavy pursuit of Dawn, with her backing away. She kept stalling him, canceling dates right and left.

I switched to the third cassette, the most tedious of the three. Browne spoke of an upcoming trip to Japan and spent a lot of time talking to a person I assumed to be his secretary. They covered administrative ground: appointments, students, grades.

Only one conversation with Dawn, the most impersonal to date. I wished I knew the chronology of the tapes.

Ironically, the main thing I got out of listening to the tapes had nothing to do with Dawn. Rather, I realized that if anyone was familiar with Browne's life, it was his administrative assistant. She made competent suggestions about how Browne should handle upcoming situations or problems or informed him that she'd already dealt with some issue for him.

Her voice sounded throaty over the phone, with a touch of a southern accent. I caught several instances of humorous banter between the two of them—the woman succeeded in making Browne sound almost human. The few times he disagreed with her, she stood right up to him. I liked her just from the way she handled herself on the phone. Browne was lucky to have found someone as level-headed and self-assured.

A knock on the door interrupted my thoughts. I propped the paint roller on the tray and opened the door a crack, leaving the key chain in place.

"Hi. Hope I'm not disturbing you."

I gawked at the man on the threshold.

"I came for the spare set of keys." Definitely my landlord's voice. "For the Jeep . . ."

He'd gotten a haircut and the beard was gone. Underneath all that hair, Jack Hamilton possessed an attractive face with chiseled features.

"Sorry, I wasn't sure it was you," I said, still staring.

"Some investigator," he muttered.

I opened the door all the way and he stepped inside. He looked at the fresh coat of primer with frank amazement.

"You don't waste any time," he said.

"No. Today's my day off."

"*This* is how you spend your day off?" He chuckled. "Interesting color you picked . . ."

"I'm glad you like it."

"I didn't realize I said I actually *like* it." He arched an eyebrow.

What was it with him, anyway? From sorting through his mail, I knew him to be in venture capital—hence I would expect him to possess decent interpersonal skills.

Wait a minute, I thought. *Venture capital.*

"Jack, may I ask you something?"

He interpreted this as an invitation to sit down. "Sure. Shoot."

"Does your firm handle biotech investments?"

"Why do you ask?"

"I'd like to talk with your biotech expert. If you have such a person."

"You're looking at him."

"You?"

"You have a problem with that?"

"No, of course not."

"Looks like I got myself cleaned up for nothing. You still think of me as a thug."

I laughed, remembering how I'd pulled the gun on him last night. Dubs was bound to hear about that. *Oh God.*

"Hey," I said lightly, "you know about first impressions. They're hard to shake."

"Well, I *may* be stretching the truth a bit when I call myself an *expert*," Jack said, "but I manage to muddle through. I was premed undergrad, did a year of medical school before realizing I didn't want to spend the rest of my life poking sick people with needles and scalpels. So I went for my masters in biology, then an MBA. I've been doing venture capital for ten years now."

Why the life history? He almost sounded like he was trying to impress me.

"What is it you want to know?" he continued when I didn't respond.

"I'm currently working a case in the biotech field, and I could use a little help. It wouldn't take much of your time."

A mischievous glint came into his eyes. "My usual rate is five hundred dollars an hour."

"Sorry. I can't afford you."

"But I could make you a deal. Have you ever been sailing?"

I shrugged. "Sure."

"How about you come sailing with me this afternoon? In return for serving as my deck hand, I'll answer your questions."

I hesitated for a mere split second. "Okay."

"Can you be ready in half an hour?"

"Deal." I went to my desk and fished his spare keys out of a drawer.

"Bring warm clothes. It'll be surprisingly cold out on the water."

It wasn't until he was gone that I felt a twinge of misgiving. After all, I didn't know Jack Hamilton from Adam.

But one glance outdoors clinched it. It was an absolutely gorgeous day. I'd have to be crazy to stay cooped up inside, painting, when I had an invitation to go sailing.

TWELVE

I hastily spread the peach primer across the remaining wall. Thus far my home improvement project wasn't much of an improvement at all; the peach color patchy and uneven. The last wall, which I'd just barely finished, looked like it had contracted some bizarre dermatological disease.

I'd fix that later. I covered the paint roller in Saran wrap and stuck it in the refrigerator, following the instructions given by the guy in the paint store. Then I dressed in a pair of jeans, a pink turtleneck, and a navy sweater. I shoved an old ski jacket into a duffel bag, just in case.

We were barreling down Storrow Drive in no time. Jack's type-A personality came out behind the wheel, as he weaved continually across three lanes of traffic. It was precisely this type of driving that gave Boston motorists their bad reputation as vehicular maniacs.

We left the Jeep in the Aquarium garage on Atlantic Avenue. As we stepped outside, the briny scent of the ocean filled my nostrils. It was a short walk to the Mass Bay Sailing Club, a yuppie establishment tucked into the ground floor of a high-rise building. While Jack talked to the attendant I watched the fleet of sailboats bob up and down on their moorings.

"There's a front moving in." Jack touched my elbow. "We can still take a boat out. We just can't venture out too far. You still game?"

I looked skyward. The weather looked fine to me, the horizon a pale blue with a scattering of white clouds.

"Sure."

Our eyes met for a split second, just long enough for my radar to pick up on something. But what? Jack's demeanor was nonchalant, but I felt an electric undercurrent.

Out on the water, I gave Jack an unschooled hand with the rigging of the boat. We got under way, Jack at the helm, an easy beam-reach into the harbor. A chilly wind hit my face.

"So what are you investigating?" he asked.

"You're probably not up to date on all the local news." I filled him in briefly on Browne's death, explaining my involvement.

"Actually, I *did* hear about that," Jack said. "And you think the wife's innocent?"

"As a matter of fact, I do."

"Why? She doesn't have an alibi."

"That's not clear at the moment. And let me remind you, Jack—my investigation is confidential."

"Christ. Who am I? The district attorney? You want my help, you need to agree that you'll trust me."

"Jack—" I began.

"Don't be so touchy. Some of my information may be confidential as well. I'll tell you what I can without violating any nondisclosures. So does she have an alibi?"

So here we were. I'll show you mine if you show me yours. I could play that game.

"Yes, I think so. I'm working on it," I admitted grudgingly.

"And the alibi is the reason you think she's innocent?"

"Among other things."

"Okay. I'm satisfied. I wouldn't want to help you if you thought she was guilty. I don't like the idea of someone getting away with murder."

"Fair enough."

Suddenly, he was distracted, looking off into the distance.

"See that plane coming in?"

Jack pointed skyward. A large passenger jet was getting ready to land at Logan. He brought the boat around. We stalled in the water, right in front of a landing strip. The plane was approaching fast. All of a sudden, a structure the size of a small office building was hanging above us in the sky. The landing gear seemed close enough to touch the mast. I cupped my hands over my ears in a futile attempt to dampen the ear-splitting roar of the jet engines, and the boat shook violently as the jets sucked the wind out of the sails. I felt a rush of adrenaline.

Jack laughed out loud. "Gets you going, doesn't it?"

My heart was still beating hard. "It sure does."

He pushed out the boom and we gradually picked up speed. "Where were we?"

"The dead man, Mitchell Browne, was on the board of Genetechnology and BioCorp. Anything you can tell me about those firms would be helpful."

"Genetechnology is one of the largest biotech companies in the world. They have a number of successful products on the market. It's a well-managed company, very respected . . . I doubt they'd be involved in his murder in any way."

"What about BioCorp?"

He hesitated. "BioCorp is a strange outfit. They've done well in their niche, which is diagnostic kits. But BioCorp's chairman is a strange duck."

"How so?"

"Everyone in the industry has good security. But BioCorp is guarded like Fort Knox. Also, Rutgers has a reputation for being xenophobic. An uncle of his got blown up at Pearl Harbor and Rutgers nurses a grudge. He refuses to deal with the Japanese in any way, or with any country in the Pacific rim. You have to appreciate how extraordinarily difficult it is to do business in the biotech field if you refuse to sell to or hire Asians."

"I can imagine."

"It's a nutty policy. Another thing, BioCorp was supposed to go public last January. Then suddenly Rutgers pulled out of the offering, leaving his investment bankers standing in the wind with their pants down. Timing-wise the market was ripe for a new issue. In fact, it would have been the perfect time to float a new stock. Needless to say, there was a lot of nasty speculation as to what happened."

"Such as?"

"Internal fraud. Rigged experiments. I'm not abreast of what's been going on the last few months, but there was plenty of talk right after the New Year."

"Fascinating."

"I have a friend who spent months working on the offering. I could find out more."

"That'd be great, Jack. Thanks. Tell me, if BioCorp had gone public, they would have come under greater scrutiny, right?"

"Of course. As a private company they operate freely. The only people they have to answer to are their private investors. Once a firm goes public, it's a whole new ball game. And at no time is the scrutiny more intense than when the stock is first offered."

It was interesting. An eccentric chairman, the tight security, the rumors of wrongdoing. I wondered what skeletons were buried at BioCorp.

We sailed without talking for a while, and I watched Jack out of the corner of my eye. I liked his well-proportioned face and strong chin. His eyes shone with intelligence, and there were blond highlights in his light-brown hair. His nose was thin, with a slight bend that suggested it might have been broken at some point. I judged him to be in his early forties. He had an air of understated self-confidence, a quiet and deliberate quality that spoke volumes.

"So how is BioCorp currently being funded?" I asked.

"Last I heard they're negotiating with Mass Bay Capital."

Mass Bay Capital. Where had I heard *that* name before? A split second later it came to me.

"Prentice Porter's firm?"

"Well, not exactly *his*. He doesn't own the fund. But yes, Prentice is one of the partners."

So our gubernatorial hopeful was dabbling in biotech investments. I had to admit that a potential liaison between Bio-Corp's chairman and Prentice was an unpleasant surprise.

Jack interrupted my thoughts. "We had better head back."

Wrapped up in conversation, we'd ignored the front pushing in behind us. The change in the weather was sudden and dramatic. Black, ominous clouds were rushing in, foreboding of a coming storm. Wind gusts hit the sails.

We came about and stopped talking, needing our wits for tacking—not that conversation would have been possible with the loud machine-gun flapping of the sails. A sudden, violent wind gust made the mere act of breathing difficult.

The boat pitched sideways as we came about. Jack offered me the tiller, yelling something about having to reef the sails. Keeping the boat on course through the churning whitecaps was tough, especially with the wind switching direction without warning. But I appreciated the slight adjustment Jack was making to the mainsail. The boat slowed and steadied instantly. We were still slicing through the water at an amazing clip, but there was less chop. Had the weather been clear and the month July instead of May, I'd have enjoyed the ride. But here I sensed danger, and the thought of the boat capsizing made my stomach lurch. Besides, riding across shipping lanes in the middle of a storm seemed reckless. I hoped Jack knew what he was doing.

We came about again.

It took half an hour of frequent tacking before we were within sight of the sailing club. The black clouds had caught up with us and there was the occasional far-off rumble of a storm.

Suddenly the wind shifted directions, and the heavens opened their floodgates. There was a bright flash of lightning, followed immediately by a heart-stopping clash of thunder.

The torrential rains I could cope with, but the lightning terrified me. Thoughts of the electrifying effects of mixing water with thunderbolts filled my head. Ending up as a fried wonton floating in Boston Harbor wasn't high on my list of life goals.

Sheets of rain pelted my face, ran down my neck, and under my parka.

"That front moved awful fast," Jack shouted across the screaming wind.

The man either had nerves of steel—or lacked common sense altogether. The jury was still out on that one.

By the time we reached the moorings we were soaked. Lightning alternated with thunder. Jack got ready to drop the mainsail and I mouthed a silent prayer that it wouldn't jam. This sudden religious conversion was disconcerting. Next thing I'd be saying a rosary.

"You'll need to pick up the mooring," Jack shouted. "You need to climb on the hull."

I stared at him. "You've got to be kidding."

"Afraid not."

"What if I fall in the water?"

"You won't. . . . You do know how to swim?"

"Of course I do. I'm a terrific swimmer. But why me?"

"You see anyone else here?" He paused. "Or would you rather steer the boat?"

I pondered that thought for a second, then shook my head. What if Jack fell overboard? We'd be totally up the creek . . .

Jack explained the maneuver to me. I cursed him under my

breath as I scooted across the hull, my bare hand reaching for an algae-covered rope attached to a painted block. A wind gust suddenly tipped the boat sideways. I slipped on the wet surface and shrieked. Jack threw the rudder into the opposite direction and grabbed my leg. A wave washed over the bow.

Great. Now I was soaked below the waist as well.

"Shit," I cursed out loud.

"Hang on to the rope," Jack yelled as he pulled me back into the cockpit.

He retrieved the slimy line from my trembling hand.

"Well done."

I glared at him. "I almost ended up in the harbor."

"But you didn't. I grabbed you just in time. Let's get the boat shipshape."

We furled the sails, doing a sloppy job. Neither of us wanted to stay on board a second longer than necessary.

By the time I climbed up on the dock I was shaking like a leaf, from the cold and from nerves.

"It's customary for the skipper to buy a round of drinks for the crew after the sail. There's a bar—"

"All I want are dry clothes."

"Okay. Rain check on the drink then?" Jack grinned.

Rain check? What a joker. Besides, I doubted one drink would do the trick. Half a bottle of something stiff was more what was required to steady my shaken nerves.

Jack laughed. "Come on. It wasn't that bad. I saw you smile."

"Look at me. I'm soaked to the bone. We almost got electrocuted. You must be nuts if you think this was fun."

"You gotta admit it *was* exciting."

"Maybe for you. I noticed that you didn't volunteer to hang over the side of the boat to pick up the mooring."

"Actually, I did. Okay, next time you sail the boat, and I'll pick up the mooring."

"What next time?"

We slogged through deep puddles on the way to the parking garage, lightning flashing overhead all the while. I was relieved when we were finally safely cocooned inside the Jeep. Jack wiped the water from his forehead and started the engine.

His cheeks were flushed. I had to admit that Jack looked terrific, even soaked. Masculine. Virile. He caught me gazing at him and I glanced away, embarrassed. I forced my mind away from him, shifting my thoughts to BioCorp instead.

Jack had confirmed Dubs's comment about the botched public offering. In addition Jack had described BioCorp's chairman as an oddball, possibly a fanatic.

I'd had a nasty encounter with a group of animal rights zealots the previous year. They had believed that saving four-legged creatures took precedence over human lives.

How far was Rutgers prepared to go to protect his company?

THIRTEEN

Lightning accompanied us all the way home. Spectacular flashes zigzagged across the Boston skyline. Steady thunder was punctuated by sporadic booms, sound effects to scare even a seasoned vampire. Mother Nature on steroids.

The windshield wipers barely kept up with the sheets of rain. An entire section of Cambridge had lost electricity, causing traffic to snarl at intersections. The Jeep's heater blasted hot air, fogging the windows, but doing little to warm me in my wet clothes. We arrived back home without incident—if you discount hitting a couple of flooded potholes at full speed.

Jack dropped me off at the door. The paint fumes inside the carriage house were strong. I opened the French doors. Outside, the rain was pounding my small deck.

My soaked jeans required the skills of a contortionist. I peeled them off and left my discarded clothes in an untidy pile on the bathroom floor. Luckily, my bathrobe was toasty, since I'd left it slung over a chair next to the radiator. I snuggled into it and ran a bath. While the tub was filling, I padded to the kitchen, still shivering as I watched the tea water come to a boil.

Tea in hand, I slipped into the bath. The herbal aroma of Crabtree & Evelyn aloe bath seeds filled the air. I sipped the tea with honey and my aching muscles began to relax. My shivering stopped. I let my thoughts swirl, enveloped in the warm, life-restoring bath.

At this moment it was difficult to fathom that water could

also kill. Of course, it wasn't strictly water that had killed Mitchell Browne. The person who'd deposited his body in the Charles had had the major hand in his death.

Somehow I couldn't see a stranger administering the Valium. Whoever murdered him, Browne must have felt sufficiently comfortable with that person to share a drink or food. It followed that Browne's killer was probably someone he knew and trusted.

Perhaps it's my cynical nature, but men being men, the most plausible reason for Browne to come down to the river in the middle of the night was for a tryst. Which brought his mistress to mind. *Dawn.* The late hour, the river. A little wine laced—unbeknownst to the professor—with tranquilizers? Why not?

Except how was Dawn profiting from Browne's death? Browne had been her mentor. With Browne gone, his mentoring would stop.

Had he stalked her? Pressured her? Enough pressure for her to want him dead?

Or had Browne had a second mistress, some woman besides Dawn? A jealous triangle? Except, on the tapes, Dawn didn't sound jealous. Quite the opposite.

The bath water was turning tepid. I climbed out, toweled myself dry, and dressed in a pair of comfy sweats.

Outside, the rumble of thunder had softened. When I was a child, during one particularly violent storm my mother had explained to me that thunder was nothing more than angels bowling in heaven. The trick had worked. Even nowadays the thought of angels bowling in heaven brought a smile to my face. There had been plenty of strikes tonight.

Back in the living room, I surveyed the walls. I retrieved the paint roller from the fridge, closed the French doors, and inserted the flip side of the final cassette into the stereo, continuing my eavesdropping on Browne's rambling conversations while

I resumed painting. A call from a student wanting a letter of recommendation, a writer scheduling an interview with Browne for a technical article, then Dawn's voice, *"Hello?"*

"Dawn, I just looked at your latest trial. Not very promising, is it?"

"No."

"You're wasting your time. I really wish you'd start working on the AIDS project."

"I'd rather work with antigens."

"You could write your own ticket with several large biotech companies if you specialized on AIDS. I know of at least three firms right here in Boston that would snap you up after you get your PhD."

"But I don't want to work on AIDS. It's too depressing."

"Okay. But Dawn, listen to me, the pay in academia is peanuts. You want to do antigens? All right. I could arrange for a V.P. of Research position with BioCorp. You'd start in the six-figure range."
At the mention of BioCorp my ears perked up.

"I really wish you'd reconsider," Browne continued.

"No, Mitchell. No AIDS. The field's already too crowded. And I sure wouldn't want to work at Biocorp."

"Why not?"

"I don't like what I'm hearing about the firm."

"Don't believe everything you hear. I'm on the board. I'd take care of you."

"No thanks."

"We're talking a big salary, a corner office. You'd get to travel all over the world. We could even work together. You could make a name for yourself. I'd help you."

"Thanks, I'm not interested. I've got to run, Mitchell."

"What about tomorrow?"

"No can do."

"You have to eat. How about dinner? The Four Seasons?"

"I'll call you."

"Lunch?"

There was a click in the line. Dawn had hung up.

Well, well, another brush-off. Except this time Dawn had actually hung up on him.

I stepped back and surveyed my paint job. I loved the look of newly painted drywall. And the color was terrific. I felt proud of myself.

The next fifteen minutes of tape were dullsville. Browne made some appointments, including one to see Melville Rutgers, Bio-Corp's chairman. Rutgers's secretary sounded snooty, a definite candidate for an attitude adjustment.

I assumed the next caller to be international, from the man's accent and the unfamiliar ring.

"Professor Browne?"

"Speaking."

"Professor Browne, I'm calling to confirm a transfer of funds."

I tried to place the man's accent. Asian, with a trace of British, spoken with a singsong intonation.

"The money is in the account now?"

"That is correct, yes. Two hundred thousand dollars."

"I'll want to transfer the funds from another account in the Cayman Islands. I'll wire instructions."

"Yes. Certainly, Professor."

Browne disconnected.

Two hundred grand in an offshore account? Browne had been speaking softly, almost whispering, like he was afraid of being overheard. Something significant was going on here.

The rest of the tape was useless. I switched to Mozart and opened the French doors. The rain was coming down softly now, a soothing backdrop to the classical music. I was finally getting into the Zen of painting, and finding I enjoyed the process.

Suddenly I got an eerie feeling, like someone was watching

me. I turned slowly and almost dropped my paint roller.

Jack was leaning against the French doors.

"Jack, you nearly gave me a heart attack. How long have you been standing there?"

"About three minutes. Your powers of concentration are astonishing."

"You shouldn't sneak up on people like that."

"I suppose so. I should be more careful, especially around you. Wouldn't want you pointing that Magnum of yours at me again."

"It's not a Magnum."

Jack smiled. "What is it then?"

"A Glock 9 mm pistol."

"Well, pardon me." He continued smiling. "What color are you painting the trim?"

"The what?"

"The woodwork."

I looked around. Did he mean the doorframes?

"I'm not going to paint the woodwork. I washed it."

"You'll have to paint it. It'll look awful if you don't."

I looked more closely. With the walls bright peach, the surrounding woodwork suddenly looked gray and dingy. Jack was right. I sighed. I didn't think I'd have the patience to deal with the countless grids separating the windowpanes.

Jack straightened. "Don't go away. I'll be right back."

He returned a few minutes later, brandishing a paintbrush in one hand, a can of paint in the other.

"Linen white. What do you think?" he said.

I looked at the paint, which was the color of whipped cream. It looked fine to me. Peaches and cream. Jack started painting the window frames while I finished the long back wall. I got rid of my paint roller, washed up, and returned to watch Jack. His paint strokes were relaxed and accurate, yet at the same time he managed to work very fast. He had nice, muscular arms.

"You're a man of many talents, Jack."

"This is how I put myself through college."

"Painting?"

"Uh-huh. I used to paint houses during summer break."

"So, Jack. Why won't you tell me where you've been the last couple of months? What's the big mystery?"

"Bugs you, does it? Not knowing?"

"Don't be silly. Why should I care?"

He glanced at me, his eyes twinkling. "I'd say it bugs you because you're a nosy busybody. Isn't that why you became a P.I.?"

"Absolutely not."

"Okay, since you don't care, I won't tell you."

"Fine. Have it your way."

Why did Jack have this unsettling effect on me?

"Would you like a drink?" I asked.

"It won't work."

"What?"

"Plying me with alcohol. It won't work."

It *had* been worth a try. Nothing else seemed to be working.

"By a drink I meant mineral water, Coke."

"Sure you did."

"How about a truce?"

He stopped. "I didn't realize we'd been at war. I thought we were having fun."

I went to the kitchen and returned with an open bottle of Chardonnay and—caught Jack rifling through the Browne's murder file, a file that belonged to me and was *confidential.*

Pointedly, I snatched the folder from his hands and shut it.

"Listen, buster. Now who's the nosy busybody?" I said.

"Is that Browne? The guy in the newspaper clipping?"

"Some of this information is protected by attorney-client

privilege. You can't just—"

"Fine. My apologies. I shouldn't have done it. But this man Browne . . . I've met him before. A few months ago."

"Really?" Intrigued as I was, I still couldn't keep the irritation out of my voice.

"He spoke at a genetic engineering symposium."

Jack sat back on the couch, stretching his legs out. "I remember being very impressed with him. You could tell he really knew his stuff. But what sticks in my mind isn't his talk, but something that happened afterwards."

I looked at him expectantly. He had me in the palm of his hand—and enjoyed every second of it. "Can we finish this, Jack? The suspense is killing me."

"I went to the men's room after the meeting broke up. I overheard Melville Rutgers talking to this man Browne. Rutgers asked him to come to his office first thing the next day. Browne said he was busy. Then Rutgers told him in this low voice, real nasty like, that if Browne knew what was good for him, he'd better clear his calendar, because Rutgers needed some answers about the dead rabbits in Section D."

"Dead rabbits?"

"Yes. Rabbits. Most biotech research doesn't happen in test tubes, it takes place in live animals—usually mice, but sometimes rabbits, or even larger mammals."

"Does 'Section D' mean anything to you?" I asked.

"No. To you?"

I drew a blank. "Did they say anything else?"

"No. As soon as they saw me, they stopped talking. In fact, the reason I remember the incident so clearly is because they both looked absolutely stunned when they realized I'd overheard them."

FOURTEEN

An hour later Jack finished painting the final pane on the French windows. I'd been sipping wine while I watched him work. He wrapped the paintbrush in plastic, perched on the edge of the love seat, and raised his own glass.

"Here's to a job well done."

Jack studied our handiwork. "I like this peach color. It's elegant, yet soft. It suits you." His gaze was suddenly thoughtful. "Macy, would you like to have dinner with me?"

"It's sort of late for dinner."

He checked his watch. "Eight-thirty. You must be hungry."

I shrugged. The wine had killed my appetite.

"Besides, you don't want to stay cooped up in here with the paint fumes. That's oil-based paint on the trim."

Great. The rest of the universe had switched to nontoxic latex while Jack was still hooked on heavy-duty, industrial-strength, macho oil paint. He *was* right about the paint fumes, though. I already felt the vague throbbing of a headache. Or maybe I *was* hungry?

"I don't know," I said dubiously. "I look a mess."

Besides, Jack had practically killed me on the boat this afternoon, and now he was asphyxiating me with carcinogenic paint fumes. What was next on his agenda? Food poisoning?

Moreover, it was pretty clear by now that more was happening than your normal landlord-tenant civility. How many landlords personally painted the woodwork in their tenant's

103

apartment? And on a Sunday night no less?

"I know a great Chinese restaurant. They deliver. We could have dinner at my place."

"Sold."

Jack departed to place the order. I shut the French doors, leaving the rest of the windows open, and changed out of my sweats. I couldn't decide what to wear. After a couple of false starts, I settled on capri pants with a Parisian motif and a fuchsia sweater. My face was a mess. I performed emergency triage using foundation to hide the windburn, and applied lipstick and mascara. My hair was a hopeless tangle. The best I could do was to run a quick brush through it before dashing to the main house through the rain.

Jack had left the front door open for me. I hadn't been inside his house before. The hall was larger, the ceiling higher, than I would have guessed from the outside. A broad central staircase swept upward in a graceful curve, the workmanship of the carved banister magnificent.

I found Jack in the kitchen. He had changed into a soft, ivory knit sweater that set off his tan and green eyes. When I got close to him I got a pleasant whiff of cologne. Had he just splashed that on? Or had I not noticed it before? Of course, it would have been easy to miss with the strong paint fumes. Two dinner settings were set on a casual dining table that was nestled inside a built-out bay window. A fire crackled in the brick fireplace. Smoldering embers, fine china, crystal wine glasses, linen napkins, Ella Fitzgerald crooning Cole Porter on the stereo. Wasn't this setup just too cozy?

The entire scene had seduction written all over it!

Or maybe Jack was just a classy guy.

"Do you prefer red or white?"

Jack's remark was innocent enough, except we'd already drunk an entire bottle of Chardonnay back at my place. Plying me with alcohol would go a long way toward leading me down the primrose path that went straight to the bedroom.

Who was I kidding? I might as well face the music. What made me so touchy around Jack was the fact that I felt incredibly attracted to him. Small wonder every little thing was becoming an issue.

I pushed my wineglass across the table. "White."

He poured the wine for both of us and started unpacking cartons of Chinese food from a large brown paper bag.

I sipped the wine. *Relax,* I told myself. *Will you just relax!*

"There's enough food here to feed an army." I surveyed the eight takeout cartons Jack had artfully arranged around the table. A scent of garlic mingled with ginger.

"I didn't know what you liked, so I ordered a little of everything," he said. "Chopsticks?"

He took a seat across from me.

"You know, Jack, I have to make a confession."

Jack made the sign of the cross.

"You were right. I *am* curious. I'd love to know where you've been the past two months."

He placed a Peking ravioli and teriyaki beef stick on my plate. "Actually, it's no big deal. I chartered a boat and sailed around the Caribbean."

"You mean you just took two months off work to go gallivanting around the islands?"

"God, you make it sound decadent."

"What you're hearing is unabashed envy. They must like you a lot at your firm."

"They love me. But that's neither here nor there. Flexibility is one of the benefits of being a partner."

We listened to Ella sing "Night and Day" while we devoured our appetizers. I was finding Jack intelligent, witty, and attractive. He even knew how to use chopsticks. Over dinner I found myself eyeing him covertly from time to time, wondering what it would be like to kiss him and feel those strong, muscular arms around me.

Was I falling for this guy? And so fast? It wasn't like me. Not at all.

When we cleared the table after dinner, our fingertips touched accidentally—or was it accidental?—as he took a dinner plate from my hands. My heart skipped a beat and I felt a slow fire spread across my solar plexus. I was embarrassed to feel strongly attracted to this man. I hadn't known him twenty-four hours. But I couldn't help myself. *But why him?*

"How about an after-dinner drink?" I heard a slight catch in Jack's voice. "Amaretto? Courvoisier? Let's see what else I've got . . ."

"Maybe a little more wine."

He poured a cognac for himself, and refilled my wineglass.

"I bet you get this all the time, but what's a nice girl like you doing working as a private eye?" He was leaning against the far kitchen counter, looking at me expectantly. I took a seat on the barstool facing him.

"I happened into it by accident. My hobby had been photography, and I was lucky to land a job as an assistant with a well-known photographer. It was glamorous—doing fashion layouts, international trips for travel magazines. But I was constantly on the road. After a while the lifestyle started to wear thin. My photography skills came in handy doing surveillance."

I didn't want to tell him what *really* got me into P.I. work. *The death of my aunt.* Not something I wanted to get into tonight.

Jack took the barstool across from me. "That outfit you're with, Investigative Enterprises. They have a terrific reputation."

"I no longer work for IE. I went out on my own."

Jack gave me an evaluative look. "That's a big step."

I thought it best to get off the topic of IE. It was still too touchy, too raw. "Tell me about the islands."

"The closest thing to paradise."

I listened to his glowing descriptions of St. Barts and Antigua. After a while, it became clear that no big seduction scene was going to happen. Neither one of us was willing to make the first move.

We'd been sitting for a while, just lazily watching the flames in the fireplace, when he said, casual-like, "There's a guest room next to the kitchen. You could spend the night. Inhaling paint fumes all night isn't healthy."

I could only imagine the look on my face.

"Listen," he continued. "Please don't get the wrong idea. I'm just being neighborly. There's a lock on that door, and I can assure you I have no ulterior designs on you." He grinned. "Especially after seeing that gun of yours. No way would I mess with a chick who packs a nine millimeter Glock."

God. Did he actually think that I'd toted the 9 mm along to protect my honor?

"I left the windows open. Surely the carriage house has aired out by now?"

"With oil-based paint, you need to give it at least twenty-four hours."

He walked to the corridor off the far side of the alcove, turned on the light, and opened a door. He beckoned to me, and I followed. Off the kitchen was a small room, a study, decorated in earth tones.

"The sofa pulls out and there are clean sheets in the closet. Look, it's up to you, Macy. But the paint fumes are bad for you. You could end up with a major headache in the morning." He took another sip of his cognac and looked studiously into his glass. "Of course, the same could be said of this stuff."

He placed his glass, still half full, on the kitchen counter. "It's getting late," he said, taking a step back. "Listen, having dinner with you was lovely. I enjoyed your company. And for what it's worth, I thought the sailing was great too, even with the storm." He backed away. "I've got a busy day tomorrow, so I'd better turn in. Feel free to do as you please. Good night."

He held my gaze for a couple of seconds, and then he was gone. I was alone in his kitchen with the crackling fire and a half-full glass of wine. With him gone, the decision whether to spend the night on Jack's sofa or go back to my own fume-infested carriage house was a no-brainer.

I wrestled the sofa bed open and found clean sheets inside the closet. There was even an oversized man's T-shirt. *Antigua is for Lovers.* My last thought as I drifted off to sleep was of Jack. Strangely, I felt simultaneously relieved and let down.

I'd be well advised not to get romantically entangled with my landlord.

I slept fitfully, waking with a start, disoriented in the dark. I'd heard a noise. The dial on my watch read two-thirty. My throat felt dry like the Sahara, signs of a mild hangover.

I listened. All was quiet. The noise must have been part of some dream. I tiptoed to the bathroom down the hall, hoping that flushing the toilet wouldn't wake Jack. I felt thirsty. I ambled to the kitchen, perused the refrigerator, and poured a glass of orange juice.

Several fortune cookies lay on the kitchen counter. I opened one. It said, *You have many good qualities.* True enough. I ate it and opened another one. It read, *Tonight you will find love and happiness.*

I chuckled softly. Well, the night had certainly had potential . . . But then it had all fizzled.

Jack's voice came from the darkness. "What's so funny?"

"Oh Jack. I hope I didn't wake you."

"No. Couldn't sleep."

He took the tiny fortune from my hand and read it.

"Hmm, love and happiness," he said. "Is that what you want?" He came closer, almost pinning me against the counter. "Maybe I could help? The love part, anyway. Happiness . . . that one's tougher."

He took the glass from my hand and placed it on the counter behind me, and pulled me toward him. I felt the terry cloth of his bathrobe as it touched me, his strong arms around me.

My knees nearly buckled when he kissed me. Oh my God, the man could kiss!

He held me, his lips and tongue exploring my mouth for a long time, our bodies pressed close together. I clung to him, feeling my breasts and thighs hot against his body, sensing his heat through the thin T-shirt. It had been a long, long time since I let a man kiss me.

This was insane. It was all too fast. It wasn't smart.

Jack lifted me in his arms and carried me to the guest room. I couldn't wait to untie his bathrobe. He was completely naked underneath.

By the time we finally drifted back to sleep it was nearly dawn.

FIFTEEN

I woke to the feel of satiny, warm skin touching my back. For a moment I thought it was a dream. But then I rolled over and saw the man sleeping beside me. Jack. God, he was handsome. In slumber, with his tousled hair on the pillow, and sleep having smoothed the fine lines on his face, he looked impossibly young.

He opened one eye and grinned at me. He traced a finger along my cheek and his face became serious. We gazed at one another, lost in time.

"You all right with what happened last night?"

I couldn't speak. I just nodded.

He pulled me close, his hands caressing my back before moving to my bare behind. He kissed my neck and I felt his hardness against my thigh and opened my legs. We made love, slowly at first. His hands and mouth were everywhere, a tangle of limbs and heat and desire. Reality receded, as our bodies entered a state of mindless ecstasy.

I was no virgin, but no slut either. There had only been a few men in my life. But none of them ever excited me the way Jack did. It was terrifying how wonderful the sex was.

Chemistry—who could explain it?

Afterwards we lay together quietly, lazily drifting back to sleep.

I woke with a start. Jack was sitting up, checking his watch. He reached for something on the nightstand and, not finding it, cursed under his breath as he ran out of the room. Seconds

110

later I heard his voice from the adjoining bathroom.

"Evan, I'm glad I caught you. Listen, I'm running late. Could you try to reschedule our meeting in New York for eleven?"

He barked instructions into the phone while I slipped into the *Antigua is for Lovers* T-shirt. When I entered the bathroom Jack's back was turned to me. He was standing barefoot on the tile floor, buck naked, the receiver in his left hand. The mere sight of his body made me inhale sharply. He turned and reached for me, his body melting into mine, cupping my breasts in his hand and nuzzling my neck as he talked. "I'll meet you at the shuttle. Yeah, the nine o'clock . . ." He wedged his hand between my legs. I moaned softly.

"Great. Sure . . . fine." He hung up the phone. "I gotta run . . ." We kissed. A hot, long kiss.

"I'm in big trouble and it's all your fault."

"My fault?" I protested. "And you had nothing to do with it?"

"No, all your fault. You're too damn irresistible, woman. I'm two hours late. How are you gonna make it up to me?"

He swept me into his arms and carried me back to the bedroom.

"Make it up to you?"

"Absolutely. I insist."

My T-shirt ended up at the foot of the bed. Then he was on top of me.

"Dinner with me," he whispered into my ear, "after I get back from New York . . . and I'll forgive you."

"Oh really!" I punched him on the arm. He cupped my breasts and kissed them. Again, I had the sensation of falling, then of heat.

"Do we have a deal?" I felt his breath near my ear. He moved his hand between my legs, caressing me. Then I felt him enter my body, with slow, almost languid strokes. What he was doing to me was too delicious.

"Say yes," he insisted, and stopped moving.

"You drive a hard bargain." My voice was a moan.

"Deal?"

"Yes, yes," I gasped, not wanting him to stop. I was so close. "It's a deal. Don't stop."

He kissed me again, and the sensations cascaded over me like ocean waves. Afterwards we held each other, trying to catch our breaths.

"You'd better get going or you'll be three hours late."

Jack let go of me. He came downstairs with me and watched as I slipped into my Parisian capri pants. We walked to the front door holding hands, a gesture as intimate as the sex we'd had. He kissed me on the doorstep.

"I'll call you from New York," he said, cradling my face in both hands. His look was intense, as if he were memorizing my features. He let go, and I stepped into the bright sunlight.

After last night's rain, the world seemed fresh and gleaming, the sky dark blue and cloudless. Raindrops caught on grass and trees sparkled like tiny prisms. The scent of the wet earth was potent and sweet. Everything seemed bright, alive.

The carriage house was chilly, with only a faint odor of paint lingering. The peach walls looked great. Beautiful even. I was tempted to skip my morning run, but willpower won out.

I ran hard, even though my legs felt like rubber.

When I returned I noticed something pink hanging from the doorknob—my bra, with a note attached. *"Dropping a handkerchief would have done the trick."*

It took me a few seconds to get it. Cute. I turned around. Jack's Jeep was gone.

I went inside the carriage house, smiling.

My smile evaporated the instant I noticed a smudge on the newly painted wall.

The smudge was located right below the window, and a damp clump of earth lay on the hardwood floor. Closer inspection revealed more sodden soil, distributed in the pattern of footsteps.

I'd had a nocturnal visitor.

Sixteen

My first thought was of my jewelry. I opened the top drawer of my dresser, where I kept a jewelry box, and rifled through the contents. Nothing seemed to be missing. My computer, TV, and DVD player were still in place. The lock on the file cabinet that held my business files looked intact. No clothes seemed to be missing. As far as I could tell, nothing had been taken.

So what had been the point of the break-in?

Or had I imagined it?

No, the smudge was real, as was the dirt on the floor. I checked the window screen. It had been forced. The frame was bent. But the person who'd broken in had replaced it the best they could. I went outside to investigate further. The soil beneath the window had definitely been disturbed; it showed two large indentations, but no distinct footprints. They'd either been obliterated on purpose or washed away by the rain.

I rushed to my car, grabbed the 9 mm from the glove compartment, retrieved the magazine from the trunk, and slammed it home. I returned to the carriage house and closed all the windows and secured their fasteners. I checked that the dead bolt on the French doors was locked. My buoyant mood was gone. I felt violated and vulnerable. Before showering, I drew down all the shades. Afterwards, I dressed in the bathroom with the 9 mm perched on the vanity and with the bathroom door locked. My actions bordered on paranoia, but I couldn't help myself.

On the way to Silverman's office, I brooded about the break-in. The motive couldn't have been routine robbery, since none of my valuables were missing. It almost had to be connected with one of my cases, most likely the Browne case.

I almost hoped it had to do with the Browne case, because the other possible scenario was too horrible to contemplate. My aunt's murderer was still at large. For years now, I'd lived with the fear that someday her killer would find me.

David Silverman's law office was some twenty stories above street level, in the newly renovated building that had once housed the Boston Stock Exchange. The floors were carpeted in a subdued shade of mauve, the walls covered with beige rice paper. John LaFarge canvasses in antique frames hung in the waiting area. An elegant décor designed to reassure upscale clients. The icing on the cake was the floor-to-ceiling view of Boston Harbor.

As I took in the expanse of azure water, I had a quick flash back to my sailing expedition with Jack. David was talking on the phone, chair tilted back, feet propped up on the side bar of his desk. The man seated next to me was about my age, but he already sported a sizeable spare tire across the middle. He wore thick lenses and had the pasty complexion of someone who spends too much time indoors. Seated on the couch behind us was a brunette in a black power suit and matching black panty-hose.

"Macy, Josh Levine, one of our accountants. Annette is my paralegal. You can get word to me through Annette when I'm in court."

We shook hands. I surprised myself by taking an instant dislike to the anorexic brunette, though I couldn't for the life put my finger on why. Maybe it was the way she looked down her gorgeous nose at me. I decided to continue leaving my messages on David's cell phone.

We sat, the paralegal retreating back to her side of the room.

"We have an interesting situation here." Josh's voice was high-pitched, a melodic tenor. "In a nutshell, Mitchell Browne had been steadily liquidating assets. By assets I mean his stock and bond portfolio."

"How much are we talking about?" David asked.

Josh pushed a printout across the desk. "Two-point-five million dollars."

David whistled. "Where did the money go?"

"Browne reinvested most of it in a company called Biosynthesis. Half a million vanished completely. I don't have a clue what Browne did with it."

For the next forty-five minutes Josh delved into the minutiae of Browne's financial affairs—his stock holdings, options, taxes, bonds, T-bills. He had documented each transfer of funds meticulously, providing more detail than necessary. When Josh finished, he made lots of significant eye contact, as if searching for our collective approval. I scribbled some notes on my legal pad just to show what an attentive listener I'd been—a trick I'd learned in high school.

"Josh, surely you must have *some* idea where all that cash went." David's tone was mildly reproving.

A pained expression crossed the accountant's face, as if not having an answer right on his fingertips was somehow letting his boss down.

David shifted the cross-examination my way. "What do you make of it, Macy?"

He had caught me unprepared, especially since I was still mentally multitasking between Browne's ledger sheets, Jack between the sheets, and the break-in. Operating on four hours of sleep didn't help.

"When cash disappears without a trace, it could mean any number of things. But usually some illegal activity comes to mind: drugs, blackmail, gambling . . ."

"My thoughts exactly."

"What about this Biosynthesis firm?" I said. "This is the first I've heard of the outfit."

David and I simultaneously shifted our gaze to Josh, who looked distraught. "I'm having trouble finding out anything about the company . . . I brought copies of the articles of incorporation with me . . ."

He gave each of us a stapled handout. I studied the pages, flipping through them quickly. They were the standard forms companies are required to file. The only truly interesting page was the one listing the investors.

"Macy, why don't you jump on this? Talk to the principals and see what this firm is all about."

I nodded with enthusiasm. This was precisely the sort of work I used to do for IE all the time, a familiar area in which I felt utterly competent.

"What's Evelyn's current net worth, Josh?"

"Her residence is worth a mil and a half. There's ten K in securities. The CDs, savings accounts, and art collection total another two K. Then there's the investment in Biosynthesis, whatever that's worth. Plus, of course, the life insurance proceeds . . . if she gets to collect."

Either way, Evelyn was a wealthy woman.

David steepled his fingers. "We *have* to track down where that half mil in cash went."

"Browne may have had an offshore account," I commented. "In the Cayman Islands."

"No kidding. How did you find that out?"

"Something Evelyn overheard," I said.

I didn't wish to betray the promise I'd given Evelyn of keeping the illegal tapes of her husband's phone conversations confidential. But I also didn't want to lie to David. It would be bad if he caught me in the fib. I knew from past experience that, above all else, David hated being lied to. In trying to do right by both of them, I was walking a fine line.

"Josh, look into his offshore account," David said. "Okay, any other questions?"

The only sound in the room was the whirring of David's computer.

David stood, towering above the rest of us.

"Great meeting. Keep up the good work, everybody."

We were dismissed. I tossed the Biosynthesis file into my briefcase. The firm sounded fishy from the get-go. And for half a million in cash to just disappear . . . Most likely Browne had hidden the money in a secret bank account in preparation for his upcoming divorce.

But there were other possibilities. I couldn't picture Browne as a gambler or drug user. But blackmail was another matter. Someone who knew about his mistress perhaps? After all, Browne had been a man with plenty to lose.

Seventeen

The downstairs lobby was a combination of polished stone, a bank of gleaming elevators, and an enormous glass wall that faced Congress Street. While I dialed Wadsworth University's main number on my cell phone, I studied the aging yuppies as they hurried by in their power suits, their demeanors all self-important, presumably on their way to important meetings. Not a hair out of place in this crowd. Dressed in my one good suit, a blue Armani, I almost fit in.

I jiggled my car keys while I waited for the Wadsworth operator to put me through to Browne's former secretary. When Jane Ramirez finally came on the line, I recognized the low, throaty voice immediately from Evelyn's tapes.

"Bio Labs, Jane speaking."

I explained who I was and what I wanted.

"You can drop by now if you like," she offered.

"I'll be there within the hour." I clicked off, pleased with her apparent eagerness.

I retrieved my car from the parking garage and paid the attendant the forty-dollar ransom. It sure was nice to have an expense account. I swung by a Greek diner and ordered two slices of pepperoni pizza to go. I'd given in to all kinds of lapses in willpower during the past twenty-four hours. Why stop now?

I parked near Wadsworth Yard and walked to my office, passing an antique bookstore, a palm reader, and a sub shop that had been cited a number of times by the board of health for sanitary violations. Your typical business establishments in the People's Republic of Cambridge.

The pizza had a thick crust and was covered with lots of cheese. I used a napkin to dab off the pools of grease floating on the pepperoni. I could almost feel my arteries clog as I chewed. It's too bad that as a species we are genetically programmed to love fat. Another one of Mother Nature's cruel jokes—right along with PMS.

I Googled Biosynthesis and got over fifteen million hits. *Wonderful.* I searched for Biosynthesis plus the various investors and got zilch. I looked for the investors in various telephone directories. There were sixteen listings for Robert Davis in the Boston white pages alone, twenty-six for John Connors. I didn't bother with any of them. The third investor, Harold Dizikian, was listed in Wellesley. I called, but got no answer. The fourth investor, Richard Kublinski, was listed in the Boston white pages, with a phone number but no address. I left a message on his machine and made a note to Google Dizikian and Kublinski later. That task out of the way, I locked the office and walked to Wadsworth Square.

The biological laboratories at Wadsworth are housed in a five-story brick building that is quite Spartan in appearance. Not a building to inspire good cheer. Two larger-than-life stone elephants guarded the entrance. Downstairs, an attendant informed me gleefully that the facility was home to twelve thousand mice. The mere thought of a few of them getting loose from their cages and running free along the baseboards of corridors made my skin crawl. I'm no fan of rodents. I don't even like squirrels.

I hoped they weren't studying hantaviruses here.

Jane Ramirez's office was located on the third floor. She was a heavy-set woman in her fifties, her skin the golden tone of coffee with cream. She wore her black hair pulled back in a bun. On her desk I noticed a framed photo of a chubby middle-aged man, surrounded by three smiling teenage boys, all of them a shade darker than her. A pair of reading glasses was perched low on her nose. She examined me over the rim of her spectacles.

"You are the private investigator?" she asked.

I nodded, extending my hand. "Macy Adams."

She didn't bother getting up and we shook hands across the desk.

"Have a seat," she said, pointing to a plastic chair.

I sat.

"Evelyn Browne hired you?"

"Her attorney did."

"Nice lady, that Mrs. Browne. Dr. B was a real busy man. Kept me busy too, what with all his calls, his busy schedule and the correspondence, not to mention the research articles he published. Students in and out all day long, asking questions, leaving messages. Too busy to remember Secretaries Day, Christmas, or my birthday. But Mrs. Browne, she never forgot. And she always got me something real nice."

With the exception of her mother-in-law, everyone else seemed to like Evelyn. That had to count for something. *Your honor, my client is too nice to kill anyone.*

Jane was real chatty, but I'd expected as much from the tapes. She smiled at me. "Last year I had this big bouquet of flowers on my desk. So Dr. B says, 'Jane, I sure hope somebody died, because if these are from your boyfriend, you'd better be careful your husband doesn't find out, or you be in big trouble.' So I tell him, 'Then you and me both in trouble, Dr. B, because the flowers, they're from *you*. Your wife sent them.' "

She chuckled, a pleasant sound that emanated from deep in her throat. Her teeth were straight and even, and perfectly white, especially for a smoker. She wasn't old, but I wondered if they might be dentures. Jane lit a cigarette before returning her attention to the high stack of letters she was sorting into folders.

"I can't believe they're trying to pin this murder on her," she said. "Well, go on with your questions. And don't mind me. I can file, smoke, and talk—all at the same time."

"I'm surprised they let you smoke at Wadsworth. How does the university escape the state law about smoking in public buildings?"

She gave me a sardonic look and arched an eyebrow.

"You a smoker, honey?"

"No."

"Well, it's my damn office. *Mine.*" She pointed to a sign above her desk. It said: "LIGHT UP—IT'S YOUR CONSTITU-TIONAL RIGHT."

Not if things in the Capitol continued the way they were currently going.

"How long have you been Mitchell Browne's secretary?"

"Almost seven years."

"That's a long time. Did you enjoy working for him?"

She sorted another letter into a file. "I did, as a matter of fact, even though he could be very demanding." She paused. "A brilliant man—that was the word around here. But he wasn't a bad guy to work for, not as long as you followed his directions to the letter, and he'd let you know exactly what was expected. He was a workaholic, and he expected everyone on his staff to bust their collective butts as hard as he did."

I nodded. "I'm trying to find out about a company Browne invested in and I'm hoping you can steer me in the right direction. The company's called Biosynthesis."

She stopped her filing for a second, searching her memory banks. "Never heard of it. You don't mean BioCorp?"

"No. Biosynthesis."

"Sorry. That name doesn't ring a bell."

It didn't make sense. Browne had sunk two million dollars into Biosynthesis. Surely Jane, as his secretary, had to know *something* about the firm. "Are you sure about this?"

Jane tapped her forehead with her finger. "My memory is excellent. But let's have a look-see, just in case."

She went through the Rolodex that was sitting on her desk. "Nope. Nothin' here with that name. There *is* BioCorp. Dr. B was on the board of directors of BioCorp."

She flipped through more cards while taking another deep drag on her cigarette. We both sat quiet for a moment. Outside I could hear the trill of songbirds.

Jane went back to her filing, the cigarette dangling from the corner of her mouth. A thick layer of smoke hung over the room. The ashtray next to her PC was full, a graveyard of ashes and spent cigarette butts.

"Okay," I continued, "while we're on the subject, let's talk about BioCorp. I heard that Dr. Browne had some differences with the chairman."

"Have you talked to Melville Rutgers yet?"

"No, I haven't."

"Oh girlfriend, you're in for an *experience*." She pointed behind me. "You wanna close that door, honey?"

I got up and shut the door while she continued attacking the pile of forms on the file cabinet. "Now there's someone right out of *One Flew over the Cuckoo's Nest*. Doctor Melville Rutgers."

"What's his problem?"

"The man's a bigot. Hates everybody. Minorities, gays, Democrats, Asians, women. Thinks that women belong in the kitchen, not in an office."

Finished with her filing, she closed the drawer and sat back down behind her desk.

"I heard that Dr. Brown and this Rutgers had some sort of

disagreement," I said.

"Oh, Rutgers and Dr. B had a regular love-hate thing going. Been going on for years. Rutgers loved Dr. B's brains and his reputation, but he hated the power Dr. B wielded over the board. They'd been buttin' heads on a regular basis. I assume you know about BioCorp's plans to go public?"

"All I know is that the public offering was shelved."

"New York Stock Exchange. Big, big deal. Suddenly Rutgers pulls the plug, leaving BioCorp broke. No funds. This Japanese outfit approaches the venture people—wants to buy BioCorp— lock, stock, and barrel. I don't remember the firm's name, but it's one of them big Japanese pharmaceutical houses. But no can do without board approval. Half of the board wants to go ahead with the deal, the other half don't. Want to guess who had the deciding vote?"

"Browne?"

"Yes, ma'am. So when Dr. B told Rutgers he was voting in favor of the Japanese deal, all hell broke loose. Rutgers actually took a swing at Dr. B. Right here in this office."

"You're kidding." This was juicy.

Jane's face turned stern and she stubbed out the cigarette. "In the end nothin' come of it. Rutgers gets himself another venture group to cough up the bucks. The whole thing blew over."

"So why didn't BioCorp go public?"

"Production problems with their test kits is what I hear."

"Could the public offering be tied in with Dr. Browne's murder in any way?"

She looked visibly surprised. But she didn't answer right away, ostensibly giving the possibility some thought.

"I really don't see how," she finally said. "Rutgers has nothin' to gain from Dr. B's death, and everything to lose. My guess is that Rutgers would have done just about anythin' to *keep* Dr. B alive and well." She reached for a stack of file folders, got up, and went back to the bank of file cabinets.

"What about here at the university? Did Dr. Browne have any enemies?"

"Enemies as in murder? No, ma'am."

"He was a very successful man. Surely there must have been people who were envious?"

"Oh sure, that would cover about half the department. Dr. Browne had speaking engagements, a best-selling book, stock options." She laughed. "Even an invitation to the White House. Oh yeah, a lot of people were envious. But not enough to kill him."

"Could his research be tied in with his death?"

"The synthetic T-cells? The AIDS vaccine? Anything's possible, but I really don't see how." She shrugged, then smiled, showing off her pearly whites.

"What about his research assistants?"

"What about them?"

"How many did he have?"

"Four."

"I heard that his involvement with Dawn Halebrook went deeper than just a working relationship."

That caused her to pause for a second, her eyes suddenly wary.

"Is that what Mrs. Browne told you?"

"Yes."

"Poor woman."

"It's true then? Browne had an affair with Dawn?"

"Well, I didn't actually see them do the nasty, but it wouldn't surprise me none."

She lit another cigarette, her third thus far. I was starting to feel dizzy just from the secondhand smoke.

"You know," she said, "Evelyn Browne doesn't deserve any of

this. I think I'm a pretty good judge of character, and that woman's no killer. It's not right for her to be accused of doing away with her husband. Why would she want him dead? I don't buy any of that 'jealous wife' motive the police cooked up. Rumors about Dr. B and his R.A.s. have been floating around for years. Evelyn knew all about them. Why kill him now, after all this time?"

I didn't think Jane Ramirez was aware of Browne's impending divorce proceedings.

"What about Dawn Halebrook?" I said. "Did she have a motive to want Browne dead?"

"I can't see that either. Browne was her meal ticket. His death messed up her research project but good. Have you talked to her yet?"

I shook my head.

"Now there's one determined young lady. She knows exactly what she wants. She knew what she was doing, getting in bed with Dr. B. She used him as a stepping-stone."

Jane made Dawn sound like some calculating man-eater who stalked Browne, when I thought of it the other way around. She noticed my skeptical look.

"Dawn ain't no damsel in distress. Don't let her looks fool you."

"Did Dr. Browne's other assistants feel that she had an unfair advantage over them?"

She looked at me quizzically.

"Dawn must have gotten preferential treatment from Browne. Did that cause resentment among the troops?"

"Most of the R.A.s have their heads buried so deeply in their research, they never come up for air. They're clueless. It wasn't common knowledge that Dawn and Dr. B had a thing going."

"I get the distinct feeling that you don't care very much for Dawn."

She shrugged. "I don't lose any sleep over that girl. But she ain't any worse than some of the other prima donnas around here."

"What sort of research is she working on?"

"Immune defense reactions to attenuated viruses. I'll say this for her, she puts in her time at the lab. No slouch, that girl."

The phone rang and Jane answered it. I made some notes while she retrieved information from the computer screen.

"Sorry about that," Jane said, hanging up.

"Not at all. I'm grateful you were able to see me on such short notice. Here's another thing I heard: that Dr. Browne and his brother had some sort of falling out a couple of years back."

She shrugged. "Dr. B wasn't one to discuss his personal life. But now that you mention it, his brother used to call here all the time. But he hasn't called *once* in the last two years. Ever since the funeral. When Dr. B's father died."

"You think they had a falling out over their father's death?" I asked.

"I can't imagine why the death of a parent would cause a rift."

"Perhaps over the estate?"

She cocked her head. "There was this lawyer called here who handled that. Hold on, I think I still have his number." She flipped through her Rolodex. "Here it is: Sullivan and Delaney, on Federal Street."

Not many secretaries would have been able to retrieve *that* piece of information after two years' time. She copied the lawyer's name on a message slip and handed it to me.

"One more thing," I said. "Do you know anything about an offshore account in the Cayman Islands?"

She shook her head. "Can't say that I do."

I slid my business card across the desk. "If you remember anything else, will you give me a call?"

She picked up the card, read it briefly, and found a home for it in her Rolodex.

"Where do I find Dawn?"

Jane checked her watch. "She's all suited up right now, in the lab. You can't go in there. She's usually home after lunchtime. Do you know where she lives?"

"Memorial Drive?"

Jane nodded.

"Is Dawn seeing anybody besides Dr. Browne?"

"Why you asking?" Her tone was suddenly cautious.

"I heard Dawn was dating some guy," I lied.

"Who told you that?"

"I think Evelyn mentioned it."

"Well, then she knows more than I do."

She took one final drag before grinding the remains of her cigarette into the ashtray.

"So as far as you know, Dawn isn't seeing anyone else?"

"That's right."

Jane wasn't a very good liar. But no point in belaboring the issue. Especially since I wanted to keep her on friendly terms.

"Thank you for your time. I appreciate it." I stood.

"Have a nice day."

"You too."

I left the door open on my way out. I figured Jane could use some fresh air.

As I walked through Wadsworth Yard, I wondered why Jane Ramirez had balked at the thought of another man in Dawn's life. Was Dawn involved with someone else on the faculty? Or with one of the R.A.s?

It beat me. But it had been the one false note in our conversation.

Jane had given me plenty of food for thought. I'd have another go at Phillip Browne, to talk about his father's estate.

I called BioCorp to set up an appointment with Melville Rutgers. His secretary said he could see me first thing the following morning, but only for half an hour. Encouraged, I tried the Biosynthesis investors once more. On the fourth ring, a woman answered.

"May I speak with Harold Dizikian?"

There was a long pause.

"He's deceased. Who is this, please?"

EIGHTEEN

The woman on the phone turned out to be the late Harold Diz-ikian's widow. She agreed to talk to me about her husband, as long as I was willing to make the trip out to her home in Wellesley.

"I don't drive anymore," she explained. "When would you like to visit?"

"As soon as possible," I answered.

"How about this afternoon then? Would you like to come by for tea?"

We settled on the time and I hung up.

Since I was heading west anyway, I might just as well swing by Concord for a brief chat with Claire Browne. I found the telephone listing for her nursery and got directions. Maybe Claire could enlighten me as to what happened to cause the rift between Phillip and Mitchell. I might even get an earful as to why Claire thought Evelyn was guilty of murder.

On impulse, I tucked one of the school portraits I'd found in Browne's desk into my purse. Perhaps Claire knew the girl in the picture.

Armed with a map, I nosed the Jetta toward the suburbs. With the traffic on Route 2 relatively light, my thoughts strayed to Jack. I experienced flashbacks of the night before—thoughts that ran decidedly toward the X-rated variety. I could picture Jack in a conference room, high up in some New York skyscraper. I hoped his meeting was boring as hell. Let him entertain steamy fantasies as well.

I'd been so wrapped up in my daydreaming that I almost missed the entrance to the garden center. The parking lot in front was full, spring being the green thumb enthusiasts' busy season. I spotted Claire Browne as she loaded a flat of marigolds into the back of a station wagon.

I climbed out of my car and walked toward her. The expression on her face changed abruptly, telling me that she wasn't at all happy to see me.

"This really isn't a good time," she said, not even giving me the chance to say hello. "It's been a madhouse all morning and I have to leave shortly."

"This will only take a few minutes of your time," I said, using my sweetest Mary Poppins voice.

"You should have called before driving out here."

I helped her load the last two flats, despite my being all decked out in Armani. Have suit, will investigate and do manual labor. I figured that had to net me a few brownie points with her. We stepped aside to let the station wagon pull out of the lot, trailing a cloud of dust.

"I came all the way from Boston," I said, laying the guilt on thick. "Could you spare me just five minutes?"

"Oh, all right. Five minutes." She crossed her arms in front of her body. Bad start.

"The other day, at Phillip's house, I got the distinct impression that you believe Evelyn killed your son. I'd like to understand why you feel that way."

She looked down and cleared her throat.

"You know, I never could understand why Mitchell married that woman in the first place. He deserved so much more. Evelyn isn't bright, and she certainly isn't attractive." She looked up. "I suppose I don't know for a fact that Evelyn killed Mitchell, but the way I figure it, the police wouldn't have arrested her unless they had some solid proof against her, now would they?"

"Their case isn't nearly as solid as they may have led you to believe," I said.

I was fibbing, but she didn't have to know that.

"Well, I beg to differ. Evelyn had one hell of a motive for wanting Mitchell dead. He'd just informed her that he wanted a divorce."

I almost let my jaw drop. Evelyn hadn't said a word about any impending divorce. This put a decidedly different spin on things.

"The way I see it," Claire continued, "Once Evelyn realized her marriage was over, she panicked. Mitchell didn't think he owed her anything. She wasn't getting any huge monthly alimony check. Without a good financial settlement, a divorcee gets dropped like a hot potato by her social circle. I ought to know, because that's what happened to me after my divorce. You find out in a hurry who your true friends are."

"You sound sure that Mitchell told Evelyn they were getting divorced."

"Isn't that what I just said?" She paused, and then let out a dry chuckle. "Oh, I get it. Evelyn hasn't told you about the divorce. Well, that just figures."

I neither confirmed nor denied it, though of course, she was right. But why add any more acid to the already caustic stew of mother- and daughter-in-law relations?

"When was it that Mitchell supposedly told her?"

"The week before he died. Five days later he turns up dead. Mighty convenient for Evelyn, if you ask me." Her tone was bitter. "Mitchell said Evelyn took the news very badly. I told him to move out of the house, but he wouldn't listen to me."

She wiped her eyes with the back of her hand. "Now if you'll excuse me, I have work to do."

She started walking toward the main building of the nursery.

I hurried after her, my high heels digging into the graveled walkway.

Claire turned to face me. "You said five minutes . . ."

"Just one more thing. Please. I got the impression that Phillip and Mitchell had a falling out right after their father died. What was that all about?"

"What falling out?" Her tone was indignant. "Phillip and Mitchell got along fine. Who said they had a falling out?"

"They stopped socializing."

"Well, they are both busy. Phillip started his own business around the time Octavius died, and Mitchell was writing his third book. With both my sons working seventy-hour weeks, it left them precious little time for socializing, as you put it. But there was no falling out."

I was unconvinced, but it seemed pointless to pursue the topic. I dug the photo I'd found in Mitchell's desk out of my bag. "Do you happen to know who the girl in the picture is?"

She took the print from my hands, but before she could answer, she started coughing. "Damn pollen," she said when her coughing fit finally ceased. "My allergies always act up in the spring. Where did you get this?"

"It was in your son's desk."

"Might have been someone he had a crush on in high school. Sorry, but I can't say I recognize her."

She put the picture in the pocket of her apron.

"Can I have that back?" I said.

"Whatever for? It doesn't belong to you."

I let her have it. I had five other photos of the girl in my briefcase.

But something in Claire's demeanor had shifted. The look in her eyes had turned crafty. "You must be *really* desperate if you think this old photo might tie in with Mitchell's death."

"I've only been at it a couple of days. I tend to solve my

cases. Whoever killed your son won't be sitting pretty for long."

She turned to walk away, and then stopped herself, touching her face in a contemplative gesture. "There *is* something," she said.

"I'm listening."

"If I were you, I'd take a closer look at BioCorp. There's something fishy about that firm. Mitchell was upset by something that happened there. What was it he said?" She paused. "Something about . . . someone stealing the firm's technology . . . tampering with experiments."

"Did he mention any names?"

She shook her head. "No names. But something at BioCorp spooked Mitchell." She sighed. "I wish I'd paid more attention. If I had known . . ." Her expression softened. "Oh hell, maybe I'm letting my dislike of Evelyn cloud my judgment. I suppose it's possible that she didn't kill him. Maybe you ought to be looking at this BioCorp firm . . ."

She checked her watch. "I'd better get back to work. Sorry I was rude to you before . . . It's just all . . . too much. You seem like a nice person. Good luck to you. I mean it."

She turned around and disappeared behind a lavender bush.

NINETEEN

I backtracked to Route 128, maybe not the shortest but definitely the easiest way to Mrs. Dizikian's house.

During the drive to Wellesley, I was fighting angry demons that threatened to destroy my objectivity. I was p.o.'d at Evelyn. She'd betrayed my trust by withholding information about her pending divorce. I had to caution myself not to jump to conclusions. Maybe Claire had lied.

Also, Claire's sudden change in attitude puzzled me. Her sudden turn-around seemed phony somehow. But then, her son had just been killed. I supposed she was entitled to some erratic behavior. As it was, I didn't know what to make of her, except to take both of her theories as to who killed her son with a grain of salt.

Wellesley is a chichi suburb west of Boston. It's considered a desirable place to live, not in small part because of the fast commute time to downtown Boston—especially at rush hour, courtesy of the Massachusetts Turnpike.

I got off 128 at the Route 30 exit and drove through tall trees for a couple miles, before hanging a left onto Cliff Road. The lots became smaller, the houses larger, and the yards manicured as I crossed over the Wellesley town line. I took a right turn, winding my way through the blossoming landscapes, cursing the lack of street signs. As I approached the side of Wellesley that abutted Natick, the houses and yards became smaller, million-dollar-estates giving way to half-a-million-dollar commuter homes.

Mrs. Dizikian lived in a smallish colonial on a winding road. The house was beige, the paint peeling off the clapboards in spots. The front of the house was overgrown with rhododendron and evergreen shrubs that at one point probably complemented the size of the house, but without proper pruning, they had gradually overtaken the space. With thick shrubbery blocking most of the windows, the house had the feel of Sleeping Beauty's castle.

The front lawn was lush and green, in need of mowing. Dandelions were taking over a large section of the grass to my left. Both the house and the yard had an air of neglected abandon.

I rang the doorbell and waited.

A lady who looked to be in her eighties opened the door. She was short and frail, a halo of curly white hair framing her head. Her eyes were a pale blue and she squinted against the bright daylight, putting up a hand up to shield her face. Her cream-colored blouse and blue skirt looked like they belonged to someone a size larger than herself, which made me wonder if she had lost weight recently.

"You must be the girl investigator," she said.

I nodded and smiled.

She lowered her hand and stretched it out to me. I noted a slight tremor, the joints of her fingers thick and gnarled from arthritis. The veins on the back of her hand were prominent through translucent skin riddled with age spots. In another forty years, if the bad guys didn't get me first, my hands would look like hers.

"Follow me, dear."

She turned around and shuffled along, supporting her weight on one of those canes that forks into four rubber-tipped legs at the bottom. The inside of the house was dark and gloomy, not only from lack of light, but also because of the dark-green 1950s vintage wallpaper. A pungent odor of mothballs hung in the air.

I followed Mrs. Dizikian into a room that must have been a screened-in porch at one point. The two large picture windows, which faced the backyard, were not overgrown with plants yet, though one ambitious rhododendron was trying. The garden beyond was lovely, with hundreds of daffodils, forsythias, and azaleas in full bloom.

"I fixed afternoon tea for us." She pointed to a door. "It's on a tray in the kitchen. Would you bring it in here?"

I followed her instructions, fetching the tray, which was artfully laid out with real china cups and saucers, cloth napkins, and a selection of tiny cookies.

"You go right ahead and pour the tea, dear."

She had taken one of the Barcaloungers. I sat down in the one beside her.

"My husband had a lovely funeral at the Methodist church. So many people came, colleagues from Wadsworth, our dear friends from Wellesley, former students . . . The sermon was very moving. Were you there, dear? I don't remember . . ."

"I'm sorry, I wasn't."

"The university sent two beautiful wreaths."

"How nice."

All this talk of funerals didn't seem to be putting a damper on her appetite. She loaded her plate with cookies and munched them heartily. We exchanged pleasantries while we ate: nice room, beautiful flowers, how did a nice girl like you become a private eye. I sampled several of the cookies, which were delicious, the kind you buy in a good bakery.

"Your husband taught at Wadsworth?" I asked.

"In the Biology Department. Were you a student of his?"

"No, I wasn't. If you don't mind my asking, what did he die of?"

"Stomach cancer." Her face contorted with pain. "He was such a wonderful man. Next June would have been our sixtieth wedding anniversary."

Her eyes turned silvery, the liquid reflecting in the incoming afternoon sun. A tear rolled down her left cheek. I looked away, embarrassed.

I always hate it when people cry in front of me, which unfortunately happens a lot in my line of work. People usually hire a private investigator in the aftermath of a tragic loss or betrayal, when their emotions are raw and they are subject to grief-stricken outbursts.

I handed her a napkin. She dabbed at her eyes and blew her nose softly.

"I'm sorry. It's just so painful," she said.

"I can imagine. Take your time."

But of course I couldn't imagine what it would feel like to lose the person with whom you had spent a lifetime. I was eager to steer the conversation in a different direction, before she had a chance to work herself into a state. I noticed a family portrait, perched on a sideboard.

"Are those your children?" I asked, walking to the photo and picking it up.

"Yes. That picture's ten years old. My son is a lawyer in New York now, and one of my daughters, the one on the right, has a PhD from Wadsworth. She teaches English literature at Wheaton College. My other two daughters are married." She gave me a faint smile. "I have five grandchildren."

"Five? That's wonderful."

"Do you have children, dear?"

"Not yet. I'm not married."

"Well, you're still young. I'm sure you'll find someone wonderful and have children of your own."

I nodded, thinking that I wasn't *that* young. For an instant, my thoughts flashed to Jack. I couldn't picture him as the father of my children. In truth, the only way I'd pictured him today was buck naked.

It was time to get down to business. "Mrs. Dizikian," I said, "your husband is listed as an investor in a company called Biosynthesis."

She looked puzzled.

"I don't remember Harold ever mentioning it."

"According to the company charter, he was one of five investors."

The confused look on her face had a lost, almost panic-stricken quality, like not remembering things was becoming a recurring theme for her.

"I'm looking to contact the other investors," I said, "but I'm having trouble locating them. I was hoping that you might be able to steer me in the right direction."

"You couldn't just call the company to get that information?"

"The only address I have for them is a P.O. box, and I haven't been able to find a telephone number."

"And you say my husband invested money in this firm?"

"Right."

She sat up straighter, her demeanor suddenly infused with energy.

"Do you think I might be able to get his money back?"

"I don't know what the financial status of the firm is," I hedged. "Possibly."

"Who are the other investors?"

I showed her the list, which she scanned carefully.

"I don't know any of these people."

"Could we have a look at your husband's files?"

"I haven't thrown anything out. He was semiretired these past few years, but he was still active as a speaker. He even published a couple of papers. And he taught a class at Wads-

139

worth. On genetic engineering, society, and ethics." She added proudly, "I used to do his correspondence."

"Why don't we have a look at his files?"

She got up, an obvious struggle for her. "Harold's study is down the hall. How much money did you say he put into that company?"

"I really don't have any idea."

She led me to a small kitchen, which looked like the "before" version you see in magazines like *Better Homes and Gardens.* The floor was covered with brick-red linoleum, which was warping and separating from the floorboards around the edges. The walls and cabinets were painted a dreadful shade of mustard yellow, the kitchen counters were stained butcher block. All of the appliances, lined up along the periphery of the room, were avocado green, a paint finish not popular since the 1960s. Nestled in an alcove was a built-in table-and-bench combo in blond pine, the bay window almost completely blocked by an industrious dogwood tree.

Dr. Dizikian's study was adjacent to the kitchen. Reddish-brown pine paneling, stained to look like cherry. The brown wall-to-wall carpeting looked shabby and dirty. The Dizikians must have had a dog once upon a time, because there were a series of deeply scratched grooves along the bottom of the study door. I couldn't imagine children doing this kind of damage to a piece of wood unless they were descended from timber wolves.

The small room was spilling over with furniture, consisting of an odd assortment of black file cabinets, Naugahyde steel chairs straight out of an old Sears, Roebuck catalog, and assorted other castoffs. Every available surface was buried under sports trophies, old books, and overgrown rubber plants. The clutter of Dizikian's study, combined with the smell of mothballs, was making me feel claustrophobic.

"You did say Biosynthesis, didn't you, dear?"

"That's right."

She took her time, searching the files thoroughly. "I don't see it."

"Could it be filed somewhere else?"

"I suppose so. Would you like to look for yourself?"

She moved aside and sat down in one of the black Naugahyde chairs, watching me as I flipped through folders. Not a single file out of place, everything neatly labeled in an even script, which I assumed had to be her handiwork. Her organizing skills beat my own hands down. If a stranger ever tried to find anything in my files, they'd be in for a long, frustrating search.

I came across a file labeled "Mitchell Browne," which contained several articles. I searched under the other investors' names. Nothing. A BioCorp file held some corporate literature and two articles. Most of the other files were bulging with data on different bacteria.

"I don't think there's anything here."

"This company, Biosynthesis. Do you have any idea how much my husband might have invested in it?" Ms. Dizikian said hopefully.

I could have sworn she'd asked me that very question ten minutes ago.

"No, I don't. I'm sorry."

"But you said my husband was one of the principals? So he must have invested a lot."

I shrugged. The idea of getting money out of Biosynthesis seemed to have lit a fire under her.

"He kept some files in his desk drawers. Why don't you look there?"

I went through his desk, which was less organized. At one point she got up and stood next to me, looking over my shoulder as I flipped through the mess. I went through every single scrap of paper, without any luck.

"There are more files in the basement. Would you like to have a look-see there?"

"Good idea."

"That goes to the basement." She pointed at a door. "The light switch is on your right."

The basement was poorly lighted, dusty, and smelled of mildew. I could make out a bank of storage shelves, three levels high. Green and black bank boxes filled the bottom two rows.

She followed me down, taking one stair at a time. I was afraid she might trip and hurt herself, so I stayed at the bottom of the stairs, ready to catch her in case she lost her footing. I breathed a sigh of relief when she had made the torturously slow descent without incident.

"The boxes are in chronological order. The year's written at the top."

I found the most recent box, covering the last two years. The folders inside were arranged alphabetically. While I looked through the contents, my hostess watched over my shoulder, visibly excited by the prospect of a windfall.

There were no files on Biosynthesis, Mitchell Browne, or any of the other investors.

I did, however, find a directory of Wadsworth alumni, which listed Richard Kublinski, one of the other investors, with an address on Marlborough Street. I made note of the information.

We climbed back up, with her ascending at a snail's pace.

"If you find out anything about the firm, will you let me know, dear?"

"Absolutely," I said. "I'd be happy to."

She took my hand when we reached the front door. "What a nice young lady you are. It's been a real pleasure having you for tea. Drop by any time you're in the neighborhood."

I said I would, even though I knew the chances of our having tea again were slim. Her loneliness was so tangible, it almost made me ache. Her children and grandchildren undoubtedly had busy suburban lives of their own. They couldn't possibly make up for the loss of a lifelong companion.

Twenty

At a service station on Route 16, I filled the tank and checked my messages. David Silverman wanted to talk to me. And there was a message from Jack. "I can't stop thinking about you. Damn inconvenient. Makes it hard to concentrate on the half a million dollars I'm supposed to dole out to this outfit down here."

My final message was from Lieutenant Pascucci, a member of the Underwater Rescue Unit that had pulled Browne's body from the Charles. I called him back and verbally genuflected until he agreed to a meeting.

"It'll cost you," he said. "Grille 23."

I winced at the thought. This would be very expensive. Then I remembered my expense account. I called Silverman. His secretary took my call. "Hello, Macy, we finally got the autopsy report on Browne. Would you like me to messenger it?"

I told her I'd pick it up personally. That way I would at least be able to scan the findings before my meeting with Pascucci.

David's secretary had left the autopsy report with the receptionist. I tucked it under my arm, took the elevator downstairs, and walked the two blocks to the Kirstein Business Library. Kirstein, which houses the largest public collection of corporate periodicals and directories in New England, is located in an aging building in the heart of the financial district, next to a narrow alleyway that serves as a nocturnal latrine for the homeless population. The library usually swarms with lawyers and consultants—and also the occasional street person looking for a place to get out of the elements. In the stacks one has to be careful not to trip over sleeping bodies, lest that body comes alive to inform you that God has witnessed your sins and you'll roast in hell.

Before settling down with the autopsy report, I checked the corporate indices and periodical listings for information about Biosynthesis. Zilch. I wasn't surprised. Cynic that I am, I'd already started to speculate that Biosynthesis was a dummy corporation. Which begged the question: what had Browne done with the two million bucks he allegedly sunk into the firm?

I made my way to the third floor, to the magazines and periodicals section, which was less mobbed than the downstairs. There were a slew of articles about BioCorp, none of them particularly informative. The news releases told me that Bio-Corp marketed a number of test kits for obscure genetic disorders. I copied the articles, put them in my briefcase, and took a seat at one of the long library tables.

The autopsy report wasn't exactly light reading. Grasping the technical jargon of the M.E. was slow going at best, and the photos made my stomach queasy.

Cause of death was suffocation, caused by wet drowning. A large volume of water and sediment had been found in Browne's lungs. There were cuts and lacerations on his face and forehead, which occurred postmortem, probably from the current dragging the body on the river floor. Weeds and sand had been found inside Browne's nose, mouth, and left ear. The toxicology report showed a level of Valium sufficient to render the decedent unconscious prior to death.

A curious side note was that several colored plastic beads were imbedded in Browne's pubic hair and the hem of his pants.

I reread the passage. Plastic beads? Where the hell had

Browne picked those up? And in such a delicate part of his anatomy?

The medical examiner pegged time of death at 9:58, which was the hour frozen on the dial of the Cartier wristwatch Browne had been wearing. He noted, however, that anytime between nine and eleven p.m. would be consistent with the condition of the stomach content, which consisted of partially digested chicken, rice, and vegetables, the meal Browne had eaten that evening. The color photographs of Browne's corpse were graphic, though as a former professional photographer I had to admire the quality of the prints, which were well illuminated and in sharp focus.

The time spent in the water had bloated Browne's features. His skin was gray and broken in places. It is difficult to look at pictures of murder victims with clinical detachment, downright impossible when we're personally acquainted with the individual. I felt some relief that I'd never met Mitchell Browne in the flesh.

While I was reading, a man had taken the chair across from me, even though plenty of other seats were available. With the thick layer of dandruff on his shoulders and the build of a couch potato, he definitely wasn't my type.

He gave me a lecherous look anyway. I swear, Kirstein was weirdo central. The man stared at me openly, grinning across the table whenever I looked up.

"Are those photos of you?" he asked. "You look like you might be a model. Can I see?"

He leaned over and got an eyeful of one particularly gruesome autopsy photograph. He packed up his papers and moved to another table.

The guy probably pegged me as some sort of murderous femme fatale who drowned her lovers if they didn't measure up—and then photographed their naked bodies as souvenirs. Or maybe he figured I worked for the FBI. Either way, he'd lost interest, which suited me fine.

I finished the report, considering it thorough and well written. Occasionally we do get our money's worth for tax dollars spent.

As I left, I was aware of a set of eyes watching me from the copy machine. Mr. Sneak-a-Peek looked at me with veiled apprehension. The expression on his face told me that he wondered whether he might get a visit from me, toting a chain saw. I was tempted to whisk out my Swiss Army knife and clean my fingernails.

The Jetta was where I'd left it, the parking meter flashing overdue, but no ticket on the windshield. I mouthed a thank you to the parking gods and drove to Grille 23.

TWENTY-ONE

Pascucci was a member of the Underwater Rescue Unit of the state police. The unit was made up of regular police officers who perform the diving services on an as-needed basis. The training and certification dives were often scheduled on weekends, to avoid interfering with regular police duties. Being a member of the unit required genuine dedication, especially during the winter months, when the water temperature turns frigid enough to induce hypothermia. The men wore special dry suits—but still. Besides which, searching for dead bodies in cold murky waters is definitely not for the faint of heart.

Pascucci once told me that he had given up diving in the Caribbean altogether. "It just spoils you for doing any diving locally, especially come January," he'd admitted.

I took a seat at the bar and ordered a martini, possibly a delayed reaction to reading the autopsy report. The waiter had just put the drink in front of me when Pascucci walked in. In his mid-thirties, Pascucci had a boyish face that was just getting some interesting character lines around the eyes. His dark, thick hair was in need of a haircut. He had the most soulful brown eyes—bedroom eyes. If he were cast in bronze, he could rival any of Michelangelo's statues.

Pascucci and I had never discussed his marital status, but for some reason I had the impression that there was a Mrs. Pascucci tucked away somewhere. He didn't wear a ring, but he exuded a well-fed at-peace aura that connoted "happily married."

He took the seat next to me and ordered a Samuel Adams.

"How'd you get involved in the Browne case?" he asked.

"Evelyn Browne's attorney hired me."

"Well, you've got your work cut out. A lot of the evidence points to the merry widow."

"Drownings involving drugs are usually tagged as accidental. Or as suicides," I answered. "What led you guys to peg this one as a homicide?"

"The car. Had it been an accident or a suicide, the car would have stayed at the scene."

The waiter returned, emptying half the Sam Adams into a frosted mug.

Pascucci took a long swallow. "Ah, that hits the spot."

"The scene? You actually know where the body went into the river?"

"Yup." He smiled broadly. "At the Cambridge boathouse."

"But that's a mile upstream from where the body was found."

"The Charles *does* have a current."

I'd assumed all along that the body had been disposed of at the Hyatt Hotel. Spooky to think of a dead body traveling an entire mile on its own.

"And how did you figure that the body was ditched at the boathouse?"

"Because Browne's car was spotted there the night he was killed."

"At what time?"

"Shortly before ten."

Right around the time that Tommy claimed he saw his mother in bed, asleep. I hoped he was telling the truth.

"Who spotted the car?"

"Joggers. Wadsworth students. They're science majors and

they jog at night, right before they run some monster of a computer program. Their names are Bryant, Yosimoto, and some Indian guy—can't remember his name. Anyhow, for starters they noticed the car. It's jade green. The color, the styling, a beautiful model. It was parked on the lawn right next to the river embankment. Odd for a car to be parked there—totally illegally. A Jaguar with vanity plates that spelled B-I-O-L-B-S. The joggers joked that it had to be a professor getting lucky with one of the students."

I almost cringed. They'd been close to the mark.

"They ran the mile and a half to MIT, then back. Two of them had made a bet how long the professorial hump would last. By the time they got back, the car was gone. They remembered the incident because they had joked about how the prof didn't have much staying power."

"So by the time they returned it was what? About ten-fifteen?"

"These guys don't run as fast as you. More like ten-twenty."

"And they're positive about the license plate?"

"Oh yes. Plus there's this huge bare spot on the embankment. The lab technicians got a plaster cast of the tire imprint left in the dirt. It's a perfect match to Browne's Jaguar. There's no doubt that his car had been parked there that night."

"Still doesn't prove that the body was ditched there."

"You may have noticed in the autopsy report that some plastic beads were found on Browne's body. Identical beads were found near the boathouse landing, apparently left over from some arts fair held earlier in the month. The way the beads were deposited suggests that the body was dragged."

"So how did the joggers come to contact the police?"

"Browne's death made the front page of the *True Blue*—that's the Wadsworth newspaper. They read it and made the connection."

The waiter inquired if we wanted another round. I looked at Pascucci.

"Just the check, please," he said quickly.

"No dinner?"

"Nah. I got Red Sox tickets."

"Maybe they were lying," I said. "Students like to play pranks."

"I don't think so. The two foreign nationals seem pretty serious. And we're talking a murder case."

"The autopsy report says that Browne weighed a hundred and seventy-nine pounds. Just how far was the body dragged? I mean, Evelyn Browne is a very small woman."

"The car was parked next to the embankment. There's a good incline at the river's edge. We had one of our smaller policewomen try it, and she managed to roll *me* down to the water without any problems. Believe me, it isn't beyond Evelyn Browne's capabilities. And once the body was in the water, it would be even easier to maneuver."

"The killer went into the Charles with the dead body?"

"Most likely."

"Ugh," I said, revolted. "That's creepy. And he better have his tetanus shot up to date."

"He? Browne's killer is a guy now? You know something we don't?" Pascucci grinned.

"I was using the generic 'he,' " I said.

"You don't think Evelyn did it because she is a woman? Browne's killer has to be a man?"

"Most killers *are* men. Wives hardly ever kill their husbands. Husbands kill their wives all the time."

Pascucci ignored my last comment. "For the body to float downriver, it had to clear the wooden landing surrounding the boathouse, which meant that whoever killed Browne had to walk the body out beyond the dock. They probably hoped the body would wash out to sea."

I thought for a moment about what he said. Most people would be leery of getting into the Charles even in daytime. Plunging into the river at night—with a dead body no less—would give most anyone the willies. Somehow I couldn't see Evelyn having the stomach for something that gruesome.

"The way we figure," Pascucci said, "Evelyn drowned her husband, then drove the car back to her house."

I suddenly remembered Browne's missing keys. Now I understood why they hadn't been in his pockets.

"We found quite a bit of dirt inside the Jaguar," he continued, "on the seat and the floor of the driver's side. The dirt matches the soil from the boathouse. We even found a yellow bead on the floor mat. It's identical to the ones we removed from the deceased's clothing. They're quite distinctive. Small, translucent, and marbled. Indigo, pink, and yellow with metallic pigments."

"All this about the car is news to me. Why wasn't the information in the police report?"

He shrugged. "Don't ask me. I'm not in charge of the paperwork. It isn't my case. I only pulled the body out of the water."

"Any footprints at the scene?" I asked.

"No."

"I assume you checked Evelyn's shoes for mud?"

"Sure. No trace of mud on any of her shoes, but she could have easily ditched them on her way home. We did find a prescription for Valium."

I couldn't think of anything else to ask. Our conversation shifted to baseball, and Pascucci went on complaining about what was beginning to look like another losing season for the Red Sox. I personally couldn't get too worked up about it— tennis was my game—but I made the appropriate sympathetic noises just to be social.

We finished our drinks and I paid the check.

"Time for the ball game," Pascucci said, making a swinging motion with his arms.

"Go easy on those hot dogs."

"Why?"

"Eating hot dogs is supposed to increase your chances of getting leukemia."

"Too late for me then. Besides, with all the diving I've done in Boston Harbor through the years, I probably glow in the dark."

"Jesus."

"We're all gonna go eventually, one way or another. Might just as well enjoy life in the meantime. To me a ball game means beer and a Fenway frank."

"Who are the Sox playing tonight?"

"Blue Jays." He drained his glass. "I wish I had better news for you, Macy, but I think you'll find that this case is a loser. Everything we've looked at says Evelyn did him."

Pascucci stood and swung an imaginary bat. "Play ball."

"What else did you find in the car?" I asked. "Hairs, fibers?"

"Car was remarkably clean. Don't know about hair and fibers. We did find two fresh cigarette butts—Marlboros."

"Any prints on them?"

"Actually no. That was surprising. No prints. They're running DNA."

He held the door for me on the way out.

I drove home. On the doorstep of the carriage house sat a glass vase, filled with a dozen beautiful, long-stemmed yellow roses. I didn't need a card to know that Jack had sent them. I inhaled the scent of the roses and felt their satiny softness against my skin. What was it about flowers that made a woman feel so utterly cherished?

I unlocked the door, kicked off my shoes and checked my

messages. Hearing Jack's voice on my machine gave me as much pleasure as the flowers.

"Well, I guess you're out late tonight. Should I be jealous . . . ? Just kidding . . . I'll catch you tomorrow. Happy dreams."

Happy dreams indeed!

TWENTY-TWO

Tuesday morning dawned with bright sunshine. The weatherman promised clear skies and a seventy-degree high.

I checked all the windows and double locked the door on my way out. My morning jog often helped me sort out impressions. Occasionally, I even get an inspired idea while I run. I could use inspiration today. Everything I was turning up made Evelyn look guilty. Her husband's intention to divorce her. The Jaguar, indisputably linked to the crime scene, parked in the garage beneath Evelyn's bedroom, practically pointing a guilty finger at her.

I worried about the break-in, still wondering whether it was connected to the Browne case. But today, only a run. No endorphins. No ideas. Only aching muscles. But I needed this.

Back home, I bolted the door and slipped the security chain in place. I checked inside the closet before removing my clothes to shower.

I decided to dress carefully for my appointment with Melville Rutgers: a dark-blue wool suit-dress with gold buttons, gold earrings, taupe pantyhose, and navy pumps. To complete the look I rolled my hair into a French twist.

BioCorp was headquartered on the outskirts of Arlington, the town adjacent to Cambridge, in a flat three-story brick structure in an office park with ample parking and dull landscaping. Remembering Jack's comment about BioCorp's security rivaling that of Fort Knox, I presumed they might spring metal detectors on unsuspecting visitors. To be on the safe side, I removed the gun from my bag and placed it in the glove compartment of the Jetta.

An armed security guard, well over six feet tall with a muscle builder's physique, opened the door. He was dressed in a black uniform and had a Glock semiautomatic strapped to his belt. His eyes were steel blue, his blond hair cropped short, and his jaw was set on extra firm.

I went to the receptionist, a woman in her forties with a permed hairdo and leathery skin whose disposition was about as mirthful as the guard's. I'd barely set foot in the door, and already I was getting a bad feeling about BioCorp. No wonder Dawn hadn't wanted to work here.

The receptionist gave me a form to fill out, a long page of small print, asking about country of birth, citizenship, occupation, company affiliations, current and past employers, universities attended, and on and on.

These people were beyond nosy! I put down my correct name and occupation. After that, I started fabricating answers left and right. They had no right to my home address or employment history. Being in the snooping business myself, I was hypersensitive to other people's attempts to infringe on my own privacy.

At the bottom of the page, in bold capital letters, was a section that stated that I was not to divulge, publish, or otherwise disclose any information learned during my visit with BioCorp. Your basic nondisclosure agreement. I signed without qualms. Good luck trying to enforce it—especially if I found anything connecting BioCorp to Browne's murder!

I handed the clipboard back to the receptionist. She checked my paperwork. Apparently satisfied, she pointed a Polaroid camera at my face. I didn't feel like smiling.

I took a seat and waited, perusing the literature provided on a side table, standard PR fare, promising innovation, breakthroughs, and profits.

A buzzer interrupted the silence. The receptionist motioned to me. "Miss Adams. Doctor Rutgers will see you now. Could I have your driver's license, please?"

"Excuse me?"

"We like to hold your license while you're in the building." She made it sound like she was doing me a favor.

"Whatever for?" I said testily.

Her face colored. Apparently she was not used to being challenged. "We keep your driver's license to ensure that you return your badge upon leaving us."

She waved a laminated badge in front of me, like a prize. The badge sported the Polaroid picture she'd taken of me. A height chart as background and an arrest number would have made the mug shot complete.

"What if I don't have a driver's license?"

She gave me an annoyed look.

"A credit card will do then."

There was a definite chill in her voice now.

No way was this lady getting her hands on my Visa card. I exchanged the driver's license for the badge, which I clipped to the lapel of my dress.

She must have communicated with someone on the inside, because the door on the far side of the lobby suddenly opened and a second security guard appeared. This one could have passed for a twin to the guard at the entrance, except for the dark-brown hair. He asked me to open my bag and briefcase and inspected the contents thoroughly. Pity that I hadn't brought something embarrassing, like a jumbo box of textured purple condoms or a copy of *Hustler*. I wouldn't have minded seeing a smile, a raised eyebrow, anything to reassure me this robotnik was human.

Next, the guard waived a metal detector around my body,

followed by another device I didn't recognize. This was like stepping behind the iron curtain before Gorbachev.

Apparently I checked out, because the guard inserted a key card into a scanner. A green light glowed and he opened the door. The hallway beyond was brightly lit and pristine. White glossy tile floor, white walls. Doors on either side were spaced about ten feet apart and painted dark blue, small white numbers serving as the only identification.

We reached a bank of elevators and rode up in silence. I smiled at the guard, but his stare remained fixed and dead. A brief thought flashed through my mind of BioCorp guards as products of some android cloning experiment in assembly-line humans.

We reached the third floor and entered a seating area furnished with Queen Anne reproductions. The guard led me to a secretary, a redhead wearing small horn-rimmed glasses and a severely tailored, long-sleeved red dress. Her lipstick and nail polish were the exact shade of fire engine red of her outfit.

She flashed a cool smile. "Doctor Rutgers is on the telephone, but he'll be with you in a minute."

Twenty-five minutes later she asked me to proceed to the chairman's office.

Rutgers was seated behind his desk in a large corner suite. He was enormous, in all directions, easily the largest human I'd ever seen. His build spoke of a passion for rich food—and plenty of it.

"Mrs. Adams. I'm Melville Rutgers."

I decided to let the "Mrs." slide.

He got up and stretched his large doughy hand across the desk. I shook it. It felt like a warm, wet sponge. After we both sat down, I surreptitiously wiped the palm of my hand on my skirt.

"It's nice of you to see me on such short notice," I began.

"As I mentioned to your secretary, I'm investigating Mitchell Browne's death."

"That's right. You're the girl detective. Oh, this should be good." He chuckled, putting his belly and double chins in roiling motion. He spoke with an accent—Kentucky came to mind.

"I understand Mitchell Browne was on the BioCorp board."

"Sure was. A girl detective. What's the world coming to? Progress, I guess. What does your husband think about you being in this line of work?"

"I'm not married." *The guy was a jerk.*

"Divorced?"

Christ. "No."

"Now see, that's what's wrong with this country. I had a discussion about this very subject last night. Where did you go to school, if I may ask?"

"B.U.," I lied, humoring him. Rutgers had no business knowing I'd gone to Yale.

"Fine school, fine school. I assume you graduated?"

"I did." Lie number two. I had dropped out.

"Now, you seem like an intelligent young lady, a college graduate and"—he actually winked—"you're an attractive individual. Someone as attractive as yourself should have children. Hell, you should have a whole truckload. You're what? Thirty? Thirty-two? And not even married yet."

I couldn't believe my ears. I was tempted to blow the interview off, and tell Rutgers where he could stick it. It took self-discipline to hold my tongue.

"Mr. Rutgers, I did not come here to discuss my personal life. I came here to talk about Mitchell Browne."

"And we will, we will. Touchy young thing, aren't you? Well. I apologize. It's impolite to ask a lady her age. Pardon my manners. And incidentally, it's *Doctor* Rutgers, not mister. But just for the sake of argument, let's say you're thirty. Get married in two years, honeymoon for a year or two. Makes you thirty-four. At thirty-four, lord knows what shape the old plumbing is in. Especially nowadays, with the rise in STDs. Pardon my being blunt, but you get my point."

What an asshole. My plumbing was none of his goddamn business. But I let him prattle on. I'd begun to think of Rutgers as only half human. Besides, I was curious to learn the extent of his lunacy.

"The only people who seem to procreate prodigiously these days are the uneducated, the insolvent, and the unemployed. Hell, they make a career out of having babies. Crank out a baby a year, end up with six, seven, in no time. Half of them are on crack or other drugs while they're making babies. So now we have a secondary problem. Drugs cause birth defects and poor parenting. Add insult to injury, these people steal to finance their drug habit. It's a disgrace. And who's picking up the tab? It's you and me, Mr. and Mrs. Taxpayer."

He paused, pointing a meaty finger at me.

"Until recently the evolution of our species was based on survival of the fittest, the brightest." He tapped his forehead. "We're taking four million years of evolution and dumping it right down the toilet. We're breeding intelligence out of the human race—"

"Mr. Rutgers, you're a busy man," I interrupted. "I was told you could only give me half an hour. We need to talk about—"

"We have plenty of time. But what I tell you this morning could change your—"

"How much time do we have?"

He checked his watch. "Twenty-four minutes."

"Dr. Browne wanted to bring in Japanese investors to—"

"Can I give you a piece of advice, young lady?"

I eyeballed him.

"This is something that'll help you tremendously in your

career as a girl private eye." He chuckled once more. "A girl private eye. I'll be . . . You know what's wrong with you ladies trying to do a man's job?" He waved his big hand in the air. "You try too hard. Now your average man would spend a little time chitchatting, breaking the ice so to speak. Something you girls just haven't learned yet. You businesswomen take yourselves entirely too seriously."

I tried not to roll my eyes. "Mister—Doctor Rutgers, you've done an admirable job chitchatting for the both of us. Can I ask my questions? I'd say the ice is pretty much broken up by now. We're definitely dealing with crushed ice."

Rutgers laughed out loud. "Now you're talking. You see how even the smallest piece of advice from a man helps? I'm sure this'll prove to be a tremendous boost in future interviews." He spread his palms. "No charge."

"Thank you. Very generous. I'd heard that you and Dr. Browne had serious disagreements about bringing in Japanese investors."

"Miss Adams, you need to understand something. Everyone says how the Japanese are these incredibly smart people. Well, I'll admit they are clever. They steal our technology, copy it, and then they turn around and sell it back to us—at double the price. I don't want that to happen with any of my products. I have no respect for the Japanese. As a people they are missing something. Something more important than being clever or working hard. Something that goes down to the core of what it means to be human. That something, young lady, is integrity. A sense of fair play. A sense of right and wrong. Did you study history at B.U.?"

"What's your point?"

"Too many people don't pay attention to history. You've heard the saying that those who don't heed history are bound to repeat it. Well, I've been a scholar of history all my life. It's my passion. History shows, again and again, that the Japanese are snakes in the grass. Remember Pearl Harbor? Sure you do. These people will stab you in the back. Now, Mitchell Browne was like the Japanese. He also was a very bright man, a clever man, disciplined and hardworking. But just like the Japanese, he lacked integrity. Honesty. Loyalty. He lacked all those values."

He shifted his massive bulk.

"What did Browne do?" I asked, intrigued.

"I do not wish to sully a dead man's reputation." Rutgers' face was a mask of piety, eyes looking upward, as if glimpsing heaven.

"Was this about bringing in Japanese investors? Or are you talking about something else?"

"Enough. The man's dead. Let's leave those sleeping dogs lie. Miss Adams, BioCorp had nothing to do with Dr. Browne's death. I know this is on your mind. But let me put you at ease. I am a peaceful man. I don't believe in violence. I believe in the Lord. I believe that He watches over us and rewards the virtuous."

He raised both hands heavenward. Dropped them and picked up a leather-bound book from his desk, turning the cover toward me so I could see it. The Bible.

"You see this Bible? I read it every morning before work. I follow the commandments—to the letter, each and every one of them, each and every day. If Browne had lived by the Good Book, he'd still be with us today."

"So where did Browne stray from the Good Book?"

He smiled. His teeth were tiny, dwarfed by his huge face.

"You're the investigator. Go investigate. Earn your money. Don't expect other people to do your job for you."

He paused. "Do you read the paper?"

"Doesn't everybody?"

"Unfortunately, no. It's a useful habit to get into: reading the paper. If you follow the news, in a day or two you'll see an announcement about our latest joint venture. We found a nice American company to do business with. We do not need the Japanese. Never will."

"You're talking about Mass Bay Capital?"

He looked at me, obviously surprised. "Well, well . . . you are well informed."

"I am a private investigator." I changed tack. "Dr. Browne believed someone was stealing BioCorp's technology. What can you tell me about that?"

"That's a new one on me." Rutgers let out a dry, tight laugh. His neck rolls jiggled. "Miss Adams, surely you've noticed this morning just how excellent our security measures are. We've gone to great lengths to protect our assets. The very idea of someone stealing technology from us is preposterous."

"If BioCorp is so well managed, how do you explain what happened to the public offering earlier this year?"

"One of our products, a test kit, wasn't performing reliably. These things happen in our industry. The problem has been fixed."

"What specifically was the problem?"

"It's quite technical. You wouldn't understand."

Time to go for the big finale. "Dr. Rutgers. Maybe you can answer this for me: What went wrong with the rabbits in Section D?"

Rutgers's face lost all animation. He stood. "Who . . . ?" His small eyes went hard. "Who *are* you?"

His hand went under his desk. I heard a buzz. A chill went down my back. The door behind me sprang open. My head swiveled in the direction of the sound. Two guards had entered the room.

My heart skipped a beat, as a wave of adrenalin rushed

through my body.

No one knew I'd come here this morning. Not a soul.

Twenty-Three

The armed guards who entered Rutgers's office looked like carbon copies of the ones downstairs. The firm was swarming with them. Maybe they *were* clones. These two looked like hired assassins in a James Bond thriller. I felt very uneasy about what might happen next. I didn't want to end up feeding the fishes in the Charles like Browne.

I had to get word to someone that I was at BioCorp. *Harry.*

I pulled the cell phone from my handbag and hit the speed dial button with Harry's number. But before I could say a word, one of the guards charged and tackled me, hurling me to the ground like a line backer. I shrieked as I fell, my head missing Rutgers's desk by a fraction of an inch as I went down. A sharp pain shot through my left side as I hit the floor. The guard landed on my back, knocking the wind out of me. I tried to inhale, but succeeded only in making sick rasping sounds.

I panicked. I could not breathe. I was a fish on land. My vision dimmed as I tried again and again to get air into my lungs. I saw Rutgers's stunned face beside me. In my tunneling vision, I felt the guard get off me. Suddenly my lungs inflated. Air. Precious air.

"Macy?" Harry's voice emanated from my hand, from the cell phone on speaker mode.

"I'm at BioCorp," I yelled. "BioCorp, in Arling—"

The guard punched me in the face. I tasted blood. He yanked the phone out of my hand. I could hear beep-beep-beep sounds as he pushed buttons at random, trying to shut the device off.

"Macy, are you all right?" Harry's voiced squawked.

"BioCorp," I yelled again.

"I'm calling 9-1-1—" Harry's voice broke off. The phone went dead as the guard threw it on the ground and trampled it with the heel of his shoe. It shattered in pieces, plastic parts scattering across the floor. Out of the corner of my eye, I saw that the second guard had drawn his gun. He was pointing it right at me.

"Enough," Rutgers's voice boomed. "Enough."

The first guard halted in midair, his foot hovering above the crushed cell phone. The second guard kept his gun trained on me.

"Why on earth did you attack her, you fools?" Rutgers yelled, about two minutes too late.

"I thought she was going for a gun," the guard said.

Rutgers shook his head, like he couldn't believe the man's stupidity. "At ease."

Both guards relaxed their stance. The second guard lowered his weapon.

"I don't know what happened that made the two of you go berserk," Rutgers said.

"But you activated the alarm."

"I buzzed you so you could escort my guest back to the entrance, you dolt."

"But the red light—"

"You were obviously mistaken. Leave us now. I'll take my guest down personally."

Rutgers waved the guards from the room.

He extended a meaty hand toward me. With misgivings, I took it. Rutgers helped me to my feet. I assessed the damage. My left elbow throbbed fiercely and my side ached when I inhaled. Broken rib, I guessed.

"I'm very sorry about what just happened." Rutgers punched a button on his phone. "Marty, the two guards who were in my office just now. Fire them."

Rutgers pulled a piece of notepaper from a dispenser and started scribbling. While he wrote, he said to me, "This was unforgivable. Accept my apologies, please. As you just heard, I have sacked those overeager morons. I can't understand what got into them. I don't know what to tell you. It's hard to find good help nowadays."

Good help? Jesus!

Just one more inanity from Rutgers. *He* had created this environment, which allowed security guards to overstep their legal bounds. I wasn't about to argue with him. I only hoped that Harry had made the 9-1-1 call and that the cavalry was on its way. All I wanted was to leave BioCorp unharmed.

Rutgers opened his desk drawer, took out a checkbook, and wrote a check. He handed it to me. "For your broken cell phone."

I looked at the amount. Five hundred bucks. Overly generous, but I wasn't complaining.

"Are you hurt?" he asked. "I can take you to our nurse's office. We have first-rate medical facilities on-site."

The very idea of coming under medical care at BioCorp sent shivers down my spine.

"No, no. I'm fine," I protested.

I trailed Rutgers to the elevator. Before we descended, Rutgers handed the note he'd scribbled to his secretary. We rode the elevator in tense silence.

Both Jane Ramirez and Jack had warned me that Rutgers was a nutcase, but I didn't think they had a clue just *how* far gone he was. That Rutgers had deadly viruses under his control was cause for grievous concern.

Downstairs, Rutgers apologized once more, stressing again

that he hadn't sanctioned the actions of the guard. Eventually, he returned to his office. I placed my badge on the receptionist's desk and snatched my driver's license from her hands. A slight grin played across her lips.

"Keep that smile while you still have something to smile about, missy. You'll be out of your job by Christmas." I watched her grin fade, with great satisfaction. Just how to make good on my threat, I had no idea.

I hurried to my car and pressed the unlock button on my remote from ten yards away, wanting to leave this place as fast as possible. I reached for the door handle. Suddenly two hands grabbed me from behind, spun me around, and pinned me against the side of the car. The guard who'd attacked me in Rutgers's office.

"You bitch," he spat. "You got me fired."

A small sound escaped my throat.

"Fucking bitch." His eyes were dark pools of hate. "I'm gonna teach you a lesson." He tightened his grip on my shoulder. For an instant I was paralyzed by fear. I had to act. I had to get my hands on the Glock. I had to get help.

As if in answer to my silent prayer, a police cruiser, sirens blasting and lights flashing, exploded into the parking lot, tires squealing as it banked sharply and sped toward BioCorp's entrance, where it screeched to a halt.

Harry's 9-1-1 call.

"I'm not done with you yet." The guard's voice was low and threatening, filled with menace. As a parting gift, he shoved me hard against the Jetta, before taking off in a run.

Two policemen were entering the BioCorp building. I waved and shouted at them, but to no avail. They didn't hear me. I climbed into the Jetta, started the engine, and brought the car around, parking it behind the cruiser. Automatically, my hand went to the Glock in the glove compartment. I pulled back at the last moment. It isn't a good idea to go into a situation with the cops while carrying a loaded weapon. Instead, I honked my horn.

The two officers rushed out of the building, followed by the receptionist. She pointed in my direction. We met up on the sidewalk.

Officers Spezzano and Donahue were thorough, taking statements from Rutgers and me, and even interviewing the receptionist. They noted the name of the guard who'd attacked me, with Rutgers stressing all the while that the guard had been given his notice, effective immediately. The two officers advised me to take out a restraining order against the man, in view of his having threatened me with bodily harm.

Twenty minutes later, with the paperwork all filled out and signed, Spezzano and Donahue let me go. Presumably they had a new emergency to attend. I called Harry to thank him and let him know that I was all right. I didn't want him to worry about me.

Shaken and bruised, I drove out of the BioCorp lot, feeling the lack of the security blanket the two police officers had provided. Frequent checks of my rearview mirror told me I had no tail. When I was sure that nobody was following me, I stopped at a gas station. I needed to pee in the worst way, and my face and hands were lathered in nervous sweat.

I felt absolutely shitty. My nerves were jittery beyond belief, my rib ached whenever I took a deep breath, and my left elbow throbbed. My psyche was shaken to the core. I bought a Coke from a vending machine and guzzled it. Instant comfort, except for a fierce stinging sensation on my tongue. I must have bitten myself when the guard punched me in the jaw.

A small park was situated across the street from the gas station. I needed to walk off the adrenaline before I went crazy. And no, I didn't think I was exhibiting signs of paranoia just because I took the Glock along.

The guard's threat kept echoing through my brain, like an unwanted mantra. *I'm not done with you yet. I'm not done with you yet.*

The creep had sounded serious, like he meant business.

What I couldn't figure out was whether he was acting alone, or whether he and Rutgers were in cahoots, the "firing" mere stage acting to absolve Rutgers from any blame should anything happen to me.

Just how dangerous was Rutgers? If he had in fact killed Browne, he wouldn't hesitate to kill a second time. With an army of well-trained security guards at his disposal, getting rid of someone who'd become a thorn in his side would be easy— with little risk to Rutgers personally.

I didn't like that thought.

In retrospect, mentioning the dead rabbits in Section D hadn't been a smart move.

I had to gather more information about the firm, starting with a list of BioCorp employees—past and present. If the way BioCorp had treated me this morning was any indication of how they did business, there had to be a number of disgruntled former employees who possessed all manner of dirt on the company.

I finished the Coke and my heartbeat returned to normal. As I climbed into the Jetta, I noticed a black SUV parked across the street. The man inside the vehicle was watching me. I looked closer, thinking I had to be hallucinating. But either my paranoia had kicked into high gear, or the man behind the wheel was the guard who'd attacked me earlier.

The hairs on my arms bristled despite the heat. My hand went to the gun in my purse. I got into my car, put the Glock on the passenger seat, and started the engine. I sped off, keeping an eye on the SUV in the rearview mirror.

I didn't like what I saw. The SUV made an illegal U-turn. It accelerated sharply, a black looming presence in my rearview mirror.

TWENTY-FOUR

I hit the steering wheel and cursed loudly. How had the SUV tailed me without my noticing? I tried to shake him by taking several quick turns. No luck. Instead of me losing him, the SUV closed the distance between us. A red light ahead. Again I cursed and slowed the Jetta. Seeing a gap in the traffic, I ran the light. The black SUV followed, speeding through the intersection without even slowing. From the cacophony of squealing brakes and blaring horns, he barely avoided a collision.

I raced on, taking sharp turns at random, with no clear direction in mind. The street I was on ended in a T-intersection. I hung a right. I got about halfway down the block, when a white van approached from the opposite direction. The van veered across the road and stopped, blocking both lanes of traffic. The black SUV screeched to a halt behind me.

A man jumped from the white van. He was dressed in jeans and a black T-shirt. Not a BioCorp guard, I thought with relief. He opened the back of the van and retrieved a long object that looked like a harpoon gun. For a moment I was confused.

Then I got the picture—and it wasn't pretty.

I grasped the Glock, slid to the passenger side, and hurled myself out of the Jetta, landing near the fender of a parked truck. My injured rib exploded in pain. From underneath the truck I saw the guy in jeans run in my direction. Simultaneously, the second man, the BioCorp guard who'd attacked me, alighted from the black SUV and cut off my escape to the rear. He had a gun.

I was boxed in, trapped.

I glanced around. The town houses behind me were set close together, with a mere strip of grass for a front yard. A short, narrow alley separated them. I made for it, sprinting for the safety of the structure in four quick steps. I edged along the perimeter to the backyard. But I didn't feel any safer once I reached the back of the town house. The bad guys were right behind me, their footsteps echoing off the concrete sidewalk.

I spotted a dense bush. No cover at all, but the plant would make it more difficult to see me. I threw myself on the ground underneath it and raised the Glock. Behind me, a wooden staircase rose to the rear entrance of the house.

I tried to figure out my next move. Heading up the back stairs of the town house was risky. The back door looked solid. On the opposite side, a brown fence separated the property from its neighbor. It was too high to jump.

The guy in jeans appeared around the side of the town house. Our eyes met and he raised the harpoon gun. I heard a whistling sound, and something struck the wooden siding next to my head. I fired the Glock. Once, twice. I heard a grunt, and the harpoon gun clattered to the ground.

Oh my God. Had I hit him?

I fired another quick round into the air. Footsteps scampered. Which guard had I shot? Was he hurt? Was he still a threat? I worried about the second guard, that he would sneak around the other side of the house and ambush me from behind.

Cowering behind the bush, I was a sitting duck, my rear completely unprotected. I couldn't hold out for long. I only had the one magazine. If I kept shooting, I'd run out of bullets.

I had to move someplace safer. And fast.

I fired off another shot while dashing up the back stairs of the house. I fired two rounds into the wood surrounding the lock. The door frame splintered. I yanked the door open and entered the hallway. I slammed the splintered door shut and slid the security chain in place.

I was in the kitchen. I grabbed the phone on the counter and dialed 9-1-1.

"Operator, there's been a break-in. I've been shot at."

"Are you hurt?"

"No."

"You're at 247 Morgan Street?"

I looked around for an address. A stack of mail sat on the kitchen table.

"Yes. 247 Morgan," I confirmed. "Please hurry. Hurry. They're breaking into the house. They'll kill me," I shrieked.

The hysterical tone in my voice wasn't an act. I *was* utterly and completely terrified.

Leaving the phone off the hook, I ran upstairs and looked for a hiding place. The queen-size bed in the master bedroom had a flowered comforter and eyelet dust ruffle. To my left was a large double-hung window. I looked down and cursed. A six-foot drop to a wooden deck—too far to jump with an injured rib. I slid the window up and left the screen open, making it look like I'd escaped to the street. Maybe they'd buy it. I squeezed under the bed, ignoring the searing pain in my rib-cage. Hidden behind the dust ruffle, I trained the Glock on the door.

How many bullets did I have left? Fear of dying was making me stupid—as well as gutless. Instead of going after the bad guys, like I should, I was hiding under a bed.

I listened intently. Nothing. No running feet. No gunfire. Maybe they'd given up.

Then, from the floor below came the sound of splintering wood.

I strained to hear, trying to figure out what was happening. Footsteps, a brief scuttling noise, then silence. I counted to ten, fifteen. Then I heard a door open, quick, sharp noises, then silence again. A door closed. A door opened. Something got knocked over. The sounds moved across the floor below me, room by room. By my estimation, my pursuers were in the living room, right below me.

An irrational fear that they could hear my breathing through the floorboards took hold of my mind. Sweat poured down my sides. I fully expected the bad guys to start taking random potshots through the ceiling.

Then the sounds below me moved on, away from where I was. I had been holding my breath. I exhaled. My heart was pounding like a sledgehammer. My head dropped to the floor. Dust motes drifted into my nostrils. I felt an almost overwhelming urge to sneeze.

Oh God, just don't sneeze. Not now.

I strained to hear. Eventually my pursuers would come upstairs. I kept my eyes on the door through a gap in the dust ruffle, expecting them to burst into the room at any moment.

The muscles of my hand were fatigued from holding the Glock in an awkward position. My palms were sweaty. I had no sense of time. It had been an eternity since I called 9-1-1 and wedged myself under the bed. The police should have arrived by now. Where were they?

I kept praying. *Don't come upstairs. Please don't let them come upstairs.*

Then footsteps, tentative, quiet, sinister, stole up the staircase. They were on their way.

A wooden board squeaked at the top of the landing. They were headed toward me. Quick steps. Then silence.

Something raced across the floor, heading right for the bed. I felt a jolt of adrenaline. A moment later something furry hit my arm. A white and orange cat—claws out and teeth bared in a silent hiss. My own surprised scream remained lodged in my throat.

The cat and I blinked at each other in amazement.

Alerted by the noise the cat made, my pursuers bounded into the bedroom. Through the eyelet dust ruffle, I could see one of them crouch to his knee, a gun in his hand. With the Glock trained on him, I tried to push the cat from under the bed with my knee. It wouldn't budge.

A hand reached for the dust ruffle. The cat scratched it and, with a loud hiss, shot out from under the bed, streaking past the two men.

I steadied my gun. I would shoot the man if I had to.

"Shit, just a stupid cat." I recognized the voice. It sent shivers down my spine.

"The damn cat scratched me," the other man cursed.

"You think she went through the window?"

I watched two pairs of feet move to the window. "Nah, we'd have heard her jump. She must be on this floor. Check the closets—and under the bed."

TWENTY-FIVE

Faintly, then louder, I heard a wail of sirens in the distance.

Police cruisers were mere blocks away, and coming closer.

A flurry of footsteps. The bad guys were scrambling down the stairs, leaving the house. Car doors slammed. A motor revved.

Seconds ticked by before the sirens stopped in front of the house. A new set of footsteps on hard-soled shoes.

A male voice shouted, "Police."

I rolled out from under the bed. "Up here," I yelled. "I'm up here."

I left the Glock on the bed.

To my delight, it was my newfound best friends, Spezzano and Donahue, running up the stairs. I continued my saga from this morning. Two more cops arrived in a second cruiser. The four men secured the scene. They walked around with me and located a tranquilizer dart, alongside a minute amount of fresh blood on the siding of the house. The crime scene unit arrived, and samples were taken, bagged, and tagged.

According to Spezzano, the fact that only a small amount of blood was present pointed to a minor flesh wound, probably caused by the ricochet of one of my shots.

"How could I have missed the tail?" I said, asking the one question that was haunting me.

"You were watching for a tail?" Donahue asked.

"Yes. Absolutely. I even drove around aimlessly for a while, on secondary streets. No one followed me. I'm sure of it. And then for that white van to show like it did . . ."

Spezzano and Donahue exchanged a thoughtful look.

"Let's have a look at your car," Donahue said.

He retrieved a large mirror from the cruiser, which he used to examine the underside of my car. He paid special attention to the right rear quarter panel.

"Aha. Transmitter," he said, triumph in his voice. He held up a tiny box.

Was this Rutgers's doing, or had the sacked security guard acted on his own? And who was the second guy in the white van?

I shuddered. I flashed back to the break-in at the carriage house. Was that also their doing? But on Sunday, Rutgers and his goons hadn't known I existed.

By the time Spezzano and Donahue left, it was nearly eleven o'clock. They provided me with a police escort to the entrance to Route 2, but from there I was on my own.

I drove into Cambridge, then to Boston, before heading west again. If I had a tail, I wanted to flush him out. Eventually, I parked in the Atrium Mall garage in Chestnut Hill, went to the bar of the Cheesecake Company, and ordered a stiff drink. So what if it was barely noon?

I called Pascucci from a pay phone, cursing the fact that my cellular lay demolished in a trash can at Biocorp. It took a good fifteen minutes to relay everything that had happened to me, beginning with my meeting with Rutgers. Pascucci listened with interest. When I finished he said he'd look into it from his end.

I returned to the bar and ate a leisurely lunch.

I left the Atrium Mall shortly after one, again checking for a tail. No one was following me. I headed east again, in the direction of the Charles River, still checking the rearview mirror.

Will I be looking over my shoulder for the rest of my life?

Dawn's apartment was on Memorial Drive. From the outside,

her building looked respectable enough, but the lobby area was shabby. I found "Halebrook" among the names and pressed a buzzer.

A female voice came over the intercom. "Hello?"

I explained that I was an investigator looking into Mitchell Browne's death, and Dawn buzzed me in. The elevator was filthy, ground-in dirt and gum wrappers littering the carpet. I emerged on the eighth floor and headed to Dawn's unit. She had left the door ajar.

I knocked before pushing the door open all the way, and entered a large living room with a wall of windows looking out over the Charles River and the Wadsworth Business School. Dawn Halebrook was perched on a stationary bike, peering at me with curious eyes, sweat pouring from her face while she pedaled at a good clip.

"If you don't mind, I'll stay on the bike while we talk," she gasped, pushing herself hard. "I only have four minutes left, and I don't want to screw up my workout."

Jane Ramirez had commented about Dawn not being a slouch. I'd been curious about the woman who caused Browne to cheat on his wife. Dawn's thin, tiny leotard-clad body was toned and sleek, muscles flexing with fluidity as she pushed down hard on the pedals. I could easily picture her as an award-winning gymnast.

Like Evelyn Browne, Dawn looked youthful for her age. But that's where the similarities stopped. Unlike Evelyn, Dawn looked to be in excellent shape. The only thing Evelyn had on Dawn were good-sized breasts. Dawn was almost completely flat-chested. Her hair was the color of wild honey and she wore it pulled back in a ponytail. With her young complexion and snub-nosed face, she looked like a high school cheerleader, not a doctoral fellow at Wadsworth. She was the type of girl—small and delicate—that always made me feel like a hulking giant.

"Have a seat," she panted.

Dawn pointed to the bar stools in front of the kitchen counter. I sat down, letting my eyes wander. Her living room was a fitness nut's dream. One big gym with mirrors. Instead of furniture Dawn had a stationary bike, Stairmaster, Nautilus machine, various dumbbells, and other assorted torture devices.

The walls were painted a bold shade of burgundy, decorated with large wooden African masks. The galley kitchen wallpaper to my right was black and white zebra stripes, completing the safari motif. The only seating in the room was a love seat placed directly in front of the windows, facing the river. The decor was unusual, yet its overall effect oddly appealing.

"What's this about? I already talked to Detective Kerrigan," she said.

"I'm a private investigator."

"Oh."

That slowed her down momentarily, her expression becoming cautious. She pushed a strand of hair out of her eyes and looked at me suspiciously, before picking up the pace of her workout again.

"Who are you working for?"

"Evelyn Browne."

Her entire demeanor changed. Her pedaling slowed and grew mechanical.

"I should have guessed. Are you talking to all of Browne's R.A.s?"

"I'm talking to a lot of people. How long had you been his assistant?"

"Two years."

"You knew him well then."

"Not really."

"Come on, Dawn. Two years? What was he like?"

"He was an absolute genius, but you've probably heard that

already. Definitely the smartest guy on Wadsworth's science faculty. He could have been a Nobel laureate."

The content of what she said rang true, but her delivery was flat.

A buzzer went off in the kitchen. Dawn stopped pedaling and slid off the bike. It was a pleasure to watch the effortless grace of her movements. She dried the sweat on her chest and back with a small hand towel, opened the refrigerator, and retrieved a can of cherry diet cola.

"Would you like something? I have cherry Coke or grapefruit juice."

"No, thanks, I'm fine."

She perched on the bar stool next to mine, opened her soda, and drank greedily.

"I'm trying to cut down on sodas. It's my one vice."

Oh sure. Cherry colas and romps with married professors. Otherwise Dawn was a regular Girl Scout.

"How is Browne's death affecting your work?" I asked.

Her face fell. The look of concentration that crossed her features made her look cute and young, with her mental processes exposed—the look of an eight-year-old who moves her lips while reading silently.

"It's been a giant blow. Getting someone of Browne's stature to be your advisor is a big deal. Suddenly you swim in offers of research grants. You get lab access. Companies line up to fund your research." She took another long sip from the can.

"And with his death you'll be losing all that?"

"Probably. One of my companies has already informed me that they won't be renewing my grant next year. Hey, they realize that someone like Browne can steer anyone in the right direction. His mind was incredible. Razor-sharp. I'd work on something night and day for months, and I'd think I'd become the expert on that little slice of the universe, and then with one sentence, Browne would put an entirely different spin on things. Even in areas where he didn't have any real expertise, he had this sixth sense of what was of real importance—often more so than the so-called experts in the field."

"That's high praise. It sounds like you really admired him."

"I did. He had an incredible mind."

"Rumor has it that you and Browne were having an affair."

Dawn laughed, but it came out nervous-sounding. "You can't be serious. That's ridiculous."

She wasn't a very smooth liar.

"Is it?" I asked.

She looked away.

"Students often get involved with their professors," I continued.

"Well, not at Wadsworth. We have a very strict code against that sort of thing here."

Her tone was sanctimonious, which grated on my nerves.

"That may be. But nonetheless, I'm sure it happens. Even at Wadsworth."

"Well, it didn't happen to me."

"Look, let's cut the bullshit and stop wasting each other's time. I *know* that you had an affair with him."

Her smile was superior. "If Evelyn Browne is spreading rumors—"

"It wasn't real smart of you and Browne to get down and dirty right on the floor of his office. Someone saw you. And it wasn't Evelyn. This person saw it all—right down to the yellow smiley faces on the panties you were wearing."

Dawn's face turned bright red. Tommy's assertion of what he'd witnessed had been right on the money.

"My preference is for us to have a quiet chat here, just us girls," I continued. "But I don't mind marching down to the dean's office and taking the issue up with him. Your choice."

"What do you want from me?" she said, her voice small and resigned.

"The truth. Tell me about the affair."

"There's not much to tell. It was over. Finished."

"Who stopped it?"

"I did," she said, confirming what I'd gathered from Evelyn's tapes of Dawn's telephone conversations. "It was no big thrill sleeping with him. He was so—old."

She averted her eyes.

"The person you're seeing now, is he aware of your sexual involvement with Browne?"

Her expression seemed genuinely puzzled. "I'm not seeing anyone."

"The talk around the department is that you're dating someone else."

"I don't know where that comes from. I'm married to the lab. I don't have time for a personal relationship. I barely have time to eat or go to the bathroom—let alone work out."

I decided to let it go—for now.

"Did Browne ever talk to you about his wife?"

"No. Except I got the impression he didn't have much respect for her. He told me once that he wished he'd married someone more intelligent."

"Like you?"

"That's crazy."

"You're an ambitious woman, Dawn. Surely it must have crossed your mind that your career would take off if you were married to someone like Browne."

She stood abruptly and tossed her empty Coke can into the trash. "Too high a price to pay. No thanks."

"Did he ever mention whether he had plans to divorce Evelyn?"

"He said he was getting a divorce. But I didn't take him seriously."

"Why not?"

"Isn't that what married guys always say? That they'll get divorced. I didn't believe him."

"But you found him attractive, at least initially. You *did* sleep with him. What happened?"

She leaned against the counter, her expression thoughtful.

"I guess at first I was dazzled by his brains. His reputation was legend. But as I got to know Mitchell better, I realized I didn't like him much. I was in several of the classes, so I saw firsthand how cruel he could be to his students. Any show of laziness or stupidity, and he could be ruthless. Students sometimes left in tears after conferences with him."

"Some of those students must have hated him."

"Hate is probably too strong a word. Dislike. The only person I can think of who truly *hated* Browne was his son."

Her answer took me aback. I'd grown fond of Tommy.

"Tommy?"

"The couple of times I saw Mitchell with him, you could cut the tension with a knife. The kid had such an attitude, always talking back. And sometimes he'd get this hateful stare in his eyes . . . Have you seen his shrink?"

"Mitchell was seeing a psychiatrist?"

"Not Mitchell. Tommy."

I felt annoyed at Evelyn for holding back. She should have told me that her son was getting professional help.

"For his kid to need a shrink irritated Mitchell no end. He was a man who prided himself on his mind, and then for his own offspring to have psychological problems . . . he was embarrassed by it."

"What are you saying, Dawn?"

"Tommy could have killed him."

"A son killing his own father?"

"Why not? You don't think it happens? Think of the Menendez brothers. I'm sure growing up as Mitchell Browne's son was no picnic. And the way Mitchell died? Drowning. Did you know Tommy is a champion swimmer? What better way to stick it to the father than in the water? Besides, Tommy isn't even his son."

I looked at her, stunned.

"Evelyn didn't tell you? God, did she tell you anything? The kid's adopted."

I felt my face flush with embarrassment and anger. What else had Evelyn kept from me? Was anything she'd told me the truth?

This was the final straw. As soon as Dawn and I were finished, I'd have a heart-to-heart with Evelyn. I wanted some straight answers for a change.

"Is there anyone else who had reason to hurt Browne?" I asked.

"No, not that I can think of."

"Where were you the night he was murdered?"

She gave me an irritated look. "At the lab. Feel free to check with the guard, if you don't believe me. I'm in the log book."

I was too pissed off at Evelyn to conduct an intelligent conversation with Dawn. I thanked her for her time and left, topping the speed limit all the way to Evelyn's house. The calming effect of the martini had worn off.

Evelyn had lied to me. Repeatedly. But had she lied to protect herself—or to protect Tommy?

My mind flashed back to my talk with Tommy, to the vehemence in his voice when he called his father a jerk. For Tommy to kill his father wasn't totally out of the realm of possibilities. Fact: Tommy had known about the Valium. Fact: he had lied to the police about his whereabouts on the night of the murder. Maybe what he'd told me was also a lie. Fact: no one could confirm his ten o'clock alibi on the evening his father was killed.

I didn't want to think of Tommy as a murderer. I liked the kid. Something about him reminded me of an old-fashioned Boy Scout. I couldn't picture him as a cold-blooded killer who'd engineered his father's death.

And from what Dawn had told me, there were plenty of other people who hated Browne's guts. In fact, the list of people who had it in for Browne was getting longer and longer.

Twenty-Six

No one was camped out on Evelyn's doorstep today. The press had given up its siege.

I rang the doorbell. Ka-punk, ka-punk, ka-punk sounds of a basketball hitting asphalt came from the backyard. I peered around the back. It wasn't Tommy practicing his dunk shots, but Evelyn. If I weren't in such a dark mood, it would have struck me as funny, seeing petite Evelyn Browne playing a tall person's sport. In her T-shirt, sneakers, and baseball cap worn backwards, she looked more like a kid than a mom.

The third time I yelled her name, she finally looked my way. Breathless, she opened a side gate. "Oh, hi, Macy. The locksmith came by yesterday, but he needs some special tool to open the desk, if that's why you're here. He said he'd come back tomorrow."

I scowled at her. "That's not why I'm here."

"Come on in," she said cautiously, reading my mood. She led me into the kitchen, where I almost stumbled over the dog that was lying on the floor.

"I talked to your mother-in-law," I said.

"I'm afraid she doesn't like me very much."

"That's an understatement."

Evelyn poured two glasses of chilled water, sliced a lemon, and deftly dropped the half moons into the liquid. She offered me a glass and gulped her own drink greedily.

"According to Claire, Mitchell told you just days before he

was killed that he was planning to divorce you."

"What?" Her head shot up. "That's a lie." She slammed the glass down so hard on the counter that I thought it might break. Her eyes blazed indignantly. Her denial looked convincing.

"Why would your mother-in-law lie?"

"Because she hates my guts. She's always hated me. Claire would say anything to make me look bad."

"She'd lie about something as serious as murder just to make you look bad?"

Evelyn shrugged.

"I also found out that Tommy's adopted."

"She told you?"

"It's true then?" I asked.

I saw no need to drag the real source of this information—Dawn—into this conversation.

Evelyn sighed. "Yes."

"I also found out that Tommy is seeing a psychiatrist."

This time Evelyn didn't even blink. "Well, sounds like you two had yourselves quite a heart-to-heart," she said defiantly. "No. Tommy isn't seeing a psychiatrist. He's seeing a psychologist. Might as well get your facts straight."

"While we're at it, is there anything else you'd like to tell me?"

Evelyn turned away and drank more water. The small dog on the floor whined softly. Evelyn sank down to the floor next to the pooch and stroked its fur.

"It's all right, girl. You'll be fine." Tears ran down her face. She made no efforts to wipe them away. I let her cry. At long last, she looked up at me. "I think she's going to pup tonight."

I didn't reply.

"Macy, you have to believe me. Mitchell never said a word about divorcing me. Please believe me."

"You've got to start telling the truth, Evelyn. I can't help you if you keep holding things back from me."

"I'm trying. I really am. But what could Tommy's being adopted possibly have to do with Mitchell's murder?"

"The people who killed Mitchell could be your son's biological parents. With Mitchell dead, and you in prison, they could regain custody."

She looked up, her eyes huge. "You think that's possible?"

"Not really. But I'm sick and tired of finding out all this crap from other people. Every day it's a new surprise. Why didn't you tell me?"

"It's ancient history. Tommy is *my* son. I couldn't love him more if he were my own. *Tommy* doesn't even know."

"This is major, Evelyn. From now on, even if something seems totally unrelated to your husband's death, you need to tell me. I won't know what's important until after I check it out. Tommy being adopted could be a factor. So could the fact that he's seeing a shrink."

"Okay, you want to talk significant? I've got Turner syndrome."

"Turner . . . what?"

"Turner syndrome. That's why I'm so short." She spoke in a tiny voice, smoothing the dog's fur as she spoke. "It's a genetic abnormality. I have an extra chromosome. Because of it, my life has been one long series of medical problems. I've never had a period. I can't bear children. You want significant? I desperately wanted a child. For two years I begged Mitchell to adopt, but he wouldn't hear of it. He hated the idea of adoption agencies and social workers . . ."

The dog gave another soft whine.

"It all right. I'm here," Evelyn said soothingly.

"So how were you able to adopt Tommy then?"

"My brother. He knows about babies born to drug addicts who don't want them." Evelyn leaned back against the kitchen cabinet and crossed her legs. "He knew this girl, she was only fifteen. She was a cocaine addict and she didn't want the baby. My brother put his name on the birth certificate as the baby's father. He knew I wanted a child more than anything. The moment I laid eyes on Tommy, I knew he was meant to me mine." More tears ran down her face. "Tommy was such a difficult baby. He cried all the time. All day long, all night long. He hardly ever stopped. I was so tired, so totally exhausted. But then, little by little, he got better."

"But how? You said Mitchell didn't want to adopt."

"He was furious. I told him I was taking care of the baby for my brother. I'd timed it so that I brought Tommy home when Mitchell was out of the country. By the time Mitchell got back, Tommy was much better. And I tried to keep the baby out of his way as much as possible. A couple of years later, Mitchell agreed to the adoption."

"And Tommy doesn't know he's adopted?"

"No, he doesn't. The point is, everything worked out. Tommy's doing well. He's healthy and strong, and he's doing well in school . . ."

"Then why is he seeing a shrink?"

"The staff at BB&N recommended that he see someone. It's not the big deal you make it out to be. A lot of kids at his school are getting counseling. This is Cambridge. Being in therapy is a status symbol around here."

Evelyn made it sound like Tommy's seeing a shrink was akin to his getting private violin lessons.

"I'd like to get your permission to talk with Tommy's psychologist."

I was startled by a voice behind me. "What for?"

Tommy was standing in the doorway. So much for family secrets.

"How long have you been eavesdropping on us?" Evelyn

asked, all the color gone from her face. She looked like someone had literally knocked the wind out of her.

But Tommy wasn't watching his mother. His eyes were on me. "I just got here. Why do you want to talk to my shrink?"

I wondered how much of the conversation he had overheard. Bad way for him to find out just how the stork delivered baby Tommy. The timing couldn't be worse. His nerves were already raw from his father's murder and his mother's subsequent arrest. On top of all that, for him to find out that he was adopted . . .

Tommy's attention focused on me. "By law, Dr. James can't tell you a thing. But to save you the trouble, I'll tell you what we talk about. We talk about my father, and how he treated my mother and me like shit. How, if he thought I'd been particularly dumb or lazy, or God forbid, disrespectful, he'd hit me. That about sums it up."

"He hit you?" Evelyn scrambled up from the floor and rushed toward her son. "Why didn't you tell me? And why didn't Dr. James report your father to the authorities?"

"Because Dad was paying the shrink's bills. And I didn't tell you, because I was afraid you'd get into an argument with Dad, and then . . ."

"Then what? What, Tommy?"

"Shit. You know. You know how he got, Mom. What's the use?" He turned away and rushed to the door. "I'll see you later."

"Tommy, wait . . ." Evelyn ran after him, but Tommy didn't wait.

"If I'm late for practice," he called from the hall, "I'll have to do an extra four hundred."

Evelyn stormed after her son, but it was no contest—he was much faster than she was. I heard the front door slam. Seconds later Evelyn returned to the kitchen.

"You didn't know that your husband beat your son?" I said.

She looked positively dumbfounded. I took her by the arm and led her to one of the stools. She sat down.

"Oh my God. My God. I never *saw* Mitchell raise a hand against Tommy. If I'd known . . ."

"Did your husband ever hit you?"

She sat perfectly still.

I turned Evelyn toward me and looked into her eyes. "He did, didn't he?" I said gently.

She shook her head. "No, not really. Just a couple of times, and he didn't hit me hard. He shoved me against a wall. And the other time, well . . . he didn't break any bones or anything . . ."

"Jesus."

"It wasn't that bad. And both times, I deserved it. I really did."

"Evelyn, is it possible that Tommy killed your husband?"

She recoiled. "No! Absolutely not. Don't you dare try to pin this on Tommy. You breathe one word of this to Silverman, and you're fired. You and Silverman both. And I don't want you talking to Tommy's psychologist. Do you hear me?"

Twenty-Seven

It took a while to reassure Evelyn that I wasn't going after Tommy. I tiptoed around the issue. I couldn't afford to get fired so soon after getting canned from IE. She finally calmed down.

We were sitting on the bar stools in the kitchen, sipping papaya juice.

"How much of our conversation did Tommy hear?" she asked.

"I don't think he heard you say he was adopted, if that's what you're worried about."

"Are you sure?"

"He would have said something if he had heard you."

"I hope you're right." She sighed. "Tommy told me about his talk with you, about what he did the night Mitchell was killed. It's good of him to want to help me out, but I don't want him to give a deposition."

I was glad to hear that Tommy had finally come clean, even if I wasn't thrilled with Evelyn's reaction to the news.

"It could mean clearing you, Evelyn."

"I don't care. I don't want any record of Tommy lying to the police. I don't want him involved. He's just a boy. He's been through enough."

The dog's whining cut her speech short. She slid off the bar stool and rushed to a dark alcove in the kitchen where the pooch had hidden. I followed her, just in time to see the first puppy make its entrance into the world. It was a wet and tiny fur ball, limp and completely helpless.

"That's my girl." Evelyn stroked the dog's head ever so gently. The dog licked the puppy, and the little fur ball promptly sought comfort at mommy's doggie takeout. Smart little critter. Evelyn smiled at me, her eyes bright, the harsh words she'd spoken only an hour before all but forgotten.

"It's a miracle, isn't it? Just look how tiny he is." She said it in the same cooing, singsong voice people adopt when talking to babies, as she gently nuzzled the little creature with her forefinger. "God, if all the other puppies look this good . . ."

Sublimation. Evelyn couldn't give birth herself, so she was beside herself at the sight of the puppies. The worry lines on her face had melted away. For the first time since I had known her, she looked totally happy and relaxed.

I had to wonder whether a woman who had such obvious respect for life was capable of cold-blooded, premeditated murder.

I frankly couldn't see it.

Except maybe to protect her child, I corrected myself. No matter how cute and cuddly, most animals, even this pooch on the kitchen floor, would kill to protect their young. How far would Evelyn go to protect Tommy? What if she *had* known that Mitchell was abusing her son? Was she capable of killing her husband to protect her child?

"Oh look," Evelyn cooed.

The small pup got adventuresome. Just minutes old and already trying to crawl.

Evelyn's smile was as broad as her face. She gently picked up the teensy puppy. It fit easily in the palm of her hand. Surprisingly, its mother seemed not to mind.

"He's a beauty," she said.

"He? How can you tell?"

"I've had lots of experience."

"He *is* adorable," I said. "What will you do with the puppies?"

"I'll keep one female and sell the rest. The sire is a champion show dog. I'll probably get five hundred apiece."

I was dumbfounded. With a litter of four or five puppies, she could be making some real money—possibly tax free. Maybe I was in the wrong business.

I reached down and stroked the little fur ball gently with one finger. He felt soft as down. The puppy's mother took offense and barked sharply at me—not a friendly bark at all. I snatched my finger away—*pronto.*

"Would you like him? I'd love for you to have him. I'd give him to you for free."

I smiled. The puppy looked so cute and loveable, and I was tempted to say yes. But then I fast-forwarded to it making mincemeat of my favorite loafers and leaving little deposits on the carpet, which brought me immediately to my senses.

"I'd better not. But thanks all the same."

The dog whined again. Something was happening. I assumed the next puppy was on its way. Midwifery definitely wasn't my thing. I didn't dare take a close look, for fear the floor show might convince me to get my own tubes tied.

I wished Evelyn good luck and saw myself to the door.

Time to get the lowdown on BioCorp. I sped down Storrow Drive in the light afternoon traffic, and left the Jetta in the brick parking garage next to the North Market building. The courtyard was packed with tourists today, the good weather bringing them out in droves. Even at this odd time in the afternoon, they were feasting like locusts.

Overall I felt frustrated. I had hoped to shore up Evelyn's defense. Instead, new bits of evidence that made *her* look guilty kept popping up like unwanted mushrooms. Furthermore, I hadn't come up with anything concrete to implicate the man who topped my suspect list, namely Melville Rutgers.

I ordered a Diet Coke from a stall and drank it on my way to the Kirstein Business Library. In front of Faneuil Hall, on the cobblestones leading to Congress Street, a juggler was hypnotizing a large crowd of spectators with his act.

I wanted to call Prentice Porter to ask him about BioCorp, but without a cell phone, there was no way for him to call me back, and I'd never reach him in person by calling his office.

At the library, I copied some thirty articles about BioCorp. Within the hour I had over two dozen names of current and former BioCorp employees in my eager hands. Rutgers was going to regret the way he'd treated me.

Next on my agenda was the other Biosynthesis investor, Richard Kublinski. I decided to pay him a visit at his home on Marlborough Street. If he wasn't there, maybe one of the neighbors could tell me where I might find him.

Kublinski's building was an elegant four-story brick structure, built in the French Academy style favored in sections of the Back Bay. The building was set back from the street, the garden out front fenced in with a black iron railing. A magnificent magnolia stood in full bloom, and yellow daffodils peeked through a thick ground cover of pachysandra.

I climbed the brick steps to the main entrance and pressed the button next to Kublinski's name. After a decent interval I pressed several other buttons, hoping to rouse somebody inside the building.

Finally a cheerful voice squawked over the speaker.

"I'll be right down."

I could hear quick footsteps in the hall, the door opening with a burst. A young man, a snazzy dresser in white trousers and a collarless black dress shirt, appeared in front of me, a huge smile on his face—which faded as soon as he saw me.

"You look like you were expecting somebody else," I said.

"As a matter of fact, I was. What do you want?"

"I'm trying to reach Richard Kublinski. I've called him several times, but I don't seem to be able to reach him."

"That's because he's in the hospital."

"Oh, really? What happened to him?"

"He's been sick for a while."

The people associated with Biosynthesis seemed to be dropping like flies.

"You wouldn't happen to know which hospital he's at?"

"Try Mass General."

I thanked the man and left. I found a pay phone a couple of blocks away, on Newbury Street. The sidewalks were busy with people window shopping and checking out members of the opposite sex—and sometimes their own sex.

The operator at Mass General put me through to Richard Kublinski's room. I hung up before he had the chance to answer.

Twenty-Eight

Mass General's main building is a large concrete structure with all the charm of a warehouse, perched on the banks of the Charles across from MIT. I managed to get lost twice on the way to Kublinski's room, trying to follow the directions the Hispanic receptionist had given me.

Kublinski looked frail. Even an untrained eye could discern that he was severely ill. I was surprised to see that he was a young man. I guessed him to be in his mid-thirties, though with his being this sick, his age was hard to judge.

He might have been attractive when healthy, but now his face was emaciated, the bones beneath his skin almost visible. Purple and black marks covered his forehead. His eyes lacked luster and had sunken into his skull.

"Mr. Kublinski?"

"Yes?" he glanced up expectantly.

"I'm very sorry to disturb you. My name is Macy Adams. I'm a private investigator."

"Come on in."

"How are you?" The phrase popped out of my mouth thoughtlessly. The instant I said it, I realized how tactless the question was, given the circumstances.

"Jeez, you're a courageous soul. People stopped asking me that. They don't want to know."

I felt my cheeks turn red.

He pointed to a chair in the corner of the room. "Have a seat."

I pulled it close to the bed and sat down. "I've been hired to look into the death of Mitchell Browne. I understand you knew him?"

"Browne's dead? I hadn't heard that. How did he die?"

"He drowned."

"Drowned?"

"He was murdered. It was in the papers."

"Murdered? My God."

Kublinski looked absolutely stunned.

"Sorry to be the bearer of bad news. Did you know him well?"

"Browne's been murdered?" He shook his head in disbelief.

He started to cough and sat up in his bed. His coughing continued and his eyes started to tear up. Eventually the coughing fit subsided.

"Don't worry, I'm not contagious. They're feeding me antibiotics around the clock. It's just fluid collecting in my lungs."

He retrieved a tissue from the night table, and spit some mucus into the tissue.

"You probably think it strange that I didn't know about Browne, but I haven't been able to do much reading lately. My eyes . . ."

"But you knew Browne?"

"Sure I knew him. I did two years postdoc work under Browne. Six years ago. So how can I help you?"

"Dr. Browne was involved with a company called Biosynthesis. I'm trying to find out more about the firm."

"I've never heard of it."

"You're listed as one of the principals."

"I am?" He looked puzzled. "Must be a different Kublinski."

"It's not a common name."

"No. It's not. Biosynthesis, you said? I've never even heard of the company. What do they do?"

He had another coughing fit. He reached for an oxygen mask and held it over his face.

"Are you all right? Do you want me to call a nurse?"

He shook his head. I watched as color gradually returned to his cheeks. "What irony," he said. "I've been studying viruses and bacteria for most of my life. Even as a kid they fascinated me. And now a virus is making a real intense study of *my* body. What's your background? Do you work in biotech?"

I shook my head. "No."

"Would you like my world-famous five-cent lecture on viruses?"

"Sure."

He seemed happy to have an audience—even if just a perfect stranger like myself.

"A virus is the smallest of living things, only the size of a few molecules. Millions could fit on the head of a pin. It's debatable whether a virus is even alive. They lie dormant, lurking, waiting, sometimes for years, until they find a victim. Disease always follows. There's nothing benevolent about viruses." He coughed once more. "Once the virus finds its way inside a living organism, it wakes up and reproduces like mad, by the billions, destroying everything in its path. Viruses are the ultimate hedonists of this planet. They kill the cells they infest. Then they ooze out and lie in wait for their next host."

It sounded like a canned speech he had recited many times before, a lecture bound to encourage a person to wash their hands before their next meal.

"Want to know what other conclusions I've reached?" he asked.

"Sure."

"We're not all that different from those viruses."

"That's a hell of a depressing thought."

"Oh, isn't it though." There was a hint of sarcasm in his voice. "We've been treating this planet like a virus treats its hosts. We've wiped out half the other species. We're polluting the earth on a scale unknown until now. There are just too god-damn many of us." He laid back on his bed, wheezing slightly, and getting more oxygen. While he spoke my eyes scanned the room. No flowers or personal mementos. John Grisham's latest novel sat on the table beside his bed, a flowery get-well card propped up next to it. I wondered if, in fact, he ever would get well.

"Can this planet support five billion people?" He continued. "Maybe the AIDS epidemic is just a way for Mother Earth to rid herself of excess baggage before we end up destroying the whole damn planet."

"That's a pessimistic view."

"Sometimes I wished I believed in God. At least then I'd have something to look forward to."

"You made it sound like you've got a death sentence," I said.

"But it is, barring a miracle. Full-blown AIDS. You probably wonder how a guy like me, who has actually been specializing in this bug, ended up getting it? You'd think I'd know better."

I didn't know what to say.

"I wish I could tell you that it was because of some accident in the lab. But it wasn't. I only have my own damn stupidity to blame." He exhaled sharply. "I fell in love. With this incredibly beautiful man. Oh yes, I *am* gay, but you've probably guessed as much by now. I thought we would be safe. We'd both tested negative for HIV. We'd made vows, sworn faithfulness. Both of us had plenty of friends who'd died of AIDS. We knew about the dangers of unprotected sex. Or so I thought."

He stopped and looked down at his hands.

"Later, I find out that he'd been seeing this other guy all

201

along." Kublinski's voice broke.

"I'm so sorry."

We sat quietly, the silence stretching on, but not uncomfortably.

"Yes, well," he continued. "Just don't let the same thing happen to you. You be careful. Take precautions. The drug cocktail doesn't work for everyone, and this is a rotten way to go."

He was right, though it wasn't something I liked to think about.

"Thanks for listening. I know I'm rambling. What else do you want to know?"

"Are you acquainted with a Harold Dizikian?"

"Zeek. Sure. Good guy. I took a couple of molecular biology courses from him—about ten, twelve years ago."

"Well, he is supposedly another Biosynthesis investor."

"No kidding? He died a few months ago. Right here, in this hospital."

"Yes, I know. I spoke to his widow yesterday. How about Robert Davis or John Connolly. Do you know them?"

"There was a Jack Connolly in my high school. But I haven't seen him since graduation."

"Probably not the same guy." I shifted in my seat. "Were you working at Wadsworth?"

"Not after I graduated. I worked in the private sector, for a company called BioCorp—in Arlington."

I held my breath. This was too good to be true.

"Then you know that Mitchell Browne was on the BioCorp board?"

"Yes. But to be perfectly honest, I don't have fond memories of the place. They canned me after they became aware of my sexual orientation."

Having met Rutgers, I wasn't surprised. "What kinds of experiments are they running in Section D?"

"Sounds like you're familiar with the firm. Section D is their antibody section. They inject animals, usually rabbits, with an antigen. Could be a virus, could be cancer cells. Then they wait for the animals to produce antibodies. What BioCorp does is to separate the antibodies from the animal's blood to use them in diagnostic tests. Tricky part is, a huge variety of antibodies are produced whenever an antigen is introduced into an animal, most of them totally useless." He sat up to clear his lungs. "If we're lucky, maybe one in a hundred rabbits will become a star producer, making a large quantity of antibodies that can be used for diagnostics. That rabbit becomes the proverbial golden goose. It's bled weekly, or monthly, to harvest the antibodies. Needless to say, that particular rabbit is treated real well, even fed caviar, if it likes it. They want to keep that critter alive as long as possible. Its life span is often twice that of other laboratory animals."

"I heard a rumor that there was a problem in Section D."

"Oh sure. Their star rabbits kept dying prematurely. They'd finally find a rabbit that could crank out the right kind of antibody, and then, bingo, it would die on them—the profits for that year down the drain." He was tiring, his voice getting raspy, his words slightly slurred.

"Did Browne have anything to do with Section D?"

"Sure. He did a lot of his AIDS research in Section D. Browne was experimenting with synthetic T-cells."

"A cure for AIDS?"

"Not exactly a cure, but another way of managing the disease, to keep people symptom-free, maybe for a lifetime."

"Why didn't you approach him? If his T-cells worked, they could add years to your life."

"I did. But Browne said he was years away from making T-cells in sufficient quantities to be effective in humans."

"From everything I hear, Browne was a real smart guy," I

said. "Was he ever able to figure out what caused the rabbits to die?"

"Nope. But they had ruled out all the obvious possibilities. It almost looked like someone was purposely tampering with them."

"Really? Why would anyone want to do that?"

He cracked a smile, the first since I had walked in the door.

"Let's just say that the way BioCorp is run doesn't inspire too much goodwill among the employees."

"So one of them might have sabotaged the lab."

"Sure."

"Who?"

"Well, the veeps and most of the managers have profit-sharing and stock options, so killing the rabbits wouldn't be in their best interest. My guess is someone further down the corporate food chain. Someone who nursed a grudge because they'd been passed over for a promotion or had some other beef with the company."

Maybe Browne had figured out who that person was, and the knowledge got him killed.

"How did *you* end up working for BioCorp?"

"Browne hired me. Sometimes he arranged for his doctoral students to use the BioCorp facilities. They have equipment that isn't available at Wadsworth. The whole setup over there is really sophisticated. In return, BioCorp got to peek over the students' shoulders, in case any of them came up with something really big—like a cure for cancer."

"Was that a good deal for the students?"

"Sure. It's a great deal all around. A win-win situation."

"There seems to be a lot of security at BioCorp. Why?"

He shrugged. "My guess? Rutgers enjoys running a police state. He's a born-again Nazi."

I smiled and he smiled back. Our mutual dislike of Rutgers

had forged a common bond.

"Could BioCorp be involved in anything illegal?"

He hesitated for a moment, as if considering the possibility seriously.

"I don't think so. Rutgers is a churchgoing, Bible-thumping kind of guy. I don't like the man, and that's putting it mildly, but I've never thought of him as being dishonest or underhanded. But I guess anything's possible."

He coughed again. "So this Biosynthesis firm, what do they do?"

"Their charter says biotech research. I don't know anything more specific than that. I'm starting to wonder if the firm even exists."

"It *is* odd." He paused. "You know, I'll probably be dead by the end of the month."

"I'm so sorry." I meant it, but my comment sounded inadequate.

"Sounds like the Biosynthesis investors are dropping like flies," he said.

"Any ideas?"

"It's almost like whoever set this firm up was looking for individuals to take the fall for something. Are you sure that Browne was in on the deal? Maybe his name was used without his knowing it as well?" His gaze was serious. "You know, I'd really hate to have my name linked to any sort of scandal after I'm dead. What if this Biosynthesis firm is involved in something illegal?"

"Harold Dizikian died of stomach cancer. His death wasn't unexpected."

"My condition was common knowledge for months. And then Browne is murdered . . ." He looked thoughtful. "Maybe all of us were chosen as charter members because we'd make excellent fall guys. Dead people can't defend themselves."

Kublinski looked tired and shrunk. I felt bad for giving him bad news. And now he looked visibly exhausted.

"Could I have some water?" he said.

I found a plastic cup, filled it, and brought it to him.

"With a lid and a straw, if you don't mind? It's easier for me."

I put a lid on the cup and inserted a straw.

"Thank you." He took the water from me and sipped it slowly. I pointed to the Grisham novel on his bed table.

"Is it any good?"

"I wouldn't know. I usually enjoy him, but with my eyes the way they are . . . I really can't do much reading."

"Just one more question?"

He nodded.

"I'd love to be able to talk to someone in Section D. Are you still friendly with anyone over there?"

"There's been a lot of turnover. Most of the staff I knew has moved on. I may still know one or two people," he finally said, "but I need to check first. Okay?"

"Sure." On impulse I added, "Do you happen to know Dawn Halebrook?"

Another nod. "She's another one of Browne's doctoral students, part of his entourage. Good-looking girl, if you go for a miniature model—with a heart to match." He paused. "She used to run experiments at BioCorp. Probably still does."

My ears perked up. Well, well. Dawn and BioCorp. Small world. Dawn would be receiving a second visit from me. And now I had a whole new line of questions for her.

"I heard an interesting rumor about Dawn," Kublinski said, a grin spreading over his face.

"Oh yeah?"

"Dawn's dating a black dude."

"Really," I said.

Maybe that explained Jane Ramirez's hesitation when I asked about Dawn's boyfriend. She probably knew the guy. Given the widespread prejudice against young black males, and defense attorneys who might look for a scapegoat, I could see why Jane might be tempted to close ranks and keep that information to herself.

"Do you know his name?"

"No. A friend of mine at Wadsworth told me about him. My friend had asked Dawn out, but she turned him down. He was a bit sore about being passed over—especially for a black guy."

"Dawn's taste in men seems to run the gamut."

"Do you believe the stereotype about black men being better in bed?"

I had to laugh. "I honestly wouldn't know."

"Well I do, and I can tell you that it's a myth. The French are right. *Dans la nuit, tous les chats sont gris.* At night all cats are gray." He smiled weakly.

I grinned back at him, glad that even with death looming he hadn't lost his sense of humor.

What a waste.

Kublinski finished his water. I took the empty cup from him and placed it on the table. I fished a business card out of my handbag.

"Would you please call me if your friend at BioCorp is willing to talk?"

He had closed his eyes and seemed to be drifting off. I placed my card on the night table, next to the get-well card, and thanked him again, closing the door quietly on my way out.

Twenty-Nine

I found my way back to the hospital lobby. From there, I called my phone number from a pay phone, wondering if despite my cell phone being broken, I could still retrieve messages. I could. There was a message from a Mr. Sullivan's secretary, informing me that he could see me at one o'clock today.

Who the hell was Sullivan? An instant later it came to me: the lawyer who'd handled the estate of Mitchell Browne's father. I'd left a message with his secretary yesterday that I wanted an appointment.

Meanwhile, one o'clock had come and gone. Rutgers was my prime suspect at the moment. But it was still important to follow up on this lead. I dialed the number and explained to the secretary why I'd missed my appointment. She informed me that yes, Mr. Sullivan was in. No, I couldn't see him later, the rest of his afternoon was completely booked. No, I could *not* see him tomorrow. And no, I couldn't see him Thursday or Friday, since he would be out of town.

Great. I probably needed no more than two minutes of his time to ask a simple question about the disposition of Browne Senior's estate. Surely Mr. Sullivan could at least take my call? No, she informed me. He was in conference and wasn't taking any calls.

Infuriated by the stonewalling secretary, I drove the short distance to the financial district, to Sullivan's office, where I paid another stratospheric parking fee. As I handed the attendant two twenty-dollar bills, I mouthed yet another silent thank you for my expense account.

The building that housed "Sullivan & Delaney, Attorneys-at-Law," had seen better days. The directory downstairs informed me that their offices were in suite 608.

I took the elevator and found Sullivan's office. The receptionist, a woman in her late fifties with salt and pepper hair, asked me to have a seat.

While she was gone, I surveyed my surroundings. Green carpeting with heavy traffic patterns, gray walls with dark scuffmarks, and none-too-clean windows that filtered the outside light to a dull gray. Sullivan & Delaney did not impress me as the kind of law firm I'd want to hire for anything more serious than resolving minor traffic violations.

A minute later the receptionist returned with a tired blond whom she introduced as Sullivan's secretary.

"Are you the lady who called earlier?" the secretary asked.

"I called about half an hour ago," I answered.

"And I told you Mr. Sullivan couldn't see you today. You wasted a trip."

She turned to leave, her manners a match for the decor of the offices.

"This is an extremely important matter. It can't wait a whole week."

She turned around. "I'm sorry, miss. But there's nothing I can do."

I doubted that very much. She disappeared into one of the offices, but I refused to budge, digging in my heels. I was determined to see Sullivan *today*. I took a seat. The receptionist gave me a pained look every couple of minutes, as if hoping I'd dissolve in a puff of smoke.

Finally, she addressed me. "Miss, why don't you run along? He won't see you today."

After a quarter of an hour the timid receptionist disappeared. I could hear murmuring in the other room. Momentarily both women returned.

Sullivan's secretary was pulling on a strand of her short bleached-blond hair, calling attention to a half inch of dark roots. Her gray suit didn't fit her well, the skirt too tight, causing the bulge of her stomach to show up prominently, making her look pregnant even though she seemed well beyond that stage of her life.

She planted herself in front of me, legs apart, hands on her hips. "Listen, miss. You need to leave. Mr. Sullivan will not see you today, or any other day, without an appointment."

"Have you asked him?"

That stopped her in her tracks.

"No. But he doesn't see people without appointments."

I gave her one of my business cards. "I'm a personal acquaintance of his. I'm sure he'll make an exception." I was lying through my teeth, but these people were giving me no choice. "I'm sure he'll be upset when he finds out he wasn't informed that I dropped by."

She took my card reluctantly, her demeanor suddenly uncertain. Then she disappeared.

I sat down and waited some more. Nothing happened.

I was starting to feel foolish as I sat for another quarter hour, staring at the dingy walls while the foam padding on the worn-out seat cushion adjusted to my contours. Maybe I was wasting my time. Maybe my being stubborn was just plain being stupid.

Suddenly an elderly gentleman appeared, briefcase in hand, wearing a three-piece charcoal-gray suit and horn-rimmed glasses. In contrast to the premises, he looked dignified, with an air of competence. His head was balding on top, a fringe of gray hair surrounding the sides. His walk was brisk. He stopped in front of me.

"Are you the young lady who insists on seeing me?"

"Yes."

He scrutinized my face, as if searching his memory banks.

"I don't know you, do I?" he asked gruffly.

I shook my head. "No."

"Well, I don't have pretty young ladies come visit my office very often. I have a meeting in chambers at the Federal Building in a few minutes. You're welcome to walk with me, if you want. But that's all the time I can give you."

I followed him to the elevator bay, where he pressed the down button. "So what's this all about?" he asked.

"I'm looking into the disposition of Octavius Browne's estate."

"And who are you?"

"I'm a private investigator."

"I know that. I read your card. I want to know what your interest in his estate is."

"Octavius Browne's son Mitchell drowned two weeks ago and his widow has asked me to look into his death. I was told—"

"Oh, so that was Octavius's son?" he interrupted. "I read about it in the *Globe*. Well, I'll be darned. I remember reading something about the professor drowning, but I didn't make the connection."

The elevator door opened and we entered.

"And Browne's widow doesn't know who inherited?" he asked impatiently.

"No, she doesn't."

"Odd that . . . I don't remember all the details. Have you checked the probate records?" His brows furrowed. "There was something odd about Octavius's will. One son inherited the entire estate. The other son was left out of the will completely."

"Really? Who inherited? Was it Mitchell Browne?"

"What was the other son's name?"

"Phillip."

He focused his gaze on the lighted numbers above the elevator doors. I helped him stare.

"I'm sorry," he said. "I don't remember which of his two sons was named in the will. It's been a while, at least two years . . ."

"Well, how about this? Do you happen to remember what the beneficiary looked like?"

"I didn't actually meet either of the Browne boys. Since I was litigating a large case at the time, and the will was straightforward, one of my associates handled the matter."

We had reached the ground floor and he started walking down Federal Street. For an old guy he moved remarkably fast. I had to take long strides to keep up with him. Since he had staked out the right side of the sidewalk for himself, I found myself having to dodge more than my share of the oncoming pedestrian traffic.

"How large was the estate?" I asked.

"Significant. I don't recall the exact amount, but I'd say well over a million."

"That's no small change."

"Actually, I think it was closer to two million. You sound like you're in a hurry for the answer. Why? You think it might tie in with Browne's murder?"

"The money might be a motive."

"Well, try probate records then. It's public information. Or why don't you ring the dead man's brother? I believe he's local. I *am* surprised Browne's widow wasn't able to help you. Surely she has to know whether her husband inherited a big chunk of money like that."

One would think so. It made me think that Phillip must have inherited the money. Maybe that's how he was able to pay for his house in Concord.

We had reached the courthouse on Federal Street, and Sullivan stopped.

"I'm sorry I can't be of more help right now, but I have an important hearing and then I'll be catching a plane. I'll be back Sunday night. Give me a call on Monday, if you still require my help."

He shook my hand and disappeared through the metal detectors inside the building, leaving me standing on the sidewalk.

This whole business was odd. It seemed a good bet, however, that the two million dollars had driven a wedge between the two brothers. But why hadn't Phillip just admitted as much when I spoke to him?

A lot of questions, and no answers. I'd have to talk with Phillip again to get to the bottom of it.

I found a pay phone next to the Old State House and dialed Phillip's number. I recognized Amanda's voice when she picked up.

"Amanda? It's Macy Adams. I have a few more questions. Would it be all right if I stopped by tonight? Just for a few minutes?"

"Sure. Phillip should be home after six. Drop by after that."

I also wanted to ask Evelyn about this latest development. Of course, with Evelyn, it was possible that she'd known about her father-in-law's inheritance all along but had chosen not to tell me.

On my way to the parking garage, I happened to pass a bookstore. Grisham's latest book was displayed in the window. On impulse I went inside and bought the audio version for Kublinski.

I hoped he'd live long enough to finish the cassettes.

THIRTY

Evelyn opened the front door. She was dressed casually, in jeans and a pink T-shirt sporting a picture of a cocker spaniel with the caption "Going to the Dogs." A rich aroma of garlic and spices hung in the air. If someone had led me into the house blindfolded, I'd have sworn I'd stepped into an Italian restaurant.

"Macy. We were just sitting down for dinner. I hope you can join us."

Despite her kind invitation, her voice sounded tense. I'd been on a roll all day, operating at a frenetic pace. While I hated to lose momentum, I really felt that I needed to slow down.

I scanned the hall. "Tommy is home then?"

"He is. Come on in."

I followed Evelyn into the kitchen. A big pot of pasta was boiling on the stove, next to a pan of bubbling sauce, undoubtedly the source of the mouth-watering aroma that was getting my taste buds all excited. A half-empty bottle of Kendall-Jackson sat on the kitchen counter. Without asking, Evelyn poured a glass of wine for me.

"By the way, have you talked to Dawn yet?" She handed me the glass.

"I have." I took a long swallow, instant elixir for my frayed nerves.

"And what did *she* have to say?"

"She wasn't very helpful."

"Did you ask her . . . about the affair?"

"Yes."

"And?"

"She admitted that she'd had sex with your husband."

"I *knew* it," Evelyn exploded. "I just knew it. I was right. You do believe me now."

"I always did," I said. About her husband's affair in any case, I added mentally.

A buzzer sounded. Evelyn removed the boiling linguini from the stove, drained it into a colander, and distributed the steaming noodles on three plates. She poured the sauce over the pasta and added a sautéed chicken breast to each plate. Finally, she decorated the plates with a sprig of parsley and a slice of lemon.

Fancy. Why can't I serve gourmet meals like that when I cook at my house? I helped her carry the plates to the table, and we sat down.

"Tommy," Evelyn called in the direction of the staircase. "Dinner's ready."

Moments later Tommy appeared, his steps hesitant. His hair was wet and slicked back and he smelled of soap. He was dressed in jeans and a T-shirt with a Wadsworth Swim Camp logo.

He stopped when he saw me. "Oh, hi. I didn't know you were here."

"Hello Tommy."

He looked at his mother, his expression guarded. She ignored him, busying herself with her napkin. Tommy shifted his gaze to me. "How's the investigation going?"

"Good."

Part of me wanted to tell them about my scrape with death earlier today, while another part didn't want to alarm them. They'd been through enough already. No need to add to their anxieties by sharing my woes.

Tommy scavenged a can of Mountain Dew from the refrigerator before sitting down. He took the seat across from me. We started the meal in silence. The atmosphere around the table seemed off to me, with Evelyn and Tommy avoiding each other's eyes.

But that didn't stop me from savoring every bite of the pasta dish that was simply to die for. The sauce was about the best I'd ever tasted, consisting of tomatoes, mushrooms, scallions, garlic, peppers, and olives. Evelyn had missed her calling. Forget the dogs. She'd make one hell of a chef.

"Evelyn," I said. "What happened to your father-in-law's estate?"

She twirled a string of linguini on her fork and shrugged. "I don't think there was much of an estate. Actually, I don't recall ever talking to Mitchell about it. Why?"

"Maybe the estate was more sizeable than you realize. Did you go to the funeral?"

"No, I didn't. The services were held up in New Hampshire, and I had come down with a bad case of the flu. I didn't want to get everyone sick."

Tommy was quiet, but he was paying avid attention to our conversation between huge mouthfuls of food.

"Is that where Mitchell grew up? In New Hampshire?"

"His father was a professor at Dartmouth."

"When was the last time you saw Phillip? Was it after the funeral?"

"No. Before. In the summer. Why do you ask?"

I filled her in on my talk with the attorney. When I finished, the silence around the table was profound.

"Two million dollars?" Evelyn sputtered. "I can't believe it. Mitchell never said one word about it to me."

"What a jerk," Tommy exploded. Mother and son looked at each other, the expression on their faces a mixture of surprise and disgust.

"So where's the money?" Evelyn said. "I can't imagine Octavius leaving it to Phillip. Octavius and Phillip weren't even on speaking terms."

"How come?"

"I have no idea. It's something I've wondered about myself." She shrugged. "So what did Mitchell do with the money?"

"Good question."

"What a bastard. What a sneaky, secretive bastard. Ugh—" Evelyn had worked herself into a state.

"Let's not jump to conclusions," I said to calm her down. "There's a chance the lawyer might be mistaken." Though deep down I doubted it. "I happened to catch the man on his way out the door, so it's possible that he got his facts mixed up with some other estate he settled."

"How do we find out for sure?"

"I'm going to talk to Phillip tonight."

"I'll come with you," Tommy interjected.

Evelyn turned to him, looking displeased. "Whatever for?"

"I haven't seen Uncle Phillip in ages." Tommy looked at me. "And you promised."

Evelyn's mouth formed an angry pout. "Where do you get off making promises to *my* son?"

"I didn't promise Tommy anything. I only said that if I needed to talk to Phillip again, I'd be willing to take him along. But the decision is yours. If you have a problem with that . . ."

No way was I getting in the middle of this argument.

To Tommy I added, "It's up to your mother."

Evelyn maneuvered a forkful of pasta around her plate before finally bringing it to her mouth.

"Please, Mom. What's the big deal?"

"The puppies? You were going to take care of them tonight."

"Please Mom . . ."

Evelyn chewed the linguini like it had turned to rubber, probably resenting the hell out of me for making her look like the heavy.

"Macy, remember what we talked about this afternoon? That I want Tommy kept out of this whole mess."

"Sure," I said.

The tension around the dinner table was giving me a stomachache.

"Did the locksmith come by, by any chance?" I asked, shifting the topic of conversation to more neutral ground.

"Uh? What? Oh yes, he changed the locks and managed to open the desk. You can rummage after dinner, if you like—"

"So, Mom, can I go?" Tommy interrupted, determined not to be headed off. "Please?"

"I want you here tonight, Tommy. It's a school night and you have homework."

"I already finished it."

Evelyn threw her napkin on the table in an angry fit, got up, took her plate, and dumped the rest of her dinner down the sink, a waste of a terrific meal if you ask me. This sudden display of anger was surprising. It seemed totally out of character.

Tommy stood. "So what *is* the problem now, Mom?"

"You always do what you want, anyway. Why do you even bother asking? You want to go visit your Uncle Phillip? Go! Just go. I'll just stay here by myself. Just me and the puppies."

Ever since I first entered the house this evening I'd had the feeling that I had arrived in the middle of a family argument. The very air had been rife with tension.

Evelyn stormed out of the kitchen. I ran after her. "Evelyn—"

"I'm going to lie down. I have a splitting headache. Just leave me alone."

"Would you like some Tylenol?" I called after her, a lame offer.

"Don't bother," she said without looking back. After she was out of earshot, I turned to Tommy. "What's with her?"

"She's upset because I told her that I want to quit the swim team. Plus, my chemistry teacher called. I flunked a test. Not my fault. Mom made me miss five days of school last week. Because of those news vans that were camped outside our house."

"But why quit the team? You love to swim."

"I do, but all my times are off. Plus everybody on the team is acting weird around me. I thought they were my friends." He shrugged. "What are we waiting for? Let's go."

"I don't think I should take you to see your uncle."

"But you promised. And Mom said I could go."

"She didn't really mean it."

I was in a quandary. It had seemed a good idea for Phillip and Tommy to reestablish a relationship. And maybe it still was—though I was starting to wonder about Phillip.

But I couldn't very well take Tommy without Evelyn's blessing. I hoped that she'd eventually calm down and come back downstairs, so we could talk it over.

Tommy and I finished our dinners. He dug in heartily, but my own appetite was all but gone. When we were done, I cleared the table and put the dishes in the dishwasher, while Tommy scooped the leftovers into Pyrex dishes and put them into the fridge.

I had wiped the counters and generally cleaned up the kitchen, but there still wasn't any sign of Evelyn. I went to the staircase.

"Evelyn," I called out, "I'm going to look through Mitchell's desk now. Would you like to join me?"

She didn't answer. I proceeded to Browne's study by myself.

A single key lay on top of the desk. I unlocked the central drawer and pulled it open. It contained several drafts of a research article Browne had been writing and several videotapes. I found a set of small keys, the type used to unlock expensive luggage. But no safety deposit keys. No secret bank account numbers. No cash.

There *was* one surprising item: Mitchell Browne's last will and testament, duly signed and witnessed, dated 14 December of the prior year, was at the bottom of the drawer. The will was straightforward, listing his son, Thomas, and his niece, Christine, as sole beneficiaries of the estate, sharing equally in the proceeds. I wondered whether the will was even legal under the Commonwealth's laws. Wasn't a widow automatically entitled to at least thirty percent of her deceased husband's worldly goods?

And how curious. Why leave half his estate to Christine? Why to *her* and not her brother? Had Mitchell meant for history to repeat itself? Had he meant to drive a wedge between Phillip's children, pitting one sibling against the other?

I wondered whether Evelyn had seen the document. Probably. But she hadn't mentioned it at dinner. I went upstairs and knocked on the closed door of Evelyn's bedroom.

There was no answer. I opened the door a crack. The shades were drawn and the room was steeped in darkness.

"Evelyn?" I whispered.

All I could hear was her even breathing. She looked tiny and defenseless in her queen-size bed. She appeared to be asleep, which seemed odd since it wasn't eight p.m. yet.

"Evelyn, are you feeling okay?"

She opened her eyes. "Migraine."

"Can I get you something?"

"No. Just dark. Quiet."

I took her hand and checked her pulse, which seemed normal.

"Take Tommy . . . to see Phillip."

"You're sure you'll be okay by yourself."

She nodded weakly. "Go. Don't worry about me."

Reluctantly, I went back downstairs. After a brief hesitation, I put Browne's will in my handbag. I didn't trust Evelyn entirely. She couldn't be happy with this latest will and might be tempted to rip the document to shreds. I didn't know what the penalty for destroying a will was.

Silverman would certainly want to see it. I'd fax it to him later tonight.

I found Tommy in the kitchen, kneeling on the floor next to the whelping box Evelyn had set up for the cocker spaniel and her puppies.

"Your mother has gone to bed. She has a migraine. Should I be worried about her?"

He swiveled on his knees and shrugged. "Not really. She has her pills. She'll be fine in the morning."

"Okay. Grab your coat, Tommy. We're going to visit your uncle."

THIRTY-ONE

On the drive to Concord, I wondered once more whether Tommy had overheard that he was adopted. I probed around the periphery, trying to steer the conversation to where the subject might come up naturally, but Tommy avoided my attempts to engage him. I finally concluded that he was unaware of the adoption. That—or Tommy was one slick kid.

I finally changed the topic.

"So what's up with your mother's migraines?" I asked. "How often does she get them?"

"Every few weeks. Especially when the weather gets warm. She has trouble with her eyes, and the pollen makes it worse."

Three days of warm weather had signaled to the plants that spring was under way. The azaleas in front of Phillip's house were in full bloom, and the annuals Claire had dropped off on the day I stopped by had been planted in flowerbeds surrounding a stone terrace. The effect was absolutely lovely. Now that I had a small patch of soil I could call my own, I should do some gardening myself.

The family had apparently just finished a meal al fresco, dirty dinner dishes still on the patio table. From the look of the leftovers, Amanda had cooked some sort of Mexican dish. Four kerosene torches around the terrace gave the setting a cozy, if not exotic air, as did the citronella candles in the pottery urns that were spread about.

Tommy bounded up the stone steps to the terrace ahead of

me, his voice exuberant. "Uncle Phillip. Surprise. I hope you don't mind that I tagged along."

"Hey, Tommy."

Phillip stood and gave his nephew a bear hug, then held him away for an appraising look. "Is that really you? I can't believe how much you've grown since the last time I saw you. You're almost as tall as I am."

"Just about." Tommy beamed at his uncle.

I was glad for Tommy, that whatever estrangement had occurred between Phillip and his brother hadn't rubbed off on him.

Phillip let go of his nephew and turned to me. "Macy, nice to see you again."

Tommy was acting shy around Phillip's beautiful daughter, eyeing her surreptitiously. The last time they'd seen each other, they'd both been mere children, unaware of the luring attraction of the opposite sex. Since then, Chrissy had blossomed into a beauty with a cover-girl face and budding centerfold body. Her shorts and halter-top were sufficiently revealing to make any adolescent boy pant with desire. Belatedly, it occurred to me that nothing except propriety would stand in the way of a romance between those two. Being cousins was a technicality. They weren't blood relatives.

Of course, Tommy didn't know that. Or so I hoped.

I noticed that Chrissy and Tommy had offered to help Amanda clear the dinner table. While they busied themselves, Phillip took me inside the house. Was it my imagination, or was Amanda casting a watchful eye my way?

Phillip led me to the family room, where we sat down and I summarized my conversation with Sullivan.

"So I was hoping that you could clarify the matter for me," I concluded. "Who inherited your father's estate?"

"Mitchell did. The old man left him the whole enchilada."

Phillip tried to sound like he didn't care, but I could hear the twinge of hurt. Being denied a large inheritance in favor of a sibling would be a gigantic slap in anyone's face, bound to cause a strain between the best of brothers.

"Why didn't you tell me this before, when I asked you whether you and your brother had a falling out?"

Phillip shifted his weight uncomfortably, seeming to shrink in his seat.

"What's the point? That was two years ago. I'm a big believer in getting on with my life."

"The inheritance caused a rift between the two of you. You *did* have a falling out. Why lie about it?"

"I wouldn't call it a rift, exactly."

"What would you call it when two brothers stop seeing each other, after they spent entire summers vacationing together on Cape Cod?"

He shrugged and brushed specs of lint from his chinos.

"Of course it didn't help," he finally admitted. "I was broke back then, and I could have used a little extra cash, even as a loan. And just because the old man left him everything didn't mean Mitchell had to *keep* it all. But why bring it up now? It doesn't have anything to do with my brother's death."

"That's what *you* say."

"Oh please." He pursed his lips. "You're really grasping at straws, you know? Are you *so* desperate to clear Evelyn that you're willing to point a finger at innocent people? I don't think Evelyn killed my brother. But I didn't kill him either. You're barking up the wrong tree."

"Am I?"

"Just so you understand. My brother's death doesn't change the disposition of my father's will. I still won't see a penny of that money . . ."

"That's where you are wrong," I blurted out. "Chrissy

inherits half of Mitchell's estate."

Phillip opened his mouth, but nothing came out. For a second or so, he looked completely flummoxed. Then the expression on his face changed to anger, his eyes flashing with indignation. "And you think . . . because of Mitchell's will? You're really way off base. That's insulting. We've suffered enough—more than you can ever know." He stood up. "I don't make it a policy to let virtual strangers insult me in my own house. I think you should leave. Now."

Anger looked ugly on most people, but somehow not on Phillip. If anything, Phillip was even more attractive when mad. He sat up straight and his eyes were alive and intense. He was a man ready for battle—and it looked good on him.

Besides, his righteous indignation seemed genuine. I almost believed him.

"Calm down," I said. "I am not accusing you of murder. I just wish you'd told me all this on my first visit. It would have saved me a lot of useless running around."

He stood and walked to the bay window, gazing out into the darkness. I could see his handsome face reflected in the black panel, see the anger drain slowly from his features.

"And you are sure that Mitchell put Chrissy in his will?" he asked.

"That's right."

For a second, I thought he would start to cry. His face contorted. Then he caught himself.

"Having been completely cut from my father's will was a monumental disappointment. Chrissy's inheriting part of Mitchell's share doesn't make up for it."

"Sure it does. It's obvious your brother felt bad about what happened."

Phillip gave a wry laugh. "I don't think so." His tone was bitter.

"What I don't get is this: Why Chrissy? Why didn't Mitchell leave anything to your son—or to you? Any ideas on that?"

Phillip didn't answer. He just stared into the darkness.

Amanda entered the room, interrupting our conversation. "Would anyone like some dessert?"

"No, thank you," I said.

"I'll have some," Phillip said.

She nodded and left the room.

"How large was your father's estate?"

He shrugged. "About two million dollars. But a lot of it was funny money. He had an art collection, real estate in New Hampshire, high-tech investments. Stuff that fluctuates wildly in value."

Amanda returned momentarily with a dish, which she handed to her husband. Vanilla ice cream topped with chocolate sauce and chopped nuts. It looked yummy.

"You'll never guess what Macy just told me," Phillip said. "Mitchell left half his estate to Chrissy."

Amanda's jaw dropped. But she looked more stricken than happy. "My God. It's too little, too late, don't you think? Don't expect me to shed any tears over his death."

Now there was an interesting reaction. I hadn't realized until now just how much Amanda must have disliked Mitchell.

Phillip gave his wife a stern look. "Let it go, Mandy."

"Why should I? We sucked up to your brother long enough. And I'm sure Evelyn will be much better off without him. You know about the affairs he had with his students. Sick." Her last comment was apparently made for my benefit, as she gave me a sidelong glance.

"Who told you about the affairs?" I asked.

"Does it matter?"

"You're saying he deserved what he got?" I kept my tone neutral.

"Well no. I'm not saying *that*. But I'm not heartbroken that he's dead either."

"Is there anything else you want to know?" Phillip asked.

"Just one thing, Phillip. Where were you the night your brother drowned?"

"With a client—" Amanda started.

"Home—" Phillip said simultaneously.

They shut up and looked at each other. Someone had gotten their wires crossed.

"My husband was with a client. A potential client actually." Amanda gave Phillip a pointed look. "The Hansens, remember?"

She smiled at me, but her eyes were empty and sad. "They're thinking of having Phillip build a house in Westford for them."

"That's nice," I said. "Where are they living now?"

"Huh? Lexington?" she said. "Isn't that right, honey?"

"Uh-huh," he agreed, but not convincingly.

"I know a Hansen family in Lexington," I lied. "I bet it's the same people. What's your client's first name?"

Amanda was quiet for two beats. "Bill."

She was a lousy liar.

"Oh, well. It's not them then." I stood to leave, doubting whether I would find a William Hansen listed in the Lexington white pages. "Thank you for seeing me on such short notice."

Amanda's smile was as phony as the rubber ficus in the corner of the family room. To his credit, Phillip didn't even try to mask his displeasure.

"I'll get Tommy," he said.

I strode briskly to the back door. Through the window I could see Tommy and Chrissy playing badminton in the floodlights that illuminated the lawn at the back of the house. They stopped when we approached. A minute later we were all assembled in the kitchen, the kids' skin pink and flushed from the exercise.

I pulled Tommy toward me, belatedly remembering his reason

for coming with me in the first place. I whispered in his ear, "This is as good a time as any. Go ahead."

Tommy looked at me, confused. He suddenly looked indecisive. Something like ESP passed between us, and his gaze steadied.

"What is it, Tommy?" Phillip asked.

"Uh, nothing," Tommy said. A hint of sadness had come into his eyes. "See you?"

"Sure. Anytime," Phillip said. "You're always welcome."

We got into the Jetta and I started the engine.

"What happened?" I asked, once we were under way. "I thought you were going to talk with your uncle about maybe living with them, in case your mother—"

"It's okay," he said quietly. "Maybe it's for the best. Maybe living with him wasn't such a hot idea after all."

"Why not? What happened?"

"Never mind," he said.

We rode the next few miles in silence. It wasn't my imagination. There was a marked change in Tommy's previously cheerful demeanor. Were teenage boys as moody as teenage girls?

"What happened?" I asked, curiosity finally getting the better of me. "Has this something to do with Chrissy?"

"No. Not Chrissy. Why would it have anything to do with her?"

"Well, something changed. Before you were gung ho about living with your uncle. And now you're not? All you did was play badminton with Chrissy. Of course I'm curious if this has something to do with her. Does she make you feel uncomfortable?"

"No. Why would she?" He sounded annoyed.

"Well, let's see. She's a girl. A very pretty girl."

"She's my cousin, for chrissakes," he protested, his voice cracking. "That's sick. No, of course it has nothing to do with her." He put one sneaker on the glove compartment door and turned away from me.

"Well, *something* is wrong."

We were getting close to Cambridge. I pulled over to the curb, stopped the car, and shifted into neutral. "Okay, let me hear it."

"What?"

"Whatever is bothering you?"

"You won't believe me."

"Try me."

"Oh, all right. Did you notice my uncle's pickup truck? It has a dent on his left fender."

"So?" I had no idea what Tommy was getting at.

"Well, I saw Phillip's truck parked on our street the night Dad was killed."

Somehow I found that hard to believe.

"How can you be sure it was your uncle's truck?"

"Well, it was the same color, and it had a dent on the left fender, just like his."

Had Tommy's real reason for wanting to visit his uncle been so that he could cook up some phony piece of information that would implicate Phillip in his father's murder?

"Tommy," I said in a stern voice. "This isn't a game. This is serious—very serious. You're implying that your uncle had something to do with your father's murder."

"You don't believe me. I knew you wouldn't."

"Why didn't you mention this before?"

"Because I only realized it tonight. I didn't know that truck belonged to Phillip. I had no idea until I saw it in his driveway."

"Well," I said, playing devil's advocate, "I find it hard to believe that you can remember a vehicle you saw parked on your street what, two weeks ago?"

"All right. Go ahead. Ask me about the cars on our street."

It seemed like a foolish game. One I did not care to play.

"The neighbor across the street drives a gray Mercedes 190," he continued. "The woman next door drives an old silver Saab. The Shermans two doors down drive this really old blue Volvo station wagon. The Baileys park their car in the garage. It's a red Alfa Romeo. Do you want me to go on?"

"No. What's your point?"

"Just that I pay attention to cars. And Uncle Phillip doesn't just drive any old car. He drives a big pickup—an F-250. No one on our street has a pickup truck, and especially not a red one. It's a really neat set of wheels. As soon as I saw it that night, I wondered who it belonged to. And then I noticed the dent."

I had to admit that his answer made a certain kind of sense. Teenage boys do notice things like that.

"Do I have your word that you're not just saying this to get your mother off the hook?"

"Absolutely not," his response was vehement. "Hey, I thought you were supposed to be on Mom's side."

"I am, Tommy. I am. But it won't help her if we start making things up."

"I'm not making this up."

"Okay, okay."

I shifted into drive and pulled away from the curb.

Up until now I hadn't seriously considered Phillip a suspect. *Cain and Abel?*

We reached Cambridge. I pulled up in front of Evelyn's house and saw Tommy safely inside. I checked on Evelyn. She was asleep. I looked for Tommy to say goodnight and found him in the kitchen, caring for the puppies.

Call me a fool, but I really liked the kid.

Thirty-Two

It was almost ten, but surprisingly, I was still wired on an adrenaline rush.

I decided to stop by Dawn's apartment. With any luck she'd be home, and I could grill her about BioCorp.

Was I stalling? I realized I dreaded going home, half expecting another visit from the demented BioCorp guard. My new address wasn't on my driver's license, I hadn't changed my voter's registration, the telephone number and utilities were in my landlord's name. Only a very determined person would be able to find out where I lived. But after the attack this morning, I wouldn't feel safe even at home.

In truth, I felt safest while I was on the move, like right now.

There was no answer when I rang Dawn's buzzer. I wondered whether she might still be at the university. I found a pay phone at the gas station next door and called the Wadsworth Bio Labs. After countless rings, an attendant answered and informed me that Dawn had left some time ago.

I decided to wait—for a little while at least. My parking spot allowed me a good view of the entrance to Dawn's high-rise.

The night air was chilly. I put the engine on idle and cranked up the car heater.

Stakeouts are boring business, ranking right up there with calculating annual tax returns and reconciling bank statements. I rummaged through my selection of music and picked out an old K. D. Lang CD. Listening to "Constant Craving," my thoughts drifted instantly to Jack. Strange how the memory of Sunday night was fading, like a photograph left too long in sunlight. Our one night together seemed already distant and unreal.

The heater was making me sleepy. I shut it off and switched to a Sheryl Crow tape.

Forty minutes later I was about ready to pack it in. It was past ten-thirty now and nothing was happening. I was just about to restart the engine, when a dark-blue sedan stopped in front of the entrance. The passenger door opened and Dawn got out. The overhead light illuminated the cabin's interior brightly. Dawn's companion was black and broad-shouldered, with closely cropped hair.

He had to be the alleged boyfriend.

The sedan pulled away quickly, barely giving me time to jot down the license plate.

There had been no kiss, no hug, nor any other gesture of endearment. In fact, nothing to indicate there was something romantic going on. Of course, that didn't mean there wasn't. Dawn's telephone conversations with Browne had been similarly lacking in passion.

Through the glass door I saw Dawn by the elevator, waiting. I locked the car, ran to the lobby door, and banged on the glass pane. Dawn turned, startled. Despite my friendliest smile, Dawn's face fell when she saw me. She pointed at her watch and shook her head. I waved to her insistently. Finally, she approached and opened the glass door a crack.

"I've been trying to reach you," I said. "I have a couple of quick follow-up questions. This will only take a minute."

"It's late," she said, her demeanor practically screaming *go away*.

"Someone told me this morning that you work at BioCorp. That's why I'm here."

I had hoped that my mention of BioCorp would put her at ease, but just the opposite seemed to be the case. She was edgy, much more tense than the first time we'd spoken. Was it because I'd brought up BioCorp, or because I'd caught her out with her date? Or "date"?

"I don't really work there," she said. "I only use their facilities from time to time. Besides, why are you asking about Bio-Corp? Aren't you looking into Mitchell Browne's death?"

"The two could be related."

"What could BioCorp possibly have to do with Mitchell's death?"

Oh, lots. Judging by the events of this morning, I wanted to tell her. But since I needed her to open up, I'd better keep my mouth shut about *that,* lest I scare her into silence.

"Just covering all the bases," I said in a soothing tone. "At this point I'm trying to eliminate possibilities. Asking about BioCorp is purely routine."

"You're wasting your time."

"What is it that you do at BioCorp, exactly?"

"It has to do with my viral project. I use equipment that isn't available at Wadsworth."

"Do you ever work in Section D?"

"Section D?" She hesitated for a moment. "No."

She was a lousy liar, breaking eye contact as soon as I'd posed the question. Her voice lacked conviction when she answered, and her color rose.

"BioCorp had some problems with laboratory rabbits dying prematurely—in section D. I was hoping you might know something about that."

"Sorry. I don't know what you're talking about."

"I was told you work with rabbits," I lied, pushing my luck. "In fact, I heard that you worked in Section D."

"I used to, but not recently. Listen, it's getting late—"

"I just wanted to see if you had any theories as to why those rabbits are dying," I continued, unperturbed. "There's a rumor that someone at the firm might be tampering with the rabbits."

She looked like a deer caught in the headlights, panicked and ready to bolt. Belatedly it occurred to me that she *herself* might have tampered with the critters.

Christ. I instantly changed tack.

"Was that your boyfriend?"

"Who?"

"The guy who dropped you off?"

"I really don't see where that's any of your business."

"What's the big deal?"

"No big deal. I just don't like having my privacy violated."

She pressed the elevator button. Unfortunately, the steel doors slid open instantly.

"What's his name?"

She entered the elevator. "Who?"

"Your boyfriend. Does he work for BioCorp too?"

"I told you. It's none of your business."

I was tempted to get in the elevator with her, but feared that it might put Dawn over the edge. The relief on her face as the elevator doors slid closed was all too obvious.

I would talk to her again, just as soon as I found someone willing to run the blue sedan's license plate through the DMV database.

Dawn had better get used to having her privacy violated.

Thirty-Three

Jack traced the curve of my spine with a yellow rosebud. We were lying on the deck of a sailboat, the sky overhead cloudless, palm trees swaying in the distance. I was really getting into the dream, when a bell on board burst into relentless clamor.

The next ring brought me to. The shrill sound wasn't coming from a marine bell, but from the telephone on my nightstand. *Who had died now?*

I groped for the receiver.

"Yes." My voice was thick with sleep. The day had already dawned, but I was dead tired. I hadn't slept well. I kept waking during the night, fearful an intruder might break in.

"Did I wake you?" Jack's voice sounded soft and intimate over the phone.

"Hmm. What time is it?"

"Just before six. Sorry to call so early, but I wanted to catch you before you left."

"Where are you?"

"Still in New York. I'll be back tonight. How about dinner?"

"Sure."

"Did you get my roses?"

"Oh yes. They're beautiful, Jack. Thank you."

"I really *am* sorry to disturb your beauty sleep," he murmured. "But I wonder if you could do me a favor. My Palm Pilot has a problem, and I need a couple of phone numbers . . . They're unlisted. I tried calling my secretary, but she must have left her phone off the hook."

Smart woman, I thought.

"And you want me to look up the numbers for you?" I said. "No problem."

"I keep an address book in my study. A spare key to the house is hidden in the garden."

He described the hiding place, gave me the code to the burglar alarm, as well as his number in New York. I pulled on sweats and surveyed the grounds for hidden assailants through cracks in the curtain. Before going outside, I had to remove the empty soda cans I'd stacked in front of the door as an early "bad-guy" warning system. I went out, my Glock at the ready.

Talk about paranoia.

Locating the flowerpot where Jack had hidden the spare key was the easy part. Lifting the damn thing was another matter. The pot was enormous and, with the soil saturated from the heavy rains, it weighed at least fifty pounds. Underneath, voila, I found a small Ziploc bag containing one single key. I felt instant excitement. The whole escapade was beginning to have the feel of a scavenger hunt.

I unlocked Jack's front door and deactivated the alarm, anticipation sending shivers down my spine. When I was a child I used to have fantasies about being invisible and sneaking into people's homes—a desire that apparently I hadn't outgrown as an adult. The idea of spying in Jack's lair, unobserved and unsupervised, was thrilling—right up there with having sex.

The morning twilight accentuated the exotic air of the big house. Jack's furnishings were predominantly oriental in style. Above the fireplace mantle in the living room hung a large portrait of a strikingly beautiful woman. She was dressed in a long, tight gown that showed off her slender body. Her features were classic—high cheekbones, straight nose, large gray-blue eyes set far apart. Her dark hair had golden highlights. She looked hauntingly familiar. I wondered who she was? Jack's mother? His sister? I looked for, but couldn't detect, any obvious family resemblance.

Countless framed family photos were strewn about the room. I picked up several at random and studied them. Grandparents, parents, lots of children. Most of the photos featured a younger version of Jack. He seemed to have come from a large family, with aunts and uncles, brother, sisters, and cousins. Nice, I thought. I loved large families. I wished I had other siblings besides my brother.

Jack's study was in actuality a library. Built-in floor-to-ceiling mahogany bookcases housed leather-bound classics. Two leather recliners in front of an ornate marble fireplace looked inviting. I pictured spending rainy afternoons enjoying a good book by the warmth of a cozy fire. They didn't make libraries like this anymore.

I dialed Jack's New York number from the phone on his desk. He directed me to the drawer where he kept his address book, and I read him the numbers he needed.

"Jack," I said, "Someone broke into the carriage house Sunday night."

"The night we spent together? While you were with me?"

"Yes."

"Did they steal anything?"

"Well no, that's the thing. As far as I can tell, nothing is missing."

"Did you check your liquor cabinet?"

"I don't have one."

"Probably some kids from the neighborhood looking to score alcohol or drugs. I left a downstairs window open last fall, and someone snuck in during the night and made off with a couple of six-packs of beer and a bottle of vodka. Keep your windows locked. I'll have ADT install a security system next week."

"You really think it was kids?"

"I do. Why? You suspect someone else?"

All along I'd been running scenarios of Rutgers and his goons breaking in, but I had to admit that Jack's theory made more sense. "No."

"And wear something dressy tonight," Jack said. "We'll go someplace nice. Can you be ready by seven-thirty?"

I agreed, and we said our good-byes and hung up.

Time to have some fun. I meandered through the downstairs, regarding the Steuben crystal vases and Meisner china on the sideboards. Not my taste, but nice nonetheless. Original oil canvases hung absolutely everywhere. Two enormous Ming vases stood sentry in the living room and multicolored oriental rugs were scattered about. The predominantly dark colors gave the house a very masculine feel.

The furnishings weren't some decorator's idea of antique reproductions—they were the real thing, probably handed down through the generations. The faint traffic patterns on the rug, the worn look of the upholstery, and the slight warping of the canvasses spoke of authenticity, which was all very lovely. But would *I* want to live here? I found the house too dark and oppressive, altogether too solemn, like a mausoleum. This place reminded me of my grandfather's house. Grandpa had been a stern individual who took himself altogether too seriously.

I had to see Jack's bedroom to make the tour complete. I bounded up the staircase, and entered rooms at random, and found—a nursery. Unlike the rest of the house, this tiny room was a bright and cheerful paradise. The yellow walls with the Peter Rabbit wallpaper border looked brand new.

So where was the baby?

This was confusing as hell. Oh, Jack, what haven't you told me?

Farther down the hall I found the master bedroom. It was certainly striking: Two large Greek statues stood at the foot of a king-sized bed. Dark green silk covered the walls. The bed itself was a canopied affair, shrouded in yards of teal-green and gold fabric. The space looked, frankly, more like a Hollywood movie set than a real-life room where someone actually slept. Strange taste. I couldn't imagine making love in this room: it would be altogether too ridiculous for words. I was glad we'd ended up in the guest bedroom.

The master bath was done up in terra cotta–colored marble, with lots of brass fixtures and an all-glass shower enclosure. Very elegant, even if the shower was a bit kinky. But watching Jack lather up in there might be exciting.

As I left the bathroom, a picture frame lying face down on Jack's nightstand caught my eye. I picked it up and stared. A wedding photo. The bride was the beautiful woman from the portrait downstairs. The groom was Jack.

I felt a sharp stab of jealousy. *Jack was married?*

Some sleuth you are, I thought wryly.

So where was Jack's wife?

In all the time I'd lived here, there hadn't been any trace of a woman's presence. Not a single piece of mail addressed to a Mrs. Hamilton had arrived, nor any items addressed to Mr. and Mrs. Hamilton.

Was Jack divorced? Recently widowed? Is that why he had taken off two months to go sailing in the Caribbean?

Dubs would know Jack's marital status. She wasn't an early riser. I'd call her after she got up.

I replaced the photo where I'd found it, face down, feeling my little bubble of happiness burst and go flat. Back in the carriage house, I wept in the shower for seven whole minutes.

Then I went back to work. I faxed Mitchell's new will to Silverman and sent an e-mail to Pascucci, asking him to run the DMV plate for Dawn's boyfriend.

I called the garden center that Browne's mother ran and

learned from a recording that it opened at eight in the morning. Maybe driving out there wasn't the most productive use of my time, but it was something to do. I put on a khaki skirt and a short-sleeved blue cotton shirt. Shortly after seven, I was on the road.

I hadn't paid much attention to Claire's business the first time I'd been here. This morning, with the parking lot nearly empty, I was struck by how pretty and well-manicured the premises were. Whiskey barrels filled with yellow and purple pansies flanked the gravel lot. The shop itself was an imitation of an English cottage in the Cotswolds, complete with thatched roof and dark decorative woodwork. To its side stood a white gazebo, surrounded by flowerbeds and hanging baskets and a small fountain with a water-spewing cherub. Several large greenhouses separated by gravel walkways stood in the back of the property.

A man, dressed in heavy work boots, a red and black rugby shirt, and dirty jeans approached me.

"Is Mrs. Browne around?" I said.

He looked at my high-heeled shoes.

"Sure thing. You'll want to see her in the office. I'll get her."

He ushered me into the store, which was filled with flower arrangements, wreaths, greeting cards, and other knickknacks. Claire's office was a small room in back.

"Have a seat. She'll be right with you," he said and left.

In stark contrast to the store in front, Claire's office was crowded and disorderly, littered with catalogs and boxes stacked on top of each other, the labels suggesting they contained insecticidal soap, fertilizer, and other gardening supplies. Ribbons, papers, invoices, and catalogs were strewn about. Claire obviously didn't believe in throwing things out until after they'd aged sufficiently.

The room felt closed-in and stuffy; a scent of secondhand

smoke hung in the air.

I rifled through the papers on the desk. One pile held order forms for bark mulch, cedar nuggets, lime, peat moss, and so on. Another pile contained delivery slips. Apparently Claire also ran a landscaping service of sorts, because there were invoices for cutting grass, cleaning gutters, clipping hedges, and spraying for gypsy moths. The dates on some of them suggested they'd been sitting on her desk for some months. A third pile contained bills. Her phone bill held special interest. Unlike my cellular plan, which showed only minutes, hers itemized the phone numbers called. I recognized one number in particular—the Browne residence in Cambridge.

My snooping was interrupted by a sudden, low-pitched growl. I turned in the direction of the sound. A large, black Doberman was standing in the doorway, teeth bared, fur around his iron-studded collar standing straight up. Something in the animal's eyes made me feel like he was ogling breakfast. I could feel the hair on my own arms spring to attention, but with less impressive effect. A large glass paperweight sat on the desk. I picked it up ever so slowly, just in case the dog decided to charge. Why had I left the Glock in the car? The Doberman's growling intensified, and my heart started to pound like a kettledrum.

The beast and I seemed to have reached an impasse, with him growling and me holding the paperweight.

"Duke," Claire called sharply from the doorway. The dog turned around in a circle, making little mewing sounds, and sat down. Mr. Hyde morphed into Dr. Jeckyl.

You big wimp. Well, that wasn't fair. Fido just happened to know who provided his kennel rations.

"Who let the dog loose?" Claire's tone was accusatory.

She filled the door frame. She was heavy, not so much obese as solidly built. Her bulk looked like solid muscle.

"I hope the dog didn't scare you," she said. "Duke is perfectly harmless."

Yeah, I thought, and rabies shots don't hurt, either.

"Well," she continued. "It's you again. My foreman thought you were the woman from Ringer Products."

She made it sound like I had purposefully misled the man.

"I don't know what gave him that idea," I said.

"So what brings you here again? I've told you everything I know."

I replaced the paperweight on the desk. Claire patted the Doberman and led him out by the collar.

"Jerry, tie Duke up out back, will you?"

She turned her attention back to me. "How about some coffee?"

"I'll join you if you're having some."

"Just brewed a fresh pot. Follow me."

I must have caught her on a day when she'd gotten up on the right side of the bed. She led the way to the back of the store, where she poured two mugs of coffee. Pointing to a carton of milk, stirrers, and sugar packets, she said, "Help yourself. I take mine black."

I poured both milk and sugar into my cup. The coffee had an unusual aroma. Hazelnut?

"Careful," she said. "It's hot."

I sipped the steaming liquid gingerly. The java was absolutely exquisite, even better than Starbuck's.

"This is really good coffee," I said with astonishment.

"We sell it in the store. Here, have a bag—on the house."

She handed me a small green vacuum-packed bag. Wasn't she friendly all of a sudden? What was going on?

"You can always buy more, if you like it. You'll have to come along to the greenhouse, if you want to talk. This *is* our busy season, and I'm up to my eyeballs."

"That's fine."

We walked the graveled pathway to the back of the property, where several glass-enclosed structures were located. Inside the greenhouse the air was hot and humid, the daylight oddly bright and diffused at the same time. The floor was a mixture of dirt and gravel.

"Have the police found any more evidence?" she asked conversationally.

"They continue to work the case. The reason I'm here is that I followed your advice and visited BioCorp. After I left, one of their employees tried to shoot me."

She gasped. "Oh my God. You were lucky you weren't hurt. Does this mean Evelyn is no longer a suspect?"

"Probably, but they haven't dropped the case against her yet." I took another sip of the delicious coffee.

She bent over six-packs of impatiens, thinning out the weaker stalks. "Shame you can't do this with people," she said distracted, "take out the bad seeds."

"What?"

"Sorry, just rambling."

"Mrs. Browne, when your husband died . . ."

"Ex-husband. We divorced years ago."

She put the crate she had finished aside, and picked up a fresh batch from below the workbench.

"Your ex-husband. I was informed that he left his entire estate to Mitchell."

"That's right."

"Why didn't your ex-husband leave anything to Phillip?"

"Who can tell? Octavius was nuts. Crazy. That's why I divorced him."

"It must have upset Phillip that his brother inherited the entire estate."

She shrugged. "Phillip was just starting his business back

then, and he was strapped for cash. He could have used the money. With Octavius's estate going to Mitchell, I decided to mortgage the nursery to help Phillip out. Phillip is a proud man, but he accepted my loan. And Phillip's kids will inherit the nursery after I die. It may not be as large an estate as Octavius's, but I possess several acres here. It'll be enough to put them through college."

She switched her attention to a tray of begonias, some of which were covered with white mold. She inspected each tray, tossing entire six packs into the trash bin. She sprayed the healthy-looking plants with a sour-smelling liquid.

"Mold. We caught it too late," she explained. "I guess Octavius's money will go to Evelyn now. So once again, poor Phillip gets left out in the cold. It hardly seems fair. That's family money."

"Actually no. The money won't go to Evelyn. I found an updated version of your son's will. He left his estate to Tommy and Christine, to be split equally."

Claire shot me a surprised look. I could see her process the information. Suddenly her eyes welled up. She turned away. While she composed herself, I sipped my coffee and listened to the chirping of the birds outside.

"Is there anything else you want from me?" she asked after a minute.

"Your son invested money in a firm called Biosynthesis. What do you know about that?"

She twisted the mug in her hand. "Mitchell didn't discuss his business dealings with me."

I couldn't think of anything else to ask, so I just thanked her.

"Told you I wouldn't be much help," she said. "Do you have a yard?"

"Just a small patch."

"Sunny or shady?"

"More shade than sun."

"Here. Get some impatiens. They do great in the shade. They're on sale right now, two bucks a six-pack. Take a whole flat, if you like."

"Okay."

"Pick the colors you want. The coral is lovely."

I bought two full trays, seventy-two little plants, all healthy-looking and blooming.

"Keep 'em moist, they dry out fast," Claire advised.

We walked back to the shop, where she rang up the sale and refilled her cup before heading back to the greenhouses.

I kept a watchful eye for the dog on my way out, but Duke was nowhere in sight. Why did Claire keep such a ferocious animal?

Thirty-Four

I drove back home to drop off the plants. I had an hour to buy a new cell phone before my meeting at Silverman's office. David had asked Evelyn to be there as well. I was concerned about Evelyn, and wondering whether she'd be sufficiently recuperated to attend the meeting this morning.

David Silverman and the accountant were already seated at the oval conference table, helping themselves to pastries and bagels that were laid out on a tray. The anorexic paralegal sipped from a bottle of mineral water. Today she wore a V-necked blouse that showed off too much cleavage for a business setting. Her breasts looked fake; they seemed too large for her small frame.

Evelyn arrived late, her demeanor quiet and subdued. The dark circles under her eyes were pronounced. She reminded me of a frightened bird.

"Shall we get started?" David said.

Evelyn nodded and flashed me a tiny smile, greatly relieving my anxiety.

"I received your fax, Macy," David said. To Evelyn he added, "Macy faxed the more recent version of Mitchell's will."

Evelyn looked at me with surprise. "Where on earth did you find it?"

"It was in your husband's desk. I came across it after you went to sleep."

"And you didn't wake me?" A hurt look came into her eyes.

"What did it say?"

"It's straightforward, Evelyn," David interjected. "Your husband left his estate to be divided equally between your son and his niece Chrissy. You can contest that, if you like. As his widow, under Massachusetts law you're entitled to thirty percent of his estate."

Evelyn looked stunned. "Mitchell left half his estate to his niece?"

"That's right," David said. "But as I said, if you have a problem with that, we can contest it."

"I'll let you know," Evelyn said. "Let me think about it."

I told Silverman about the two million dollars Mitchell supposedly inherited from his father. A look of annoyance crossed David's face.

"Why didn't *we* pick that up in Browne's financials?" he asked, addressing Josh.

Josh flushed. "It didn't show up in any of—"

"Now I get it." Evelyn spoke up suddenly. "I finally get it. That's why Mitchell kept me away from his brother. It had nothing to do with me. He didn't want me to find out about his father's estate." She snorted. "And all along, he'd made it sound like it was my fault. By slipping him the Valium, I played right into his hands."

"You didn't know about your father-in-law's two-million-dollar estate?" David said.

"No, I didn't."

"Your late husband seems to have been a very deceitful man." David's soft tone belied the sharpness of his words.

"So where did all that money go?" Evelyn asked.

"Good question. Macy, what have you found out about Biosynthesis?"

I explained my suspicion that Biosynthesis was a dummy corporation, summarizing my visits with Kublinski and the late

Professor Dizikian's widow.

David looked at Josh. "What do you make of this?"

"I would tend to agree with Macy. I've tracked down the company's supposed bank account." He pushed his half-eaten bagel aside and handed out a set of bank statements. "No payroll, no checks to suppliers, no rent or utility payments. Browne transferred money out of Biosynthesis to several foreign banks. The paper trail stops in the Cayman Islands."

"That must be the offshore account you talked about, Macy," David said.

"I don't understand any of this," Evelyn interjected in a small voice.

"It looks like your husband transferred money out of the country in order to hide your joint marital assets."

"He wanted to cheat me out of my divorce settlement?"

"In a word, yes."

"You mean millions of my husband's dollars are sitting in some banana republic, and I won't be able to get it?"

Josh nodded. "Precisely. And without the account numbers, we may never be able to access that money."

Evelyn's face fell. She looked about ready to crumple to the floor.

"Don't panic, Evelyn," David's voice was smooth. "The account numbers are bound to be in your husband's files. Macy will find them."

I wished I was half as sure as David.

Time for another search through Browne's belongings—with a fine-tooth comb this time. Evelyn and I agreed to rendezvous at her house, after I stopped by my place to change into more casual clothes.

I tried calling Dubs once more, from a conference room in Silverman's office. I had to get the goods on Jack Hamilton. I finally reached her at the office.

"Macy, I'm so glad you called," her voice chirped cheerfully as always. "Are we still on for tennis on Sunday morning?"

"Sure."

"I'll book a court for nine. Or is that too early?"

"No, that's fine. Listen, the reason I'm calling, Jack Hamilton's back in town."

"Oh, so you met him. He's great, don't you think?"

"He seems real nice. What's his story? Is he married?"

"Very much so." She paused. "You haven't met his wife yet?"

"No, I haven't even seen her."

At least not in the flesh, I added in my mind.

"Well, wait 'til you do," Dubs bubbled. "Jack's wife is Celestina Berenson."

"Never heard of her."

"Macy! She's a big-time supermodel. Looks to die for. She was on the cover of *Vogue* a couple of months ago. You'd recognize her."

I was stunned. If Jack was married to a gorgeous supermodel, what did he need me for?

"I wonder why I haven't seen her," I said. "They're not getting divorced?"

"No, no. She travels a lot. You know, supermodel. South Beach. New York. London. Paris."

Dubs was a sucker for fame and status.

"You've met her, then?" I said.

"Couple of times. Pretty cool, don't you think? To have a celebrity live right next door to you. You'll get to meet her soon enough, I'm sure."

When hell freezes over would be soon enough.

I hung up and fought the urge to throw the telephone receiver against the wall.

What a bastard. Jack Hamilton, you are a despicable bastard.

I felt a red surge of anger. I entertained visions of Jack falling overboard in Boston Harbor, of his Jeep crashing into a bridge abutment, of a tree falling smack on top of him in a thunderstorm.

Then I listened to the voice of reason. *Okay. I had been stupid. I hadn't done my homework. I should have done what I always advised my clients to do: Check out the people you get involved with thoroughly before embarking on a personal relationship. If I wanted to attribute blame, I only had to look into the mirror.*

By eleven o'clock, Evelyn and I were camped out in Browne's study, going through the contents of his desk once more. Except this time I knew precisely what I was looking for: a series of numbers resembling an access code to an offshore bank account.

At the bottom of his desk drawer, slipped underneath the array of hanging folders, I found a hidden manila envelope I'd missed before. Inside it were the Biosynthesis articles of incorporation, including some legitimate-looking business plans for the firm. I put the envelope aside.

I unlocked the top drawer, where Browne had kept a year's worth of American Express statements, which itemized his expenditures. They showed him dining at a number of local restaurants, upscale places like 29 Newbury, Blu, Pignoli, and the Bristol Lounge at the Four Seasons. The dollar amounts indicated he hadn't dined alone. Evelyn didn't recognize any of these establishments. They listed a number of purchases at Victoria's Secret and Cachet, women's clothing stores. Evelyn's face registered dismay when she spotted the charges. Whatever Mitchell had bought there, it hadn't been for her.

There was a two-thousand-dollar charge from Tiffany on the December statement, which Evelyn also didn't recognize. She handed the credit card receipts back to me, her eyes downcast.

"It's so damn blatant," she said. "His unfaithfulness. I know I shouldn't let it bother me. But it does." She pointed to the pages. "It's all there, in black and white. I can't remember him ever buying *me* anything from Tiffany—or from any jeweler, for that matter."

I fished the set of small keys from the drawer. "You recognize these?" I said. "They look like luggage keys."

Evelyn took the keys from me and shook her head. I returned them to the drawer.

I removed the videotapes from the back of the drawer. The labels showed a yin-yang sign and numbered codes. P-9-1487. P-8-9633. I handed one to Evelyn.

"Do you have any idea what's on these?"

"No. Probably something to do with his work."

"Might as well take a look, since he kept them so well hidden."

"There's a VCR in the family room."

I followed her into a room next to the kitchen, separated by a half wall. The color scheme was white and green, with pink accents. An ivy-leaf pattern ran throughout: ivy curtains, upholstery fabric, with a stenciled ivy border along the perimeter.

Evelyn inserted the tape and hit play. It started innocently enough: a middle-aged man asking a little girl for directions. She got into his car. It was right about then that it dawned on me what type of tape this was. I turned the tape off when the man dropped his pants, the camera closing in on the little girl on the bed. The little girl's eyes were empty, dark pools.

Evelyn let out a stifled gasp and ran from the room.

I found the remote control and fast-forwarded through a section of the tape. What I saw was graphic—and extremely disgusting. When the man started in on the kid, I couldn't stand to watch anymore. I switched it off and ejected the tape.

I felt physically ill, a visceral reaction to what I'd witnessed on the TV screen.

I called Evelyn. She didn't answer. She wasn't in the living room or kitchen. I went upstairs and found her curled up on a love seat in her bedroom, staring into space.

I entered the room. Evelyn turned away from me. "I want to be alone," she said quietly.

"I know this is hard for you. But we need to talk."

"Please go away . . ." Her voice broke and she started crying. I was torn as to whether I should stay or leave. Maybe the best thing was to give her a few minutes to herself.

"I'll fix something to eat," I said.

Downstairs in the fridge I found turkey cold cuts, juice, bread, even some cookies. I boiled water for tea. Under different circumstances I might have enjoyed playing house in Evelyn's beautiful kitchen. As it was, I hardly noticed what my hands were doing. My mind was spinning, trying to make sense of this latest piece in the jigsaw puzzle of Browne's murder.

Browne had been a closet pedophile. I suppose there were other possibilities, but they seemed far-fetched. With twenty-twenty hindsight, the facts had been there all along. Both Evelyn and Dawn, with their small, delicate physiques, were childlike. In dim light, both of them resembled children.

I could only imagine what sick fantasies must have played in Browne's head.

Had Mitchell ever acted out these impulses and actually molested children? If he had, it could send the scope of the investigation in entirely new directions. Mitchell could have been targeted for blackmail. In fact, maybe that's where all the cash had gone. The Cayman Island account might not be Browne's at all. It could belong to a blackmailer whom Browne had been paying off to keep his sick obsession a secret.

I wondered about Tommy. Since the videotape was of a little girl, I assumed Browne's taste ran that way. But then again, I didn't know much about pedophiles. Maybe they were interested in children, period. Boy or girl. Maybe the real reason Tommy was seeing a shrink was to deal with the trauma of sexual abuse?

Had that thought occurred to Evelyn as well? I shuddered.

I took a tray up to the bedroom. Evelyn was on the love seat, her legs curled up underneath her body, a tissue clutched in her hand.

"Lunch?" I asked. I looked for a place to put the tray, the bed the only available surface.

"I don't want anything."

"Okay, but we need to talk."

She shook her head.

"Have something to eat, then. You'll feel better."

She picked up half a sandwich, took a small nibble and chewed mechanically. She replaced the sandwich on the plate, wiped her eyes, and let out a deep sigh.

There was no other chair, so I sat down on the wall-to-wall carpet.

"You know, when we first got married, Mitchell would buy me these outfits. They looked really young—jumpers, gingham. Some looked like school uniforms. He'd ask me to wear them to bed. It was bizarre, creepy, but I went along with it, thinking it had to be a harmless idiosyncrasy of his. It never occurred to me that he was pretending he got it on with a child."

I wasn't so sure. Somewhere, deep down, she must have known. She just couldn't admit it to herself.

"To your knowledge, did he ever act those fantasies out?"

"What?" She looked startled. "Oh, my God, you mean with children?"

I nodded.

"No. I don't think so. I hope not."

But she didn't sound convinced.

"Those tapes," I said. "You can't just buy them in a store.

People who sell those types of tapes often provide other services."

"What are you saying? Child prostitution? That Mitchell was involved in something like that?"

I nodded. "It could explain the cash withdrawals from his account. Maybe he used the money to pay for his sickness. Or someone could have been blackmailing him."

I poured tea for both of us, adding sugar to my cup. I sipped the hot liquid carefully.

"Evelyn, we need to share this information with the police. Mitchell's sexual perversion may be the thing that got him killed."

"You can't be serious. We can't go public with this. We just can't. Tommy would die of shame if this came out. The kids in his school would put him through hell. It could destroy him."

I hated to ask my next question. "Do you think your husband ever molested Tommy?"

The look in her eyes was one of utter surprise. Then she actually gave it some thought.

"No," she finally said. "I don't think I would have missed *that*. Tommy and I are very close. I would have known." She shook her head emphatically. "I'm sure nothing like that ever happened."

Her voice was firm this time and she looked me straight in the eyes. She believed it.

Which didn't mean it didn't happen.

I let it go. I reached for a turkey sandwich and munched.

Evelyn slid down on the floor beside me, cradling the teacup in her hand. She blew on the liquid and took small sips.

"I feel so ashamed."

"There's no reason for *you* to feel ashamed. Your husband's the one who was sick."

"But don't you understand? He touched me. We had sex.

And not just that. My name has been dragged through the mud. Now this. Cambridge is a small community. When I go out, I hear people whisper, and I see the sly glances in my direction. I know they talk about me. *There goes the woman who murdered her husband.* And now they'll add *her husband was a pedophile.* They'll wonder whether I knew. They'll think I'm a monster."

"Beats going to jail, Evelyn."

She fell quiet.

"It'll be hell for Tommy if word gets out. Parents won't let their kids associate with the child of a pedophile. They'll figure this sort of thing runs in families."

She had a point. It did.

"Macy, you *can't* tell anyone. It has to remain our secret. You have to promise."

"Tommy's stronger than you think, Evelyn. And we don't have the luxury of keeping this a secret. Not when it might tie in with Mitchell's murder."

"I'd rather go to jail than have Tommy bear the shame."

"And who would raise Tommy if you are incarcerated? Have you thought about that? Tommy could end up in foster care."

Evelyn picked up her cup and sipped the tea in silence. I sensed she was coming around.

"Who all would need to know?"

"Silverman, for starters. The investigating homicide officer."

"So you'll bring in the cops?"

I nodded.

"We'll be in the tabloids again. 'Wife of Wadsworth Professor Kills Him after Discovering He's a Pedophile.' " She shivered and pulled down on her hair. "God, I hate the press."

I stretched my legs out in front of me, resting my back against the side of the bed.

"You know, the biggest fight Mitchell and I ever had was after I got breast implants."

Some of my tea went down the wrong way and I coughed.

"I shocked you." Evelyn smiled. "With Turner syndrome, boobs aren't part of the package. I always looked like a little girl up top. I thought Mitchell would be thrilled when I got a bigger set of boobs. Aren't men supposed to like big breasts? It was my Christmas gift for him."

She stared at her hands, which were folded in her lap. "I couldn't understand why he got so angry. Instead of being pleased, he was furious. He smashed a Stuart Swan cocktail table."

"Oh, Evelyn—"

She waved my sympathy aside.

"That's when the affairs and the long trips started. I drove him right to it."

"No, Evelyn. You didn't drive him to it. He did that himself."

She shook her head vehemently.

"Well, to be honest, I didn't get the implants just for him. I wanted to feel like a real woman. I was sick of looking like a little girl."

Evelyn put her teacup on the floor and gazed at me. "Mitchell stopped having sex with me after that." She fiddled with her hair.

"I finally understand why," she added bitterly.

THIRTY-FIVE

I called David Silverman and told him about the kiddie porn tapes.

"Did you handle them?"

"Well, yes. I had to—otherwise we wouldn't have found out what was on them."

"Okay. Don't touch anything else in Browne's office. And don't handle the tapes again. I need to think about this for an hour." He paused. "Boy, this really changes things. I can use this. I'll bury the D.A. with this." He sounded energized. "But we have to figure out how to get the maximum leverage out of the tapes."

"You're just the man for the job."

"Okay, Macy. I'll get on it. Meanwhile, here's what I want you to do. Sit tight. Don't touch anything in Browne's office. Don't touch the tapes. I'll send a forensic guy to you as soon as I locate someone I can trust. Meanwhile, you and Evelyn stay put. You babysit her. Don't let her touch anything."

I hung up the phone, understanding David's concern only too well.

I shouldn't have touched the tapes without gloves. But how was I to know beforehand what explosive secrets they'd reveal?

We needed to find Browne's prints on those tapes. His prints had to be there, for Evelyn's sake. Because otherwise there would always be that lingering specter of suspicion of the defense team planting the tapes as false evidence.

Jack showed up on my doorstep at seven-thirty sharp, looking disgustingly handsome dressed in a navy suit and striped red-and-navy tie. I could feel my palms grow sweaty and my stomach do flip-flops when I opened the door. His smile was broad.

"Great dress," he murmured.

The black silk cocktail dress I was wearing was nothing special, but the way Jack's eyes surveyed my body made me feel self-conscious, like the dress was too sexy or too clingy—which it wasn't.

The moment of truth was here. I had no idea what to expect from the evening. What I longed for was for Jack to tell me that his supermodel wife was history.

He opened the door of the SUV for me and helped me climb in, no mean feat in a dress that tapered at the knees. The sacrifices we women make to look attractive to the opposite sex.

Jack tried to hold my hand during the short drive downtown, but I pulled away as soon as he shifted into third. Yet even this brief contact with his fingers made my stomach lurch, the way it does when I ride a Ferris wheel.

The "nice" place Jack had selected for dinner was Cafe Budapest, the corniest of the old-fashioned restaurants in Boston. Where else does one find strolling violinists serenading your table in this day and age?

We exchanged pleasantries while we waited for our drink orders. The couple seated next to us was gazing deeply into each other's eyes, like two lovesick teenagers. They started French kissing openly, an embarrassment to the other patrons in the restaurant. The two waiters who were serving the couple giggled and winked up a storm. Thankfully, the man whipped out his credit card before the groping under the table reached a heating point sufficient to set the tablecloth on fire. From the guy's dazed facial expression, I could have sworn his woman had unzipped him and was sticking her hand up his fly.

While all that was going on, we sipped our wine. Jack seemed mildly amused by the goings-on at the next table. I felt just plain annoyed and distracted.

But Jack was sharp. He picked up on my cool mood right away.

He covered my hand with his. "What's going on?"

I pulled away. "I talked to Dubs earlier today. She happened to mention your wife. I didn't realize you were married, Jack."

"Separated."

Separated. I let that thought run a few laps through my brain, and found that it ferried in a whole new set of emotions, all too complex to sort out over dinner.

He lifted his wine glass and swirled the liquid in a circle. "I should have told you. But I honestly hadn't foreseen that we'd get involved so fast. I thought the last thing I wanted right now was another relationship. But there you were."

His talk was way too smooth, which bothered me.

Jack's eyes turned somber when he caught my expression.

God, I loved those intelligent blue-green eyes of his. I could lose myself in those eyes.

Despite my good intentions, I felt my pulse accelerate. Damn him.

"Can you imagine how I felt when I found out, Jack. You deceived me. In all fairness, I hadn't asked you whether you were married, but from the way you came on to me, I just assumed there wasn't anyone in your life."

"You're right. I should have told you."

"I mean—what was the other night all about? A little fling to tide you over while you decide what to do about your marriage?"

He winced. "Give me more credit than that, Macy. God, is that what you think of me?" He exhaled, a look of anger in his face. "I certainly hope that what we have is more than a little fling, as you put it. I want to keep seeing you."

I swallowed. Of course, this was what I wanted to hear. But what if it was all a lie?

"Why did you separate from your wife?" I finally managed to say, my voice not sounding like my own.

"You really want a play-by-play?"

"Yes, I do. I need to know where things stand."

"You're one tough lady. Nosy, too."

He smiled and touched my nose with his finger.

His touch both angered and delighted me. He was making light of things, almost condescending. But I couldn't seem to help myself. Just being near Jack made me feel giddy.

The waiter refilled our glasses, topping mine off before I had the chance to put my hand over it to indicate I didn't want any more. I needed to keep a clear head. Replacing the bottle in the ice bucket with a fluid motion, the waiter left discreetly.

"Not a pretty picture, my marriage." Jack paused, as if he didn't know where to start. He cleared his throat. "You already know that I spent the past two months sailing in the Caribbean. What you don't know is why. I left because I was too damn angry with my wife to stay here."

He kept swirling his wine glass, looking into it as if searching for answers.

"Celestina and I met seven years ago, at a party. Every guy in the room had his eye on her. She was easily the most beautiful woman there. Dubs told you she's a model?"

I nodded.

"But Celestina wasn't just a pretty face. I found her to be charming, intelligent, and quite witty. I asked her out on a lark, not thinking for a minute she'd even consider dating an old, stodgy guy like me. I was floored when she said yes."

Ouch. I felt another stab of jealousy. But I kept my face immobile and hoped my eyes weren't turning green with envy.

"We were married a few months later. I hadn't given it much thought, what it would be like to be married to a famous model. I assumed she'd be traveling a lot. But so was I, so that didn't seem like much of a problem. What I was unprepared for was Celestina herself. She had seemed to have it all—on the surface. But inside she was as insecure as they come. She only let me see *that* side of her after we were married. Modeling is a high-pressure job. And she's old by industry standards. She's getting her first wrinkles, in a profession that idolizes youth. She also has trouble keeping her weight down. It's an obsession with her. She starves herself, then she overeats, then she throws up. She weighs herself constantly—sometimes twenty, thirty times a day."

Nutcase. But if my livelihood depended on tipping the scale twenty pounds below my normal weight, I'd probably behave in weird, obsessive ways too.

His fingers traced circles around the rim of his wine glass. "It took a while, but it finally dawned on me that Celestina has an eating disorder. It seems bulimia is an occupational hazard with models. I wanted her to see a doctor. She claimed she had things under control. It wasn't any big deal, just a way to enjoy food without it ending up on her hips."

I listened intently. The first time someone had told me about a girl in school sticking her fingers down her throat to bring up lunch, I thought they were telling me a sick, sophomoric joke. The thought of upchucking on purpose was too repulsive to fathom. Of course, since then I'd learned legions of prominent women suffer from bulimia—if talk shows are to be believed.

The waiter brought a breadbasket and spreads and asked if

we wanted another bottle of wine. Jack looked at me. I shook my head.

"I guess not," he said. The waiter left. "Where were we?"

"Bulimia."

"Right. Then three years ago Celestina's career stalled. She wasn't getting any significant bookings. We decided it was time to have a baby. To my surprise, she conceived right away. Four weeks after we found out she was pregnant, her agent called and told her she landed a big contract as spokeswoman for a major cosmetic line. We argued nonstop over whether she should take the job or not, especially since it meant spending most of the summer touring the world."

"I'm surprised a cosmetics firm would agree to hire a pregnant model."

"A clause in the contract Celestina conveniently ignored; she wasn't showing yet. She took off for New York, then London and Paris. A month later she called and told me she miscarried. Much as I tried not to, in my heart I blamed her for losing the baby."

"Why?"

"Because she wasn't taking care of herself. I wondered if she'd had an abortion, but she swore she hadn't." Jack's voice was bitter.

Easy for him to criticize. Having a baby was less disruptive for men than for women. They didn't have to agonize over careers, morning sickness, or stretch marks.

For a model, a pregnancy would be a complete show-stopper.

Sensing a break in the flow of the conversation, the waiter approached and asked if we were ready to order. We hadn't even looked at the menus. I was too riveted on the conversation to bother perusing a lengthy list of food selections.

"Do you serve goulash?" I asked.

"Of course. The best you can find, Madame. Specialty of the house."

"Goulash for me," I said, handing back the menu unopened.

"Make that two," Jack said.

The waiter bowed politely before disappearing. Jack crossed his arms in front of his body and sat back in his chair.

"After she returned from New York," he continued, "We fought constantly. Not about the miscarriage—well, at least not on the surface—even though maybe that's what the fights were really all about. Celestina's career was taking off. She was suddenly *the* hot model, swamped with job offers and magazine covers—which meant she was working harder than ever to keep her weight down. She was exercising constantly. I was sure that her bulimia was totally out of control, but she kept the bathrooms so well perfumed, I couldn't tell. Plus, of course, I had no way of knowing what she did on the road. But I watched her like a hawk at home."

He laughed, a mirthless laugh. "Hard to believe now, but I stooped as low as going through her trash. She turned me into a certifiable lunatic. I kept track of what she ate—junk food, mainly, and tons of it. She couldn't have maintained her weight eating all that crap, not without throwing up. We fought over her eating. But she always had a good excuse. She'd say, *I only ate three cookies. I put the rest down the disposal so I wouldn't be tempted.* Once she figured out that I was sorting through her garbage, the empty ice cream containers, potato chip bags, cookie and candy wrappers disappeared. I don't know what she did with her trash. For all I knew she'd started eating sensibly . . ."

Jack shook his head sadly. "I'm sure all this sounds absolutely pathetic to you."

"Not at all," I said.

Of course it was pathetic.

But I was fascinated. As bad as I felt for Jack and his wife, I couldn't see him married to a head case like her. He seemed too sane.

"People don't lead perfect lives," I said. "You'd be surprised by some of the things I see as a private investigator."

"Perfect lives? I'd settle for average."

"So what made you finally leave her?"

"I came across a prescription for some heavy-duty painkillers. I was immediately concerned, of course. I called the doctor's number, which was listed on the prescription. When I dialed the number, I reached a clinic known mostly for performing abortions."

"Your wife had an abortion?"

"The clinic wouldn't confirm it, but it was obvious to me that she did. Which made me realize that I was probably right to wonder if she had aborted our baby three years ago in Paris. It was just too damn convenient for her to miscarry right after landing a big modeling contract."

Jack picked up his glass and sipped some of the wine.

"I confronted Celestina. She denied it. But I threatened to have my lawyer subpoena her medical records. She finally admitted it. She'd aborted our baby—not once, but twice. It made me sick to my stomach. I felt like someone had taken a two-by-four and slugged me in the gut. I wanted children more than anything in the world."

Jack's eyes were moist. He took a deep breath. I looked away, the yellow room with its stuffed animals and Peter Rabbit wallpaper border dancing through my head. Jack must have painted and wallpapered the room himself, a labor of love. He was that kind of guy.

"I told Celestina then and there that it was over," he continued. "I tossed some clothes in a suitcase and stormed out of the house. I can't even remember where I spent the night. I got totally plastered. All I remember is sitting in an airplane to Antigua the next day, nursing one mother of a hangover."

The waiter brought our dinners, two scrumptious-looking plates of goulash.

"Have you seen your wife since you got back?" I asked.

"No."

"Spoken to her?"

"No. I don't even know where she is."

We were both quiet for a long while, just picking at our food. The food was excellent, but it wasn't going down well.

A waiter ambled over, concern written all over his face. "Is everything all right?"

Like the chef might have slipped up on the salt.

"Yes, just fine," Jack replied tersely.

With Jack going through all this turmoil right now, it was the worst possible time to get involved with him. By the time he'd finally worked through his emotional baggage, he wouldn't want to associate with anyone who'd been part of this painful stretch of his life. I'd be smart to stay clear of him.

"You can't avoid her forever," I said. "You *are* still married."

"I know that," he snapped. He paused a beat, then softer, "Sorry, it's just that the mere thought of her makes me mad as hell."

There didn't seem to be anything left to say. Neither one of us had enjoyed the meal. How did my mother ever survive three—count them, three—divorces? No wonder she'd always been so skinny.

We drove home in silence. How much simpler life had been before I knew about Jack's marital woes. It's true what they say: ignorance is bliss.

He parked the Jeep in the graveled driveway, turned off the ignition, and faced me.

"So where does that leave us?" he asked.

"Nowhere."

I was about to elaborate when I noticed a dark figure leaning against the door of the carriage house. Jack followed my gaze. The guy separated from the wall and approached the Jeep. I could just barely make him out in the beam of the Jeep's headlights. He was a black man, dressed in a conservative suit and tie.

Jack said, "You know this guy?"

"No."

"Let *me* handle it. And keep that gun of yours out of sight."

Fat chance. Not after what had happened yesterday morning. My fingers were already curled around the butt of the Glock.

Jack rolled down the window. "Can I help you?"

The man approached the Jeep and looked straight at me.

"Macy Adams?"

"Yes?"

"I'm Dawn Halebrook's friend. She said you wanted to talk to me."

I relaxed. Jack and I both got out of the SUV. To my right I spotted the sedan with the license plate that I'd asked Pascucci to run. Jack looked at me, his eyes uncertain.

"Are you okay with this?"

"I'll be fine, Jack. I would like a few minutes alone with this gentleman. Mr. . . ."

"Johnson. Troy Johnson." The man extended his hand and we shook. The palm of his hand was warm and dry. "Pleased to meet you, ma'am."

Jack remained where he was, studying the sedan parked in front of his house. Some misplaced protective instinct must have kicked in, because he seemed reluctant to leave me alone with this stranger.

"It really *is* okay, Jack."

"I'll see you as soon as your meeting is over?"

"Sure. Thanks for dinner."

Reluctantly, Jack turned and walked away, but not before taking one long, hard look at the license plate and the strange man. I watched him go.

Then I turned my attention to Troy Johnson.

"So what did you want to talk about?" he asked.

Good question, I thought.

THIRTY-SIX

Troy Johnson was about six feet tall and on the thin side. His bearing reminded me of military personnel.

"Can we talk inside?" He motioned to the carriage house.

I would have preferred to meet somewhere other than in my bedroom, but I had no choice but to invite him in. I tried to remember in what state of disorder I'd left the place. As best as I could recall, dirty sweats and lingerie were scattered everywhere.

He seemed to catch my hesitation.

"I work for the FBI," he said, removing a wallet from his pocket. He flipped it open, displaying the shiny, contoured brass insignia nestled in black leather. He turned the flap, revealing his two-card FBI I.D., with the bureau logo in one-inch turquoise letters on top, his photo and FBI seal on the bottom. It looked like the one Harry used to carry.

"Excuse my place. It's a mess," I said as I unlocked the door. "You may want to close your eyes."

He chuckled, "Not a problem. Believe me, I've seen worse."

I charged ahead of him, nonchalantly nudging pantyhose and an underwire bra underneath the bed on my way through the room. Surely he'd seen racier undergarments on his girlfriends. I brushed my sweatpants and long-sleeved top off the couch to make room for him, then picked up the garments and dumped them unceremoniously into the clothes hamper. He took a seat.

The brass FBI insignia, stiff-starched shirt, muscled body,

and observant eyes spoke of professionalism. Competence. This guy took himself seriously. What did he think of me, a grown woman living in a one-room studio with an unmade bed and dirty underwear strewn about? I bet his own place was ship-shape at all times, his bed linens made up to hospital specs.

He had to figure that any investigation I'd pursue would be as haphazard and disorganized as my living quarters. If, on top of that, he guessed that I slept with my landlord, possibly to get a discount on the rent, he'd have to add to his assessment that I possessed the morals of an alley cat. Private investigators aren't respected by professional law enforcement to begin with. In Johnson's estimation, I probably rated as a rank amateur.

I glanced up and caught him staring at my legs. So he was human after all.

"How did you locate me?"

"Arlington Police report. You left quite a paper trail. It's late, so let me get right to the point," he said, cracking his knuckles and leaning forward. "I'm working on an undercover assignment in conjunction with the Federal Trade Commission. We're investigating unauthorized transfers of U.S. technology to foreign countries."

He detailed how a few months ago BioCorp had called on the FTC, complaining about knockoff versions of their diagnostic kits. A DNA trace revealed that the antigens used in BioCorp's own kits were one hundred percent identical to the knockoffs, meaning that the fraudulent kits were an inside job.

Everything Johnson said confirmed my feelings that something illegal was going on at BioCorp, and that Browne's death was somehow tied in with it.

"It took several months to create a cover for me to get inside BioCorp. Your snooping into Mitchell Browne's death is jeopardizing my investigation, putting all my hard work since January at risk."

I listened quietly. I knew where this was headed. Johnson was on a cease-and-desist mission.

"We're asking you to stay clear of BioCorp," he said, confirming my suspicions.

"And what do I get in return?"

He smiled, showing a row of brilliant white teeth, brightened further by the contrast to his ebony skin. "We'll allow you to continue operating as a private investigator in the Commonwealth of Massachusetts."

He stared impassively. I waited for the punch line. "And . . . ?"

"That's it."

"How generous of you folks."

"Please, Miss Adams. Consider this an official warning. We tend to pull licenses of private operatives who interfere with ongoing FBI operations."

"Can you actually do that? Pull my license? Maybe I should talk to my lawyer about that."

Johnson's features hardened. This had been the wrong thing to say. He was getting annoyed, not the reaction I had aimed for.

Where was all my hostility coming from? This wasn't like me. I realized belatedly that Johnson had become a magnet for the suppressed anger I was feeling toward Jack.

"Go ahead. Talk to your lawyer," he said. "If he's smart, he'll advise you to give it up."

"But you can't stop my investigation."

"Yes we can. I already told you, we can pull your license."

He eyes shifted away from me. I followed his gaze and noticed a pair of black lace panties draped over the arm of the couch, right below eye level, directly in his line of vision. I felt my face color.

He smiled a knowing smile, as if sensing the cause of my discomfort.

Any sense of professionalism I might have felt up to this point was utterly blown. But what he said made me angry. He was talking about my livelihood. This wasn't something I would give up lightly.

But anger wouldn't get me anywhere. I changed tack.

"Do you know Harry Luger? He used to work for the Bureau?"

"I know him."

"I used to work for him. At IE. If you talk to Harry, he'll vouch for me. He'll tell you I'm discreet."

"I've already talked to Harry about you."

I was taken by surprise. For a moment I didn't know what to say.

"Okay . . ." I paused, trying to organize my thoughts. "Evelyn Browne is looking at a murder charge. I firmly believe that she is innocent. So far, everything you've told me only convinces me further that BioCorp is somehow tied up with Browne's murder. How can I possibly let this go? For that matter, how can you?"

"BioCorp had nothing to do with Browne's murder."

"Well, Troy? May I call you Troy?"

He smiled. "Sure, Miss Adams."

"Macy, please."

"Okay. Macy."

"What makes you so sure that BioCorp isn't involved?"

"We've been on the inside at BioCorp for some time."

"I have this theory about BioCorp. I know about the dead rabbits in Section D. I think Browne discovered the identity of the person who killed the rabbits."

Troy Johnson was quiet. By not denying it, I read his answer as a yes and continued.

271

"After Browne discovered the bunny killer, he got murdered. They killed him to shut him up."

The FBI agent shook his head. "That's not what happened."

"How can you be sure this isn't how it went down?"

"We'd been keeping a fairly close watch on Browne."

Again, his answer was totally unexpected. *A close watch on Browne?* Something shifted in my mind. Why would the FBI keep taps on Browne? They wouldn't—not unless they suspected *him* of killing the rabbits. That didn't make any sense.

Or did it?

"You had Browne under surveillance?" I said.

Johnson was quiet, his face not giving away a thing.

"Why? Did you think he killed the rabbits?"

"You're laboring under a misconception. The rabbits weren't killed."

I flashed back to my conversation with Kublinski about Section D. *Rabbits that produced the antigen . . . one in a hundred . . . the proverbial golden goose.*

I was getting it now.

"Are you saying that the rabbits were nabbed? Or switched with dead rabbits? You suspected Browne of kidnapping the rabbits? Is that why you had him under surveillance?"

Again, the FBI agent stonewalled me. But I could see a glint in his eye. I was on the right track.

"Since Browne was under surveillance, did the FBI actually witness his murder?"

He looked at me as if I'd just beamed down from Mars.

"Heavens." Johnson shook his head emphatically and laughed out loud, a real belly laugh. "This is rich. Miss Adams, I'd say you've been reading too many thrillers."

He was definitely laughing at me, not with me.

"Help me out here," I said. "We're talking a potential life sentence for an innocent woman. You know *something*. All I'm asking is that you throw me a bone." He didn't respond. I pressed on. "I'll settle for a clavicle, for God's sake . . . A bone spur . . ."

Troy Johnson looked thoughtful.

"You might want to pull Browne's telephone records for the night he was murdered."

I thought for a second. "The FBI had a wiretap on Browne's phone?"

I'd struck a nerve. I could see it from the sudden tension in his face.

"There's your bone," he said softly. "Now do I have your word that you'll stay clear of BioCorp?"

"Okay. You have my word."

I stood up. Johnson was already heading toward the door. I tried to catch up with him, almost tripping as my right heel snagged on the rug. I would have fallen if he hadn't caught me.

"Had a few drinks tonight?" he asked, his tone amused.

"Just a couple of glasses of wine," I said. "How do I get in touch with you, in case I need to?"

"There'll be no need to call me. I've already told you more than I should have."

He opened the door.

"So what will the phone records tell me?"

"Good night, Miss Adams."

"Wait . . ."

I stepped into the open doorway, effectively cutting off his way out. He stepped backwards, bumping against the wall. We were practically dancing. I took another step forward. "Who nabbed the bunnies? Did Browne do it?"

He sidestepped me and made his way out the door. "Please, Miss Adams. The rabbits have nothing to do with Browne's murder. Just drop it."

I closed the door behind him, leaning against it, feeling pretty good. I'd gotten a new lead: Browne's phone records. I walked back into the room, plopped down on the couch, and put my feet up on the coffee table.

Why hadn't the FBI given the information about the phone records to the detectives investigating Browne's murder? Was it just a case of the various police departments not talking to each other?

I thought back on the conversation. Johnson's demeanor had changed distinctly as soon as I mentioned the word "wiretap." But why? Surely it had to be authorized and legal? I couldn't see Johnson not going strictly by the book. But what if—?

My thoughts were interrupted by a knock on the door. I scanned the room for any items Troy Johnson might have forgotten. Nothing that I could see. I hoped it wasn't one of Rutgers's goons.

I grabbed the Glock and approached the door warily. I looked through the peephole. Jack was standing on the threshold. I put the gun on a side table and opened the door.

"I, uhm, wanted to make sure you're okay."

"Oh, Jack." I was touched by his concern. He must have watched the carriage house closely, because he'd come the second Johnson left.

"So what was *that* all about?"

"Stuff having to do with the Browne murder case."

"Is this what being a private eye is like? People camping out on your doorstep at all hours of the night?"

"Not usually."

"Well, I was worried. I don't want anything to happen to you."

He stepped across the threshold and wrapped his arms around me. I melted against his chest. It felt so good to be engulfed in the warmth of his strong arms. Oddly, what I felt wasn't sexual at all.

Reluctantly, I pulled away. "I'm not a home wrecker, Jack. I still remember how hurt my father was when my mother took up with another man. It broke his heart. I'm not going to come between you and your wife. I wouldn't want to cause that kind of pain."

"You aren't coming between Celestina and me. My marriage is over. It was over long before you came along."

"You don't know that. You haven't even talked to your wife since you got back."

"I don't want her back. Not after what she did to me."

He talked a good game, but he didn't sound entirely convinced. Not to my ears.

"I wish I'd known about her before I met you," I said.

"No, you can't wish that." He was serious. "Then we wouldn't have found out how great we are together."

He pulled me close, his lips caressing my neck. I pushed him away.

"You need to decide what you want to do about your marriage, Jack. Trust me, it's better if we don't see each other."

"You're giving me the brush-off?" he asked, his voice thick.

"You know damn well how attracted I am to you. But I don't sleep with married men."

His face softened. "I guess I can live with that. What's another month or two?"

He suddenly pulled me close again, kissing me on the lips. This time I could feel the heat rise between us. I pushed him away.

"I mean it, Jack. I'm not going to be the *other woman*."

As I said those words, Dawn popped into my mind.

Dawn. Of course.

Dawn wasn't BioCorp. Technically she wasn't even a Bio-Corp employee, so I wouldn't be breaking any promises I'd made to Johnson if I talked to Dawn, now would I?

Troy probably wouldn't see it that way, but who was going to tell him? Not I. Not Dawn.

I disentangled myself from Jack's arms and checked my watch. Ten-fifteen. Late for a social call, but so what?

"I've got to go." I grabbed my coat, handbag, and the Glock and herded Jack out the door.

"You can't be serious? Where on earth are you going at this hour?"

"No time to explain."

Jack walked me to my car. "Do you want me to come with you?" he asked.

"No, Jack. How would you feel if I asked to tag along to one of your meetings?"

He touched my elbow. "It's late. Should you be out by yourself?"

"Jack, this is what I do for a living. I'll be fine."

Jack didn't know the half of it. He didn't know about my near-fatal run-in with the BioCorp goons, or my being shot at with a tranquilizer gun.

My last glimpse of him was in the rearview mirror. He stood in the driveway, a solitary figure, watching me as I hung a right into the street.

THIRTY-SEVEN

On the way to Dawn's house I thought maybe, just maybe, my mother and I weren't all that different after all. She had busted up three marriages, and here *I* was, lusting after a married man.

The first marriage she'd wrecked had been Jorge Almeida's. Jorge was a rich, suave Brazilian millionaire whose wife was history the moment my mother appeared on the scene. Jorge had been tall, dark, and handsome, an impeccable dresser who spoke with a devastatingly charming accent. I'd assumed that my mother saw mainly dollar signs when she looked at him, but one glimpse at them *together,* and I realized that the love bug had bitten my mother hard.

Jorge and my father had been as opposite as the North Pole is from the equator—or Boston from Rio. Where Dad was self-contained, self-disciplined, and stuffy, Jorge was passionate, romantic, and charismatic.

After their respective divorces were finalized, Jorge spirited my mother away to Brazil—and convinced her that her offspring would be better off staying behind in the U.S. of A. Never a PTA type to begin with, with Jorge front and center, Mom all but forgot she even had children. My brother and I spent two summers in Brazil, but during the school year we were at different boarding schools. Tucker and I had always been close, and I missed him dreadfully. I was slow to make friends at school, and consequently my secondary school experience was lonely—the pits. I had sworn back then that I would never be party to a divorce. Yet here I was: Jack was married.

Eventually Jorge broke my mother's heart. She found him in bed with a younger woman. What comes around goes around, I guess. The shoe was on the other foot, and it hurt. Mom promptly divorced Jorge and immediately found another married man: a wealthy insurance company executive this time. But Marvin must have bored her to death. Their marriage was over almost as quickly as it had begun. They were divorced within a year. Marvin tried to get back together with his ex-wife, but she wouldn't have him.

A regular little home wrecker, my mother.

Miraculously, she had found happiness with husband number four, Gerald Aronsen, a Hollywood studio executive. They'd been married for over ten years now.

I pulled into the gas station in front of Dawn's place, parked, and set the Jetta's kill switch, a toggle lever I'd asked my dealer to install beneath the dash to foil any would-be car thief.

I assumed Dawn knew that Troy Johnson was working undercover. But what if she didn't? I'd have to tread carefully. Dawn answered the doorbell within seconds, her voice sounding small and tinny over the intercom. "Hello."

"Dawn, it's Macy. May I come up?"

I was surprised when she buzzed me in without further explanation or protest. She waited for me upstairs by the door, dressed in gray sweats, her honey-blond hair hanging loosely around her shoulders. God, she looked young. So young, she made me feel old.

"Did you talk to Troy?" she asked.

"Yes. We talked a little while ago." I felt greatly relieved. She'd given me the perfect opening. "Troy agreed that in exchange for my cooperation, you'd talk to me."

A complete lie. I had to be out of my mind. I prayed I wasn't making a colossal mistake.

"He said that?" She sounded surprised.

"Yup." I tried to keep my voice casual. "You can call him, if you like."

I held my breath. If she decided to call Troy, yours truly was going to be in a big pile of doo-doo. Hell, I was digging myself in pretty deep even if she didn't call. Troy Johnson probably *did* have the authority to yank my license.

On the other hand, he'd told me to stay away from BioCorp. Not from Dawn.

"All right," she said. "If that's what he said. What do you want to know?"

Open Sesame. I felt like kicking up my heels and shouting hallelujah. She motioned me to a couch overlooking the river. A half-empty wine bottle sat on the cocktail table, with one solitary glass.

"Lovely view," I said, glancing across the water, which reflected the floodlights along Memorial Drive.

"Thanks," Dawn said. She was fetching a second glass for me. "I'm glad you dropped by. I hate drinking by myself."

"Don't we all."

She poured wine for me and we clinked glasses.

"I got some really bad news today. I've been trying to line up grant money. A state sponsor came back negative this afternoon. I struck out everywhere."

I nodded understanding and put my glass on the table.

"You must miss Browne's mentoring."

"Oh yeah." She sighed.

"Why would Browne get himself involved in this mess?" I'd purposefully left the question vague, hoping Dawn would fill in the blanks.

"Maybe he saw it as a way to get out from under Rutgers. Mitchell *had* been responsible for every single breakthrough BioCorp's R and D department ever made. But Rutgers paid him peanuts. The firm was bleeding money because of the counterfeit kits. I guess Mitchell figured this was a way of getting what was rightfully his."

I tried to make the mental connections, but too many pieces of the puzzle were still missing. I still had only a foggy idea what she was talking about.

"If Browne hated working for Rutgers so much," I said, "why didn't he just pull up stakes and do his research elsewhere?"

"A lot of Mitchell's own money was invested in BioCorp. If Mitchell were to leave, Rutgers could tie him up in court for years—intellectual property, proprietary rights. That's why Mitchell wanted the firm to go public. And when that didn't pan out, he tried to bring in the Japanese. Mitchell wanted out. Trouble was, no investment bank was going to touch BioCorp— not after the recall fiasco."

Recall? What recall? "Incidentally, how did that happen?"

"Rutgers put pressure on his staff to ramp production up too fast. They cut some corners." She shook her head. "What a moron. Penny wise and pound foolish. Mitchell went absolutely ballistic when he found out that Rutgers had fudged the data. I'm sure that's why he got Rutgers's son involved in his scheme."

My ears perked up. Another clue, and this time I had absolutely no idea what Dawn was talking about. But anything that could bring Rutgers down was riveting.

"Rutgers's son and Mitchell were in cahoots?" I said.

"Looks that way. Payton has been working at the lab for a year. Blatant nepotism, you ask me. The boy's only in his early twenties, and a follower. Point is, he couldn't have thought up the scheme to nab the rabbits by himself. That's why I think Mitchell was involved."

"But what would be the point? Why take the risk of involving Rutgers's son? What if the kid went to his father and spilled the beans?"

"Mitchell had his back covered. He left no evidence that linked him to the rabbits. You ask me, Mitchell did it to embarrass Rutgers. Maybe to pressure Rutgers to resign as chairman."

I was still in the dark. "So how did Browne hook up with Rutgers's son?"

"Well, again, you won't find anything concrete to link Mitchell to young Payton. But the whole scheme was so clever. Nab the rabbits, replace them with the dead ones, then produce knockoff kits overseas and sell them in the original BioCorp packaging. Payton ran the outsourcing department. It was his signature on the orders for the knockoff kits. All very clever. Too clever for Payton. That's why we think Mitchell was involved. Payton denies everything, of course. He swears someone set him up. But his fingerprints are all over the deal."

"So Rutgers may have killed Browne?" I recalled Rutgers's beady, cold, little eyes, staring out of his fat face. "I bet he was livid when he found out Mitchell had set up his son."

"But that's the beauty of the scheme. Rutgers never connected Mitchell to the deal. Nobody did. The whole business had been set up through a third person in the Pacific rim. And Payton denies everything. In any case, I can't see Rutgers killing Mitchell. Mitchell was the driving force behind BioCorp. Without him, the firm would have gone down the tubes. His synthetic T-cells project is going to be a real breakthrough. Bio-Corp owns the patent, but Mitchell was the only one who could pull it off."

"And Rutgers realized that?"

"Oh sure. That's why he would never murder Mitchell. Not in a million years. Rutgers had Mitchell by the balls. Mitchell signed a very restrictive contract with BioCorp. For better or worse, they were stuck with each other. And Rutgers will throw Payton to the wolves if it means keeping the firm."

"His own son?"

"I don't like Rutgers, but he isn't a crook. If his son was involved in something fraudulent, Rutgers won't save him. The kid will go to jail."

"So what happens now?"

She shrugged. "Payton has disappeared. My guess is that he's working on his tan in some South American backwater."

"Beats doing laundry for inmates at some Club Fed for the next ten years."

She ran her fingers through her hair. "Unfortunately, Rutgers will continue as chairman of the board."

"What happens with Browne's synthetic T-cells?"

"It's sort of academic at this point. The results of Browne's experiments are stored on BioCorp's servers, but they've gotten infected with a computer virus. Files keep disappearing. Even the backups don't seem to be immune. A little more of Browne's T-cell research is disappearing every day. It's very discouraging."

"Jesus. How could this happen?"

"My guess is that Mitchell put a virus into the system that self-activated. I think he put it there as insurance, to make sure Rutgers couldn't get his hands on Mitchell's research, should he ever get ousted from BioCorp's board."

Unbelievable. This was a corporate soap opera.

"Browne feared that Rutgers might steal his research?"

"Right."

"So who killed Browne?"

"That's the sixty-four-thousand-dollar question."

"Troy suggested I look at Browne's phone records for the night he was murdered. Were the Feds listening in on Browne's calls?"

"Well, Troy never admitted that they had Mitchell's lines tapped, but he warned me to keep it strictly business when I called him."

"How did you get involved with the FBI, Dawn?"

"I was the one who figured out that the rabbits had been switched. I didn't know who to trust at BioCorp. It was such an obvious inside job. So I went to the FBI."

"You and Troy must have discussed Browne's murder. Who does he think did it?"

"Troy never tells me anything. He's like all the other agents," she complained.

I felt like I was getting very close to solving the case. But some crucial pieces were still missing.

"Dawn, the affair you had with Browne. Why did it end?"

She stiffened. "Oh God. Not that."

"Why did you sleep with him? He was old enough to be your father."

For a while she said nothing, her expression unreadable. "Have you ever noticed how men are into bodies, and women go for the mind?"

"Hmm."

"I was in awe of Mitchell. The man was brilliant." Dawn finished her wine, sipping slowly.

"Would you have guessed that I grew up on a farm?" she asked out of the blue.

"No."

"Yeah, well, I did. I was always different from my brothers and sisters. Hard to believe we swam in the same gene pool. Maybe my mother had her own personal Bridges of Madison County, or maybe the milk man was smarter than he looked." She smiled. "I was reading books by the time I was three, while my brothers and sisters struggled through the alphabet in first grade. I did everything better than they did, and boy, they hated me for it. They treated me like a freak."

"How did you end up at Wadsworth?"

"I knew I had to get out of the hick town I grew up in. My

parents barely scraped together the money to pack the oldest two boys off to the local community college. They weren't going to waste a college education on a *girl*. I was a good gymnast. Once I found out about athletic scholarships, I began training hard—four, five hours a day. And I got lucky. A former Olympic hopeful lived in my town, and he trained me for free." She ran her hands through her silky blond hair. "God, I never talk about this stuff. It feels good to talk." She smiled. "Did you ever consider becoming a shrink?"

I shook my head, amused. "No."

"Anyway, getting into Wadsworth was nirvana. I wasn't a freak anymore. I was just like everyone else."

"There must be lots of eligible men who want to date you. Why Browne?"

"The power."

"How did the affair end?"

"Things got strange," Dawn said.

"Strange how?"

She lifted her shoulders. She was no longer meeting my eyes. "You know . . ."

"I might. But I'd like to hear it from you."

"The sex," she said. "It got strange."

"We found some videotapes at Browne's house. Of children."

Dawn shivered and pulled her arms tightly around her. Her lips opened and she started to say something, but then she stopped herself. She looked down.

"I guess I knew it had to be something like that," she said. "I told myself I was imagining it. Then I told myself it was harmless, just a fantasy. But it freaked me out. He brought clothes he wanted me to put on, clothes that made me look like a child. And then there was the sick, patronizing way he talked to me. It got so it was always there when we did it. He was a father doing it to his daughter."

THIRTY-EIGHT

Dawn and I chatted for another half an hour or so. I wanted to keep it light, calm her down. Girl talk. By the time I left she was pretty much in the bag, in an alcohol-induced stupor rendering her almost comatose on the couch. I nudged her toward the bedroom before leaving her apartment at a quarter past midnight.

Downstairs, I got an unpleasant jolt. Troy Johnson was leaning against the fender of my car. The look in his eyes alerted me instantly that he was in a rotten mood.

"I could have your license for this."

"You said for me to stay away from BioCorp. You didn't say anything about Dawn."

"What did she tell you?"

"That sex with Browne sucked."

"Did she say anything about BioCorp?"

"We talked about Mitchell Browne."

"What did she say about BioCorp?"

"We talked about her childhood, why she got into gymnastics. Our conversation had nothing to do with BioCorp. She confirmed what you said, that she doesn't think Rutgers is involved in Browne's murder. Ask her if you don't believe me," I said, though I prayed he wouldn't. Hopefully, most of tonight's conversation would vanish in an alcoholic haze and Dawn wouldn't remember a thing in the morning.

Troy's face still looked angry. I didn't want him to pull my license.

"Browne was involved in child pornography," I said, trying to worm my way back into his good graces. "That's why I needed to talk to Dawn."

If this was news to him, he didn't show it, his face a perfect blank. Not being able to read the man was unnerving.

"You go near *anyone* associated with BioCorp again, and I will go after your license. That's a promise."

"Fine. Okay. I won't."

He pushed himself off my car, got into his sedan, and slammed the door.

It had started to drizzle. I scurried to the Jetta. I turned the key, but the ignition ground away uselessly, the engine failing to turn over. *Not tonight. Not car trouble.* I was too tired to deal with this. I could already feel the dull pain of a headache.

Belatedly, I remembered setting the kill switch. I disengaged the little toggle, and the motor fired right up.

My temples throbbed. I desperately needed a good night's sleep and I wasn't going to get it at home, where there was no guarantee I wouldn't receive further visits from the FBI, from Jack—or worse, from Rutgers's tranquilizer-gun-toting goons.

The Sonesta hotel was a mile downriver. I checked in, sinking into the dead sleep of a shipwrecked sailor who'd finally found a safe harbor.

I slept late. The hotel offered a terrific breakfast, consisting of eggs, bacon, home fries, toast, juice, and coffee. Nice to feel well rested and pampered for a change. I checked in with Silverman to see what was happening. David was in a meeting, but Annette, his anorexic paralegal, wanted to talk to me. Urgently.

Now what? I thought while I waited for the receptionist to put her on the line.

"Macy, where are you? I've called everywhere, trying to reach you. You really should get a pager. Or at least keep your cell phone turned on."

Just what I didn't need: A lecture from someone with fake boobs.

"What's up?"

"There's an emergency at Evelyn's. She's going crazy. You need to get over there."

"What happened?"

"I'm not sure, but Evelyn's totally freaked out. She's been asking for you. You had better get your butt over there. Somebody needs to calm her down."

I paid my hotel bill and sped to Evelyn's house. Silverman wouldn't be happy when he learned that I'd been incommunicado until ten in the morning. And Annette would be sure to tell him. My fault. I'd bought a new cellular phone, but I'd left it in the trunk of the Jetta. With so much happening yesterday, I'd forgotten to charge the phone battery.

Even from half a block away, I could see why Evelyn was "freaked out." Garbage was strewn all over her front lawn. Whoever did this, they'd done a thorough job. By my estimation, the contents of five or ten bags had been spilled, making a big, disgusting mess.

A stray dog was rooting through the garbage. He growled when I approached. I picked up a half-full plastic water bottle from the lawn and flung it at him. "Get," I yelled. "Get."

The bottle hit him on the nose and he scampered away.

I rang the doorbell.

Seconds ticked by. There was no answer.

"Evelyn," I yelled. "It's me, Macy. Open the door."

The door opened. Evelyn fell into my arms. "Ohmigod, ohmigod," she gasped. "Oh Macy, who would do this?"

Only then did I notice the crude cardboard poster that had been affixed to the latticework beside the door. Uneven capital letters: "MURDERERS BELONG IN JAIL DIE BITCH."

I tore the sign from the lattice, took it inside, and closed the front door. Evelyn burst into tears as she read the message. Had she not seen it before? I didn't understand why, after everything else she'd been through, this was pushing her over the edge. I put my arms around her and tried to console her, rocking her like a child.

"We'll get this mess cleaned up, Evelyn. Okay?"

"What if they come back?"

"I'll shoot them."

Evelyn looked at me with alarm. I smiled.

"Come on. Get me some trash bags. And do you have a rake?"

Evelyn found a rake, and rubber gloves for me. We ventured outside, where she kicked an empty milk carton across the lawn. "What a bloody mess."

"Maybe we should call the cops," I said.

"What if it was one of my neighbors?" Evelyn said. "If I call the cops, it'll just make it worse. Because then the press would get wind of it."

She had a point. The silver lining—if this cloud had one—was that no newspaper photographers had shown up to splash this latest incident on tomorrow's front page. Or at least not *yet*.

I started raking the mess into piles, using a snow shovel to lift the debris into garbage bags.

"Probably the Evans kids," Evelyn said. "Real little bastards, all three of them. They live just down the street. Damn them." Her mood seemed to be lifting, now that we were doing something concrete about her spoiled front lawn.

The vandalism of the yard and the threatening note was upsetting. But I agreed with Evelyn's assessment: neighborhood rowdies acting up. Or Tommy's classmates at BB&N. The optimist in me wanted to believe that it had been kids. The same optimist also hoped they wouldn't have the balls to do anything more damaging than hurl garbage.

Evelyn and I spent the next half hour raking up the debris, none too pleasant a task. While scooping up trash, I thought with guilty irritation about my overdue tetanus booster. Recalcitrant bits of coffee grounds, rice, cherry pits, and other pieces of organic matter stayed imbedded in the lawn despite our best efforts. The birds and ants in Evelyn's yard would have a field day. On the bright side, maybe Evelyn would find a budding cherry tree sapling in her front yard come summer.

While we were raking, a pickup truck stopped at the curb. The truck was shiny and new, with a bright red paint job, its truck bed filled with garden waste. The driver rolled down the window and offered to haul our garbage away, five bucks a bag. I agreed, and he tossed the three bags we'd already filled into the truck bed. We became best buds when he helped us clean up the rest of the garbage. After we were done, I thanked him and gave him forty bucks, which he pocketed.

When Tommy mentioned seeing a pickup truck on his street the other night, I hadn't believed him. But now I gave his comment more credence. I knew nothing about trucks, but seeing this pickup parked at the curb, I noticed how powerful and macho a machine it was. It made sense somehow. Of course Tommy would notice a set of wheels like this. Sexier even than a girl to someone Tommy's age, a new big, shiny truck like this might well be the boy's vehicular version of a wet dream.

I found myself staring at the behemoth.

"You like my wheels?" my buddy asked, giving his truck a proud, proprietary glance.

"Yeah, I do."

"You'd look good in a Ford. Should get yourself one. There's something real sexy about a lady who can handle a truck."

"I'll think about it," I said cheerfully, giving the truck's tailgate an affectionate pat before he started the engine. The man looked puzzled for an instant. Then he smiled brightly.

At that moment I believed Tommy. Now I needed to figure out what to do about it.

THIRTY-NINE

I decided to canvass Evelyn's neighbors. She insisted on accompanying me—with her cocker spaniel. The pooch wagged its tail full speed when it saw me. In a flash, the canine broke loose, leash trailing behind it like the tail of a kite, barking merrily. The dog didn't stop when it reached me. It jumped, digging its sharp little doggie claws into my jeans, its tongue licking my hands vigorously.

"Happy to see me, buster?" I said, peeling the pooch off me and putting it back on the ground. I knelt down and petted the silky fur while trying to dodge the wet, pink tongue darting for my face.

Evelyn laughed out loud, a laugh that sounded bell-like, like a child's. "I didn't realize you two had become such good friends."

"Neither did I." I pointed to the bag in her hand. "What have you got there?"

"It's the puppies." She opened the canvas bag for a peek inside. The four pups, looking larger with their fur dry, were huddled together, their little eyes still closed. "Buffy won't leave the house without them."

It seemed pretty clear who the boss was. More power to Buffy for putting down her paw.

Late morning turned out to be a lousy time to go knocking on people's doors, asking if anyone remembered seeing a red F-250 pick up truck parked on the street the night Browne was killed. The few residents who were home had trouble remembering anything at all about the night in question. Two weeks was too long a time span. None of them recalled *any* red pickup truck parked on their street recently.

We rang doorbells, without any luck, with Evelyn getting a lot of oohing and aahing over the puppies. One neighbor offered to buy one of the toy-sized canines.

"It's the perfect gift for my niece," the woman cooed. "Oh, look at this little fellow, with the brown ears, isn't he just too cute. How much do you want for him?"

She started to reach into the bag, but was stopped by mama dog's ferocious bark. Only when Evelyn took the bag out of the woman's reach did the barking ebb to an occasional growl.

The lady didn't even bat an eyelash when Evelyn mentioned the five-hundred-dollar price tag. They agreed that the puppy should remain in the care of mama dog for a few more weeks. Poor Buffy, I thought. Unbeknownst to her, her offspring had been put on the auction block right in front of her soulful eyes.

My patience started to run thin by the time Evelyn finished explaining the feeding and hygiene routine for a puppy, reassuring her neighbor that she was welcome to drop by her house anytime she wished to see her latest family addition.

I told Evelyn we could skip the rest of the houses. If I had to listen to another ten minutes of puppy talk, I'd blow my stack.

We returned to Evelyn's house, where I called David Silverman, reaching him this time. I explained about the nature of the garbage emergency, and how I'd dealt with it.

"We still need to find those account numbers, Macy. Can you keep on looking?"

"Sure."

"And if you find any more tapes, don't touch them. I'd love to have a kiddie porn tape with just Browne's prints on it."

I told him that I understood. "David, one more thing. We

need to get Browne's phone records for the night he was killed. The sooner, the better."

"And you don't know anyone at the phone company?"

"David, even if I did, I can't ask for Browne's records. It's illegal."

"Okay, I'll get a subpoena."

"It could turn out to be the key to this entire puzzle."

David said he'd get on it, and we disconnected.

"I suppose it's too early for a drink," Evelyn said when I hung up the phone.

"It is for me, but you go ahead."

"I don't like to drink by myself. Makes me feel like a lush."

"I want to go through the rest of your husband's belongings. His clothes and stuff upstairs."

"Right now?"

"It's as good a time as any."

"I've been meaning to pack his clothes to donate to the Salvation Army. But I just can't get myself to touch any of his things. I haven't even been in Mitchell's room."

"Let's get started then."

Evelyn paused and her expression hardened. "Ever since you found those tapes, all I think about is what a sad excuse for a human being Mitchell was. I don't want to keep anything he touched."

Clearly, she wished to exorcise Mitchell from her life. And I couldn't blame her. We climbed the staircase. Mitchell had claimed the largest of the bedrooms as his own. The walls were painted a dark gray-green, with polished cotton drapes the shade of tobacco trimmed with gold fringe. On top of the nineteenth-century sleigh bed lay a plaid comforter whose stripe pattern picked up the gold tones of the curtains. Two sepia-tone landscapes hung above the bed, rimmed by jade-green matting, both set in identical dark-brown wooden frames. A dresser, a large chaise, and a TV/VCR combo on a stand completed the furnishings. The room gave the impression of having been professionally decorated, but the dark color scheme made it feel oppressive and claustrophobic—in stark contrast to Evelyn's smaller bedroom, which seemed bright and cheerful in comparison.

I immediately checked inside the TV stand, located the VCR, and touched the eject button, thinking with disgust that this was where Mitchell had inserted his sick tapes. The stand was empty, except for a couple of outdated *TV Guides* and the VCR remote control.

"Where do you want to start?" Evelyn asked.

"How about the dresser."

"You go ahead. I'll be right back."

There's something melancholy, if not downright creepy, about going through the belongings of the departed. Browne had been a meticulous organizer. Socks, briefs, and shirts were stacked neatly, arranged by color and pattern. Evelyn reappeared momentarily with a large cardboard box, and we got into a rhythm: I would take an item out of the drawer, shake it out, check any pockets for valuables, and hand it to Evelyn, who would refold the article on the bed before piling it into the cardboard box.

We finished the dresser quickly. Besides undergarments and shirts, I found a handful of coins, half a dozen professorial bow ties, and three pairs of cuff links. No videotapes. No slips of paper. No deposit box keys. No secret account numbers.

Browne's closet proved equally uninteresting. His taste in suits had run toward tweedy jackets, corduroy pants, and a few boring gray and blue dress suits, slightly shiny at the seat and elbows. A quick search through the pockets yielded a ballpoint pen, a slip for unclaimed laundry, and credit card receipts from ExxonMobil and Borders books.

There were several pairs of penny-loafers, size eight. "Never trust a man with small feet," my mother used to say. No sneakers or athletic shoes, confirming my suspicion that Browne hadn't been a big believer in working out.

Browne's ties were dull, a collection of understated small prints in drab colors. The only colorful tie in his collection was one of Santa Claus and his reindeer.

A wistful smile played across Evelyn's face when I handed it to her. "I can't believe he kept this." She folded the tie carefully. "Oh my, this brings back memories. My present for Mitchell six, seven years ago, when Tommy was still in grade school. I wanted to make Christmas special that year. I hoped the tie would do the trick, put Mitchell in the Christmas spirit." She sighed. "I don't think he wore it once."

She fumbled with the tie until it emitted an electronic rendition of "Joy to the World."

I myself had possessed a pair of Christmas socks that played a musical chime. The socks had been a great hit at parties—until I put them through the wash.

"It still works. What do you know?" Evelyn smiled. "Tommy used to play with this tie endlessly, used to drive Mitchell crazy. I had to keep taking it away from him." She set the tie aside on top of the dresser. "Joy to the World" chimed an encore. "Who knows, Tommy might still get a kick out of it."

I checked the top shelves of the closet, which held several old sweaters and two battered suitcases. Tags from a "Hotel Europe" attached to the handles of Browne's luggage caught my eye.

"Evelyn, do you know where this Hotel Europe is located?"

"I think it's in Thailand."

"Did you go with him?"

"No. He didn't want me on those trips."

"How long was he gone for?"

"A week, ten days. Why?"

"No particular reason."

I didn't see much point in enlightening Evelyn about the reputation of Thailand as a destination for people seeking unusual sex-for-sale experiences.

I rummaged through the side pockets of the suitcase, which netted an orphaned sock.

We worked steadily for another hour and managed to empty the closet of everything, leaving only empty hangers and dust balls. The stripped closet looked forlorn: more evidence of Browne's existence had been wiped off the face of the planet.

The space was large enough to step inside. I ran my hand along the back of the upper shelves to make sure I hadn't missed anything small—like a safety deposit key or scrap of paper. I came back with dust on my hands.

We did a quick check of the bathroom: nothing there except the standard toiletries one would expect to find. Evelyn threw the entire collection into a black trash bag.

Back in the bedroom, Evelyn picked up the Christmas tie and tossed it in with the rest of her dead husband's belongings.

"You changed your mind about the tie?" I said.

She nodded. "The idea of Tommy wearing anything that my late husband laid his hands on makes my skin crawl." She closed the flaps of the box, her mouth set in a determined line. "Want to take a break?" she asked.

"I'd just as soon get it over with. Where else did your husband keep things?"

"Well, there's the attic."

"Lead the way," I said, feeling a second wind.

We climbed the narrow staircase that led to the loft. It was chilly, dusty, and dark upstairs; the attic nothing more than an unfinished, uninsulated storage space. The slanted roof timbers were raw wood, darkened with age and stained in a couple of spots from water seepage. The small area between the rafters was crammed with junk: old toys, a crib, baby paraphernalia, kids' sporting equipment—remnants of Tommy's younger days.

I followed Evelyn to one tidy corner of the attic.

"These are Mitchell's boxes. I honestly don't have a clue what's in them—I've never opened them."

Evelyn watched me pull the first box out of the stack. It was very heavy. As soon as I opened it I saw why: it was filled with textbooks.

"Chilly up here," Evelyn shivered visibly. "I'll go get a couple of sweatshirts."

She headed back down while I continued rummaging through the box, emptying it completely, placing the books on the attic floor. After I was satisfied it held nothing of interest, I returned the contents and set the box aside, going on to the next one, which contained yearbooks, photos, and term papers from Mitchell Browne's high school days.

Evelyn reappeared.

"Here," she said, handing me a bulky long-sleeved shirt. I thanked her and pulled it on. I assumed I was wearing one of Tommy's castoffs. Somehow I couldn't see Evelyn as a walking advertisement for "Mortal Kombat."

"Found anything?" she asked.

I handed her one of the high school yearbooks.

"Well, look at this." She sat down on a box, leafing through the book. "There's Mitchell. God, he looks young. I find it hard to believe he was ever a kid himself."

A tear sprang into her eye, which she wiped away quickly with the back of her hand. "What a mess. I had such hopes when I married him. We were going to be so happy together. Nothing worked out, did it?"

"You have Tommy," I responded.

She smiled through her tears. "You're right. I guess I should be grateful. Something wonderful did come out of this stupid marriage after all."

The next box was small and contained cancelled checks, all over a decade old. A long shot. I set it aside. Maybe I'd return to it later if nothing else panned out.

There were another dozen or so boxes containing old clothes, paperback books, biotech magazines, and other junk. No videotapes. No safety deposit box keys. No bank account numbers.

"Let's take a break," Evelyn finally said. "My hands are frozen and I'm hungry."

The search hadn't yielded the hoped-for results. My back was stiff from bending over and lifting heavy boxes, the dust in the attic had wormed its way into my sinuses, and I felt frustrated. Outside, the light was fading, and the forty-watt light bulb suspended from the ceiling gave scant illumination. I hated to give up, but it made no sense to continue rummaging through the attic in the dark.

We descended the staircase. On the second floor I caught a glimpse of Tommy, hunched over his desk. The sounds of a "classic rock 'n' roll" station came from his room.

"Wine or tea?" Evelyn asked in the kitchen.

"How about both?"

Evelyn pulled a bottle of Chardonnay from the fridge. "I hope you'll stay for dinner. I'm making beef tournedos, my favorite recipe. It's wonderful."

I was grateful for the invitation. While I sipped the wine, Evelyn started a kettle with water. The music upstairs had stopped and it was very quiet in the house, except for the street noise muffled by the distance. Evelyn brewed tea and I watched her stir olive oil, garlic, scallions, and mushrooms in a pan. In a separate skillet she browned the beef, and the wonderful aroma of home cooking filled the kitchen. She retrieved a covered Pyrex dish from the refrigerator and placed it in the microwave.

Evelyn worked in silence, concentrating on her tasks. Rather than being awkward, the lack of conversation felt comfortable.

Something made me turn around. Tommy was standing in the doorway, a big grin on his face.

Tommy cleared his throat. "Mom, my science fair project got picked as a finalist. I get to exhibit it at MIT next month. The governor will be there."

Evelyn went to her son and put her arms around his shoulders, giving him a big hug.

"Congratulations," I said. "That's great."

At first, I felt genuinely pleased for Tommy. It sounded like a major accomplishment.

Then I thought about how the media would exploit this, should Tommy actually win. "Murdered Professor's Son Takes First Place in Local Science Fair, Follows in Dead Father's Footsteps." I could see the headlines now.

"Well done, Einstein," I said. "Do I see a Nobel prize in your future?"

"Hardly," he said, his voice cracking.

I quizzed Tommy about his project while Evelyn served the food and we sat down for dinner. The tournedos were nothing if not divine: Evelyn hadn't exaggerated. They were served with a mushroom sauce, accompanied by red bliss potatoes and string beans.

Evelyn's portion, like herself, was tiny, and she chewed every bite with great care. I ate heartily, feeling the rejuvenating effect of the food. Tommy wolfed down everything on his plate and went for seconds. Ten minutes after we'd started eating, Tommy asked to be excused and fled the kitchen, leaving Evelyn and me to linger over coffee and dessert, which consisted of scrumptious raspberry and kiwi tarts with a clear glaze. I could get used to this.

Sated, the feeling returned that I'd missed something during my search of the house. Where had Browne hidden his secrets? Where do most people hide stuff?

In plain sight? No, not likely, not with Evelyn having the run of the house. More likely I'd find a secret hidey hole in Mitchell's bedroom. Or maybe a hidden safe?

"Let's keep looking," I said.

Evelyn groaned, but she followed me upstairs, where I checked behind the framed sepia prints. No hidden safe. I examined Mitchell's closet more thoroughly.

"But it's completely empty," Evelyn said.

I stepped inside the closet and knocked on the cedar planks. The sound echoing back was hollow. I tried a spot six inches away, knocking again on the cedar. Hollow. I kept moving and knocking. Hollow, hollow, solid, solid. I stepped back and examined the shelves. Nothing. I pushed a chair into the closet, climbed, and checked the space above the shelves.

"There's a lock at the back of the closet," I said, my voice breathless. I peered closely at the keyhole. It was very small. "Those keys in your husband's desk—"

"I'll get them." Evelyn rushed out of the room. She reappeared a minute later, keys in hand. The third one fit the lock.

After some trial and error, I got the wood panel to snap back, and then the entire floor-to-ceiling cedar assembly slid sideways, revealing built-in shelves, a closet within a closet, the carpentry so seamless that the compartment was completely invisible from the outside. Browne's cubbyhole contained a veritable video library. There had to be well over a hundred tapes and CDs. But I was more interested in the four small cardboard boxes.

This time I'd brought a pair of plastic gloves, which I donned. I lifted the boxes one by one and carried them to the bed. The first one contained statements from two bank accounts in the Cayman Islands and in Switzerland. When I totaled up the amounts in both accounts, it came to over three million dollars—all money that Mitchell had squirreled away.

The second box contained a number of pornographic magazines. The third contained a large number of computer CDs labeled "T-CELLS." A fix for the virus-infested computer files? I set that box aside, having no intention of handing it over to the police, where it might be tied up in some evidence locker for months, if not years. Silverman could help Evelyn figure out what to do with the CDs. Maybe David could get Evelyn a better deal than Mitchell had been getting from Rutgers.

But it was with the fourth box that I hit pay dirt. This one contained hundreds of photographs of young girls—primarily Polaroids. I judged all of the girls to be eight or nine years old, and most of them were brown-skinned and exotic looking. Thai, I assumed. But it was a padded envelope at the top of the box that absolutely riveted my attention. It contained photographs of Phillip's daughter Chrissy—over fifty of them. Most of the pictures showed the girl on the beach, wearing a frilly pink-and-black polka-dot bathing suit. A few were close-ups of her face, with Chrissy first smiling at the camera and then looking slightly annoyed.

But most disturbing were the dozen or so candids of the girl asleep, her covers tossed carelessly aside and her nightgown hiked up over her hips, her legs splayed apart. Several of these photos were limp and dog-eared, like they'd been handled repeatedly.

Evelyn flinched when she recognized the photos for what they were.

The photos explained more eloquently than words why Phillip no longer associated with Mitchell. They also made it clear why Mitchell had left half his estate to Chrissy.

FORTY

I shoved Chrissy's photos back in the envelope, except one, which I put in my purse.

Motive. Could this be the motive for Browne's murder? Mitchell's niece was an incredibly beautiful child. Had he crossed the line?

The thought was too painful to contemplate, yet the photos gave credence to the idea.

Maybe the falling-out between the two brothers hadn't occurred over their father's estate, but over some ugly incident involving Chrissy. With that in mind, Phillip's pickup parked in front of Mitchell's house the night he was murdered took on a more ominous meaning.

Despite my reluctance to do so, I had to confirm my theory. I thought about talking to Amanda and Phillip, but they would probably deny the whole thing. And by talking to them, I would put their guard up. My best bet was to confront Chrissy directly.

One thing puzzled me. Why had Phillip waited two years to get even?

Had something else happened more recently? Had Mitchell made another overture? Or had Phillip just found out recently? Sometimes rape victims had flashbacks years after the original incident.

My mind was racing. I needed answers—and proof.

Opportunity. I had to show that Phillip was at Mitchell's house the night he was murdered. Tommy's account about spotting the pickup was all good and dandy, but I sensed it might not be enough.

Maybe I could get Phillip to admit he had been there. On tape. Tonight. Of course, taping a conversation without the person's knowledge was totally illegal in Massachusetts. It certainly wouldn't be admissible in court. But it would get the cops' attention—after they chastised me severely.

"What are you going to do with all this stuff?" Evelyn interrupted my thoughts.

"I'm trying to figure that out." I turned to Evelyn. "I'll let David sort it out. In the meantime, let's put everything back where we found it."

To make sure that the closet would remain locked, I pocketed the keys. I didn't totally trust Evelyn not to rummage around, thereby destroying or absconding with evidence. I headed to Tommy's room. He was sitting in front of the computer, concentrating intently on some schematic on the screen.

"Hey, Tommy."

My voice startled him and he almost knocked over a can of soda.

"Shit," he said, catching the can at the last moment.

"Sorry. I didn't mean to sneak up on you."

I sat down in the chair next to him and gave him my best Mary Poppins smile.

"Tommy, remember what you told me about your uncle's pickup truck?"

"Sure."

"Could you show me exactly where you saw it parked?"

He shrugged. The three of us headed out to the street. Tommy hung a left and stopped four houses down. He stepped into the road, stretching his arms out on both sides.

"It was parked right here," he said, "sort of blocking the driveway, and I remembered thinking that Mr. Russell—he's an ancient guy who drives a big boat of a Caddy—would have a fit if he saw the pickup in front of his driveway."

"Tommy, get back on the sidewalk," Evelyn shouted, her maternal instinct kicking into high gear as a car approached.

"I'd like to borrow your son for a couple of hours, Evelyn, if that's okay with you?"

After I finished explaining my plan, Evelyn said, "I'll come with you."

Just what I didn't need: a crowd. Or maybe I did. There was security in numbers.

"Okay, Evelyn, but you need to do exactly as I tell you."

I was thinking my plan would work even better if Evelyn tagged along.

We went back inside. Tommy, Evelyn, and I grabbed our coats and left in the Jetta, swinging by my house so that I could pick up the tape recorder and change into some clean clothes. I also double-checked that my pistol was loaded and ready to go, stowing it in my right coat pocket. It was my responsibility to keep Evelyn and her son safe from harm. Thus armed, I felt ready.

On the way to Concord I explained to Tommy and Evelyn what I was planning to do, and we rehearsed what I needed them to say. Then we ran through his spiel twice more.

"There's just one thing I don't understand," Tommy asked after a short silence. "Why would Uncle Phillip want to kill my father?"

"Well, it all goes back about two years, to when your grand-father died." I explained about the will, hoping it was sufficient to satisfy his curiosity. I did not want to get into a discussion of his father's perverse sexual proclivities.

After I finished, he said, "Two million. We'll be rich." But there wasn't any mirth in his voice. Any other thoughts he had on the matter, he kept to himself.

Minutes later we arrived at Phillip's house. The red F-250 stood in the driveway—big, new, and shiny, except for the dent on the right fender. Just as Tommy had described it.

Amanda's features went from surprise to dismay when she opened the door and saw Evelyn. Amanda's face looked like she'd taken a bite from an apple and discovered an unexpected worm.

"Hi. Hope you don't mind our dropping by," Evelyn said. "Tommy has some fabulous news he wanted to share with you."

In a glowing voice Tommy explained about his science fair project, finishing his speech by inviting Phillip and Amanda to the banquet with the governor. He was a terrific little actor.

I had instructed Tommy to keep Phillip and Amanda talking while I went in search of Chrissy. I hoped the awkwardness of having Evelyn there would serve as an added distraction. Tommy spoke about his science project, just as we'd rehearsed, and I asked Amanda if I could use the ladies room. She pointed toward a corridor off the kitchen. As soon as I was out of sight, I snuck upstairs in search of Chrissy.

I found the girl in her bedroom—a room all done up in bows, ribbons, pastel wallpaper—stuffed animals everywhere. She was lying on top of a canopy bed, on her stomach, her upper body propped up on her elbows and feet swinging back and forth in the air. Not a comfortable position for reading, but it seemed to work for her.

I clicked on the tape recorder inside my pocket and closed the door. I would only have a minute or two alone with her, so I had no choice but to be abrupt.

"Hello, Chrissy."

She looked up, her expression cautious.

"Your Aunt Evelyn and I went through your dead uncle's belongings today, and we found a bunch of pictures of you."

Her face contorted into a pained smile, but her eyes looked

terrified, with all her facial muscles seeming to bunch up. She was suddenly holding on the edge of the bed as if she were on a roller coaster, afraid of falling off.

I wished my tape recorder had visual input. Her body language said it all. Unfortunately she wasn't saying a word. She just sat there, looking terrified. I felt like a toad for torturing her like this, but at least now I was reasonably sure something bad *had* happened with her uncle.

"Look, I'm sorry to have to get into this, but I have to know. Your uncle Mitchell, he molested you, didn't he?"

She blinked hard, but still didn't say anything.

"Chrissy, for God's sake, tell me. Did he molest you?"

"Yes." She said it in a choked whisper. I hoped the tape would pick it up.

"This was when? Two years ago?"

Tears had started rolling down her cheek.

"Where did he molest you?"

"At Grandpa's house."

"Before your grandfather's death?"

She shook her head. "No. After. The day of the funeral."

Good God.

She started sobbing in earnest. I knelt down beside her and put my hand on her back. "It's okay now, Chrissy. He's dead. He can't hurt you anymore." A box of Kleenex sat on her nightstand. I pulled out a couple of tissues and handed them to her.

"He gave me something to drink. I couldn't stop him. I was like, limp."

I patted Chrissy back. "Did he molest you again after that day?"

She shook her head from side to side.

"I'm sorry I had to hurt you by asking, but I needed to know. Just one more question, Chrissy. Do your parents know what your uncle did to you?"

306

She didn't answer. She was crying into her comforter.

God, I hated doing this to her. Hated even more what this would do to Phillip and to her family. Sometimes I don't like myself when I have a job to do. How could I possibly make this turn out right?

"Chrissy, please. I need to know. Did you tell your mom or dad about what happened with your uncle?"

She nodded yes just as the door behind me opened.

"What the hell is going on here?"

My head snapped around. Amanda was standing on the threshold. She looked pissed, teeth clenched, hands on her hips.

"Chrissy and I are talking about her dead uncle."

Amanda took in the crying girl on the bed, me kneeling beside her, the box of tissues in my hand. "You had better leave. You've caused quite enough grief for one night."

Chrissy was sobbing openly. Amanda grabbed my arm and physically shoved me out the door. I was surprised that she didn't stay to comfort her daughter. Instead, she herded me down the stairs.

In the family room, Phillip, Tommy, and Evelyn were sitting on the sofa, involved in what looked like an animated conversation. Phillip's pleasant expression fell when he caught sight of his wife. A wealth of nonverbal communication flashed back and forth between husband and wife in a split second.

"Macy wants to leave," Amanda announced.

I couldn't wait to get out of there, but I still had my most important question to ask.

"Phillip," I said, "I found out that you went to your brother's the night he was killed. Why did you go to his house?"

Phillip looked stunned.

"How did you—"

"Phillip didn't go see Mitchell that night," Amanda cut in sharply. "He was with a client. We already told you that."

I tried hard to keep my voice casual when I spoke. "The neighbor two doors down from Evelyn, a Mr. Russell, called the police to have your pickup towed. Your vehicle was blocking his driveway. He lives in the fourth house south of the Browne residence."

It was a lie, but a good one. I waited a few seconds, feeling the tension in the room build. "That made you the last person to see Mitchell alive, Phillip. What did he say to you?"

"Mitchell wasn't home. I didn't get to see him."

Gotcha, I thought. I had Phillip admitting that he'd been at Mitchell's house the night he was murdered. Better yet, I had it on tape.

"Too bad," I said. "I was hoping he might have said something important to you. What time was it when you dropped by?"

"Err—around nine." Phillip's tone sounded defensive.

"Are you sure it wasn't later," I said. "The police report says that the neighbor called around ten."

I could see tiny beads of perspiration form on Phillip's forehead.

"Phillip was home by nine-thirty. I can vouch for that," Amanda cut in sharply.

"I see," I said. "What made you swing by? It must have been important, after not seeing him for nearly two years."

He shrugged. "I just happened to be in the neighborhood. I don't need a special reason to see my brother." He tried to smile, but his facial muscles refused to cooperate.

Likely story, I thought. If Tommy and Evelyn had not been with me, I would have asked Phillip point blank whether he killed his brother because he found out that Mitchell had molested his daughter. But I didn't want to get into the pedophile thing with Tommy present—nor did I want to do anything that might push Phillip over the edge, for that matter. It was my responsibility to deliver mother and son safe and sound back home. I'd let the cops handle Phillip.

"It's a shame you didn't catch Mitchell at home. He might still be alive if you had."

Phillip looked perturbed, his face a dark, brooding mask.

If there was going to be trouble, it would happen now. My hand closed firmly around the butt of the Glock inside the pocket of my coat.

Tommy had stood up. "I'm glad both of you can make it to the banquet," he said in a hopeful tone with just the appropriate hint of uncertainty in his voice.

The kid was a regular Laurence Olivier. But beneath his veneer of nonchalance, I bet his heart was racing.

We left without incident.

"See, I told you I wasn't lying," Tommy said when we reached the bottom of the driveway. But there was no mirth or triumph in his voice. "What happens now?"

"The police will handle it."

He paused for a minute. "Did you get everything on tape?"

"I hope so. Let's drive down the road a bit before we check the recording."

I watched the rearview mirror. The road behind me was empty. When I thought it was safe, I pulled into a driveway. I rewound the tape part way. The quality of the recording was surprisingly clear.

Tommy turned and looked at Evelyn. "You think this'll get Mom off?"

"Oh, I hope so," I said. "I sure hope so."

But I wasn't feeling jubilant, because, underneath it all, I thought Phillip wasn't a bad person. Just a man who'd been pushed too far.

And then there was Chrissy. Her uncle had put her through hell. It would take years for her to regain her trust in men—if ever. And now I would be sending her father to prison. None of it seemed right.

FORTY-ONE

When I woke Friday morning I felt out of sorts. This whole business with Chrissy was making my stomach churn.

I had tried to shrug it off, to no avail. Becoming sentimental wasn't part of my job description—not if I wanted to continue functioning effectively as a private investigator.

I made my bed and picked up all of my discarded clothes before heading out for my customary run. During the quick tidy up, I noticed a piece of paper wedged under the front door. A note. I unfolded it.

"Since your car is back, I gather you're still among the living. If you feel like going for a jog this morning, call me. Jack."

It was a tempting offer. Having Jack along would add some bounce to my stride. I could use some cheering up this morning. I reached for the phone.

When he stopped by ten minutes later, Jack looked much too handsome, dressed in black running shorts and a jade top that matched his eyes.

"You think you can keep up with me?" I teased him.

He laughed. "And I was going to take it easy on you. Forget it."

I ran a little faster than normal, pushing myself hard, and he *did* keep up, though I could tell by his labored breathing that it was a strain. Well, he *had* asked for it, and I *did* ease up after the first mile.

When we got back to the house, he bent over at the waist.

"Not bad . . . for a girl," he said, between deep gasps.

"Not bad yourself—for an old guy."

"Ouch."

"I usually lose 'em after the first quarter mile."

"Do you do this all the time?"

"Do what?"

"Torture men?"

It was my turn to laugh, not so much because of his line, but the expression on his face was priceless.

"What are you?" he gasped. "Some sort of college track star? You should have warned me."

"Hell no. A girl likes to keep a few secrets."

"Want to stop by my place for some coffee? I'm buying."

I felt tempted. But I would not set foot in his house again.

"Listen Jack," I said. "It's over. We'll be just casual acquaintances from now on."

He shifted his weight. "How's the murder investigation going?"

"Good. It's almost wrapped up."

"Really? I'm impressed. So who did it? The butler?"

"No, the brother."

"Wow." He whistled. "Not exactly a *Leave-It-to-Beaver* family."

"No, not at all. And you don't know the half of it."

"Is he behind bars?"

"Not yet. Hopefully that'll happen sometime today."

"Well, I'll say one thing. I'll be real glad when they put this character away so I can stop worrying about your safety."

"Jack. You're a sweet man. I hope you and your wife work things out."

"And if not?"

I dashed off to the carriage house, waving to him over my shoulder. Damn it, part of me still longed to pull him into my room and rip his clothes off. But I suppressed that thought and took a lukewarm shower instead.

I shifted my thoughts to more pressing matters. When I last talked to David Silverman, he told me he'd be in charge of orchestrating events this morning. All I had to do was show up at Evelyn's house around nine.

By the time I arrived, half the "orchestra" had already assembled in Evelyn's living room. It consisted of the fingerprint guy, Wilson, part of David's forensic team, and several of his associates. David's anorexic paralegal was filing her nails on the settee. David himself presided over a "strategy session."

Evelyn entered from the kitchen, carrying a tray of coffee fixings and muffins. She seemed to be in her element, smiling at everyone as she arranged food, napkins, china, and silverware on the sideboard.

The cops showed up shortly thereafter. I was happy to see Pascucci among them. He gave me a curt nod. After brief introductions were made, I took everyone upstairs and unlocked the hidden compartment in Browne's closet. The cops went to work, cataloguing the contents. My presence seemed entirely superfluous.

David pulled me aside. "I have the phone records you wanted."

"So fast?"

"It helps to have friends in the right places."

He handed me an envelope. Inside was a list of incoming calls for the night of the murder, five of them, all from the 508 area code. The first call came in at 8:59, the last at 9:46. I immediately recognized Phillip's home number: he had rung three times, all three calls coming shortly after nine p.m. He had obviously lied when he told me he dropped by the house at nine. It must have been earlier—or later.

Unless Amanda made the calls. That *was* another possibility.

From the sheet I noticed that the conversations had been short, about thirty seconds each. Except the last one, which was about three minutes long.

But wait a second, I thought. Who had answered the phone? According to Evelyn, they didn't get home from dinner until after 9:30.

"Grab a muffin before they're all gone, Macy," Evelyn interrupted my thoughts, playing hostess.

"Evelyn, you're positively spoiling me. But I love it."

"I could teach you how to make these."

She handed me a muffin on a plate. It had a very rich, lemony flavor. Heavenly.

"Evelyn, these are sensational."

"Coffee?"

"Sure," I said, distracted. "Evelyn, the night your husband was killed, what time was it when you got home from the restaurant?"

"Around nine-forty," she said. "I add some grated lemon peel. That's how the muffins get that tangy flavor."

"They're the best muffins I've ever had. Honest. Nine-forty, you said? Was Tommy home?"

"No." She looked puzzled.

"Did you get any telephone calls?"

"No."

I showed her the printout. "Someone picked up these calls."

She furrowed her brow. "Must have been Mitchell's machine."

"Mitchell had an answering machine?"

"Well, not an actual machine. He had voice mail, you know, from the phone company?"

My God. The messages from the night of the murder were still sitting somewhere in voice mail cyberspace.

"Do you know how to access his messages?"

"No. I don't. Why are you asking?"

"Phillip called your husband a bunch of times the night he was killed. Whatever he said was undoubtedly important."

David had been eavesdropping on our conversation. I turned to him, but he had already picked up the phone.

Five minutes later a small group of us was gathered in Mitchell's study. David put his contact from the phone company on the speakerphone.

A quiet hush preceded the first message. Finally a voice came from the squawk box. *"Mitchell, Phillip. I have to talk to you. It's urgent, please call me as soon as you get in."*

The operator's voice went through the standard announcement before the second message came on. *"Mitchell, Phillip again. Please call. It's urgent."*

I was surprised at the third message. *"Mitchell. I need to see you. Call me."* A woman's voice, with a lot of static in the background. The voice sounded familiar somehow, but I couldn't place it offhand.

The next message was another one from Phillip. *"Mitchell, if you're there, pick up . . . Mitchell? Oh, hell. I'm coming over."*

The following call was a hang-up. There had been four messages. I wondered about the fifth call. The one that came in at 9:46. Mitchell must have picked it up personally.

David thanked his contact at the phone company. After he hung up, David left us and went to a quiet corner of the room to confer with a man whom—by the impeccable cut of his suit—I judged to be a lawyer. Maybe someone from the D.A.'s office? I watched as the two conversed intently. Everyone else dispersed. With no one paying any particular attention to me, it dawned on me that my role in this drama was finally winding down. I took a seat in the living room, thinking about my next move, when Pascucci walked in.

"Why so glum?" he said. "You ought to be celebrating. You did what the police couldn't do."

I shrugged. "You think it's enough to exonerate Evelyn?"

"That's up to the D.A., but my guess is that this new evidence pokes too many holes in their case to take Evelyn to trial."

"Is Phillip Browne going to be charged?"

"Not yet. They won't want to end up with egg on their faces twice on the same case."

"So what's the next step?"

"We'll be bringing Phillip in for questioning this afternoon."

I must have looked pretty downcast, because Pascucci sat down on the sofa next to me and put an arm around my shoulder.

"So why the long face?"

"Nothing, everything's just fine," I said. "Oh, hell, it's the thought of Phillip incarcerated at Walpole for the next twenty years. It doesn't strike me as . . . right."

"Why? You think he's innocent?"

"At least on some level, yes. I can see why he did it."

"That's a bunch of baloney, Macy. Where would we be if every time a private citizen thought he had a problem, he took the law into his own hands?"

"Oh, I don't know. I think the concept holds a certain appeal."

He dropped his arm from my shoulder and gave me a sharp look. "Be careful what you wish for. Phillip did have other options. He could have gone to the authorities to get redress from a court of law."

"Yes, but in order to do that, he'd have put his daughter through hell. Think about that. She was very young at the time. Think about her having to relive all the ugly details, in a public forum. Think about her having to face her accuser. It's like getting raped twice."

"They make it easier on victims now. The court would have let her testify in chambers, on videotape."

We both fell quiet. The seconds ticked by.

"What time are you bringing him in?"

"After lunch." He stood. "I think you're being too hard on yourself. Get over it. You did the right thing."

I found David Silverman in the kitchen, talking to Evelyn. I asked him if he needed anything else from me. He thanked me for doing a fine job and said that if something else occurred to him, he'd let me know. But for now, I could take off.

I left. It was in the hands of the lawyers now, with the wheels of justice grinding away ever so slowly.

Back at the office I found several messages. Dubs had called to ask me to join her and a few friends at The Country Club for dinner on Saturday night. I called her back.

"Imagine," she said, "the guy I had a date with tonight cancelled at the last minute. What's wrong with Boston men? Maybe you and I should move somewhere else. New York, California . . ."

"I prefer being dateless to living through transportation strikes, earthquakes, fires, mud slides, and riots. Besides, Dubs, I'm getting too old to acquire a whole new set of friends."

Boston men indeed. Well, there was Jack. Maybe Boston had some potential after all. Or maybe not. I didn't want to think about it.

I started typing my report for David Silverman, a vague sense of dissatisfaction still gnawing at my gut.

Why didn't I feel a sense of closure? The case was solved, wasn't it?

Maybe it was because I still had unanswered questions. At best, I could speculate about what had happened the night of the murder. And who was the mystery woman that called Mitchell the night he was killed? I sure wished I'd been able to identify her voice.

And what about the alleged appointment with the potential

client Phillip claimed he had that evening? Had Amanda made that up? That would have been stupid. It would be so easy to check.

On impulse, I grabbed the phone book off the shelf and found a listing for a David Hansen in Arlington. I dialed the number. A woman's voice answered, "Hello?"

"Hi, my name is Macy Adams," I chirped. "I'm calling on behalf of Metropolitan Life and Casualty regarding an insurance claim. Could I ask you a few questions?"

"What's this about?" she asked, guarded. She sounded wary, like I might be some telemarketer trying to sell her something she didn't want.

"A red pickup truck was involved in a hit-and-run Friday night, two weeks ago. An eyewitness got the first two digits of the license plate. One of the vehicles pulled up by the DMV computer belongs to a Phillip Browne. I spoke to Mr. Browne earlier today, and he claims that he was at your house during the time of the accident. I'd just like to verify his whereabouts on the night in question. Was Phillip Browne at your house Friday evening, that would be the fourteenth?"

"Yes, he was."

"What time did he arrive at your house?"

"Around eight."

"I see . . . and when did he leave?"

"At eight-thirty. He received an urgent call from his wife. That's why he had to go. He said there was some kind of family emergency."

"Short meeting. You're sure it was eight-thirty?"

"Oh yes. He was right on time and stayed only half an hour."

Interesting, I thought. Very interesting. If he left the Hansens, he could have dropped by Mitchell's house and still made it home by nine-thirty. Or had Amanda lied?

"Well, thank you, Mrs. Hansen. I really appreciate your help."

I offered a quick good-bye and hung up.

I included my conversation with Mrs. Hansen in the report for David. After I finished typing the document, I readied my final bill for services rendered and attached it with a paper clip.

Having nothing better to do, I decided to drop by the police station to see what, if any, new information I could pick up.

Inside the precinct, I found an empty seat on a bench near the entrance. I watched the stream of human shipwrecks as they made their way through a sea of attorneys.

I stood when they brought Phillip in. He looked stoic, not even glancing my way as he was being led past.

Shortly after, Claire Browne rushed into the precinct, alongside a lawyerly-looking man. Even from down the hall I could hear her voice. "This whole circus is ridiculous."

They disappeared through a closed door.

I caught Pascucci on his way to the interrogation room.

"Could I talk with you?"

"Make it quick," he said.

I briefly told him about my telephone conversation with Mrs. Hansen.

"Listen, Macy," he said. "Please don't think that we don't appreciate the cooperation you've given us on this case. But from now on, it would be better if you let the police handle it. You've done all you can. Let it go, for your mental health, if nothing else. I can tell this case is depressing the hell out of you."

He patted me on the shoulder and hurried away.

How patronizing! It wasn't my mental state Pascucci was concerned about. It was a turf issue, plain and simple. He wanted me, Miss Private Citizen, to butt out of what had become strictly a police case.

I was debating whether I should bother staying. Phillip would be here for hours, and even after he was finished, it was questionable whether Pascucci would tell me anything that had been said behind closed doors. Especially in view of the way he had just treated me.

Claire Browne's voice snapped me out of my reverie.

"Oh, it's you again. This is all your fault."

I looked up. She was standing in front of me, her eyes hot with anger.

"Are you proud of yourself, getting an innocent man dragged down here? You know what you are? A disgusting busybody. A repulsive troublemaker. That's what you are. Can't you see that Phillip is the *one* decent human being in this whole sordid mess? But you just had to smear him with your lies. There's one thing I'd like to know: How do you sleep nights?"

Her voice had turned shrill. She pointed a finger at me. "You'll pay for this. You'll rot in hell."

She turned on her heels and stomped out of the building.

FORTY-TWO

Claire Browne's words reverberated inside my head as I left the police station. *"Phillip is the one decent human being in this whole sordid mess. How do you sleep nights?"*

The temperature outside the precinct was cool, the weather overcast and gloomy, matching my mood. I slid into the Jetta and started the engine, driving away deep in thought. Something kept gnawing at me. I had a feeling of incompletion. What had I overlooked? I felt like some crucial fact was lodged in my subconscious, where it failed to float to the surface.

From experience I knew that the more I thought about it, the further it would recede.

At home, I took off my dress, peeled off the tan pantyhose, and slipped into an old pair of khakis. I went to the kitchen and brewed a cup of Claire's wonderful coffee. Then I rounded up the various notebooks, reports, and scraps of paper that I had accumulated on the Browne case. I wasn't sure what I was looking for, but something in this pile had to spark a memory.

I started with the autopsy report, glancing first at the gruesome photos, then rereading the text carefully. There was the Valium. Right away, it felt wrong. Phillip was strong and muscular from working construction. He would use his fists instead of drugs to knock out his brother. Especially in a fit of anger. I wrote down *Phillip . . . Valium . . . NO!*

Poisons and drugs were methods favored by *women* when doing away with someone. That was the stereotype, at least. The

Valium was the reason the police had immediately suspected Evelyn. Was there another woman with the motive to kill Mitchell? I wrote down the word *woman*, underlining it twice. Then I wrote *Amanda?*

Next I went through my notes of the eyewitness reports. Mitchell's car had been spotted at the Cambridge boathouse around ten o'clock. Phillip's last call from his house was made at 9:29. Was that enough time to travel from Concord to Cambridge and take Mitchell down to the river? I wasn't sure. The timing seemed tight. Of course the eyewitness account could be off by a few minutes. Still . . .

I wrote down *travel time Concord/Cambridge at 9:30 p.m.?*

In the notes I'd taken after my first conversation with Pascucci I found an item I'd completely forgotten. The cigarette butts in Browne's car—two Marlboros.

Phillip didn't smoke. Neither did anyone else close to Mitchell that I could remember—except his secretary. There could be a perfectly innocent explanation for the butts. Maybe Mitchell had given Jane a ride at some point. Or maybe Jane had been the person with him by the river that night. Maybe Jane had killed Mitchell? I wrote down *Jane Ramirez.*

I couldn't think of a motive why Jane might want to dispose of her boss. But that didn't mean there wasn't one. Another thought surfaced. Would the killer have been stupid enough to leave cigarette butts behind? Very unlikely—unless he or she had been in a hurry. Or been interrupted . . .

Mentally I went through the list of the other women in Mitchell's life: Evelyn, Dawn, Amanda. My impression was that all of them were nonsmokers. Or maybe not a woman, but a teenager experimenting with smoking? Tommy? No, that didn't make any sense at all.

Where else had I seen cigarette butts? I drew a blank.

For all I knew the discarded cigarettes could have been in

Mitchell's car for some time, if he were the stereotypical male who'd wait until hell froze over before bothering to clean out an ashtray. Cleaning up was probably Evelyn's job.

Okay, the cigarette butts were probably a dead end.

I'd been so absorbed in my thoughts that I'd almost forgotten to drink my coffee. I gulped it down while it was still hot, mentally thanking Claire for giving me the free sample of her exquisite brew. Thinking of Claire reminded me of the impatiens, which were still sitting in the plastic trays on the brick patio out back. I'd completely forgotten to water them—let alone plant them. It was while I sprinkled water over the flowers that a sudden insight surfaced: Claire Browne was a smoker.

I was stunned for a moment, almost dropping the watering can. Had I actually seen her smoke? I wasn't sure, but I was certain I had smelled the scent of secondhand smoke on her clothing. Which didn't mean the Marlboro butts in Mitchell's car were hers. Or that she'd killed Mitchell, for that matter. After all, a mother killing her own son? It was a stretch.

I went back to the kitchen to refill the watering can. Going back outside, I noticed that the sky was opening up, a few patches of blue peeking through the gray clouds.

A thought kept churning in my mind while I continued watering the plants. What had Claire said the morning I talked to her, when she was thinning out some of the weaker stalks? *Pity you can't do this with people?* To whom had she been referring? To her own son? Was it possible?

The Valium would certainly fit. But had Claire known that Evelyn slipped tranquilizers into her husband's butternut squash? Most likely Phillip had told her all about it. Phillip was her favorite son, as were his children. What if Claire found out recently—say two weeks ago—that her oldest son had molested her granddaughter? She'd be outraged. I myself had witnessed her acid temper, remembering her outburst at the police station. Also, Claire definitely possessed the requisite physical strength for dragging a dead body into the river. Her horticultural job kept her in great shape.

Claire's behavior had been erratic from the first time I talked with her. Initially, she'd as good as accused Evelyn of murdering Mitchell. Then Claire had tried to steer me in the direction of BioCorp. And Claire had insisted that Mitchell told Evelyn he was divorcing her, when even Mitchell's divorce attorney didn't believe that Evelyn had been aware of Mitchell's plans.

I checked my watch. Just past six. It would bug the hell out of me all weekend if I didn't get to the bottom of this. I could return to the nursery tonight, under the guise of buying more plants, to see if I could find any spent cigarette butts in Claire's office. If she smoked Marlboros, I'd consider Claire more seriously. If not—I'd drop the whole idea. I grabbed my car keys and my pistol and drove to Concord.

By the time I got there, however, the nursery was already closed. Not a single car in the parking lot. So much the better, I thought. I donned plastic gloves, retrieved the lock picks from the trunk of my car, and started working the dead bolt of the back door.

After ten minutes I gave up. The skin on my knees felt raw from kneeling on the rough wooden stoop, and I nearly had a heart attack each time a car drove by. I'd never really gotten the hang of using the picks. So much for finesse—I'd have to do this the old-fashioned way: break my way into the place. Unfortunately it would alert Claire come morning that she'd been burglarized.

I spotted several masonry bricks that someone had used to prop up a display of flowerpots. I dislodged one of them and smashed a glass panel of the rear door with it. Reaching inside, I twisted the dead bolt open, careful to avoid the jagged edges of glass.

I listened for an alarm. But the quiet was profound, except for a dog barking off in the distance. The barking stopped, and the ensuing silence was almost eerie. It was so still that I could hear my own heartbeat.

The air inside the store was stuffy. It smelled of dried flowers and earth, mixed with a pungent chemical odor. Insecticides?

I closed the door, which left the inside of the shop in almost complete darkness. But I did not dare turn on the fluorescent overhead lights. I pulled a penlight from my handbag and turned it on. Its scant light cut a sharp beam through the dusty air. I moved swiftly to Claire's office at the back of the store.

Sure enough, there *was* an ashtray in the middle of Claire's desk. I shone my penlight on its contents. A veritable graveyard of cigarette butts, all the same brand: Marlboros. Using a letter opener, I maneuvered several butts into the Ziploc bag I'd brought. I was pretty sure what a DNA comparison would show.

My eyes stopped on a piece of paper on top of the desk: Claire's cellular telephone invoice. There was Mitchell's phone number—twice. The last call had been made at 9:46 the night he was killed. So Claire had been the mystery caller Mitchell had spoken to right before he was murdered. I wished I'd made the connection earlier.

I began checking the desk drawers. I didn't have to look far: cramped into the back of the top right drawer was a vial of Valium and a key ring. The patient listed on the tranquilizer prescription was Claire Browne. I recognized the gothic insignia on the key ring immediately: *PRU-DEN-TIA,* Wadsworth University's motto. Attached to it a car key, embossed with a slanted L in an oval, which I bet would fit snugly into the ignition of Browne's Jaguar. The key next to it on the key ring was an old-fashioned skeleton type. The key to Mitchell's desk?

Why hadn't Claire gotten rid of this incriminating evidence?

I was putting the Valium and key ring back in the drawer,

when I heard a low sound. I froze. The noise was tiny, like claws scraping on wood. Mice?

The hair at the nape of my neck prickled. Something was out there. I felt I wasn't alone. I pointed the penlight toward the entrance of the room. Beyond the office door, in the corridor, some good ten or fifteen feet away, the beam of the penlight picked up shiny, black fur. Claire Browne's Doberman let out a low growl when I shone the light in his eyes.

The dog seemed as confused by my presence as I was by his. Maybe he recognized my scent from before, but couldn't quite place me, and was uncertain whether I was friend or foe. We both stood stock still, staring at each other. I took the Glock out of my pocket. Gun in hand, I moved toward the door in slow motion. After a few steps the dog caught on. As if someone had sounded an attack bugle, it took off. Both of us scrambled toward the door, reaching it at about the same time. Just as I was slamming the door shut, one hundred pounds of dog energy smashed into it on the other side. The impact pushed me back slightly, and for a moment I wasn't sure whether I would be able to hold the beast off. But then the door latch snapped shut. Lucky me that Dobermans couldn't twist doorknobs.

The dog made a few half-hearted running attacks from the other side, crashing into the wood. Then he began to scratch the door vigorously.

After a minute of scratching, he gave it up. Ever resourceful, the Dobie started barking ferociously. The sound was threatening and primal, and it made my skin crawl with dread and fear.

I checked the window. It was high up and small. I didn't think I could fit through it.

Terrific. I was being held hostage by a howling dog. I'd pay a thousand bucks for a quarter pound of ground sirloin right about now. I could take a page out of Evelyn's book and mix a couple of Valiums into the sirloin, which would do wonders for the beast's overzealous disposition. I didn't care if he ate the evidence.

I had my Glock. I could shoot the dog if I needed to, but I didn't have the heart to kill an innocent animal.

Then I had another unpleasant thought. Where was Claire Browne?

Maybe I should call 9-1-1? But no. When I smashed the window, I'd taken that option out of play. I had broken the law. A B&E on my record could cost me my P.I. license.

I was contemplating my next move, when the door flew open. Claire Browne barged into the room, a shotgun in her hand. She fired into the ceiling above my head, sending a shower of broken plaster over me. I hit the floor, my ears ringing from the blast.

"Don't shoot," I shouted. "It's only me."

The dog let out a low, menacing growl and I could hear him pace, his claws making the scratching sound I'd heard earlier.

"Get up," Claire ordered.

I stood, hands raised in the air.

"What the hell are you doing here?"

"I—" My brain went completely blank.

The dog started barking again.

"Shush, Duke," Claire shouted. "Bad dog." The Dobie kept up his howling, however. She nudged him in the side with her left knee. "Sit. Shush. Bad dog."

While she was trying to quiet the dog, I had pulled my right earring off and dropped it on the floor next to the desk.

"Well?" she addressed me again.

"This is sort of embarrassing," I stammered, "but I was look-ing for an earring. I must have dropped it when I was here the other day. Trouble is, the earrings don't belong to me, they belong to a friend. They are heirlooms, real gold and valuable, and my friend needs them back tonight because she's having dinner with her grandmother . . . who had given her the ear-rings." I was rambling. "So I came by, thinking you'd be open. When I got here, the place was closed. I'm real sorry about the window. I'll pay for the repairs, of course."

God only knew what she made of my story. I hoped she was buying it.

From the look on her face, she seemed to be at least consider-ing what I had said.

"Back up, all the way to the corner," she ordered gruffly.

I moved back slowly, keeping my hands in the air.

She walked around the desk, keeping the shotgun trained on me. Then her eyes wandered to the Glock on the desktop. I could see a shift in the expression on her face. She gave me a look filled with pure hate.

"Were you thinking of shooting my dog?"

"No, no. Of course not."

"Back up further. And keep those hands in the air," she com-manded.

Again I complied. She took a seat in the chair behind the desk, keeping the shotgun aimed at my chest.

"So what were you really looking for? And I don't buy that earring story for a second, so save it."

Her eyes fell on the open drawer. "Oh, so you already found what you were looking for. Clever. That's too bad—for you. Curiosity killed the cat, you know."

"What do you mean?"

"Don't play innocent. I see the Valium and Mitchell's keys. So did *you*."

"Why didn't you get rid of the stuff?"

She shrugged. "Insurance, in case the police decided to pin this on Phillip."

She came around the side of the desk and pushed the drawer shut. "I won't let my son take the rap for me. If the D.A. doesn't drop the charges, I'll come forward and confess. These two items are insurance, so they'll take me seriously. So what tipped *you* off?"

"The cigarette butts in Mitchell's car."

"They don't prove anything."

"No, they don't. But they showed me that you were with him."

"Stupid of me. I should have cleaned them up."

"They'll charge Phillip with murder."

"I wouldn't be so sure. All the evidence against him is circumstantial. I'm sure they'll drop the case. Of course, nobody would have thought of Phillip in the first place if it hadn't been for your snooping. And you lied. There was no police report about Phillip's truck blocking a driveway."

"Why did Phillip go to Mitchell's house that night?"

"He came to head *me* off. He was too late, of course. By the time he got there, Mitchell and I had already left." Claire backed away. "Where are your car keys?"

"In my coat."

"Take your coat off, nice and easy, and toss it on the table. And keep your hands where I can see them."

I did as she commanded. Claire fumbled through my coat pockets, found my keys, and threw them on the desk.

"You drive. And keep your hands in the air."

I complied. She herded me outside, occasionally prodding me in the back with the shotgun. We must have cut quite the picture, hostage and captor. Unfortunately, there was no passing driver to see it. My bad luck.

"Open the passenger door," she ordered.

The barrel of the shotgun remained aimed at my head while I walked around the car and slid into the driver's seat. She pulled my own gun out of her pocket and pointed it at me, stowing the shotgun in the back seat.

"Where are we going?" I asked, surprised at the eerie calm I felt. It was as though this whole thing was happening to somebody else. What was wrong with me? Claire was probably going to kill me.

"You'll find out soon enough. Take Route 2 West. And keep both hands on the wheel."

The moon was almost full, a light breeze pushing banks of clouds across its yellow orb. The road and its surrounding landscape were alternately illuminated in sallow light or thrown into opaque darkness as the clouds shifted overhead.

The flow of traffic on Route 2 was too fast to chance engineering a car accident, too great a risk of turning both Claire and me into crash dummies. My mind was racing feverishly, trying to think of a way to get my hands on the gun. I needed to create some sort of diversion. But how?

Claire had two inches and about forty pounds on me, all muscle. I doubted whether I would win a wrestling match with her. The only bit of good luck was that she'd left the dog back at the nursery. The mere thought of a Doberman's choppers attacking my face made me feel faint. And though I was a fast sprinter, I harbored no illusions about being able to outrun a large dog.

"Don't speed," Claire warned.

Without my noticing it, the speedometer needle had crept up. Adrenaline.

"So why did you do it?" I asked her.

"You already figured that part out. You know what Mitchell did to Chrissy."

"But he was your son."

"So what? That's no excuse. He was despicable, every bit as twisted as his father."

"Your husband was a pedophile?"

She was quiet. Miraculously, talking with her eased my fear.

Claire seemed so calm and rational. She wasn't acting like a crazed killer. I figured if I could just keep the dialogue going, maybe I could talk her out of whatever she was planning to do to me. After all, the idea of turning herself in had already crossed her mind.

"Did your husband molest his sons?" I asked.

"Ex-husband," she snapped. "And I said he was a pedophile, not that he was gay. He molested my daughter."

"Mitchell had a sister? How come no one ever mentioned her?"

I suddenly noticed Claire's hair, which for once wasn't covered by a bandana. It was blond and crinkly. I'd seen the same type of hair before—in the old photographs from Mitchell Browne's desk.

"That girl in the picture I showed you. She was your daughter?"

Claire didn't answer. Now that I looked at her more closely, I noticed even more of a resemblance. She had the same jutting chin and the same high broad forehead as the girl in the photo.

"Keep your eyes on the road," Claire admonished.

"Where's your daughter now?"

"She's dead," she said in a whisper. "She killed herself on her seventeenth birthday."

"Because of what your husband did to her?"

Again, she didn't answer.

"Is that why you divorced him?"

There was a faraway look in her eyes. I was losing her.

"Why didn't you stop him? Why did you let him do that to your daughter?"

That got her. "Because I didn't know. I had no idea. Back then, we didn't have talk shows that paraded all sorts of sickness in front of the general public. To think that a father would . . . with his own daughter . . . well, it was simply inconceivable. It never occurred to me that a man might be capable of doing something so utterly perverse. By the time I found out, it was too late. It wasn't my fault."

There was genuine anguish in her voice. It was obvious that she *had* been blaming herself for her daughter's death, that she'd been living with that guilt for decades. Finding out about Chrissy must have finally pushed her over the edge.

"I had no idea what Octavius had done to our daughter until I read her suicide note," she said, her voice quavering.

We drove in silence.

"Why did your husband disinherit Phillip? Did that have something to do with your daughter?"

"No, it had nothing to do with her. He found out that Phillip wasn't his child."

For some reason, her admission of Phillip's illegitimacy threw me for a loop. Claire was so plain. With her air of no-nonsense, pillar-of-the-community arrogance, it was a real stretch to envision her as a seductive siren engaged in an illicit love affair.

Not having the same father explained the lack of a family resemblance between Phillip and Mitchell.

"So who was Phillip's father?"

"The gardener."

"And what happened to him?"

"He got married and raised his own family. I never told him about Phillip. And he wasn't smart enough to figure it out for himself."

"Does Phillip know?"

"No. Take the next exit," she said, the authoritative tone back in her voice.

FORTY-THREE

The exit coming up was west of Littleton, in a rural area I'd never been to before. Nothing looked familiar.

A sense of dread rose in my gut. Being buried in a shallow grave in an isolated wooded area was not how I'd envisioned the culmination of my career as a private eye.

"Take a right, at the clearing, behind the trees."

Claire pointed to a small dirt path. I followed the narrow lane, which went all the way to a lake, the path ending in a concrete decline that was probably used as a boat ramp in the summer.

I was beginning to discern her plan. Macy Adams was a nuisance that Claire wished would disappear. Claire would dispose of me in the same way she'd disposed of her son—in the water. Then she'd drive my car back to Cambridge and park it somewhere. It might be days before I'd be missed.

And months, if ever, before my body was found.

Except that I didn't intend to go down without a fight. Even if she succeeded in killing me, she wouldn't get away with it.

Instead of downshifting, I left the car in third, coasting along on the clutch, which I released abruptly. Predictably, the car stalled.

Both of us were thrown forward by the sudden halt. In what I hoped was an unobtrusive motion, I flipped the kill switch I'd asked the dealer to install under the dashboard to the "off" position. I wouldn't be able to start the car again. Neither would

Claire. So much for her getaway plan.

"I think we just ran out of gas," I said.

"Nonsense, the gauge says the tank's half full. You stalled the motor on purpose."

She pointed the gun squarely at my forehead.

"Start the engine," she snarled.

I turned the ignition key, but the car just made a sick, grinding noise, the engine refusing to turn over.

"I don't know what's wrong with it," I said, trying to make my voice sound panicked. "Honest." I feigned another attempt at starting the motor.

"I'm going to count. By the time I get to ten, you had better have this thing running, or you'll have a bullet in your head."

"The carburetor sticks sometimes," I ad libbed. Never mind that I didn't even know what a carburetor was.

"Then fix it."

"I'll try," I said, unbuckling my car seat.

I opened the car door and popped the hood lever, scooping up some sand with my left hand as I climbed out. Claire kept her distance from me, the Glock pointed at my head.

I lifted the hood, favoring my empty right hand, and leaned into the engine. I unscrewed something, having absolutely no idea what. But suddenly I held a car part in my hand.

"Didn't you say it was the carburetor?" Claire asked suspiciously.

Damn, she probably knew more about cars than I did. In fact, she was probably one of those women who could fix a motor in a pinch. I put the car part on the fender and angled slightly to my left.

Claire had narrowed the distance between us. She was right behind me now, the Glock in her hand almost close enough for me to touch.

Moving in a flash, I ran into her and grabbed the wrist of her gun hand, simultaneously tossing sand into her face. The gun went off, and the stray bullet hit something. A tree? By my surprise maneuver I'd neutralized her superior strength, and Claire was momentarily off-balance. I jammed her gun arm into the edge of the open hood. The impact with the metal must have hurt, because she grunted and let the gun drop. I heard a series of clanking noises as the gun dropped into the innards of the motor.

Unfortunately, Claire recovered quickly. She yanked me by the hair and tried to slam my head into the engine block. I resisted, and hit the open hood of the car instead. A sharp pain exploded at the back of my head, and I cried out. I put my hands around Claire's neck and pulled myself close to her face—and bit down hard on her nose.

She let out a blood-curdling scream and let go of me, bringing her hands to her face. Blood streamed from her nose. I could taste Claire's blood in my mouth. I spit it out and kicked her in the shins. She stepped back and pulled something from her pocket. The object glinted in the moonlight—a small pair of pruning shears.

Claire made quick, stabbing motions in my direction. I backed away. Keeping the sharp edge of the shears pointed in my direction, she rounded to the passenger side of the car.

The shotgun. Ohmigod. I remembered her stashing it in the back seat.

I took off in a run. The light of the full moon lit the forest to almost obscene brightness. I ran for my life. There were no large trees to hide behind, no walls or fences. The vegetation consisted mainly of light brush. It seemed that no matter which direction I chose to go, I'd be silhouetted by the moon, making me a perfect target.

The lake was my best option.

I ran like mad, making for the jetty. I reached it, ran out onto it, and dove into the lake. The water was chilly. So frigid it took my breath away.

I stayed underwater, gliding in long strokes, keeping parallel to the shore and making for a stony outcropping that I hoped would obscure Claire's view of the lake beyond.

I surfaced and inhaled greedily. Claire was standing on the jetty, scanning the water. She spotted me and, just as I dove under, she fired a round.

I continued underwater, trying to vary my path in a zigzag pattern. I stayed underwater until my lungs felt ready to burst. Then I had no choice. I had to come up for air.

This time I didn't see Claire. She wasn't on the jetty. She was on the move, probably heading in the same direction I was.

I contemplated swimming across the lake, away from the shore. But there was the moon. If I headed straight out into that beam of moonlight, my outline would be easy to spot each time I surfaced. I'd be a dead woman. My best bet was to keep close to shore, where the rocks and sea grasses sheltered me from view. If I moved slowly, and avoided disturbing the glassy surface of the water, I'd be near invisible. I gasped for air and sank back beneath the surface once more.

The next time I came up, I saw Claire reload the shotgun. She had climbed a rocky outcropping, which gave her a panoramic view of the entire lake. She was looking in my direction. I wondered if she could make me out? Was I leaving a wake?

She aimed, and I didn't even have time to dive. She almost got me that time, the pellets hitting just inches away. A spray of water splashed up in my face. I took a deep breath and sank down, swimming along the bottom of the lake and counting the seconds. Twenty, thirty, forty.

I was out of air.

This time, when I resurfaced, I came up slowly. I saw Claire.

The shotgun was aimed in my direction. I drew a fast breath, not getting nearly enough air, and sank back under.

Damn. I cursed the bright moon. I cursed the freezing water. I was starting to shake from the cold, my teeth chattering. How did Claire manage to see me? How could she always know where I was?

I heard the next shot. The sound seemed far away this time, quieted by my being underwater. For all I knew, she'd missed me by inches.

I had one happy thought. Somebody was bound to hear the shots. I prayed they were dialing 9-1-1 at this moment.

When I surfaced again, the moon was gone. A large, heavy cloud had moved across the sky, obscuring all light. I took a quick breath, and this time I sank all the way to the bottom of the lake. With cold and shaky fingers I untied my shoelaces and kicked my sneakers off.

I had to come up for air again. It was still pitch black. I couldn't see Claire, or anything else on shore. I struggled out of my jeans and started swimming across the lake, careful to remain underwater as much as possible. On the opposite shore stood two houses, their lighted windows beckoning to me like beacons.

My skin was numb from the cold, my arms stiff and sluggish. After a while I doubted whether I'd be able to reach shore. I feared passing out from hypothermia.

The bright moon returned. A cold gloom of despair seeped into my bones. The opposite shore seemed as distant as ever, the lake much larger than it appeared from shore. Swimming underwater was proving to be slow and exhausting, but I had to keep swimming, to keep moving, or Claire need not bother with shotgun pellets. The cold alone would do me in.

With the moon shining brightly again, I expected another round of gunshots. But there was only the soft quiet lapping of the water. I continued to swim.

By the time I reached the opposite shore, I had no sensation in my limbs. They'd gone numb with cold and fatigue.

I stumbled over rocks, dead leaves, and broken branches, walking, then crawling until I reached the safety of a house. I rang the bell and collapsed on the doorstep.

I don't remember anyone opening the door. I'd passed out.

EPILOGUE

When I woke up in a hospital room the next day, Jack was sitting by my side, holding my hand. The doctor told me that I'd suffered a mild case of hypothermia. There would be no permanent damage, he assured me.

All charges against Evelyn Browne were dropped. At my suggestion, Evelyn compiled a cookbook. With the notoriety of the murder case, she quickly found a publisher. I didn't relay David Silverman's suggestion for a title to her: *Cooking with Valium*.

Tommy was the runner-up at the M.I.T. science fair. The governor shook his hand, and college recruiters swarmed to him like bees to honey, even though he was only starting his junior year that fall. Currently, Stanford tops his list of college choices.

Later that fateful evening which almost saw me turned into a human cryogenics experiment, the police found Claire Browne at her home, a bullet lodged in her brain. To my dismay, she'd chosen my Glock as the instrument of her death. Ironic for Claire's life to end the same way as her daughter's, by her own hand. She'd written a suicide note and left it propped against the banker's lamp on the blotter of her desk. In it, she confessed to killing her son Mitchell, with a cryptic explanation that she didn't want history to repeat itself—an allusion to her daughter's death that only Phillip's family and I fully understood.

Claire had also left a sealed envelope for Phillip. Its contents were never made public.

Sadly, even after Claire Browne's confession, the press still described Phillip as a "person of interest" in the murder of his brother. The *Boston Globe* kept speculating that Claire Browne had taken the rap for her youngest son.

Surprisingly, the fact that Mitchell Browne had been a pedophile never made it into any of the Boston papers. Which may explain why Mitchell Browne's murder remains shrouded in mystery in the public's mind to this day.

BioCorp continues to thrive. Rutgers and Silverman reached a favorable financial agreement over the disposition of the CDs Browne had secreted away in his closet, and Rutgers found a new boy genius at MIT to continue Browne's work with synthetic T-cells. Troy Johnson and I agree that the goons trying to take me out of the picture that fateful Tuesday morning had probably been in cahoots with Rutgers. But we could never prove it, and the BioCorp guard whom Rutgers supposedly fired that day was never found. Payton and his father reconciled their differences.

The impatiens I bought from Claire have flourished into colorful knolls of immense beauty, a final flowering legacy. Jack had planted them while I was recuperating in the hospital. Maybe I should have uprooted them—because they remind me of the dead woman whenever I look at them. For the rest of my life, I'll probably think of Claire Browne whenever I see impatiens in bloom.

May she rest in peace.

ABOUT THE AUTHOR

Sibylle Barrasso, a graduate of UCSB, finished her postgraduate education with an MBA from UCLA. She's lived in Europe as well as in Brazil, where she worked for IBM. A job offer from Bain & Company tempted her to give up the eternal sunshine of California for the ever-changing seasons of the Northeast. Her consulting work in the high-tech area, including the biotech industry, became the basis for *Dark Waters*. She was a contributing editor for *New Mystery Magazine* and collaborated on a nonfiction book about mysteries set in the Southwest, titled *Bad Boys and Bad Girls in the Badlands*. At the Santa Barbara Writers Conference, she received an award from Sue Grafton for her novel *Obsession*, and was twice a finalist in the St. Martins Press Best First Private Eye Novel. She served on the board of the New England Chapter of Mystery Writers of America, on the steering committee for the New England Crimebake, and is a member of Sisters in Crime and International Thriller Writers. She lives in Boston, Massachusetts, with her husband and son. In her spare time, she enjoys playing tennis and golf. Visit the author's Web site at: www.sibylle barrasso.com